OPERATION ROMANOV

OPERATION ROMANOV

Richard Ashton

The Book Guild Ltd
Sussex, England

First published in Great Britain in 2002 by
The Book Guild Ltd,
25 High Street,
Lewes, East Sussex
BN7 2LU

Typesetting in Times by
IML Typographers, Birkenhead, Merseyside

Printed in Great Britain by
Antony Rowe Ltd, Chippenham, Wiltshire

A catalogue record for this book is
available from The British Library

ISBN 1 85776 601 6

CONTENTS

ACKNOWLEDGEMENTS

*My appreciation is extended to the following people for
their wisdom, encouragement and enthusiasm in the
writing of Operation Romanov;*

Peter Whitbread

*Jenny Hewitt and Doug Watts
both of the Jacqui Bennett Writers Bureau
and
The Russian Orthodox Diocese of Sourozh
for their advice and guidance.*

*And by no means least
my wife
for her patience and understanding.*

PROLOGUE

St Petersburg, 1998

They had both felt impelled to come and witness the final ritual burial of the Tsar Nicholas, the Tsarina and three of their children.

Neither the grey-haired man in the wheelchair nor his woman companion was related to the imperial family, whose bones were at last being laid to rest. Each had been drawn to this city of spires, legacy of Peter the Great and which proudly still bore his name, St Petersburg, because for them, the ceremony held a significance beyond belief.

As the eight tiny oak coffins, holding what remained of the royal family and their three servants, were borne into the great St Peter and Paul Cathedral, their thoughts went back over three decades to a time when they had been engulfed in a vortex of blind hatred and greed. For those are the very passions the name Romanov is capable of conjuring up.

Now, it was as if the funeral itself marked an ending. Not only for the pitiful remains about to receive their final benediction, but also for themselves.

Difficult though it was from the confines of a wheelchair, the man leant towards the woman.

'Would anyone believe us?' he whispered, 'It happened so long ago.'

'No,' she replied, 'and it's better the past remains the past.' Yet she knew he would never be content with that. Silence followed, as she again became absorbed in watching a strikingly handsome man standing close to the coffins.

'I feel she is here.'

'Who?'

'Elizabeth.'

'She probably is,' she replied, after a moment's thought.

'Do you think she is pleased with us?'

'With you . . . no doubt.'

'She didn't quite pull it off,' he said, almost to himself, 'but I think she is well satisfied. After all,' he rambled on, 'half a loaf is better than no bread.'

The woman had obviously heard him because, somewhat dryly, she replied, 'I've never heard a royal princess referred to as half a loaf before.'

He chuckled. 'You know something? When we get home I'm going to put it all down on paper.'

'They'll never believe you.'

'No,' he sighed, 'they probably won't, but I'm going to, just the same.'

She squeezed his hand.

1

'Bring the Girl to Me ...'

It was the year of the Profumo scandal, an era when we were told 'You've never had it so good,' of CND and the birth of a new word, 'Beatnik'. It was also the time of gathering clouds over Europe, the Cold War ...

* * *

The note, written on heavy expensive paper, embossed with the writer's address, had no signature, only initials. The words 'Bring the girl to me,' leapt out at Olga as she fingered the enclosed crisp banknote. Fifty thousand roubles – more money than she could earn in a year! Clutching such riches to her chest, she again peered at the address. Appenzell, Switzerland. Neither the initials or the address meant anything to her. She quickly reached the only possible conclusion. The fame of the gorgeous Natasha had travelled further than even Olga had dared hope, that much was obvious. She digested the rest of the note written in a lazy scrawl with increased excitement – 'train and air tickets will shortly follow also travel documents ...'

* * *

Kolomyja, an obscure town on the borders of Poland, Russia and Romania, had little claim to fame other than, since time

1

immemorial, it had suffered invasion from all three. Vladimir Gollitzin, accepting Russia as the largest and present incumbent, had been granted citizenship shortly after the war.

His wife, after years of toil, had died at fifty, unlamented, and received as little love in death as she had received in life. This unforgiving and pitiless attitude in those around her was the catalyst whereby Natasha, their daughter, although very young, had learnt her first lesson: the need to survive whatever the cost and, by surviving, justifying the means. Her gradual metamorphosis into a strikingly attractive woman, together with her ability, without effort, to attract men, was not lost on Vladimir. As Natasha was soon to learn, his approach to his family was governed by their abilities to keep him in good vodka.

'Granny' Olga, his long-time associate, wore an aura of dread as easily as she wore her cloak. Doors closed and curtains were drawn when she walked the streets of Kolomyja. She was an active Communist, and people had disappeared through incurring her wrath. As a midwife she was adept at introducing life into the world or, if to her advantage, terminating it; she also engaged herself in other more dubious activities far removed from Moscow and her duties as a party official.

Her particular forte, known to a select few, was preparing young girls for prostitution. Therefore, it was to 'Granny' Olga that Vladimir turned when, in spite of his vodka-induced stupor, he began to recognise Natasha's potential. The examination of Natasha was held in the privacy of Olga's own home. Never, she would recall later, had she received such a subject, or a more compliant one, to work on. Natasha was the embodiment of all she could wish for. How different, she reflected, from the girl's heavy-limbed, featureless and clumsy elder sister, Valma. Olga, giving Natasha a hundred roubles to spend, rushed breathless to her partner.

'Vladimir,' she crooned, 'you have a diamond.' And then, mindful of her future interest in her protégée, 'She will require the most sensitive of polishing and the very best tuition, but a diamond nevertheless.'

2

Watery eyes, all but concealed beneath coal-black eyebrows, stared back at her, as a hand with veins like cords reached for the attendant vodka bottle. After what seemed an age to the impatient Olga, the silence broken only by the sound of vodka hitting the bottom of the glass, Vladimir's mouth, like the entrance to a dark cave, formed a reply, 'Usual terms?' This, following a release of wind that made even Olga, not easily embarrassed by the diverse actions of the human body, look away in disgust.

'Not this one, Vladimir,' her voice barely above a whisper, but incisive, 'for this one – half of everything.'

* * *

Throughout a freezing winter Olga taught Natasha the arts necessary for luring men like bees to pollen. And, once entrapped, the seduction would be followed by their permanent servility and adoration. Such magnetism, Olga knew, was only lying dormant; it required little of her skills to release it and with it the ultimate any man could wish of a woman: perfection.

Olga had learned that courtesans at the court of Louis XIV had indulged in exercising chained monkeys as a means of enhancing their own attraction. Never reluctant to employ any proven method of seduction, she accepted the role of monkey to Natasha's beauty. The exquisite loveliness of her pupil, made more appealing by a naive charm, achieved that purpose.

Frequently, they were seen together at any event considered by Natasha's mentor worthy of their patronage. Her protégée's sensuous figure was always garbed in creations meticulously chosen to cultivate erotic fantasies in the most effete and palsied of men – fantasies all the stronger because they were hinted at and implicitly unattainable.

The impact created was, as Olga reluctantly admitted, somewhat self-defeating and merely confirmed her mounting suspicions that the men of Kolomyja were not worthy of such a delectable creature. Wealth of the kind she envisaged did not exist there, and she was resigned to looking further afield to achieve her goal, but to accomplish it required money. Already the cost of preparing Natasha for her new role in life, as an enchantress of men, had drained the coffers dry. A patron was needed . . .

2

Appenzell, Switzerland 1963

Olga's perusal of the hastily borrowed school atlas revealed that Appenzell was a small town close to the banks of Lake Constance. She dismissed initial thoughts that some expensive whorehouse had decided to recruit her protégée – unlikely in a town so small. No, she concluded, excitement mounting, without doubt some wealthy party official (all such people were retired party officials in Olga's experience) wanted to avail himself of her; and so he would, she mused – at a price. Such a solution appealed; after all, did it not promise greater riches to come? Hurriedly, she called Natasha to her.

'Soon we are going on a journey, my beloved. Pack only your best clothes, the rest can stay in this miserable hole, and not a word to a soul, you understand?' The last said as a command which Natasha, in the time they had been together, knew better than to disobey.

* * *

Natasha was tired. It had been a long and tiresome journey, not helped by the reticence of her companion to divulge even the barest of reasons for the sudden excursion in, what for Natasha, was a great adventure, nevertheless tempered by the uncertainty of its outcome.

'Money, my sweet,' was all Olga had volunteered, 'more

money than you have ever dreamt of.' Certainly, Natasha thought, the advent of riches after a life of unremitting poverty would be wonderful. But she knew Olga well enough to have no doubts who would earn that money and where the lion's share would go. Until now the pleasuring of men had been something that was distant and intangible and brought to life only through the teachings of Olga. She had no doubts the reality would be very different.

With the air of a man casting pearls before swine, the taxi driver at the airport opened the cab door for them, but not before insisting on payment in advance. Although disconcerted and muttering an oath, Olga brushed aside the inference and laboriously counted the money from her purse, which, like a sporran, hung from her heavy leather belt.

They had expected a large house, but nothing had prepared them for the magnificence of the building now spread out before them. As the taxi made its way up the broad driveway, ornamental fountains came into view, each one depicting, with its surrounding sculptured figurines, some scene quite foreign to them both but nonetheless splendid. Green lawns surrounded beds of flowers, awe-inspiring in their variety of colours, and stretching endlessly wherever they looked. A colonnade led to a heavy wooden door complete with a large lion's head brass knocker. They alighted, Natasha clutching Olga's hand tightly and, ignoring the sneering comment of their driver, Olga raised the knocker to its fullest extent and released it. The resultant noise reverberated round them as if the sound itself was rebuking them for their intrusion. The silence that followed did little to relieve Natasha's nerves as the door, with agonising slowness, opened to reveal a tall, heavily built man with greying hair, wisps of which peaked out from below a white skullcap.

The sight of the man reduced Olga's agitated state somewhat. She was right after all, now it was simply a case of striking the best bargain she could. With growing confidence she waved the note under his beaklike nose. The man said nothing but with an imperious wave of the hand ushered them inside.

Whereas the approach to the house had created a tremendous impression on them, the inside was, to their eyes, even more opulent. From high in the ceiling hung a huge chandelier, its myriad lights bathing what was obviously only the entrance hall in a cascade of brightness. Huge paintings vied with multicoloured tapestries on every wall, and at each window – windows that climbed high into the ceilings – hung massive drapes of brocade curtains. As they followed repeated imperious waves of the man's hands, their feet sank into a carpet of luxuriant depth.

Without any word from their guide they were ushered into a room with even more evidence of affluence. But before they could digest this, their attention was drawn to the far end of the room as a door opened to admit a grey-haired woman leaning heavily on a walking stick. Purposefully, she advanced into the room and gently lowered herself into a high-backed chair. Pointing her stick at Olga, she commented on the obvious.

'So, you've finally got here,' and then, 'you may address me as Duchess or Your Highness. And this person,' now directing her stick at the guide, 'as Igor.'

With introductions evidently completed she turned her attention to Natasha. For what seemed an eternity to the impatient Olga, Natasha was subjected to an intense evaluation. The silence was finally broken by a command.

'Turn around, girl, and walk over to the bureau.' Natasha, not sure what constituted a bureau, walked across the room on legs that seemed no longer to belong to her.

'What do you think, Igor?' Igor said nothing, but nodded appreciatively.

Olga, with Natasha centre stage, grasped the opportunity to study the woman. The order to walk across the room and, in particular, the opinion sought from Igor, was reassuring. Now she was on familiar ground. It was plain they were weighing up Natasha's potential, prior to the bargaining. Her confidence restored, Olga considered the most suitable opening price.

She eyed her adversary, now sitting straight-backed with both

7

hands resting on the handle of the stick, her fingers adorned with a multitude of rings, their individual beauty and lustre made even more vivid by the opaque whiteness of the skin. Olga's mind leapfrogged; she recognised there was no going back to Kolomyja – not now. In her mind's eye she saw the cold stare of her Commissar as she attempted to explain her sudden dash to Switzerland. No, she had burnt her bridges, there was no going back. Two hundred thousand, a quarter of a million? She grappled with the sums, each more outlandish than the first. She glanced across at Natasha, now standing rather forlornly in the centre of the room. Her beauty, notwithstanding the limited haute couture available in Kolomyja, still radiated through, even in these most luxurious settings. Dismissing her first thoughts, she would settle for one hundred and fifty thousand, after all she still had the bulk of the fifty thousand roubles in her pouch. Negotiations, she decided, would begin at two hundred thousand to allow room for the inevitable bargaining. With her mind made up, Olga awaited the old woman.

'You are probably wondering why I invited you here,' said the Duchess, directing her gaze back at Olga. Again the tenuous feeling of uncertainty assailed Olga. 'Well, I will tell you. You know the girl as Natasha Gollitzin,' she said. 'Although such a name is on her Certificate of Registration, that is not her true name.'

Wide-eyed, Natasha sat down on the nearest chair, clearly fascinated by what she was hearing. Olga shuffled her feet, her confidence of a moment ago gone and nervously aware that something was dreadfully wrong.

'When she was a baby,' the woman continued, 'she was lodged with the Gollitzins – incidentally, how is the old sot? And her sister Valma?'

Olga muttered that Vladimir and Valma were well.

'Vladimir was paid a retainer to raise her as his own ... you understand?'

Olga again muttered that she did understand.

'You are now asking yourself "Why?" are you not?'

8

Olga, after a brief pause, mumbled that she was indeed.

'For the answer we must go back to what you,' here the Duchess fixed her with a look of such ferocity that Olga involuntarily took a step back, 'called the Glorious Revolution, an era of blood-letting that has continued to this day. Millions have died because of you and your Bolshevik friends, and all Russia has become but a cesspool of gulags.' Continuing, her voice now high-pitched, 'You have the blood of our beloved Tsar and Empress and family on your hands. One man,' now spitting out the words, 'one man alone could have saved us. That man...' here her voice dropped to a mere whisper, as if the mention of his name was a blasphemy in itself, 'was Gregor Rasputin.' Then, in a voice once again pitched to the height of intensity, 'And there,' pointing dramatically with her stick at Natasha, 'is his granddaughter.'

Whilst the tirade was continuing, Igor had surreptitiously moved behind Olga and begun to unwind a length of silken material that, until then, had served as a cummerbund. With the faintest of nods from the Duchess, he quickly knotted one end and slipped it, imperceptibly, around Olga's throat. Her eyes, still registering incredulity at what she had just heard, flashed in alarm but all too late as Igor's knee drove into her back with ferocious force. An almost imperceptible click reached Natasha, sitting dumb-founded, only feet away, as Olga, without a sound and with her head now lolling like a broken doll's, slid to the floor.

'I'm sorry you had to witness that, my child,' said the Duchess, her voice now matter-of-fact, and then to Igor, 'remove the kulak.'

Without a word Igor reached down and, gripping Olga's leather belt, lifted her and disappeared through the door so recently entered by the Duchess.

'You have no need to fear,' comforted the Duchess, addressing the white-faced and shaking Natasha. 'Tonight you'll sleep between silken sheets with Igor at the foot of your bed. You need not concern yourself over him, he is a eunuch and quite harmless. In any event,' a smile spreading quickly to her eyes as she extended her arm, 'it is only proper that a princess should sleep with a dog at her feet.'

3

More Revelations – and Natasha Says Farewell to the Duchess

Sergei Poznansky, a devout monarchist and one-time childhood friend of the heir to the throne of all the Russias, Tsarevich Alexi, glanced round at the incredible lavishness of the Duchess's house. He had expected the sister of the Tsarina to live comfortably, but this – his gaze returned to the aged lady seated before him ... how frail she had become but still as defiant as ever. Almost unbelievable, nearly fifty years after the event, that she had survived in the same pit that had claimed the lives of the Grand Duke Mikhailovich and four other Romanovs. Although equally as bloody as the atrocity at Ekaterinburg, the deed had escaped the publicity surrounding the deaths of the Tsar and his family.

Sergei's thoughts of the past were cut short as, leaning forward in her chair, the Grand Duchess Elizabeth began to speak.

'I've been very foolish, haven't I, Sergei? I have neglected my duties where the girl Natasha is concerned. I trusted Vladimir far too much for far too long. You know he intended to put her into prostitution – anything for a bottle of vodka and the kulak was to act as her ponce. Heaven only knows what damage has been done to such a young susceptible girl.'

'Perhaps it would have been wiser to have let the kulak live,' Poznansky sighed, 'the KGB has a long arm, and Switzerland and your American passport won' t protect you forever.'

She interrupted him. 'If I could, I would kill them all for what they did to my beloved sister and her family.'

As tears moistened her eyes, Sergei, aware of her mounting distress, leant forward, taking hold of her hand.

Her eyes, which but a moment before had been gathering pools of sadness, flashed coldly and with such sharp intensity as to all but freeze him into inertia. Recovering quickly, he removed his hand.

'Remember who I am, Sergei,' she remonstrated. 'In the unlikely event I should wish you to touch me, I will be the one to hold out my hand.'

It was the Grand Duchess Elizabeth speaking, sister of the Empress of all the Russias, not a crippled, weary old woman in her nineties who, for the better part of her life, had lived with the knowledge that death, or worse, could come at any time.

'Forgive me,' he whispered.

'I know, I know,' she replied, 'you are right – after all, we are not in the Catherine Palace at Tsarskoe Selo now. It's 1963, a different world.'

'Indeed,' replied Sergei, and then, 'let us review the facts as we know them. Olga Semyonov, by no means a senior party official, is missing and, with her, the young unknown girl Natasha Gollitzin. No great worry there. No, the danger is Vladimir Gollitzin and how much he knows . . . or suspects. Only you know that.'

'You know Natasha's history as well as I do, Sergei. I had to act as I did . . .' her voice died away as her eyes seemingly recalled an episode that time would never erase.

'I have often wondered why you didn't keep the girl with you?' The effrontery of his question made Sergei breathless.

'You have never been hunted, have you, Sergei? If you had you would know better than to ask such a foolish question. I knew she was safe with the Gollitzins, after all, even the secret police would hardly look for a royal princess with a peasant family – and in such an out of the way place as Kolomyja.'

'You were right, of course, and I'm sorry I doubted you. But to return to Natasha, how did you know of Gollitzin's plans for her?'

'There are many who sympathise with the cause, Sergei, and a few roubles distributed here and there keep me informed.'

'You mean there are others who know about Natasha?'

'Don't be an idiot, do you think I've shouted it from the house-tops? Only a handful know who she is and what she is.'

'Vladimir Gollitzin,' continued Sergei, somewhat chastened, 'if the KGB pull him in, forgive the Americanism, he'll sing like a bird...'

'Then he will sing on one note, Sergei, he knows little or nothing of any importance, only that he was asked to give the child a home in exchange for a retainer.'

'Even so, you know how persistent they are, and there is always the search for the gold to spur them on.'

'What of it?' she replied as a smile crossed her face, a smile that reminded him of the first snows of winter glistening on the steppes. Playing on her obvious change of mood, he adopted a more servile manner and moved closer to her.

'Your Highness, come with us to Paris, you, the girl and Igor, there we will all be safe.'

'Safe?' she exclaimed, 'You of all people must know that can never be. No,' her voice firm and decisive, 'my presence would only inhibit you, and above all it is the safety of the girl that matters – without her there is no monarchist movement, you understand?' Sergei nodded. 'No, you will take her to Paris, I will remain here.' Then, with a look that was more a grimace, 'It will be interesting to meet that pig Derevenko again, after all these years.'

'Derevenko? Wasn't he responsible for the death of the Grand Duke?'

'He was,' she said, again with that faraway look. 'There is the blood of many Romanovs on his hands.'

She stood up, signifying the discussion was at an end. Momentarily, she looked at him again, and as her features softened, stretched out a hand with the grace and dignity of a time long past. Sergei knew it was the final goodbye, he would never see her again, this living embodiment of all that was left of those once closest to the Tsar and Tsarina. With as much formality as he could muster and with just the very tip of his fingers, he guided her hand to his lips.

*   *   *

The Duchess Elizabeth, her face deep in concentration, listened to Sergei Poznansky speaking from Zurich.

'It will not be easy, Natasha lacks a visa for entering France – but,' he reassured her, 'money will unlock all doors. She and Igor will meet here, and together we will fly to Paris via Rome.'

'You are confident?'

'Yes, Your Highness, provided we all keep our heads.'

'Then let it be.'

As if on cue, Igor escorted Natasha into the room. Again the Duchess marvelled at the translucent loveliness of the girl, now more suitably attired in new clothes.

'You are flying to Paris, girl, Igor will be with you, together with an old and dear friend of mine, Sergei Poznansky. You will lodge with a family of the French nobility who will instruct you in the arts and graces of a royal princess ... you understand?'

Natasha nodded. It was all too much; from a home little more than a hovel, to this ... and now Paris ... her head was spinning. The night before, lying in that huge bed, engulfed in the luxury of silken sheets with, from somewhere out in the darkness the soft, incessant snoring of Igor, cruel thoughts assailed her. Perhaps it was all a mistake – the old woman had mixed her up with some-one else and soon she would be sent back to Vladimir and the sister she hated. Her mind went from one possibility to another. And Olga ... she missed Olga, sly and cunning though she was. And that awful ... killing ... what was it all about? Everyone seemed so concerned about her well-being – she, a princess! It couldn't be, but if it meant opulence beyond her wildest dreams, then why question it?

She felt the Duchess eyeing her. Perhaps she should have been more appreciative of the title 'Princess'. Obviously, the Duchess considered it the very highest ... had she then inadvertently offended her? Her fears came to naught as the woman suddenly began to laugh. At first, no more than a chuckle erupted from deep within her. Then reminiscent, recalled Natasha, of the winter winds of Kolomyja, she burst into a gale of laughter that shook and convulsed her fragile body. The laughter, infectious in itself, spread to her and, unable to contain herself, a girlish giggle soon became uncontrollable, near hysterical, laughter.

Lowering herself on to a chaise longue, the Duchess wiped her tear-stained face, drank deeply from a medieval, jewel-encrusted goblet, then, moving aside, motioned Natasha to join her.

'Forgive the outburst, child, but looking at you,' the deep-throated chuckle beginning again, 'made me realise what must be going on in your head – utter confusion, I'm sure. I should not have been so thoughtless.' With that the Duchess looked straight at Natasha and clasped her hands in a grip that reminded her of when Olga, as had often happened, lost patience with her during one of their lessons.

'Now listen carefully, Natasha.' The use of her name by the Duchess sent a thrill of excitement through her. It was as if their relationship, so nebulous until then, had become something special to them both.

'This will be the only opportunity I shall have to talk privately to you. You must be so very confused by what you have heard and seen here, and for you to understand, I shall explain it as simply as I can. On the night you arrived here, in my excitement, I told your kulak friend that you were Rasputin's granddaughter. That can never be proved. However, it is an indisputable fact that your paternal grandmother was the Tsarina Alexandra.'

Silence followed this statement as Natasha's eyes widened in disbelief. It was too incredible and fantastic for her mind to accept. Until a day or so ago, she was nothing more than a poor peasant girl. Now she was being told she was the granddaughter of the last *Matushka*, the little mother of all the Russias.

Pausing only to drink from the goblet, the Duchess began again.

'Your mother was the Princess Eugenia, fifth daughter of the Tsarina. What do you know of your mother's half-sisters?'

In a whisper, and with four fingers raised, Natasha counted them off, 'Olga, Maria,' she hesitated, then with a smile, 'Tatiana and Anastasia.'

'Well done,' exclaimed the Duchess clapping her hands, and then with a complete change of demeanour, 'and what do you think of the Communist Party?'

Natasha looked blankly at her.

'Good, I can see from your expression such matters have never entered your head ... as it should be. One other matter,' using her stick for leverage she rose from the chaise longue and, for one brief moment, she was back at court in the Winter Palace. Standing perfectly straight, she announced:

'I am the Grand Duchess Elizabeth, sister of the last Tsarina, Empress Alexandra, God rest her soul. My life is dedicated to restoring the monarchy to my beloved Russia; and to avenge dear Nicholas, Alex and her family, all brutally murdered at Ekaterinburg.'

Breathing deeply, the Duchess sat down and reached for the goblet. Natasha, having listened to the awe-inspiring denouement, wondered whether some response was expected. Uncertain of what form the response should take, she remained silent.

'Now Natasha,' said the Duchess. Again that thrill of excitement swept over her as the Duchess called her by name. 'To go back to those terrible days prior to the revolution, Rasputin's influence within the royal court, and in particular where my sister was concerned, was bitterly resented by the masses. We were at war with Germany, Nicholas was at the front with his troops. The birth of your mother would have been viewed with much scepticism by the people, so the birth was hidden and known to but a few. Your mother, but a day or so old, was smuggled out of the palace and, under my direction, placed in the care of an obscure but trusted court official.'

Her voice implied that, even after fifty years, and as if it were yesterday, the magnitude of what she had done remained with her.

Natasha waited patiently, half-believing, half-disbelieving what she had just heard.

'Inevitably, Natasha, there are many who lay claim to the throne, some more genuine than others, but none, my dear, can challenge your birthright. You have only to look at the top of your right thigh and there you will see the mark of the Romanovs, it will be with you for life – you will do well to remember that.'

Natasha momentarily basked in the thought of a life of power where her slightest whim would be a command, and where she would be surrounded by sycophants whose only desire was to please.

* * *

Over dinner, served by Igor on magnificently embossed plates, each bearing the emblem of the House of Romanov, the Duchess, in a tone that boded no questioning, returned to the subject of Natasha's future.

'Tomorrow morning you will leave with Igor for Zurich. From there you will fly to Rome and then on to Paris. The Comte de Toulouse, a sympathiser to the cause, will take you into his home and your tuition will begin. The Comte has a son and two daughters, so you will not be without company. Do as you are bidden, Natasha, uphold the honour of Russia and stay true to the monarchy.'

The Duchess again drank deeply from the ever-present goblet.

'May I ask some questions?' Natasha's voice betrayed her nervousness. 'How old am I, and where are my mother and father?'

'You were born on the seventeenth of August, nineteen forty-two, so you are twenty-one. You have the warmth of the summer

17

sun in your veins. Your dear mother, never strong, died giving life to you. Your father was killed in the war flying with the Luftwaffe – the German air force.'

Now adopting a more pensive mood, the Duchess reached across the table and, clasping Natasha's hands, whispered, 'Trust no one. Always be on your guard. Only to Igor, whose loyalty is beyond question, can you safely entrust your life.'

Signifying the talk was at an end, the Duchess rose from her chair and, half-turning, looked at her. It was a look that Natasha sensed was final. She would never see this infirm, fragile old woman, who claimed to be the living soul of the Romanovs, again. A woman who had brought about such an extraordinary and, even now, unbelievable change in her life. She felt no sadness at the parting, only impatience at the thought of what the morning was to bring – Rome ... Paris ... perhaps even the throne of all the Russias.

4

Where There is One There Must be More . . .

Natasha decided the house was not nearly as imposing as the old woman's – she couldn't get used to calling her the Duchess. As they alighted from their car, Igor, punctilious in his duties, checked their baggage whilst Sergei, eyes everywhere, surveyed her new home.

Paris – it really was true, she was here. As Natasha looked around her she had a feeling of disappointment. Identical houses spread away to right and left, nothing remarkable about them – but, even so it was . . . *Paris*.

At the top of a flight of steps a door opened and a distinguish-looking man appeared with a woman on each arm. He descended the steps, then, leaving the women, approached Sergei and with an extravagant gesture kissed him on both cheeks.

They spoke excitedly for a moment or two before the man, at Sergei's invitation, came over to her.

'*Bonjour, comment allez-vous?*' Natasha, by way of response, did a bob, halfway between a bow and a curtsy. He smiled and spoke rapidly in French. '*Comment vous appelez-vous?*' Totally unsure, Natasha returned the smile.

'*Parlez-vous français?*'

To her relief Sergei stepped in. 'Mademoiselle Natasha speaks very little French.'

'*Bon*, then we will all help her,' he said, smiling again, and with that beckoned the two women over and introduced them, but this time he was far less voluble. The older of the two, as Natasha had surmised, his wife, was Madame Suzanne who, extending her hand, murmured, '*Enchanté Mademoiselle*,' again the bob, and again as she was introduced to Mademoiselle Celestine, his daughter. The formalities concluded, the party moved up the steps and into the house.

The Comte's son, Marcel, then greeted them. Dark, with pronounced black eyebrows which emphasised his sallow complexion, he confirmed the image Natasha had always held of Frenchmen. The faintest trace of garlic emanating from him added the final Gallic touch. His, '*Enchanté*,' followed by '*comment ça va?*' as he held her hand decidedly longer than necessary, sent shivers up and down her spine as she replied, 'Très bien, merci.'

The Comte was at pains to point out that his youngest daughter, Eugénie, was at day school but would he home that evening.

With Natasha now safely ensconced with the Comte and his family, Sergei, in conversation with the Comte and Comtesse, stressed how important it was that he met with the Chairman of the Russian Nobility Association.

'In the final analysis, Henri, the attitude of the Association towards her claims to the throne will be crucial in obtaining the endorsement of the Duma in exile.'

After further discussion with the Comte, it was agreed that he would fly to London the following day. The Comtesse had expressed her concern.

'Surely, Sergei,' she had said, 'you must be tired after your long journey from Zurich. After all,' looking at the plump grey-haired figure before her, 'you are no longer a young man.'

Again Sergei had impressed on her the importance of an early meeting, and so the day after their arrival in Paris he had flown to London.

* * *

The offices of the Nobility Association were drab in the extreme.

20

Located in a backstreet in Holborn, only the district code, WC2, gave them any semblance of respectability.

Sergei Poznansky eyed the man sitting across from him with interest. Dmitri Sokolov, Grand Chairman of the Russian Nobility Association, was the epitome of everything Russian. It required no imaginings of Sergei's to envisage him riding, scimitar in hand, across the rolling steppes of the Ukraine, his half-wild horse breathing fire whilst he cut and thrust at all who crossed his path. Such musings were entirely false. Dmitri Sokolov was an intellectual who had probably never ridden a horse in his life. A Professor in Modern Sciences, he had lectured at the University of Leningrad until Beria, head of the NKVD, had begun to take an interest in his monarchist activities, when he had fled to London.

'How is the Grand Duchess?' Sokolov's resonant voice interrupted Sergei's thoughts.

'She is well.'

'Good, good, and is she still enjoying the finer things of life?'

Sergei remained silent.

'I have never depreciated what the Duchess has done on behalf of the cause. My only criticism,' Sokolov smiled thinly, 'is that it could have been done more cheaply.'

'As sister of the Empress, it is only to be expected she would maintain a lifestyle in keeping with her position.'

'Such lavishness,' muttered Sokolov, examining his thumbnail with interest, 'when so many of our countrymen are living in poverty.' Then looking directly at Sergei, he said, 'tell me about the girl Natasha.'

'I delivered her to the house of Henri, Comte de Toulouse, yesterday,' said Sergei, immediately regretting volunteering her location.

'The Comte de Toulouse – very interesting. May I ask for what purpose?'

'To be taught the arts and graces of the Russian nobility,' replied Sergei, beginning to feel uncomfortable. 'As a simple kulak she has a lot to learn.'

Sokolov, silent for a moment, erupted into a volume of laughter which shook the small room like a thunderclap. Recovering, he said, 'You cannot be serious,' wiping his eyes with the backs of his hands. 'Really, Sergei, I expected better than that from you.'

'I disagree,' replied Sergei, 'as the granddaughter of the Empress every care must be taken with her tuition.'

As Sokolov leant across his desk the sigh was clearly audible.

'I repeat, you cannot be serious. Are you really hoping to persuade the Grand Council, the Duma in exile, to adopt the girl as Heir Apparent to the throne of the Tsars? This kulak, on your say-so.'

'And the Duchess's.'

'Her account can never be proved.'

'Surely the word of the sister of the Empress, the Grand Duchess Elizabeth, would be accepted?'

'Very unlikely, Sergei. You see, the Duchess in her latter years, has been intensely disliked. One of the old school, Sergei – put her on the throne and we would be back to the revolution. No, listen to me, and avoid ridiculing yourself in a hopeless cause.' Seeing the look of defiance in Sergei's eyes, Sokolov continued with even greater emphasis.

'There are at least four reasons why the Council would never consider endorsement.' Sokolov counted them on his fingers: 'One, her lineal descent cannot be proved – even if it were, imagine, Sergei, the effect. The Council would be branding the last Empress as an adultress. Two, no bastard child would ever be recognised by the Holy Church. Three, even the remotest connection with Rasputin would have the masses in open revolt. Finally, Sergei, as you know only too well, only a male heir would be acceptable.'

'Then there is little more to be said.'

'Perhaps, Sergei, you should have given more thought to the ambitions of an old and embittered woman driven on over the years by her fanatical hatred of the Bolsheviks and, more to the point, the inevitable effect of senility.'

22

For a few moments the two men looked at each other, then Sokolov spoke again.

'What about funds?'

'Not as much as I had hoped – you see, the Duchess lived years behind the times.'

'Strange, is it not Sergei, all that opulence . . . but no money?'

'I agree.' Rising, Sergei gripped the proffered hand, the parting words of Sokolov slowly registering as he closed the door.

* * *

Sergei, finding a café conveniently close, ordered a coffee and reflected on the day's events. The Foreign Accounts Manager at Coutts had been sympathetic. 'Quite definitely only twenty thousand pounds had been deposited by Letters of Credit from Zurich.' Incredible to believe that the Duchess had been so out of touch. The commitment for Natasha's tuition was one thousand pounds a month. In a little more than a year and a half the money would be gone, then what . . .?

Should he cable the Duchess? But to do so would compromise their position. The girl would have to be told. What a let-down – one minute heir to the throne of all the Russias, the next nothing. And what of himself? No job, no prospects and little money, also the matter of entry on a forged passport. God, what a situation to be in. Sergei lit a cigarette and ordered another coffee. Those last words of Sokolov's, *All that opulence and no money*, reverberated through his mind. It simply didn't make sense; whatever Sokolov's opinion of the Grand Duchess, all that talk about age and senility, he knew the Duchess was no fool. All the planning and care she had undertaken in the interests of the girl and the monarchy, to come to naught because of lack of money. It didn't ring true. Again he went over the Duchess's last instructions. *Contact Coutts either in Paris or London. They will have all the funds you're likely to need.* Supposing she had intended to do more but had been stopped before . . .? Derevenko, killer of many

23

Romanovs, had he got to her? The thought brought him out in a cold sweat. He had no illusions if that were the case, he could be next.

*   *   *

A nondescript building, close to the Kremlin in Moscow, houses the infamous Internal Section of the KGB. In the building, in an equally nondescript office, resided the head of the section, Alexis Sternov. As Sergei quietly drank his coffee in far away London, Sternov was wrestling with a conundrum.

Yet again he sucked on his pipe, an unconscious habit when faced with a seemingly insoluble problem, reflecting on the irony of having to refer to documents nearly fifty years old.

'Bull' Sternov was by any standard a large man. On this occasion, his size was given additional emphasis as, with shoulders hunched, be towered over the tiny desk, his huge hands moving spasmodically across a collection of papers that all but obliterated its spotless blotter. The papers were the contents of two file covers, both of some vintage, as witnessed by their all but indecipherable lettering and worn, frayed edges.

He drew on the unlit pipe and the peculiar sucking noise penetrated the otherwise silent room, as at random one piece of paper was selected to receive his intense concentration, only to be discarded and replaced with another. A knock on the door interrupted his studies. With a gruff 'Come!' – Bull Sternov never used two words when one would do – he returned the latest object of his inspection to its companions and looked up.

Mikhael Derevenko entered the room and with exaggerated care closed the door behind him. His 'Evening, Comrade Sternov,' was addressed more to the closing door than his superior. Not that it mattered, as the greeting was ignored anyway.

'Well?' barked Sternov, eyeing his subordinate with obvious distaste. 'Anything to add to your report?' He had never been impressed with Derevenko. Too often he had let personal preju-

24

dices outweigh his judgement, and his latest debacle emphasised the point. True, be had built up an enviable reputation with the old NKVD, but that was in the past. Now, in Sternov's opinion, he was living off past glories and should have been put out to grass long ago.

'No, comrade, I've traced them to Rome where they changed planes and then on to Paris, but there the trail ended,' and then quickly, 'but I've no doubt I shall pick it up again soon.'

What a dispirited creature he looked, mused Sternov. White-faced, with his left arm in a sling, hardly the stuff to inspire confidence. Ignoring the optimistic forecast, he decided to turn the screw.

'What a mess – a mess that so easily could have been avoided. Your orders were explicit, bring the girl or the Duchess, preferably both, to Moscow. We have neither! What is worse, the Duchess is dead ... dead people are silent people, Derevenko.'

'All I did was defend myself,' Derevenko replied, tenderly feeling his left arm, 'how was I to know she had a swordstick? And anyway, the girl had already flown.' A pause. 'In any event, from my enquiries both here and in London she presents no threat. Neither the Russian Orthodox Church nor the Nobility Association will recognise her claim.'

Here, Derevenko allowed himself a smile, the smile of the condemned given a last-minute reprieve. Only the ticking of the clock, somewhere high up on the wall, intruded on the silence.

'You fool,' Sternov snapped, his voice like whiplash. 'Did you really believe we were not aware of that?' Derevenko fidgeted nervously. 'The girl and the Duchess were the means to an end – the real prize the missing Romanov gold, valued at two million in 1920 – guess its worth today? I will tell you, in excess of twenty million! All hidden away by the Grand Duchess Elizabeth, the Duchess you've so conveniently killed.'

Like a newly caught fish, Derevenko's mouth opened and closed but no sound ensued. Sternov studied him afresh; small and incredibly thin, he aroused in Sternov feelings of contempt –

feelings often held by very large men for the unprepossessing of their number – returning the papers to their respective files, the finality of his actions was not lost on Derevenko.

'You're off the investigation, Derevenko, it's now a matter for Section H of the Foreign Bureau. Anything you have on the Duchess or the girl is to be handed to them.'

Again the ticking of the clock was discernible.

'I cannot accept that, Comrade Sternov, you see my honour is at stake.'

'What has honour to do with it?'

'I swore vengeance,' gently touching his arm again, 'as the Duchess lay dying, I swore to kill the girl – whatever it takes.'

'Precisely,' said Sternov, between his teeth. 'There is no place, Derevenko, for such dramatics in my department, and, irrespective of the take-over by the Foreign Bureau, I would have dismissed you anyway.' Derevenko bowed and moved towards the door.

'A word of warning, Derevenko, the matter of the gold bullion has gone all the way to the First Secretary.' Sternov stood up, dwarfing his subordinate. 'Any interference with the procedures to recover it will incur the most dire consequences.' Derevenko, making no comment, quietly closed the door behind him.

For a while, Sternov, his fingertips pressed closely together, gazed at the ceiling, then he reached for the telephone.

'Sternov, Department S. Mikhael Derevenko...' a pause ... 'arrange for his arrest. Charges? Actions prejudicial to the State ... yes, I will present the necessary report.'

Sternov then sat back – but continued his contemplation of the ceiling.

*　*　*

Utterly despondent, Sergei returned to Paris and the home of the Comte.

'I am only a minor official at the Credit Lyonnais,' said the

26

Comte, after hearing of the disastrous outcome of Sergei's visit to London. 'There is no way,' he continued, 'I could support the girl, still less meet the costs of her schooling.'

'Henri and I have quite a struggle as it is,' added the Comtesse, eyes rounded in supplication. 'It is quite out of the question.'

'If she could get herself a job modelling or something,' suggested the Comte, only to see Sergei raise his hands in horror. Ignoring the gesture he continued. 'When this arrangement was entered into with the Duchess, we assumed money would not be a problem...'

'I understand,' sympathised Sergei, 'I'm equally at a loss – as you are ... it never entered my head.' Sergei's face was a mirror of despair.

'Henri's suggestion is not so bizarre, there are many couturiers who would welcome Natasha; she is, after all, a very beautiful woman. I – ' The Comtesse never finished, as their attention was drawn to Igor, whose appearance from the far side of the room was as unexpected as it was unwelcome.

'Not now, Igor,' remonstrated Sergei. Igor's reply was incoherent, as he laid on the highly polished dining table a small oblong parcel wrapped in a grimy covering of newspapers.

'Really, Igor, do you have to?' said the Comtesse, eyeing her highly prized table.

'Duchess give,' mumbled Igor, turning away.

The word 'Duchess' appeared to have no significance other than to Sergei, who, rising from his chair, moved quickly to the table and began tearing at the covering of newspapers. Soon an object the size of a bar of household soap was revealed ... suddenly breathless, Sergei, ignoring its dirt-encrusted exterior, held it aloft.

'If it's what I think it is, our troubles are over.'

*   *   *

Dmitri Sokolov, head on one side, squinted again at the small

27

oblong piece of metal which, without objection from the Comtesse, now adorned her table.

'Without doubt,' he said, fingering his beard, 'it is part of the Romanov bullion – the mark of the double eagle confirms that. What do you think it's worth, Henri?'

'Difficult to say until it's assayed, but at a guess possibly thirty thousand sterling. But you must remember, because of what it represents, we would have to accept well below the market price, in other words the black market valuation.'

'Of course, of course,' agreed Sokolov, fingertip touching fingertip and obviously deep in thought. 'But where there is one there must be more . . .'

Silence followed this as each contemplated such a possibility.

'You say Igor produced it out of his hat, as it were?'

'Yes,' Sergei replied. 'He brought it, unknown to us all, all the way from Zurich, and through the customs.'

'Remarkable,' said Sokolov, again feeling his beard, 'then we must speak with Igor.'

'That may be difficult, Igor is not quite . . .' said Sergei hastily, '. . . he is a child in a man's body; it won't be easy.'

'Nevertheless, it must be done. Where is he?'

'In the garden with Natasha,' volunteered the Comtesse. 'He rarely leaves her alone – I'll fetch him.'

'Whilst we're waiting I must tell you, Sergei, just before leaving London I heard from Zurich, the news from Appenzell is bad. The Duchess, to quote the official report, "died from a gunshot wound to the head" some three days ago . . . Derevenko of course, but the Swiss are stating it was accidental. Not only that, but from our own sources it appears the house was ransacked – searching for that,' Sokolov inclined his head in the direction of the gold bar.

'I did warn her,' said Sergei quietly to himself.

Sokolov sighed. 'It was inevitable, Sergei. In my last letter to her I implored her to get out whilst she could – America, or even here she might have been safe, but you know how stubborn she was.'

The appearance of the Comtesse, followed closely by Igor and Natasha, brought the discussion to an end.

'I think it would be wiser and in the best interests of the girl if she was not a party to this,' said Sokolov, assuming the role of inquisitor-general.

'I agree,' said the Comte. 'Suzanne, take Natasha to your room,' and then, as Igor shuffled on behind them, 'not you, Igor, you stay here.' Sergei, glad that the leadership had passed to Sokolov and the Comte, remained silent.

'Now, Igor,' began Sokolov in his most condescending manner, 'tell us what you know about that,' pointing at the bar.

Igor, shoulders hunched and looking wary, mumbled, 'Duchess give Igor.'

'Yes, yes, we know that, Igor, but where did your mistress get it?'

'Mistress find.'

'Find? Where did she find? Think carefully, it is most important.' Then, in a flash of inspiration, 'Natasha's future depends on it.'

'Igor love Natasha.'

'Then you must tell us.'

'Igor go in car, dig with spade, Mistress open box, many bricks, Igor given one.'

'Could you take us there? Where the bricks are.'

'Long way.'

'We're getting nowhere with this,' interceded Sergei. 'They could have driven for hours and finished up within minutes of the house; Elizabeth was a wily old bird, she would never have given the hiding place away to Igor, of all people.'

'I'm inclined to agree, Sergei, but of one thing I'm certain. Somewhere there exists the clue to the gold. Knowing the Duchess, she would have not wanted it lost; it had one sole purpose, to further the cause,' here, Sokolov could not resist a sneer, 'as well as keeping her in the manner she considered her birthright.'

'Sokolov, if the gold were found, would that improve Natasha's chances with the Council?' Sergei's voice was deep with intensity.

'They would have sympathy ... at a price,' was the somewhat distant reply.

'Then,' said Sergei, with a degree of force that surprised him, 'we must honour the memory of the Grand Duchess and find the gold.'

'Always assuming you found it, what then? If its value is what I believe, it could weigh over a ton – try getting that through customs.'

'Impossible,' contributed the Comte.

'It has been done,' proffered Sergei, 'with careful planning.'

Never had much time for him, reflected Sokolov, a little man, who, even now, he still viewed with some suspicion. Particularly his motives for being involved with the monarchist movement. True, the Duchess, in entrusting the girl to him, must have had faith in his reliability. But his doubt remained. And what of Igor? Something very strange there he could not quite put his finger on. The man appeared an imbecile, but it could be pretence and a clever one. After all, twenty million in gold was a lot of temptation.

'I am convinced,' said Sokolov, recovering from his reverie, 'that the girl is the key. If nothing else it would appeal to the Duchess. We must go over with her everything she and Elizabeth did whilst in Appenzell, what they talked about, where they went – everything, gentlemen. I have no doubt she is totally unaware of the secret she carries – but carry it she does.'

* * *

At the time the sample of Romanov gold embellished the dining table of the Comte de Toulouse, a meeting was taking place in a grey, unprepossessing building not far from the Kremlin in Moscow.

Sternov needed no reminding that a summons from Vladimir

Semichastny, head of the KGB and the most feared man in Russia, was no accolade. Even when Semichastny, surprisingly, rose from his chair and greeted him affably, it did little to calm feelings of foreboding.

'Alexis,' began Semichastny, thin lips forming a smile, 'tell me, any new developments concerning the vexing issue of the Romanov gold?' A pause, whilst fingers turned a sheaf of papers contained in a bright red folder 'And the girl ... Natasha Gollitzin?' Expressionless eyes peered at Sternov over rimless spectacles.

'Comrade Semichastny, as you are aware, Internal Security gave little credence to the existence of the gold until recently.'. Only the rustle of turning pages disturbed the silence.

'That isn't what I asked!' The menace was tangible.

'We now have proof the cache exists,' stammered Sternov, desperate to recover, 'and we have a lead where the girl is concerned.'

Semichastny, intent on studying one particular page, remained silent until, with a voice little above a whisper, he spoke again. 'Then don't you agree, Alexis, we must recover it...? and the girl.'

'Indeed, comrade.'

'Has it not occurred to you that the key to the puzzle may well be the girl, Gollitzin? Love and hate, Alexis, ignore them at your peril, they are very powerful motivators.' Extracting a page, Semichastny squinted across at the discomforted Sternov.

'Take the girl and the Duchess Elizabeth – love and naked ambition, either one a sufficient motive to ensure the Gollitzin girl has every possible resource. Now, consider hate, as represented by Mikhael Derevenko; put them together, Alexis, and we will solve the riddle.'

'Comrade Derevenko allowed personal feelings to cloud his judgement, comrade, that is why –'

Semichastny interrupted.

'It was a mistake to dismiss Derevenko. He nurtures hatred, a very powerful aphrodisiac when harnessed to such a task.'

Having secured the folder, the thin smile again creased his face. 'I have decided to reinstate Derevenko. His orders are to play a waiting game – let them have the gold, Alexis, after all it will be much simpler to take it from them than search for it ourselves ... don't you agree?'

Sternov agreed.

'One more thing, Alexis. You will shortly be receiving special orders prepared by the First Secretary and myself. Orders, Alexis, of a highly confidential nature. I think when you receive them matters will become a great deal clearer...'

'I will be honoured, comrade.

5

An Invitation
(Three Months Later)

With the likelihood of further funds becoming available the Comte and Comtesse's attitude to the proposed tuition of Natasha softened. It was agreed, following the emergence of the gold bar and the possibilities it presented, that she should remain with them for three months. During that time the Comtesse would undertake to ensure that Natasha was taught the refinements and etiquette necessary for her new position in life.

Sergei, deciding London was immeasurably safer from the attentions of the KGB than Paris, found for himself a small flat in an unfashionable part of Edmonton. However, mindful of his obligations to the dead Duchess, he made frequent visits to the home of the Comte and Comtesse and was soon marvelling at Natasha's transformation from an almost illiterate peasant girl to that of a sensuous and sophisticated woman.

'Her English is improving, Sergei, and her French ... to be honest, she is an admirable pupil in every way. In fact, I'm beginning to feel very proud of my accomplishment, particularly in so short a time.'

'You've achieved wonders, Suzanne, and it is so important because at last I have persuaded Sokolov to present her to the Duma in exile – you know how vital it is that she obtains their endorsement as the true heir.'

'Do you think that's possible?'

'The endorsement? I see no reasons why not, after all who have they got at the moment, only that waster Prince Michael and his obnoxious surrogate mother.'

'So fingers crossed, Sergei.'

'As you say, Suzanne, fingers crossed.'

* * *

Enveloped in the warmth of her bath, her body indulging itself with the caress of the limpid water, Natasha's mind wandered back over the past few months of cataclysmic change. The journey from Kolomyja, with Olga impatient at every delay. Then Olga's murder, followed by the flight to Paris. The teachings of Suzanne – more gentle than Olga's but nonetheless determined. The temptations presented by Marcel, who within a few days of her arrival at the home of the Comte had declared his undying love for her. All flashed through her mind like pages in a photograph album.

Even now, in spite of all the fuss and fawning bestowed on her, she found it all but impossible to believe what the old woman back in Appenzell had told her. That she was the granddaughter of the last Tsarina and one day would ascend the throne of all the Russias.

As Igor gently stroked the base of her neck and shoulders, she recalled the teachings of Olga. The lessons of seduction given in the bleak surroundings of Olga's tiny flat, back in Kolomyja, seemingly a million miles away from the luxury she now enjoyed. How she still admired poor Olga and her grasp of human nature and particularly its fallibilities. Her understanding of what was required to release the baser instincts lurking in all men and women. Yes, as with Suzanne, she had learnt her lessons well.

Then there was Sergei, dear quaint Sergei, who had remained uncompromising in his devout loyalty, as typified by the gorgeous flat he had found for her and Igor. How quickly she had ingratiated herself into the party scene since her arrival in London – in spite of dear Sergei's protests. Then the chance meeting with Bill Webster,

34

who had become a willing door-opener and provider of many adventures.

Igor's gentle strokes descended slowly from the nape of her neck and shoulders until, as if by accident, they brushed most exquisitely against the soft rim of her breasts. She sighed, and through half-closed eyes watched his reflection opposite in the full-length bath mirror.

Igor, imperturbable, distant, cloaked in mystery but with an indefinable menace. She remembered an incident in Paris when, unannounced, she had walked into his small attic room to find him whistling quietly whilst hunched over a table – a table which displayed an armoury of guns. His attempts to belatedly cover them with a cloth was not lost on her. Neither was that brief aura of intelligence, far removed from the bumbling Igor she was used to.

Tired of her daydreaming she signalled to Igor, who, unperturbed as ever, reached for two large bath towels he had draped earlier over the radiator. He watched, with complete indifference, as she rose from the bath, the water cascading from her until only driblets remained – each one descending in channels, marking her body as if even they were jealous of her leaving.

Draping the towels round her Igor began his ritual of drying her. His rubbing assailed in her a physical response which, as always, he studiously ignored.

'Igor,' she teased, 'don't you find me attractive?' said as she slowly removed the towels and stood naked in front of him, before turning and adopting various poses calculated to arouse even the most sterile of men.

Again there was no response from the enigmatic Igor. Frustrated at such indifference, Natasha kicked the towels into the corner of the bathroom and flounced out – fortunately, or otherwise, she failed to notice the glimmer of a smile which slowly replaced the previous set features of Igor's face.

*　　*　　*

Whilst commenting, rather smugly, that the district code was wrong, 'We're NW8 here,' Peter Canning read the letter through again. Meanwhile, Emma pirouetted gaily round the room. He could see that, as far as his wife was concerned, the invitation was already accepted. Carefully replacing the letter in its envelope, he forced a weak smile.

'I would love to go, pet, but it's a difficult time for me,' he began, his face now assuming that strained expression which in the past had helped him out of many a difficult situation. 'I promised Charles a round of golf on Sunday, and then there's that meeting Saturday morning.'

'But you don't have to go to the meeting,' complained Emma, the first flush of excitement already fading from her face. 'You said yourself it didn't really involve you.' Lips pouting, she quickly slipped her arms round his neck, her closeness stretching Peter's strained expression to the limit. 'You like Janice,' she purred, 'I know you do, and you went to law school with Bill, so you're bound to have a lot to talk about...' with that she reached upwards, her mouth searching for his.

Peter, brow furrowed, avoided the inviting lips and slowly freed himself from her embrace. No longer was he in his sitting room with his wife but sweating on a couch in his private room at the Temple, a dark witch of a girl beneath him, clawing at his back and muttering words Emma had never heard and, if she had, never uttered. Then that awful moment when Bill, the same Bill now married to Janice, had walked in...

*   *   *

As Bill and Janice Webster met them in the driveway of their home, the prospect of a weekend with Bill and his wife was not helped by his greeting and the use of the words 'Old reprobate'. Lunch, following a brief sojourn in the local pub, passed quietly without any of the expected innuendoes and Peter began to feel more relaxed. It was, after all, no more than an indiscretion.

Perhaps he was making too much of it after all and, from what he had heard, Bill was no saint. Such reassurance was cut short when Janice placidly announced, as she rose from the table, that one of the dinner guests was to be a Natasha Gollitzin. 'Fascinating girl, very attractive, part Russian I believe. You'll have to watch Peter, Emma, she's a real *femme fatale*. Bill met her at the Raybournes, one of their dinner parties, you know how they love to spring surprises when entertaining...' her voice died away as she disappeared in the direction of the kitchen.

'You remember Natasha, Peter,' said Bill with a smile. The faint trace of malice in his tone was not lost on Emma, who shot a quizzical look at her husband. Peter, conscious of the rising colour in his cheeks, muttered incoherently into his already empty coffee cup.

Alone in their room, as they prepared for an afternoon walk, Peter braced himself for the inevitable questions.

'I've never heard you mention Natasha Gollitzin,' began Emma, her eyes round with curiosity. Peter's attempts to explain their meeting away failed miserably. After a final pronounced flounce in front of the mirror, his wife, with a look her husband knew only too well, said archly, 'I'm looking forward to meeting this Natasha, *femme fatale* and all. You will introduce us, won't you, Peter?'

Peter shuddered as the bedroom door closed behind her with a bang.

*   *   *

The afternoon walk was like the calm before the expected storm. Bill had declined the invitation to join them and, as the girls had gone on ahead, Peter was alone with his thoughts. It was impossible to believe that he and Natasha were to meet up again in such circumstances.

Once more he saw the look of astonishment on Bill 's face that evening. Only Natasha seemed oblivious to the situation. With eyes still reflecting her animal passion of moments before, she had gathered her clothes together and, pressing them to her naked body, made a gesture of contempt by blowing a kiss in Bill's direction.

Peter's thoughts returned to his wife. How traumatic it would be if she learnt of his infidelity whilst they were staying with Bill and Janice – not that he cared overmuch for Emma's friend. Janice was a daddy's girl who had everything. First Roedean, then a finishing school in Berne . . . and Bill, made a senior partner in her father's multimillion-pound law firm within a year of their marriage. Their six-bedroomed house, the two cars. Why was it Emma made so much of them? He could never compete: a junior partner in a solicitor's practice, it would be years before he could hope to match them. And why did Emma always assume that he and Bill were such friends? Yes, they had studied law together but their relationship had never amounted to much. Bill was deep, he knew that, and he had no doubt he had been set up where Natasha was concerned. Almost certainly Bill had had her himself before passing her on, and he was convinced he had been watching them long before making his presence known. Yes, without doubt and amongst other things, Bill was something of a voyeur.

*　*　*

Bill had watched them leave from his bedroom window. First, the two girls, their inane chatter reaching up to him in the crisp autumn air, then Peter, his overcoat done up to the collar, hands deep in his pockets. What a fool, he had thought, how Natasha had ever fancied Peter was a mystery. But then – a wry smile creased his face – Natasha had been pissed out of her tiny mind and he had ensured all the right ingredients were there – Peter hadn't needed any persuading, and Natasha . . . well, Natasha had peculiar tastes, so unlike the inhibited English women he had known. His thoughts turned to the delicious minutes he had watched them perform. Peter had been quite out of his depth, as he had expected, but even so it had been quite a delightful cameo.

The evening promised a wealth of delights with the two of them just across the dinner table. Peter, like a fish, was already on the hook. How he played him would be a source of endless amusement. Natasha, totally unaware of her party piece, would provide him with further enjoyment as the sprat to catch the mackerel.

The arrival of the caterers, earlier than expected, meant that further luscious thoughts were left in limbo, as a fussy little man boasting a drooping moustache, which gyrated alarmingly every time he spoke, insisted on inspecting everything. It was one of the few occasions when Bill was more than pleased to see his wife walking up the driveway, Emma, as ever, hanging on her every word.

Their walk had emphasised Emma's feelings of awe about Janice.

'I understand you've never met Natasha Gollitzin?' Janice had said when they stopped to admire some swans gliding majestically across a lake.

'No,' Emma had replied, trying desperately to appear uninterested.

'I believe Peter has,' Janice had said, clearly delighted to be in a position to impart such knowledge. 'They met whilst he and Bill hosted a farewell party at the Temple; they say she's related to Tsar Nicholas – but you hear these tales, as you know. But she is a most delectable and sweet creature ... such presence, makes me feel quite inadequate.'

The thought of Janice ever feeling inadequate had intrigued Emma to the point where she was determined to pursue the subject of Natasha Gollitzin further. Janice, however, had obviously decided otherwise. 'We'll be eight for dinner, a nice number don't you think?' – said with a sideways glance. 'I've brought in outside caterers, so much easier, no rushing in and out of the kitchen.' Emma, heartened by this admission of some deficiency on the part of her hostess, had agreed.

*   *   *

39

They joined their hosts for an aperitif in the drawing room, where they were quickly introduced to Bill's near neighbours George and Hilda. As Peter sipped his sherry, all his sensitivities were concentrated on the door from where she would appear. Not even the vociferous George, large, with a manner to match, or the twitterings of his diminutive wife, distracted him.

As if by some secret signal, conversations ceased as, declining Janice's arm, Natasha entered the room. Once again Peter experienced twin sensations of self-loathing and rapturous longing. Her approach for the formal introduction caused him to shiver with anticipation as, with superb disdain, Natasha held out her hand to him. The simple black dress she was wearing looked far from simple on her; in body and soul Natasha could never be that uncomplicated. Her fluidity of movement reminded Peter of a ballerina's combination of precision and poise. In her hand she delicately balanced her sherry glass and in an infinitesimal moment, as their eyes met, the tip of her tongue caressed its rim.

'Peter, how nice, we meet again.' Her scarlet lips, wet from the sherry, served to emphasise the width of her mouth.

Before he could conjure up a sparkling reply he was conscious of a hand gripping his, as, in an act of obvious possession, Emma said abruptly, 'I believe you know my husband,' her voice betraying her uneasiness.

'How you say? Ships that pass in ze night,' came the reply, enriched with a heavy accent which in itself conveyed promises of dark mysteries still to be unveiled. And then as she moved away, 'But it was very pleasant.'

Although by now Natasha was across the room, Peter still drank deeply of her perfume – a fragrance which reminded him of the scent of a tropical plant – a plant known only to flower at night – a black orchid.

The scream of tyres in the driveway announced the arrival of the final guest, Jamie, younger brother of Janice and still at university, met in the hall by Bill, his words of welcome clearly heard.

'You might at least have worn a tie, James, and your trousers look as if you've been to bed in them.'

Janice quickly joined her husband. 'Rubbish, Bill, I told Jamie not to bother to dress, it's quite informal.'

'I had no idea he had been invited,' replied Bill, with heavy emphasis on the '*he*'. James, obviously stung by his brother-in-law's remarks, hit back, 'Well, if that's how you feel about it, I'll shove off.'

Janice, suddenly aware that the drawing room door was open, gently closed it.

'Really, you two,' she began again, 'don't you know I've a room full of guests in there? Bill, you rejoin them, and Jamie, go upstairs and tidy up and enough of this nonsense.'

As they both turned away to do her bidding Janice was keenly aware that only a limited truce had been called. Both would need careful watching over dinner, she mused, as smoothing her hair she prepared to rejoin her dinner guests.

*   *   *

In sepulchral tones, 'Drooping Moustache' announced dinner. Diffidently, they followed their hosts into the dining room. With the mystique of her perfume still lingering in his mind, Peter, much to his barely concealed annoyance, found himself alongside the insipid Hilda, whilst, to his chagrin, Natasha was escorted by James. A James, he noticed, with mounting despondency, already responding to her attention and the heat of her personality.

To the accompaniment of the popping of champagne corks, each bottle deftly handled by the white-gloved caterer, warm asparagus was served. Fascinated, Peter watched as Natasha fondled hers in the manner of a love goddess at the altar of the mighty phallus, her fingernails reminding him of an occasion when, like tips of blood-red spears, they had ploughed deep furrows in his bare back.

*   *   *

Damn him, thought Bill, as James and Natasha went into dinner chatting together as if they were lifelong friends, damn him to hell. All his perverse planning for the evening, whereby Peter, in front of the simpering Emma, was to be reduced bit by bit to a floundering shadow of a man, had come to naught.

How he envied men, he reflected, who had the capacity to interest her, however tenuously. Sitting at the top of the table, outwardly the perfect host, only served to conceal the torment within. As Bill looked at her, he again remembered their first meeting at the Raybournes, a couple who prided themselves on being with-it. To John and Connie Raybourne, the acquisition of Natasha Gollitzin to grace their dinner table was indeed a triumph. Avid supporters of CND and anything that attacked the Establishment, they were also renowned as connoisseurs of all things beautiful and bizarre. Their dinner parties, the envy of many, were frequently attended by the avante-garde of the West End theatre. Added emphasis, undoubtedly, would be Igor, who went everywhere with her – the beauty and the beast – incongruous but, to the Raybournes, the *pièce de résistance* for them and their guests. How and when they had discovered Natasha remained a mystery, although, Bill suspected, it had probably been by chance.

Janice had declined their invitation, and, as luck would have it he had been seated next to Natasha at dinner. He remembered how, long before the coffee and brandy, he had become so fascinated by her mix of childlike simplicity and adult sophistication, both masking a wanton sexuality, as demonstrated by an uninhibited exhibition of eating a cherry as if she were performing oral sex, he had become hopelessly addicted. Then, his accepted offer to escort her home, his inept fumblings in the back of the taxi followed by, surprisingly, the open invitation to her bed ... the sensation, combined with an all-embracing sense of triumph, that he was to have her and then, at the peak of her intensity, his utter failure and humiliation, followed by utter degradation, as she laughed.

Over and over he had relived that moment when awareness had

dawned that he could never possess her. And so, as if in compensation for his own failure, he hoped for similar failure in others, the willing but feeble Peter Canning providing his first solace at the farewell party in the Temple. Peter, as Bill had suspected, proved incapable of coping with her demands and excesses. From such failure in others he had drawn but a modicum of satisfaction, for in the depths of his mind lingered the unacceptable but nonetheless bitter realisation that he was imperfect. Such a manifestation, born of failure, boded ill for Natasha Gollitzin.

* * *

Janice surveyed her guests. Apart from Bill continuing to glower at poor Jamie, and Peter, who for some indefinable reason seemed to be enjoying a private sulk, the party appeared fine. Satisfied, Janice continued her cautious but profoundly interesting study of Natasha Gollitzin.

Contrary to what she had told Emma earlier, this was the first time they had met. From Bill's description, she had expected a tarty *femme fatale*. After all, in her opinion, it was no great accomplishment to entice men into bed. She guessed that Bill had already availed himself of that opportunity. Not that such an assumption worried her – Bill in bed, she smiled to herself, left a lot to be desired. Looking at Natasha, she surmised that she would be in no hurry for a repeat performance.

Rarely, reflected Janice, had she seen a face with such delicate bone structure. The wide expressive mouth and evenly shaped teeth were enhanced by scarlet lipstick, its colour offsetting a milky-white unblemished complexion. But it was the eyes that fascinated. Dark, brooding and quite hypnotic in their intensity. Eyes, Janice immediately felt, that were the mirrors behind which lurked a mind schooled in depravity. Her hair, thick and as black as pitch, hung loosely on bare shoulders, providing a subject any artist would relish.

Jamie was clearly dazzled by her attentiveness, much to Bill's evident annoyance. Peter continued to glare balefully at all and sundry. George was being George, when Hilda wasn't looking, and as for Hilda herself, well it was obvious what she thought of Natasha.

How hopeless men were, Janice mused, at concealing their feelings. It was inevitable that Natasha, enjoying some remark of Jamie's, should turn laughingly in her direction. Their eyes met, and in that infinite moment a message flashed between them and was understood by both. Janice, looking away, experienced a stirring that both frightened and excited her.

Shuffling in her chair and with downcast eyes, Janice recalled an earlier time, three years ago, when that same recognition signal had passed between her and a lissome blonde teenager; as if by mutual consent, a dark secret was shared and enjoyed and what was most disconcerting for Janice, a promise to be fulfilled. In spite of her reluctance, Janice's thoughts greedily returned to the school in Berne when she had crept into the girl's bed. How the soft, warm, supple body pressed close against hers had aroused physical longing and animal-like sensations unbelievable in their intensity.

The excuse she had fed herself since, that her intentions had been to comfort the girl, who was obviously suffering from homesickness, was, she now realised, a blatant untruth . . . and now this, an invitation in Natasha's eyes, momentary, but nonetheless explicit in its intentions, that had overwhelmed her body like an electric shock. Then, to her growing apprehension, the realisation that she herself had given an instant response, a response so clear as to send a shiver down her spine. Carefully avoiding further eye contact, Janice, aware that her hand was shaking, drank deeply from her glass.

*   *   *

Hilda Fawcett, of Fawcett Pie and Sausage fame, made a mental note to speak to Janice. The beef was just a tiny bit underdone, and the plates could have been hotter. Peter Canning, her dinner companion, had been a bore all evening. Having tried to engage him in conversation, she had finally accepted how hopeless it was, as she watched him moodily chase a pea round his plate.

Not for the first time, she turned her gaze on the most interesting member of the party, Miss Gollitzin. She certainly was a most strikingly attractive woman – of course she knew it, but one should not blame her for that. East European at a guess, even east of the Danube from her heavy accent. Hilda cracked her knuckles, a habit when deep in thought, and continued her assessment. It was blatantly obvious she had all the men eating out of her hand. Even George, silly old fool, was attempting to engage her attention with his stories of how he had opened his first butcher's shop – as if she were interested. One had only to look at James, barely out of his teens but already bewitched. No, she decided, she most certainly would not have invited her to the party. Even the caterer, simpleton that he was, had succumbed to her devastating smile and had totally ignored her request for French mustard. Having Miss Gollitzin at the dinner table was rather like introducing a stick of dynamite into a child's box of fireworks with the touch-paper already sizzling.

*   *   *

'Big George' Fawcett, all of eighteen stone and over six foot, towered over the dinner table like some monolithic sculpture. A man with a gargantuan appetite, he devoured his food as he did life, with enormous gusto. Although his fleshy face and buck teeth gave him an unfortunate resemblance to a well-known cartoon character, they had been the spark to ignite his financial ambitions. At an early age he had accepted that such physical liabilities could be compensated for only by money. Money, he had quickly learnt, was both a persuader and a provider.

Hilda, a David to his Goliath, had been the provider in the early days. Now the owner of six shops with an interest in a further three, George had become a pursuer of the good things in life and, in particular, women. None too keen to accompany his wife to the Webster's dinner party, he had been persuaded in the knowledge that Janice Webster kept a good table. Although, he accepted, 'hoity-toity' Janice Webster was beyond his orbit, being Hilda's goddaughter, she did possess long, shapely legs, so the evening would have its compensations.

Then the evening's surprise package Natasha Gollitzin. His kind of woman. Sophisticated, but with a touch of childlike simplicity, which he found unbelievable in its temptations. And then there were those eyes, eyes of such depth and full of such promise as to entice him into imaginings foreign even to him. He had to have her. In his experience every woman had her price; in her case he guessed she wouldn't come cheap, but what the hell, it was only money. A weekend in Paris might tempt her, plus a shopping expedition . . . it had never failed in the past. But how to get to her? Hilda, ever-watchful Hilda, had taken an obvious dislike to the woman – only to be expected, of course. Then there was that kid Jamie, still wet behind the ears but nevertheless a threat; some women liked a young boy. A lot would depend on how he played his cards at the coffee and brandy stage; until then he would simply continue drinking in her exotic perfume and fantasise over that delectable wide red mouth.

*   *   *

'They're a rum lot in there,' said Marlene, the caterer's assistant, nodding in the direction of the dining room as she began loading creme brulée onto the silver serving trays. ''Ave you ever seen anythin' like it, all those men slobbering over that black bitch?'

'She's not black,' corrected Henry, his moustache twitching.

'You're as bad as the rest of 'em,' countered Marlene, 'I've seen you leering at 'er and taking a peek at 'er tits . . .'

'That's enough of that,' replied Henry, somewhat sourly. 'Just remember we're paid to do a job, we're not 'ere to comment on the 'ouseguests,' said with a touch of pomposity as, with some disgust, he eyed his assistant now perched on the edge of the kitchen table. Not bad in bed when she'd had a skinful, but the woman in there, now she was something . . . the nasal voice of Marlene interrupted further thoughts.

'Oh gawd, I've laddered my new stockings. Only bought 'em at Marks yesterday, now look at 'em.' With that she spread her legs to examine the damage. Henry, already aroused with his thoughts of the 'black bitch', had unexpected views of black stockings and suspenders climbing to pink thighs – thighs fringed with the frothy lace of panties now stretched wide.

Conscious of his interest, she quickly responded. 'You can forget that,' she mouthed, 'we won't be 'ome before three. Tell you what, chat her up, she looks as if she could cope with half a dozen.' Her laughter following this aside was a mix of coarseness and the culmination of too many cigarettes, as her voice dissolved into a bout of coughing.

'Stop guzzling that champagne and 'elp me with these puddings,' chided Henry, now concentrating on the job in hand.

Marlene, having smeared butter over the run in her stockings, again defiantly lifted the magnum to her mouth. 'She's Russian, you know, as sure as eggs.' Having made such a profound statement, she contemplated its possibilities. 'Do you think she's a Commie sent over 'ere to lure men to their deaths? I remember a film once, it was ever so good, she were a Mati Hari.'

'A Mati what?' he interrupted her.

'You know what I mean, anyway,' continued Marlene, not in the least discouraged, 'she was killed in the end with 'er lover in 'er arms.'

'Before, or after?'

'Oh shut up,' she said, 'all you think about is sex, sex and more sex.'

'Amen to that,' was the rejoinder.

* * *

47

Alone in the scullery Igor listened to the banter coming through from the half-open door of the kitchen. His thoughts, although in a very different vein, were also concentrated on Natasha and the dilemma she had created since their arrival in London. It was obvious she had taken to her new life like the proverbial duck to water. Not surprisingly, he had to admit, when such naive charm was combined with irresistible beauty. Her head had been turned. Really, his thoughts continuing, you could hardly blame the girl, catapulted as she had been from a life of abject poverty to riches beyond her wildest dreams. Now, he recognised, they had a Frankenstein on their hands. Should he speak to Sergei or confront her himself? Either way his cover, so diligently prepared, would be gone, and Igor would become Charlie Tuttle, one-time member of British Military Intelligence but now committed to an outrageous scheme hatched by someone within the environs of the CIA. He recalled his first meeting with Elizabeth, of how she had resurrected his life and given him a sense of purpose whilst engendering in him the spirit of defiance and belief that one day her beloved country would recover its soul.

Seated at the bare wooden table with the ludicrous ramblings of the caterers as a background, his thoughts again returned to Appenzell and the Duchess. How she had chuckled when, in their early days together, he had adopted the persona, both in dress and speech, of the eccentric Igor. Then, inevitably, their last meeting came back to him. He gently rubbed the knuckles of the hand she had gripped so tightly as he recalled her words 'Natasha is our only hope, guard her as you have me, with your life...' He had given his word – all that he had to give her. She had said nothing in reply, but her eyes, trusting and with a shining implicit faith, told him more than words ever could.

* * *

The Websters' drawing room was very spacious, ideal for entertaining. Two four-seater sofas and numerous easy chairs vied with

48

each other to tempt the guest – all enjoyed the proximity of the large open fireplace with its marble surround. That evening, for the comfort and ambience of her guests, Janice had ensured a good supply of logs, which kept the fire a brilliant red, its warmth reaching out to the furthest extremities of the room.

Emma and Janice exchanged a grimace. It was obvious to Emma the dinner party was not the success her hostess had hoped. Not surprisingly, she reflected, with that woman receiving all the attention. Long ago she had decided that Natasha Gollitzin was a man-eater. A man-eater with an insatiable appetite, who, in all probability, had already digested her husband and very likely Bill as well. Curiously the thought of Peter in bed with Natasha did not worry her unduly. Marriage to him, she had to admit, was a disappointment. In the early days, whilst at law school, he had been full of optimism and fun with his ideas and grandiose plans for the future – all, sadly, had turned out pie in the sky. Now, as a junior partner in a small practice, with promotion dependent on dead men's shoes, she had come to accept that the years ahead would merely be mirrors of years past.

Looking at Natasha, languidly sipping a brandy, legs loosely crossed, she could well understand if Peter had fallen by the wayside. Although James and George's conversation had ended on George being despatched to the library, James's eyes continued to stray across and devour the reclining Natasha. It needed little imagination to conjure up a vision of Natasha in bed, fulfilling any man's fantasies, plus, she smiled inwardly, a few of Natasha's thrown in.

* * *

Declining pudding, much to the annoyance of Janice, Bill and Peter had adjourned to the library.

'Thank you for joining me, Peter,' said Bill as he closed the library door behind them. 'I think I would have strangled that kid if–'

'I felt the same,' cut in Peter, 'what on earth does she see in him?'

'You know Natasha, Peter, it's simply a case of fresh young meat.'

'Do you really think she would hop into bed with him?'

'Don't you?' responded Bill.

Silence followed as both conjured up the image of James trying to cope with Natasha's eccentricities in bed.

'Did you notice her tattoo when you were . . . you know?'

'Yes,' replied Peter, his face slightly flushed. 'Mind you, I've seen similar ones before – usually on high-class prostitutes.'

'My, you've been around haven't you?' A hint of admiration entered into Bill's voice. 'I never thought you had it in you.'

'Oh, it's a long time ago, water under the bridge.'

Having poured himself a brandy. Bill joined Peter on the leather sofa.

'Sure you won't have one?'

'Perhaps later,' replied Peter, obviously still suffering from withdrawal symptoms over the loss of Natasha to James.

'Tell me,' began Bill again, his earlier intentions to ridicule the man put aside, 'when you had sex with her, what was it like?'

'Really, Bill, that's a bit much.'

'Was she too much?' Bill's attempt at humour failed miserably. 'Seriously, what is she like in bed?'

Peter looked directly at him.

'If you must know, she's insatiable. I felt totally drained, every bone in my body ached,' Then, half to himself, 'But I couldn't wait for more.'

'Did you satisfy her?'

'Bill, this really is too much – I don't know.' Then softly, 'I don't think any man could.'

'Did you know, Peter, that it's not just men with the delectable Natasha – she likes the taste of the fair sex almost as much.'

'How do you know all this?' countered Peter.

'I've been making a study of Miss Natasha Gollitzin. Believe me, she's best left alone.'

'Easier said than done,' said Peter, 'the mere thought of another man –'

'Or woman,' teased Bill.

'God, did you have to tell me?' exclaimed Peter, his eyes downcast.

'There's something else, Big George was licking his lips all evening.' This was said as he moved to the bell-pull.

'She would never look at him.'

'Where Natasha's concerned, the more the merrier ... anyway, Peter, have a brandy and drown your sorrows.'

'Was there somethin'?' enquired Marlene, her frizzy hair showing round the library door.

'Yes, coffee, please.'

Peter, crossing to the decanter, helped himself to a large brandy as Marlene returned with their coffee.

'Anythin' else?' She posed before them, legs unnecessarily wide apart.

'No thank you, Marlene, we'll ring if we need you.'

They both watched whilst she minced out of the room, her bottom gyrating alarmingly, as if trying to liberate itself from the tightness of her skirt.

'That's more your mark, Peter,' as the door closed behind her. 'Women like Natasha are way out of your league. As a matter of interest, how many times have you been to bed with her?'

'Only the once, in my room at the Temple. You ought to know, you were there.'

'Sorry about that, did your back take long to heal?'

Peter gave him a long look before answering, and, to Bill's surprise, confronted him.

'You've slept with her, haven't you?'

'Surely you are not as naive to think you're the only one?'

'You bastard,' said Peter, rising to his feet, 'I might have known.'

Red-faced, Big George entered the library. 'I've been ordered to fetch you both,' he said, as he began pouring a brandy, 'the natives are becoming restless.'

51

Lumbering over, he collapsed alongside Bill.

'I say, she's ravishing, ravishing I say. Where did you find her, Bill?'

'Who? Marlene?' replied Bill, exchanging a wink with Peter.

'Marlene? Who the 'ell is Marlene?'

'The waitress, George, the girl who waited on us at dinner.'

'The serving wench? The days I troubled myself with serving wenches are long past. No, I'm talking about the black piece,' he said pouring himself another large measure of brandy. 'Never seen anything like it in twenty years, and believe me I've seen the lot: Paris, Rome, Amsterdam and the Far East.' Looking around as he gulped his brandy, droplets of which rested on his chin, he exclaimed, 'What's this then, a wake? You both look as miserable as sin.' Laughing uproariously, he again slumped down alongside Bill. 'Now come on, Bill, where did you find her?'

'She's a friend of a friend, George, nothing more or less,' he replied, trying to placate him.

'Well, name the friend then.'

'You wouldn't know if I told you.'

'Why all the bloody secrecy? I thought we were all friends together,' replied George, somewhat ruffled, as the door of the library opened.

'Oh there you all are – if the devil were to cast his net now...' Hilda's laboured humour was ignored. 'Janice would like you to join her in the drawing room.' Her voice and air of authority was in no way diminished by the lack of repartee from the three. Standing in the doorway, eyes behind bifocals examining each in turn, she presented a formidable figure. 'And you, George, have had enough brandies for one night.'

'Coming, my love,' as the three rose to their feet. George's conciliatory tone was not matched by his expression, as each of them replenished their brandy glasses before trooping across the hall in the wake of their self-appointed Pied Piper.

* * *

'At last here they come,' said Janice, as Hilda, still officiating as the Pied Piper, led the recalcitrant trio into the room.

'What's all this...? Cannot live without us for five minutes – for five minutes, I say, what do you make of it, Bill? – Perhaps they do love us!'

For once, Janice was grateful for George's buffoonery, coarse at times though it was.

'You see, George,' she said, 'I've kept your seat warm beside Natasha.'

'Well, I say, I'm grateful for that, I say,' as with a lurch, which all but precipitated his brandy over the still-reclining Natasha, he sat down. Natasha, moving to an upright position, managed what was for her a rather watered-down smile of welcome – the inference, though, was totally lost on George.

Bill surveyed the field. Big George, fortified by the brandies, was making his long-delayed move. Not that he would bed the lovely Natasha tonight, oh no, mused Bill, not with Hilda's gimlet eyes watching every move. No, he would try for an assignation somewhere far removed from here. He was probably, guessed Bill, offering 'sweeteners' right now, but from the indifferent response, illustrated by the barely concealed yawn, it was heavy going.

Peter? Possibly, but here again 'Emma the Mouse' – he laughed inwardly at his private joke – would present an insurmountable problem. Neither had tried to hide the frigidity that existed between them both during dinner and since, Natasha being the catalyst – no, there was little hope for Peter tonight.

But James? Now, if he were to lay odds he would be favourite. Bill recalled their animated conversations during dinner, he was young and virginal, and he had no encumbrance – free as a bird was dear James. Yes, he was the one most likely to stealthily walk the corridors tonight. Bill studied the callow youth now in conversation with Emma. His pink cheeks and uncut hair, thought Bill, were the epitome of the youth of today. A self-confessed fan of Bob Dylan and Tommy Steele – you couldn't be much more diversified than that – indicating a mind similar to that of a jack-rabbit. Although engaged with Emma, he was betrayed by his eyes, which at every opportunity drank in the gorgeous Natasha. Bill again suffered that tightness of the throat experienced whenever the prospect of a new male, obviously capable of arousing her, hove into sight. The thought of the kid being devoured by Natasha's uninhibited lovemaking created in Bill feelings of utter frustration, combined with an overwhelming desire to be a part of it – if only as a voyeur.

The appearance of the caterer sufficed to stifle further agonies as, with suitable deference, Henry, at the door of the room, awaited Janice's attention.

'Henry,' she said, 'thank you for a splendid meal, it was excellent.'

Henry inclined his head in acknowledgement. 'All the rooms have been prepared, ma'am, including...'

Janice cut in, 'What would I do without you, Henry. Now you get off home. Have you rung for a taxi?'

'I'm about to. Would eleven tomorrow be satisfactory?'

'Perfectly,' she replied, 'as you know, we're only having a cold luncheon, so eleven will be fine, and Florrie will be here at eight to prepare breakfast.'

'The table has been laid and I've put a note out for the milkman.' Henry, always susceptible to praise, awaited further blandishments. Unfortunately, they were not forthcoming as Hilda's shrill voice interrupted.

'Is the fire on in our room, Janice? You know how I feel the cold.' As if anticipating her question Henry, in a superior tone, stated fires had been lit in all the guest rooms.

'Thank you for that, Henry, and goodnight to you.' Henry, aware that he had no further excuse for prolonging the interview, inclined his head once again and quietly closed the door behind him.

* * *

54

Janice, banishing any feelings of guilt to the back of her mind, was thankful that months ago she and Bill had decided to have their own bedrooms. Opening her bedroom door, she listened – the house was as silent as the grave, only the street lights, creating light and shadows of their own along the darkened corridor, gave her any sense of reality.

Gently she tried the door. It opened as if it itself was a willing partner to her intentions. Crossing the floor, she was soon at the side of the bed, the outline of Natasha's body made clear and distinct by the dying embers of the fire. Reaching up to her was that all-consuming scent at once familiar – an aroma that created sensations that danced up and down her spine, tantalising her with their rich promise. She reached out with her hand and felt the silky softness of an exposed arm. Slowly she bent down-wards . . .

The voice was harsh and as cold as steel. 'I think, Mrs Webster, it would be better for us all if you returned to your room.'

*   *   *

As the weekend guests prepared to depart, Janice invited them all to attend her drawing room for the last time. Adopting a position with her back to the fire and ensuring she avoided Natasha's eyes, and in particular Igor's, she made an announcement.

'It's Jamie's twenty-first a week Friday, and after discussing matters of the celebration with daddy, it's been decided that Bill and I will hold a dinner party in his honour. You are all invited,' gushed Janice, 'seven-thirty for eight, and this time I think we'll make it black tie.'

'Are you sure you want the work, Janice?' said Hilda, eyes widening behind the bifocals. 'Surely James would prefer a party with his own age group rather then be surrounded with us old duffers.'

'Nonsense, Hilda, before he left Jamie said he would love it – he's planning to bring his latest, Penelope Charters, Sir Humphrey

55

Charter's daughter, and anyway Daddy's giving him a party at the Vic, Saturday, when he can invite all his friends.'

'Well, if you say so, Janice, of course we would love to come.'

'Nothing like a party organised by Janice, I say, wouldn't stay away for anything ...' George's voice rang round the room.

'We would be delighted,' contributed Emma, her eyes glancing at Peter.

'Natasha?'

'It would be, how you say, veree nice, *merci*.'

'That's settled then – and don' t forget to let me know if you want to stay overnight, no problems with beds. Well, may I now wish you a safe journey home and God bless.'

6

An Innocuous Event?

History is littered with occurrences when, as a result of some quite innocuous event, a chain reaction occurs which profoundly influences or even resolves what, until then, has appeared insoluble.

Just such an event happened when Natasha, returning to her flat after leaving the Websters, stumbled on the stairs, grazing the top of her thigh. Fortunately, Sergei was present, having just concluded negotiations with the landlord involving a further short-term let for Natasha and Igor. Applying sticking plaster to the wound, he saw, for the first time, the iniquitous tattoo placed there by the Duchess years before when Natasha was but an infant. Familiar with the centuries-old insignia of the House of Romanov, he was immediately aware of the many inaccuracies depicted in the tattoo. Such a scale of deceptions would have never been permitted by the Duchess unless ... mumbling incoherently, Sergei rushed out, to return minutes later brandishing a large magnifying glass. For what to Natasha seemed an age, he scrutinised the mark, instructing her, as he did so, to adopt various positions and to spread, with her fingers, the skin surrounding the tattoo, thereby keeping it taut.

Lying, as she did, full-length on the sofa, her dress hoisted and crumpled at the midriff, and aware of the erogenous position she had been asked to adopt, Natasha could not resist chastising him.

'Reeley, Sergei, eet ees veree naughty, *non*?

Sergei said nothing. Having completed his inspection, he

walked across to the window. Natasha, her head supported by an arm bent at the elbow, watched him with rounded eyes.

As if reaching a momentous decision, he turned and with a purposeful stride retraced his steps. Looking down at her, he swallowed deeply and then, in a voice choked with emotion, said, 'Natasha Gollitzin, granddaughter of the last great Empress of all the Russias, you've been carrying the key to the Romanov gold on your thigh for the last twenty years.' A pause, as he desperately sought to control himself, then, 'And you didn't even know it!' Another pause and then in a tone of suppressed excitement, 'That tattoo is nothing more or less than a map ... a map giving the exact location of the hidden gold.'

* * *

Sergei was troubled. His mind was continually going over and over the events since leaving Appenzell – searching for a solution that just would not come. The major worry without doubt was Natasha, who had taken to her new life with an enthusiasm, which, if not controlled, could spell the end to any prospect of support forthcoming from the Grand Council.

Another matter, he reluctantly admitted to himself, and one he would have to come to terms with, was the knowledge that since their time at Appenzell – *was it really but three months ago?* – he had fallen in love with her. He, approaching sixty, now revered this slip of a girl who, apparently without effort, had men falling over themselves in their desire for her. Problems mounting on problems, and now the discovery of the map – what was he to do about that?

Another thought which came and went, like some recurring nightmare, was Derevenko. Sooner or later, Sergei was certain, he would put in an appearance ... what then ... what of Natasha? Her safety, always paramount, was even more so now, he couldn't bear the thought of anything happening to her. At times he found himself wishing he had never heard of the Romanov gold, or the

Duchess or, for that matter, the whole monarchist movement. But then there would be no Natasha.

His thoughts returned to the map and what it contained. In spite of himself, he found his mind dwelling on ideas he never dreamt possible. Why not get the gold, or at least some of it and, with Natasha, flee to America. There they would both be safe. No, what of his word to the Duchess? How could he possibly live with himself afterwards? But he knew the seed had taken root; whether it died or blossomed would depend on circumstances – circumstances he recognised over which he probably would have little or no control.

*   *   *

After considerable time on the telephone to both the Comte and Dmitri Sokolov, Sergei arranged for a meeting to be held in his sparse bed-sitting room close to Natasha's flat. He also bought himself a camera and took several photographs of the tattoo, much to the amusement of Natasha.

'I trust, Sergei,' said Sokolov, somewhat wearily, 'this is not just another attempt to persuade the council to endorse the girl. I have to admit the whole business is getting to me. We're too old for this sort of nonsense, aren't we, Henri?' said to the Comte de Toulouse as he slumped into the only chair in the room.

Not to be outdone, the Comte smiled back at him and in a torrent of French expressed concern at his enforced absence from Paris.

'Gentlemen, please,' said Sergei, 'I couldn't possibly tell you over the phone what I have discovered for obvious reasons, but please, Dmitri, have a look at this.' With that be placed the photograph of Natasha's tattoo on the bed.

With what, to Sergei, appeared to be agonising slowness, Dmitri Sokolov produced a pair of spectacles and peered at the tattoo, with the Comte, anxious not to miss anything, leaning over his shoulder. Sergei, meanwhile, in a vain attempt to contain his impatience, paced the room.

At last, after he had studied the photograph for the umpteenth time, Sokolov laid it down.

'Assuming it is genuine, we still have to recover the gold, and that won't be easy.' The Comte said nothing, but moving over to the window, gazed at the suburban scene below.

'Henri,' said Sergei, ignoring Sokolov, 'tell me about the plan we discussed in Paris when we found the ingot . . . tell him, Henri.'

The Comte cleared his throat. 'For some time now my *Amicale de l'Ordre Francaise* has been running food, medical supplies and blankets to the Kurdish minority in western Turkey. This has been done with tacit approval of both the French and Turkish governments. It would not be impossible to vary our route whereby we follow the frontier of Germany and Switzerland. Gentlemen, we could divert, say two vehicles . . . cross the frontier at Basel, from there to Zurich, Zurich to Appenzell. We're talking of no more than a hundred miles.'

The Comte paused to allow the portent of what he had said to be digested. Then, continuing in an adopted conspiratorial tone, 'Two three-ton trucks could be in, loaded, and out of Appenzell inside twelve hours.'

The silence in the room was almost tangible as Sergei and Sokolov, eyes staring fixedly in front of them, envisaged riches beyond their imaginings. It was Sokolov who spoke first, his face etched with concern.

'Whoever goes will be taking one hell of a risk. They're bound to be watching the house . . .'

And the frontier,' volunteered the Comte.

'Yes, but think of the rewards,' said Sergei, his obvious enthusiasm dismissing Sokolov's wariness out of hand, 'There must be twenty million in gold just waiting to he picked up. You must support the enterprise, Dmitri, think what it would do for the monarchist cause.'

'One thing is certain,' said Sokolov somewhat mournfully, 'no word must leave this room. If Sternov or Derevenko were to get wind of it we would all be finished – kaput.'

*   *   *

Mikhael Derevenko decided that he disliked England and, in particular, its weather. Since his arrival at Heathrow it had rained incessantly, and his reception at the Embassy that morning had done little to improve his demeanour. Instructions as to procedures did nothing to encourage any change in this feeling of despondency. It was obvious from the attitude of the Third Secretary, who, apart from taking great delight in telling him how he had been made a Hero of the Soviet Union, had contributed little in defining what support he could expect to receive – in fact, he had come to the conclusion that he was very much on his own. Ostensibly, he was a bona-fide member of the trade mission currently visiting the country that was to be his only cover. Reporting was to be direct to Moscow by diplomatic bag.

Wincing as droplets of ice-cold rain penetrated to his shirt collar, he waited for what appeared to be a non-existent taxi to take him back to his seedy hotel in what was called Earls Court. In spite of the deluge, Derevenko smiled to himself. Not for the first time be began to wonder just how much of the Romanov gold, assuming he found it, would really end up in the coffers of the Soviet Union, and what would be his reward? A medal perhaps? Again the smile. And at the end of it all a small flat and an equally meagre pension. Well, not this time. This time Mikhael Derevenko was going to take care of himself. He would fix the girl after he got to know all she knew, that went without saying, the pain in his left arm would ensure that . . . at last, a taxi drew up, its wash soaking the bottoms of his trousers and arousing in him such indignation as to have his hand moving, almost imperceptibly, towards his shoulder holster. However, the driver's cheerful 'Where to, guv?' disarmed the provocation.

*   *   *

Colonel Sir Rupert de Quincy, Bt, late of Haileybury and the

Coldstream Guards, waved a piece of paper in the direction of his assistant, Captain Edward Farrar, at the same time commenting 'Yet another one, Teddy; these blasted trade missions, nothing more than a glorified exercise in spying. This must make it close to fifty requesting diplomatic immunity.'

'Yes,' came the reply, without elaboration.

'What do we know of this fellow?' looking again at the paper adorned with the red hammer and sickle in one corner and the address of the Russian Embassy, emblazoned in gold, in the other. 'One Mikhael Derevenko.'

'Not a lot, first time over here, we're doing the usual checks, but he's something of a one-off. No military intelligence record that we know of, in fact, no intelligence record at all – least not here.'

'Somewhat worrying, don't you think? It's unlike the Bear to send over a novice with the Third Strategic Strike Force coming over from the States later this month, not to mention the Starstreak. Do a visual on him – usual circulation but include the French.'

'As you wish, sir,' responded Farrar with something of a sigh. 'Shall I invite observations?'

'The lot,' came the response. ' It only needs one to slip through, and I have an itch at the nape of my neck about this chap – you know what that means...'

Captain Edward Farrar said nothing but strode purposefully through the door in the direction of the communications room.

*   *   *

What really shocked Sergei out of his euphoria at finding the map was a telephone call from the Comte after his return to Paris.

'Money up front, Sergei,' he had said 'The Ordre Francaise would not carry the burden of such an expedition alone.'

Sergei admitted to himself that he had not fully thought through the practicalities of the plan, the cost of such an enterprise totally eluding him. First and foremost, his concern had to be for Natasha.

The perfunctory response he had received from Sokolov when requesting an undertaking that the gold, if recovered, would ensure the Council's endorsement, worried him. Until then, he had assumed the gold to be Natasha's trump card. Admittedly, Sokolov had said that the Council might possibly look favourably on her aspirations, but only if evidence were found that Tsar Nicholas was her grandfather. Such evidence, as Sokolov well knew, would be impossible to find and near impossible to fabricate. Although Sokolov had not mentioned it, Sergei also knew that Prince Michael, son of the Grand Duke Michael, had already been accepted as the true Heir Apparent. Imperceptibly, and without that earlier feeling of shame, his thoughts returned to recovering the gold for himself and with it, feeling to safety with Natasha.

7

A Little Bird Sings!

If any building fashioned by man were to survive in an ever-changing world, considered Alexis Sternov, then that edifice would be the Lubyanka prison. Sitting in the back of his official Zil limousine, the solid grey double doors of the prison stared back at him uncompromisingly, their bare façades scarred by the depredations of the weather, as if in sheer frustration at such a solid and enduring structure.

As the great doors swung open, the car's headlights revealed an inner courtyard frequented by shadowy figures and outlines of high walls stretching away into the blackness of the night. As he stepped from the soporific atmosphere of his vehicle, a dog, as if in torment, howled from somewhere out in the darkness. Sternov shivered involuntarily. The silence that returned broken only by the sound of frozen snow crunching under the weight of heavy footfalls as a figure slowly materialised before him.

'Good evening, Comrade Sternov,' said a voice, releasing thin wisps of condensation into the freezing night air.

'Good evening,' replied Sternov, as he studied the figure swathed in a belted overcoat done up to the neck, the only embellishment being a single red star that adorned the centre of a peaked cap.

'Take me to your Commissar's office.'

* * *

'So you are interested in the man Gollitzin,' said the Commissar whilst pouring Sternov a large measure of Johnny Walker whisky. Then, as if in answer to the look of surprise on Sternov's face, said, 'Got it during the Berlin airlift – two crates of it. Good stuff, don't you think?'

Sternov agreed as he took a further long draught. At the same time his attention was drawn to the Stalingrad Star decorating the Commissar's chest. Sternov nodded in its direction.

'Ah, that,' said the Commissar, as if it were of little consequence. 'I guess I was one of the lucky ones.'

'Now you have your reward,' said Sternov, looking around at the plush furnishings of the office.

'Are you intending to interrogate him in his cell?' asked the Commissar, as if anxious to change the subject.

'I see no reason why not, and by the way, have you a bottle of vodka? I believe Gollitzin is an alcoholic.' The Commissar's hand, as earlier, disappeared into an ornate cabinet and reappeared clasping a large bottle.

'You see,' said Sternov, 'I'm an advocate of the carrot and the stick.'

A wintry smile creased the rough features of the Commissar's face. 'Excellent,' he said, 'and I will lend you Boris,' indicating a well-built uniformed man sitting at a desk by the door. 'He will provide the stick.'

His laughter roared out at this aside, and, apart from advice to 'Wear this,' as he threw a heavy quilted coat in Sternov's direction, continued as Sternov and his new companion closed the office door behind them.

* * *

Vladimir Gollitzin was sitting hunched over a bare wooden table as the cell door swung open. Draped over his shoulders was a dirty brown blanket of the type issued to troops in the field. As a protection against the damp icy conditions in the cell, it was worse than useless. He barely looked up as Sternov and the guard entered.

65

'Now Vladimir,' said Sternov heartily, 'how are they treating you?'

Eyes, all but hidden behind coal-black eyebrows, looked up; for a few moments they appeared not to register Sternov's presence as, fixedly, they were drawn to the bottle held loosely in his hand.

'Here,' said Sternov, undoing the cap and passing the vodka to him, 'try this.' Hands, shaking in anticipation, grasped the bottle and in one movement raised it to a mouth, a mouth hidden behind a tangled web of a beard.

'That will do for now,' said Sternov a few moments later, as he forcibly removed the vodka. 'More later.'

Gollitzin, wiping his mouth with the back of a hand, watched as the bottle was placed on the floor by the cell door.

' Answer my questions truthfully, Vladimir, and it will remain here,' said Sternov. 'Lie to me, and I will know when you're lying. Not only will you never see another bottle, but you'll have a beating you'll remember to your dying day. Have I made myself clear?' Vladimir nodded.

'Good, now tell me all you know about Olga Semyonov and the girl called Natasha.'

* * *

Incredible, thought Sternov, as he sank back once more into the luxury of the car, but so incredible as to have a ring of truth. So the girl Natasha was no more related to the last Empress than he was. A simple gypsy girl, bought for a few hundred roubles to replace an infant placed in Gollitzin's care, which, to his dismay, had died of diphtheria within a few months. Faced with the prospect of losing his retainer, he had sought a substitute. All this had happened in 1946, a year of turmoil, when all Europe and most of Russia was in a state of upheaval, as a seething mass of displaced people searched for the unobtainable.

What was perhaps even more incredible, thought Sternov, was that the Duchess Elizabeth had suspected nothing. That year after year she had continued to pay Gollitzin in the mistaken belief that her protégée was alive and well.

One thing was for sure, decided Sternov, as he completed writing up his notes, the girl Natasha could not possibly have any recollection of her antecedents – whether or not the Duchess had confided in her about the whereabouts of the Romanov gold was another matter. Notwithstanding what he had learnt today, the girl remained the key element in the search for the bullion. Well, that was up to Derevenko...

With a sigh, Sternov snapped closed his notebook, settled back into the soft cushions and closed his eyes.

* * *

'What is it?' enquired Colonel de Quincy, his voice barely concealing his impatience at the interruption.

'The dossier on Mikhael Derevenko,' replied Captain Farrar. 'It makes very interesting reading.'

'Tell me.'

'We were right, no history of military intelligence, but what is curious is that he was working for a number of years with the Internal Security Section of the NKVD.'

'So?'

'Well, sir, one must ask the question what is he doing here?' Without waiting for a reply, Captain Farrar continued, 'His particular duty was surveillance of the monarchist movement.'

'I didn't know there was one.'

'It's been active both here and in Paris for some years, certainly since the war. At one time we gave it tacit support, some funding, that sort of thing, but recently, because of Khruschev's virtually impregnable position, we've rather lost interest.' Colonel de Quincy, no longer hiding his annoyance, laid his hands flat on his desk.

'This is hardly a matter to concern us, Farrar. I suggest you file the report and concentrate on that Military Attaché who's been sniffing around.'

'But, sir,' protested Farrar, 'something is going on. Derevenko has done a runner. He was supposed to be at that tractor demonstration up at Peterborough yesterday; he never appeared, and their Embassy is being very evasive.' Farrar waited momentarily to allow the import of what he had said to sink in. 'There is more. We've had a report from Zurich that the Grand Princess Elizabeth was killed during a robbery – murdered, of course.'

'Duchess Elizabeth, wasn't she related to the Tsar?' asked the Colonel, his interest finally aroused.

'Sister of the last Empress,' said Farrar, somewhat smugly.

'Still, it's hardly a matter for us.'

'We are picking up rumours, sir.'

'What rumours?'

'A mixed bag, but one that keeps occurring, the Romanov gold.'

'That hairy chestnut...'

'Hairy chestnut or not, rumour has it that it's worth twenty million sterling.'

'Now that may be of interest. Anything else?'

'Only that another heir to the throne has turned up.'

'Not Anastasia?' said de Quincy, with half a smile.

'No, this one appears to have more going for her – she is reputed to be the granddaughter of the last Tsarina.'

'Really, Teddy,' said the Colonel with a sigh, 'this is all we wanted right now. You had better do a report for the PM; doubtless if the Queen gets to hear of it, questions will almost certainly be asked. Give him the best briefing you can. As for Derevenko, you never know what the bastard might be up to. Put out an ASR on him, and when you've found him, have him tailed.'

* * *

Mikhael Derevenko was very pleased with himself. In less than forty-eight hours he had contacted his 'sleeper' operating within the Council of the Russian Nobility Association. It would be simple, he was told, to trace Natasha Gollitzin: the whole movement was talking about her and her aspirations for the throne.

Tenderly he felt his left arm just above the elbow. The pain was constant and worse when he tried to lift it above the waist. But soon he knew he would have his revenge. Again he recalled the dying face of the Duchess as she lay spreadeagled on the thick carpet, her blood already discolouring its rich motif. No doubt she had heard him as her life's blood ebbed away. Yes, she had heard the oath he had screamed at her, to kill the girl Gollitzin whatever the cost – the look in her fast-fading eyes had convinced him of that . . . soon now, it would all be over.

8

The Twelve Apostles

Had they been present, the guests at the Webster's house party of a day or so ago might have been highly amused but not necessarily surprised to see Big George Fawcett, having alighted from a taxi at the top of St John's Wood Road, his head all but obliterated by a huge bunch of red roses, stealthily approach the door of Natasha's flat. Lifting her door knocker he glanced to the right and left, as if expecting Hilda to appear at any moment. Satisfied that such materialisation was highly unlikely, he released the knocker. The two heavy thumps reverberated in the silence that, until then, had shrouded the doorway and himself with very welcome anonymity.

Guilt, like an icy finger at the nape of his neck, assailed him. What if Bill Webster was with her? Then to Hell with Bill Webster. He had been no help. All he wanted was to keep her under wraps for himself: there was no share and share alike in his make-up. With his confidence returning he considered be had been very adroit in obtaining her address from the kid Jamie ... the door opened and the vision that was Natasha smiled at him.

'Why, Georgy, how nice,' her vermilion lips all but putting the red roses to shame. 'For me?'

'I just happened to be passing,' he stammered, the newly won confidence draining away, 'so I thought why not call upon Mademoiselle Natasha.' (George thought the French bit most appropriate.)

Her smile, as usual, was devastating.

'You like a café?' she pouted, stepping aside.

'I can't think of anything better,' he said, a broad smile enveloping his face as he thankfully closed the door behind him. He followed her up a flight of stairs that obviously led to her flat, his gaze fixed on her slowly rotating hips. Even something as mundane as climbing a flight of stairs was, for Natasha, an unconscious act of such sensual promise that George's already overworked imagination reached fever pitch.

*　*　*

'Now, what shall I wear?' said Emma, eyeing her husband across the breakfast table. 'I know, that blue dress you took such a dislike to, the one you said made me look like a tart.' Peter lowered his paper.

'You've changed your tune – what was it you called her?'

'Yes, a Russian whore, and I meant it, but that was yesterday. I've slept on it since then, and anyway, I think the Russian whore could do with some competition, don't you agree?' Her silky tone of voice in no way deceived him. He knew well enough that what was to him but a minor indiscretion had, to her, mushroomed into something far greater and probably beyond his capabilities to control.

'Personally, I think the further we're away from Jamie's birthday party the better!'

'Yes, you would say that, wouldn't you? After all, you've already had her so you've nothing to gain and everything to lose, a typical man's attitude. Well, we're going, I shall ring Janice shortly and confirm we're coming.'

With a sigh, he laid his paper down. 'You know you're playing with fire, don't you?'

'That's what makes it so tempting, that just for once we are going to do something different and escape from this stifling existence of ours and live a little.'

'If entering into competition with Natasha Gollitzin is your idea of living, then you can count me out.'

'Oh no, my dear,' as she began clearing the table, 'Daddy's had his fun, now it's Mummy's turn.'

*   *   *

James Lawrence was particularly pleased with himself. After the departure of his sister's guests, including the ravishing Natasha Gollitzin, he had indulged himself in a long phone call to his latest girlfriend, Penelope Charters. Pen was an extremely modern young lady. She smoked quite openly, using, as Princess Margaret did, a long cigarette holder, drank pints of beer and, when wishing to create an impression, used four-letter words with abandon. However as her father was ' big' in the City and her mother rode to hounds, she was more than welcome in the Websters' household. James's conversation with her had been eminently successful, as she had agreed to cast aside her inhibitions and sleep with him after the party. This, following the interest shown in him by the wonderful Natasha, was a triumph indeed. (He would keep Natasha in mind for some future occasion.)

He had been trying to bed Penelope Charters for weeks, and anticipation of the weekend filled him with a heady sense of well-being.

When discussing the arrangements for his twenty-first he had deplored Janice's idea of a fancy dress party as being *de trop*. Although not mentioned, he recalled a recent rag ball when his costume had been reduced to tatters, resulting in a bill of fifty pounds from the enraged owner of the hire firm. A dinner party would be much more sophisticated and in keeping with the image he liked to project of himself of a more mature man. The presence of the delectable Natasha could only enhance this.

So, to an amused Janice, he had insisted on her being invited, thereby ensuring a most stimulating evening. *Little did he know*, thought Janice, *how stimulating!*

*   *   *

Big George, by now delirious with expectation, balanced his coffee cup and saucer precariously on his knee whilst gazing adoringly at the incomparable Natasha. Her dark forbidding eyes, with their seeming ability to expose even his most innermost thoughts, held his with hypnotic intensity. Eyes that had the capacity to create and fashion in his mind extreme sexual desires, such desires being heightened in the knowledge that it was she who was the creator and he merely the servant.

'You have present for Natasha?' she said, remembering Olga's teachings. George, finding a home for the offending cup and saucer, produced his wallet and was extracting two or three notes from a thick bundle when hands, acting in concert with a whispered 'Georgy, for me?' closed over his and gently removed the entire package. With the dexterity of long practice, half the contents were removed and his wallet returned to him as her mouth, now but inches from his, breathed, 'Georgy, you're so generous.'

'Georgy', smiling the smile of a man whose head was only just above a torrent of rising waters, managed a weak, 'Oh I don't know,' as she took hold of his arm and propelled him towards the doorway leading into her bedroom.

A shouted, 'Natasha, where are you?' penetrated through to them both.

Natasha's response was swift in the extreme as 'Georgy' found himself back on the sofa so recently vacated by them both, and a fully composed Natasha was greeting the interloper with honeyed words, 'Sergei, how lovely to see you...'

From the kitchen window Sergei followed the hurried departure of Natasha's devastated guest. If it were not so pathetic, thought Sergei it would have been deemed comical to observe Big George furtively move from one corner of the street to another as if, by doing so, he somehow became featureless and anonymous in the extreme.

Sergei turned away from the window and, declining Natasha's offer of a café, returned to the sitting room. Without preamble and adopting what he hoped was the severest of expressions, he began to speak.

'It has to stop, Natasha, you understand? It has to stop.' Natasha, seated on the sofa so recently occupied by her and Big George, blinked, as if suppressing rising tears. How lovely she was, thought Sergei, already beginning to weaken. Even dressed in workaday clothes, her beauty radiated an incandescent glow of warmth which, without effort, reached out to him. Gathering himself together and avoiding those terrible bewitching eyes, he began again.

'If you persist, Natasha, with these flagrant acts of,' Sergei paused, as though uttering the word itself were a sin, 'prostitution, then your chances of becoming a princess of the royal household of the Romanovs will be gone forever. To be recognised as a princess, Natasha, you must conduct yourself as a princess, you understand?'

Natasha nodded.

'Do you want to be a princess, Natasha?'

'Oh yes, please.' Her childlike response again had him weakening.

'Then you must solemnly promise no more of this nonsense.'

'I promise.'

'If you fail me, Natasha, then you will be returned to Kolomyja.' He should have tried that one before, he thought, judging by the look of horror on her face.

'Now, where is Igor? He's been told never to leave you alone.'

'He has gone to the cinema, he loves the cinema, he goes every day ...'

'That must stop. When he returns I want you both round at my room, you understand?'

Natasha, very meekly, said she did understand.

'Another thing, Natasha,' continued Sergei somewhat pompously, 'the Duma have finally agreed to give you an audience. I cannot emphasise enough, Natasha, the importance of this; to go before them is itself an honour ... you understand ...' again Natasha, very meekly, said she did understand.

'Good, the audience will take place Friday morning, you realise the significance of a Friday, don't you?'

'It is a holy day.'

'Excellent – it is essential you create a good impression. Wear something fairly simple, no jewellery, but do get your hair done, and I shall be round with a taxi at eleven. And, yes, Natasha, inform Igor of my displeasure and tell him I want to see him in my room.'

Natasha nodded.

*   *   *

Natasha fidgeted with her lace handkerchief whilst Sergei, standing behind her chair, gave an appearance of calm he was far from feeling. What on earth had possessed the girl? Again he looked down at the tight blonde curls which, as if by some obscene miracle, had replaced that flowing cascade of rich blackness – if she had ever had a chance of endorsement, it had almost certainly evaporated under the devilish influence of some obscure hairdresser.

The Duma in exile, for both convenience and economy, shared the same building in Holborn as the Russian Nobility Association. This suited Dmitri Sokolov admirably, as it enabled him to keep a close ear to the ground without it necessarily being too obvious. He again glanced across at the blonde apparition that had once been the Natasha Gollitzin he knew and chuckled inwardly. With his knowledge of the 'Twelve Apostles' as he called them, it wasn't difficult to guess what their reaction would be ... something akin to horror at the thought that they were being invited to endorse this *strumpet* as heir to the throne. However gleeful he was at the forthcoming downfall of the girl, he knew it was in his interests to remain a supporter. Since the unveiling of the ingot his thoughts had barely left contemplation of the hidden twenty million – what was it he had said, yes, *Where there was one there must be more*. Indeed there must be, and the girl, Natasha, was the key, of that he was certain.

75

Natasha shivered involuntarily as the raw damp of the late November day penetrated the room, its high ceilings absorbing what little heat two inadequate stoves at each end struggled to provide. Whilst being guided to their seats opposite a long table, which, to Natasha, seemed to stretch endlessly in front of her, a priest of the Russian Orthodox Church entered. Wearing a black shift and headdress, he immediately started to scatter water from a round bowl, which be swung, somewhat alarmingly, on the end of a cord, chanting as he did so.

'He's blessing the meeting,' volunteered Sergei in Natasha's ear. Natasha, however, made no comment as, wide-eyed, she continued to absorb the scene before her. At each corner of the room, long thin candles, held in wall brackets, spluttered and danced some macabre ritual as they fought to survive against the cold draughts of air that periodically invaded the room. Again Sergei whispered, warning her that when the Duma entered everyone was required to stand. Natasha acknowledged this with the faintest of nods. She was far too engrossed in the huge backdrop of the Imperial Eagle draped behind the table to pay him much attention. It was magnificent in its grandeur, providing, in an otherwise bare and unpretentious room, a splash of colour, brilliant and awesome in its splendour. On either side were life-sized portraits of the Tsar Nicholas and the Empress Alexandra and, further to one side, an enlarged photograph, restricted to head and shoulders, of the accepted pretender to the throne, Prince Michael. His blue eyes, below a curly mop of blond hair, seemed to return her admiring gaze with equal fascination. Natasha's stomach churned at the thought that, as a royal princess, their paths would undoubtedly cross.

A disembodied voice, from somewhere in the dark recesses of the room, commanded everyone to stand and greet the elected Duma of all the Russias. Natasha, on legs that no longer seemed her own, rose to her feet.

* * *

Back in Natasha's flat, in the mundane environs of St John's Wood Road, Sergei Poznansky admitted to himself he was a very disillusioned man. The audience arranged for Natasha had confirmed his worst fears that the Duma – the Twelve Apostles, Dmitri Sokolov called them – were merely going through the motions. The paucity of their questions directed at Natasha and the constant reference to her as 'my child', had only added to his conviction that the whole business was a charade. As far as they were concerned, she was nothing more than a distraction, a lovely distraction possibly, but nothing more.

Prior to Natasha's presentation Sokolov had warned him that the Romanov gold must not be mentioned, and certainly not the map. He was convinced, Sokolov had continued, that the KGB's intelligence gathering had penetrated the Duma – like the original twelve, he had smiled, they had their Judas.

So where now, contemplated Sergei? Natasha's chances of any official recognition seemed remote. His mind went back to that last meeting with the Duchess. What a fool he had been to be so taken in by an old woman's dreams. It was obvious she had built her hopes on sand, ignoring all the practicalities, and had become infatuated with her grand design to put Natashia on the throne.

But what of the gold? Certainly it existed. Igor hadn't simply picked up an ingot worth over twenty thousand pounds sterling; she had given it to him. As Sokolov had commented, '*Where there was one there must be more.*' But even if it were so, recovering it was as far away as ever.

Sergei looked across at Natasha, asleep on the sofa and oblivious to all the fears and doubts assailing him. So sleep the innocent, he thought. Perhaps, after all, she would have been better off left in Kolomyja – even a life of prostitution was better than being killed for a cause she would never understand.

The Duchess, she was the cause of all of this – her ridiculous aspirations for Natasha, which might have a catastrophic outcome for the girl. No, he no longer felt he had allegiance to the Grand

Duchess Elizabeth. He had done all he could and more; now it was a case of self-preservation for himself and Natasha.

*   *   *

As in London, Moscow's leaden skies gave promise of the harsh winter to come. And, although separated from Sergei Poznansky by hundreds of miles, Alexis Sternov, Internal Security, KGB, was experiencing similar conflicts of the mind as to the best course of action to take. His confidence had been shaken by the terse response from Vladimir Semichastny to his report that the Gollitzin girl was nothing more than a common gypsy girl and therefore an impostor bought for a handful of roubles to serve the purposes of a confirmed drunk. Semichastny's reply had been brief to the point of dismissal: 'I disagree,' he had written in his own spidery scrawl.

Sternov was under no illusions as to his fate if he failed to produce. Failure in the eyes of men like Vladimir Semichastny was dealt with swiftly and ruthlessly; he himself had dealt with many faceless people who, if their lives were spared, were banished to the frozen wastes of Siberia, all condemned to a life of unremitting hardship – from which few, if any, returned.

Obviously, from his abrupt reply, Semichastny knew a lot more about the girl than he was prepared to admit . . . restlessly, Sternov sucked on his pipe, concentrating on what, up to now, he had discarded as an irrelevance: the murder of Olga Semyonov, the lowly party official. His eyes looked up at the ceiling, a habit he had when deep in thought, as he again went over every detail of Derevenko's report. The murder was an irrelevance but an irrelevance that could be turned to his advantage – barely containing his excitement, he reached for the telephone.

9

Betrayals

It was a day or two after the abortive meeting with the Duma and, whereas it was within Sergei Poznansky's character to dither, once having made up his mind to a certain course of action, he was unwavering in his determination to see it through. Therefore, the apparent lack of interest shown by the official in the vestibule of the Soviet Embassy in no way deterred him.

'The information I wish to give to the Ambassador will be of great value to the Union,' he said in faultless Russian. 'Please arrange for me to see him.'

The man appeared to remain sceptical and obviously continued to harbour doubts but, after a pause during which he observed the tenacity of purpose clearly etched in Sergei's eyes, he relented and reached for the telephone.

'His Excellency wishes to know the nature of your business, sir?' Such was Sergei's state of mind that only now did he notice the man was wearing the ribbon of the Hero of the Soviet Union, and that he had no left hand. It had always amazed him how millions of his fellow citizens had died and countless other millions had been maimed in the war Stalin had called the great patriotic war. It made no sense that so many were prepared to make such sacrifices to keep such a despot in power.

'Your business, sir?' said the man, holding the telephone in his only hand, his voice betraying his impatience.

'Tell him,' said Sergei, followed by a moment's hesitation, 'that

I wish to talk to him about the Romanov gold.' There, thought Sergei, it was done. Now it was just a question of keeping his head and remaining steadfast through whatever lay ahead. Surely, as his motives were honourable, God and his faith would see him through.

* * *

Dmitri Sokolov eyed the three figures hunched around his dining table.

'You're certain you weren't followed?' he said.

'Positive, Dmitri, we all came by different routes and in separate taxis. Anyway,' continued the spokesman of the three, 'why all the secrecy?'

'Because,' said Dmitri, 'there is twenty million in gold at stake!' As he had expected, the effect of such an announcement created immediate attention. No longer were they displaying their annoyance at being dragged halfway across London in the middle of the night.

'You mean the Romanov gold?' Again, it was the spokesman.

'Precisely,' replied Sokolov, 'that is why I invited you here. You have each been hand-picked because you have the right connections. 'You, Paul,' addressing the bald spokesman, 'have relatives in Berne. Vladimir, you have a brother living in Zurich.' Then, turning to the last member of the trio, 'And you, Magyar, lived in Switzerland for some years.'

'Get to the point, Sokolov,' said Paul.

'Certainly, gentlemen. The point is I know where the gold is buried. Buried by the late Duchess Elizabeth in the mistaken belief that you,' pointing to each of the three in turn, 'as members of the Duma in exile, would endorse her protégée, the girl Natasha Gollitzin, as heir to the throne.'

'Such nonsense,' growled the heavily-bearded Magyar, silent until now. As you know, Sokolov, we met her a few days ago. Good for a ...' with that he made an obscene gesture with his forearm, 'but heir to the throne, the Duchess must have been mad.'

'Who else knows about this?' questioned Paul, still the spokesman.

'Fortunately, only myself and Sergei Poznansky. He is considering, with the help of the Comte de Toulouse, a joint expedition to recover it. Two lorries to divert to Appenzell, load it and return.'

'Wouldn't last five minutes,' said the red-haired Vladimir. 'What is he expecting – the KGB to gift-wrap it for him?'

'Exactly,' agreed Sokolov. 'But we are not going after all of the gold, however inviting. Three ingots apiece would ensure that we could all live the remainder of our lives in comfort. If we get greedy, gentlemen, we shall all pay the price. You, Paul, could give up that miserable little newsagents you run all hours, and you Vladimir, your so-called Russian delicatessen.'

'And I would not have to drive that infernal taxi for twelve hours a day to get anything like a decent living,' interceded the bearded one.

'Then we are agreed,' said Sokolov. Three heads nodded in unison. 'Needless to say, gentlemen, not a word of this must leave this room. We'll meet again shortly, until then absolute secrecy.'

His new accomplices having left, Sokolov relaxed with a large brandy and his thoughts. How easy it had been to persuade the three to join his venture. He had never rated the Duma very highly, an oligarchy of men exiled from their mother country, each with their own political ambitions and nursing grievances, both real and imaginary, against the Bolsheviks. Much the same as his Nobility Association. Neither had any sort of future, only twin federations which allowed men to dream their dreams of eventual glory. No, he had no feelings of guilt, why should he? Such were his thoughts as he poured himself another brandy. An opportunity had presented itself, a once in a lifetime opportunity, he would be a fool not to grasp it.

* * *

81

The shrill demanding ring of the telephone, in an otherwise silent room, sent shivers of anticipation chasing up and down Sergei's spine. Tentatively, he lifted it to his ear. For what seemed an age only silence greeted his 'Hello,' then, 'You have information?' The thick Russian accent accentuated the menace in the voice.

Sergei, by an effort of will, remained calm. 'Yes, for certain considerations.'

'Then we must meet,' was the reply, 'Say in one hour on your Waterloo Bridge.'

'But it's past midnight,' objected an astonished Sergei, 'and anyway how will I know you?'

'I will know you,' said the voice before the faintest click indicated the line had gone dead.

* * *

'Sir, have you read this?'

The Head of Section 10, British Military Intelligence, looked up. 'What is it, Teddy? You've been sniffing round my desk all morning.'

Ignoring the remark, Captain Farrar began to read from a sheet of paper and purposefully again ignored his chief's gesture of impatience.

'*Report of Inspector D. Waters, CID, attached to the Department of Immigration, Home Office.*

Arrived at illegal immigrant's address, 14, St John's Wood Road, St John's Wood, at 10.00 hours accompanied by Mr Duncan Gray, Home Office Official.
Met at door of flat by illegal immigrant who identified herself as Natasha Gollitzin. Miss Gollitzin shown Home Office Order and invited to pack a suitcase and accompany us. Escorted detainee into flat. On reaching sitting room adjoining door opened and a male, clothed in what appeared to be a

82

black cloak and wearing a white skull cap, attacked Mr Gray, forcing him to the floor in a judo hold. The man warned me in English that to interfere would result in Mr Gray's back being broken. Whilst still securing him he instructed me to release the woman I had just handcuffed. In consideration of Mr Gray I released the detainee. Both the man and woman then left flat. I understand on reaching street level my driver was rendered senseless by what I believe was a professional karate chop to the side of the head. My vehicle was then taken and last seen heading in the direction of South London.

Report ends. Distribution Scale E.
D. Waters, Inspector CID, New Scotland Yard,
Attached HM Home Office.'

Teddy Farrar began to laugh.

'I see nothing funny in it,' said Colonel de Quincy testily. 'Duncan Gray will be off duty for at least three months as a result of injuries to his back.' Shuffling his papers, he looked up. 'In thirty years in the field, Teddy, I've only known one man who used such a judo hold. It's called the *Tiako*, collapses the spine like so much tissue paper; believe me, that man Gray was extremely lucky. It has all the hallmarks of an old friend who was supposed to have died in the Congo years ago.'

Colonel de Quincy's eyes now assumed a faraway look, as he recalled a time when he was but a novice in the world of espionage and counter-espionage.

'Charlie Tuttle,' he said with a reverence Captain Farrar had never heard from his chief before. 'One of the finest field agents I have ever known. Spoke six languages fluently and was a master of disguise.' Smiling, to himself, he continued, 'Whenever he was introduced he always said "Charlie Tuttle ... rhymes with scuttle."'

The Colonel sighed audibly, 'They don't come like that any more, Teddy, more's the pity.'

Then, coming back from his private reverie, he held up a cellophane bag.

'You know what's in here, Teddy?' Teddy Farrar shook his head. What next, he thought, was his chief about to reveal to him from his distant past?

'The remains of Charlie's nose.'

'You cannot be serious, sir.'

'Not his nose per se, but a damn good imitation, made up of resin and a mix of plaster of Paris, the sort of thing theatricals use.'

'But,' objected Captain Farrar, 'I'm somewhat confused, you said just yourself not an hour ago that it was purely Home Office business.

'Not any more, Teddy,' more shuffling of his papers, 'the Home Office is insisting that the guilty man was the missing trades mission fellow, Mikhael Derevenko, I know differently. One thing is certain: if Charlie is involved, then it's big. Not only that, but the Minister himself rang me this morning. It appears our friends are asking for the girl to be returned to Moscow – invoking an extradition treaty – a hangover from the war years. Rich, isn't it?'

'On what grounds?'

'Well, according to him she's wanted on a capital charge, accessory to murder no less.'

'There you are ... I said there was more to it than meets the eye with that Derevenko fellow over here.'

'You're probably right, Teddy, but it's still not a matter for us – at least not at present.'

'Couldn't she apply for asylum?'

'What, with a capital charge against her? No chance. No, within a week she'll be back in Moscow and then it's Goodnight Vienna, as they said in the old music hall days.'

'What about your agent extraordinaire, Charlie Tuttle, do you think he's working for the Commies?'

'Charlie Tuttle, never, but involved somewhere, yes without a doubt. Somewhere,' continued Colonel de Quincy, 'there is a link

with the girl Natasha Gollitzin and through her this fellow
Derevenko, I'm sure of that. Teddy, get on to the Home Office,
speak to the Minister if you have to, I want a complete blackout on
this, no press coverage, nothing. Quote National Security to him
... that will do the trick.'

'As you wish, sir,' said a smiling Captain Farrar , as yet again he
made his way to the Communications Room.

*   *   *

It was the sort of rain, although not heavy, that gave Sergei
Poznansky the impression he was walking through an impenetra-
ble mist, the dampness penetrating through to his very bones.
There was no wind and the resultant stillness was almost real as if,
without effort, he could reach out and touch it. The lights of the
bridge, distinct though they were, only emphasised the unknown
terrors lurking in the hidden depths of the menacing darkness, a
darkness their brightness never reached.

As he slowly walked across the bridge, the sensation that every
movement was being watched grew with every step. Reaching the
centre he stopped, and as he did so a dark shadow, motionless until
now, moved to block his path.

'Come here under the light.' The voice, although speaking in
English, had the same heavy Russian accent as the man on the
telephone. Sergei walked a few yards until he was bathed in the
harsh glare of one of the lights. It was then he saw the ugly snub
nose of a pistol levelled straight at him.

'There's no need for that,' he said in a voice he barely recognised.

The figure made no response but continued to look at him.

'Sergei Poznansky,' he finally said, breaking the silence. ' I
should have guessed.'

'Its been a long time, Mikhael,' Sergei replied, confidence
slowly returning. If Mikhael Derevenko was taken aback at the
recognition, he did not show it. Moving in closer, so close that

Sergei could smell a mixture of stale tobacco and damp body odour, he ran his hands over Sergei's body.

'If you're looking for a gun, I never carry one.'

Derevenko made no reply immediately, but as if by sleight of hand the gun disappeared.

'Good, now tell me all you know about the Romanov gold.'

'I know where it is.'

'Appenzell?'

'Possibly.'

'You have a map?'

'Better than that, a photograph, enlarged, a child could follow it.'

'What are your terms?'

'Half a million in American dollars.'

'Now I know you monarchists are crazy,' Derevenko said, with a short, high-pitched laugh. 'I could persuade you for nothing . . .'

'No, you couldn't. You could kill me now, but no Poznansky, no gold. It's in a safe deposit box – look, here is the key, but, as I'm sure you know, there are over three hundred banks in the City alone. Now which one could it be? And under what name? No, Mikhael, this time you are going to have to accept that I hold the aces.'

'Half a million dollars is out of the question, my friend. However, I will go this far, fifty thousand in dollars, in cash, here tomorrow night, you bring the photograph'

'And get a bullet for my pains? No, you'll have to do better than that, Mikhael.'

Derevenko smiled. If a snake ever smiled, thought Sergei, it would be exactly like that.

'All right, I will arrange something better. In the meantime, Sergei, remember who I am,' said, as the darkness of the night once again enveloped him. Sergei turned and began to walk away – curious, he thought, that he hadn't noticed the rain had stopped.

10

Turmoil

Sergei Poznansky was worried. Approaching Natasha's flat, he had immediately noticed a police car drawn up outside, with a uniformed constable stationed in the doorway. Trusting that he looked just a casual passer-by, he had crossed over to the other side of the road and continued walking. Convinced he had aroused no interest, he rushed to his room with the intention of calling Natasha, only to realise that 'they' would quickly trace his call. Dashing out again, he began to search for a phone booth. The first displayed an 'Out of order' sign, and beginning to feel desperate and fearing the worst, he continued searching.

At last finding a usable phone, he quickly dialled her number and waited breathlessly as the tone told him the number was ringing. As the ringing ceased he guardedly whispered into the mouthpiece, 'Hello.' Silence followed, then a voice he had never heard before said, 'Who is that?' Sergei, with a sense of dread, quietly replaced the phone.

* * *

Janice Webster could be forgiven for feeling uncomfortable. As a hostess par excellence, she was aware of the importance of a congenial atmosphere to any party. Watching her guests, now gathered in her drawing room quietly sipping their aperitifs, it would be apparent to any observer, she conjectured, that a comparison of the drawing room with a funeral parlour would not necessarily be amiss.

As she again looked at the gathering, she mentally compared their present demeanour with the last time they were together; how very different it was then. Could they possibly be the same people? Even Big George, usually so dependable when it came to injecting some life into the proceedings, was unaccountably morose and withdrawn. Then there was Emma, wearing a dress eminently unsuitable and more appropriate for the back streets of Kings Cross than her drawing room. And Peter, admittedly never the life and soul of a party, was on this occasion obviously engaged in open warfare with his wife. The newcomers, Ben and his wife Audrey – Ben, as a business associate Bill had insisted he was asked – were both strenuously trying and failing hopelessly, not to notice the barely concealed antagonism going on around them.

Finally, there was Natasha, but not the Natasha of the earlier party. Her luxuriant shoulder-length hair as black as pitch was gone and with it that all-prevailing air of mysticism. Her new ash-blonde tresses of dazzling silver, although emphasising her black compelling eyes, destroyed that dark magnetism which was so unique to her.

But then, not only was she outwardly different, but unknown to her hostess, her mind was in a turmoil. The last twenty-four hours had destroyed any sense of security and permanence she had felt since leaving Kolomyja.

Incapable though she was of understanding the reasons for, and the consequences of, her and Igor's headlong flight the day before, she was not so naive as to believe that it was the result of some terrible mistake. Even now, in the comparative safety of Janice's drawing room the memory of the two implacable faces continued to haunt her. Tenderly she felt her wrists which had felt the cold hard steel of the handcuffs, and shivered at the recollection. And what of Igor? Recalling the sight of his crushed nose and sudden transformation from a simple-minded, quiet, loveable friend into an obvious clear-thinking resolute man, added to her utter confusion.

Now he no longer obeyed her every whim, but commanded her with a voice of such authority that it overwhelmed her completely. As she slowly sipped her sherry she again relived the scene of a few hours ago, when she insisted on attending the party. His face, red with anger, was so far removed from the gentle Igor she had come to know and trust that it served only to add to her fears, not lessen them.

Janice, inexplicably, had been cold and aloof. Even Bill and Peter had assumed attitudes which compared with the earlier weekend party, were both distant and mystifying.

*   *   *

For the tenth time in the past five minutes Janice looked at her watch. Damn Jamie, she thought, it was his birthday party after all, and he should have made an effort. She had particularly asked him to arrive in time to welcome his guests. Instead, that role had fallen on her shoulders. As for Bill, what an asset – missing when she wanted him and when he had made himself available, behaving like a spoilt child.

Desultory conversation, punctuated by painful periods of silence continued as, with a despondent look at Hilda, Janice again went out into the hallway in the vain hope that by doing so Jamie might magically appear. As she turned to retrace her steps, struggling with yet another disappointment, a thunderous hammering on the front door halted her.

On opening the door her first thought on seeing Jamie's white shirt and hands stained a deep red was that it was some sort of university joke. In bad taste, but nevertheless a joke. But his voice, no longer the soft drawl she was used to, was now so intense and loud that for a moment confusion created a paralysis of the mind. Conscious of her own inertia but seemingly powerless to act, she continued to stare in helpless shock at the bloodied figure of her brother.

'Get a doctor,' he screamed at her, 'Pen's been shot!'

As he half-entered the hallway, her view of the driveway was no longer obstructed. Some distance away and lit by the driveway's fitful lights was a crumpled mass of pink. It was only the white outstretched arm pointing towards her, as if in supplication, that told her it was a body...

*   *   *

'May I introduce myself,' he said politely, producing his warrant card. 'Chief Inspector Reynolds, Hendon CID,' and, turning to the thickset man at his side, 'this is Detective Sergeant Andrews.'

'There's no need for that, Chief Inspector,' said Janice, as she waved away his warrant card. 'May I get you something? Coffee perhaps...'

'Thank you, but not just now, perhaps later,' he replied, glancing round at the people assembled in the drawing room.

With a vague sweep of her hand, Janice, anticipating his question, said, 'Everyone is here except my brother, James, he's upstairs with my husband. Would you like me to fetch him?' She paused, 'He's very upset...'

'No need, we've already spoken to him.'

'Miss Gollitzin is missing,' exclaimed Hilda, her voice incapable of concealing a note of triumph.

'That has been noted, Miss...'

'Fawcett,' came the quick reply, 'Mrs Hilda Fawcett. And may I ask when we will be allowed to go into dinner?'

'You won't he detained a moment longer than is necessary,' replied the Chief Inspector in a matter-of-fact tone. 'I do have some good news for you,' he continued, addressing them all. 'Miss Charters's injuries are not life-threatening and I understand she is, under the circumstances, quite comfortable.'

'Thank God for that,' murmured Janice to the accompaniment of a similar chorus of relief.

'She was very lucky,' added the Chief Inspector rather unnecessarily. 'Now,' he continued, 'you will each be required to give a short statement to my Sergeant and your names and addresses. Once that is completed, you may go.' Then, turning to Janice, 'Is there somewhere we can talk privately?'

'Certainly' she replied, 'the library, we are unlikely to be disturbed there.'

'Good, and I'll have that coffee now if I may.'

*   *   *

The library, with only one lighted table lamp, seemed to Janice only too appropriate for the continuation of her own personal nightmare. Never her favourite room, tonight its shadowy corners and massive bookshelves, rising to the ceiling, were more a setting for some macabre plot than a haven of learning. As the Chief Inspector settled in a leather armchair, Janice curled up on the chaise longue opposite.

The opening of the library door to admit Marlene with the coffee hindered the start of their discussion. This was further delayed by the obvious reluctance of Marlene to withdraw.

''Ave you got him yet?' she blurted out in thick nasal tones, 'you know, 'im in the black robe and white 'at.'

'Really, Marlene, this is too much, will you please leave us,' said an agitated Janice, hardly believing what she was hearing.

'No, no,' said the Chief Inspector, as he helped himself to sugar, 'let me hear what the girl has to say.'

'The girl' the Chief Inspector referred to, needed no second invitation. As an avid movie-goer, and as Henry could testify, capable of an imagination so vivid that it defied all logic, Marlene was in her element. Ignoring Janice's raised eyebrows, she promptly sat down at the Chief Inspector's feet, displaying, as a consequence of the limitations of her skirt, red suspenders topped with a fringe of white lace panties.

''E's the killer,' she said in her thick nasal drawl, 'sure as eggs.'

'So far,' said the Chief Inspector dryly, 'nobody has been killed.'

'Yer know what I mean . . . 'e 'ad a go, didn't 'e?'

'This has to stop, Marlene. Will you please leave us,' said Janice, rising from the chaise longue and for the first time noticing the figure of Henry, clearly in a state of agitation equal to her own, at the library door. 'Henry, will you please remove your assistant before I completely lose my temper, and I'll speak to you later.'

'Olright, I'm goin',' said a disgruntled Marlene, 'but you'll see if I'm not right about what I said.'

The Chief Inspector, with an attempt to pour oil on troubled waters, called after the receding Marlene that he would interview her later.

'That girl,' said Janice, as the library door finally closed, 'I am so sorry. What must you think?'

'Mrs Webster, the world is full of amateur detectives, don't worry about it, and anyway the girl meant well. As a matter of fact,' continued the Chief Inspector, 'I was about to ask you about the man in the black robe,' this with a smile. 'I assume he does exist?'

'Oh yes, she was referring to Igor, Miss Gollitzin's manservant. Quite harmless, but to an impressionable girl like Marlene he could be construed a threat. You see, his dress is rather eccentric.'

'Miss Gollitzin's manservant? The lady who is missing?'

'Yes.'

'Tell me about her, describe her for me.'

'Coal-black hair, no, I'm sorry, she's recently gone blonde.'

'Wait a moment, this might be important, you're saying she is normally dark?'

'As dark as pitch.'

'But now blonde?'

'Yes.'

'The girl who was shot this evening, Penelope Charters, she is dark?'

'Yes, she is,' agreed Janice, and then after a moment's thought, 'You don't think . . . ?'

'It is a point, and a very valid one in view of the fact that Miss Gollitzin has gone missing.'

Henry, having quietly opened the library door, again stood in the entrance and waited patiently for a break in their conversation. Catching Janice's eye, he took a few steps towards her.

'Ma'am,' he began apologetically, 'the dinner, if I don't serve it soon it will be ruined.'

Janice, after momentarily covering her face, managed a weak smile.

'Henry, I'm so sorry, by all means announce dinner and tell them I shall join them shortly.'

'And the birthday cake, ma'am?'

'No, Henry, no cake. I doubt James will join us, leave it at that for now. Just announce dinner ... for those who might want it,' said with a wintry smile at the Chief Inspector.

'Very well, ma'am,' said Henry withdrawing.

'This was a birthday party?' enquired the Chief Inspector.

'Yes, my brother's twenty-first.'

'I'm sorry. Now, Mrs Webster, tell me all you know about Miss Gollitzin.'

'Well, I've only known her a short time, she was a guest of my husband at a recent weekend house party. She is a very attractive young lady, very striking, East European I believe. In fact, I heard recently that she has pretensions, as a princess, to the Russian throne. Perhaps my husband could tell you more.'

'So you know really very little about her?'

'Yes, very little. . . I suppose.'

'I notice some hesitation. Mrs Webster, I must ask you to be frank with me. I'm sure I've no need to remind you that we have an attempted murder on our hands, for all we know he may try again. You're sure there is nothing more you can tell me?'

'Not really,' began a decidedly uncomfortable Mrs Webster, 'except that, as I said, being such an attractive girl she probably had many . . .' again, the hesitation, 'boyfriends.'

'You think one of them possibly, perhaps out of jealousy . . .'

'Yes, I think that's certainly possible.'

'Well,' said the Chief Inspector, looking at his watch, ' I don't

93

see we can achieve much more tonight, and doubtless,' giving Janice a smile which noticeably failed to reach his eyes, 'you will want to get back to your guests. Tomorrow, I should like to have a word with your husband and a further word with your brother, who will need to sign a statement.'

'We'll be here,' said Janice, suddenly feeling very tired.

'And, oh yes, your maid Marlene.'

'She's not my maid, Chief Inspector, she's the caterer's assistant and only here for tonight, but I have her address.'

'That will do, and thank you for your frankness, Mrs Webster.'

It was only after he had gone and she was pouring herself a generous measure of brandy, that she pondered about the Chief Inspector's parting words – 'thank you for your frankness'. She knew that he knew she had been anything but that.

*   *   *

To Janice, the second shock of the evening was almost as traumatic as the first.

As she smoothed her hair in front of the large oval mirror above the fireplace prior to joining her guests, a sound reached her from the furthest extremity of the room. It was a part of the library that, whatever time of day, was always in shadow. Tonight, with the light of only one table lamp it had become the dwelling place of the night creatures that exist in all imaginations, the small recesses between the multitude of bookshelves resembling entrances to the blackest of pits.

The noise Janice heard coming from one of the recesses was of sobbing.

'Who's there?' Janice found herself saying, as she fought to contain nerves strained to breaking point.

It's me, Janeece,' came the reply between much louder sobs, 'Natasha.'

'Natasha!' exclaimed Janice, her voice a mixture of relief and utter surprise. 'What on earth are you doing there?'

Out of the gloom appeared the figure of Natasha. Not the Natasha of poise, elegance and beauty, but a distraught young girl who, with the aid of a limp handkerchief, was attempting to repair the ravages of a tear-stained face, the cheeks of which displayed streaks of black mascara like the adornment of some native savage.

'Oh, Janeece, what am I to do?' she wailed, further tears swelling up.

'First of all,' replied Janice, making an effort to control herself, 'you had better have a brandy. You look as though you need one.'

With a degree of normality established, Natasha, both hands grasping her brandy glass, between further sobs repeated the question, although this time even more forcibly.

All intention of returning to her guests abandoned, Janice sat down on the chaise longue and motioned Natasha to join her but not before she, too, had helped herself from the decanter.

'Now, Natasha, what is this all about?' she said as she produced her own handkerchief and began repairs to Natasha's face. 'I hope you don't mind a little spit,' she remarked, endeavouring to inject a touch of humour into the situation. Natasha, quiet now, submitted to her administrations with a smile, but a smile far different from its usual devastating brilliance.

'There, that's better,' said Janice, returning her now discoloured white lace handkerchief to the hip pocket of her dress.

'Now, Natasha,' she began again, 'listen to me, you must tell me just what this is all about.'

'I'm so frightened, Janeece.'

'Well, if that man meant to kill you, you've every reason to be ... was he your lover?'

Natasha shook her head.

'Do you know him?'

'I think,' said Natasha, screwing up her handkerchief into a ball, 'he was the man the woman was frightened of.'

'What woman? Really, I think you had better start from the very beginning.'

As she heard of Natasha's early days back in Kolomyja, a look of incredulity came over Janice's face. Of her sharing a bed with Valma, her sister. The brutal drunken Vladimir – who frequently abused her. Then the emergence of 'Granny' Olga and her lessons in seduction, the journey to Appenzell and the meeting with the Duchess, the murder of Olga ... to Janice it sounded like some adventure story taken from a best-seller. Then the amazing denouement that Natasha was the granddaughter of the last Tsarina and therefore likely heir to the throne.

All was related in such a manner that Janice, however bizarre it appeared, had no doubt the story was true. And then the revelation of the Romanov gold, her near arrest only a day ago, and with it the incredible transformation of Igor.

'Look,' said Natasha, lifting her dress waist-high to reveal the tattoo etched at the top of her thigh. 'This is the map of where the gold is hidden.'

Perhaps the close proximity of Natasha and the overwhelming feeling of sympathy she had for her, together with the not inconsiderable amounts of brandy she had consumed, all conspired to produce in Janice sensations which, throughout the evening, had lain dormant. It was the sight of the top of Natasha's thigh that aroused the flood of feeling beginning, as always, with a pronounced tingle in her lower abdomen. Before she could restrain herself the tips of her fingers, which earlier had been exploring the map, began their inexorable climb. Slipping under the tight elastic of Natasha's panties, they reached the soft warmth of their goal. Leaning across her, Janice was conscious of the reluctant movement of Natasha's legs, which widened only slowly to receive her ever more demanding fingers.

The sound of Natasha's childlike voice pleading, 'Not now, Janeece,' acted on Janice like a douche of cold water. What was she thinking of? Trying to seduce the girl with a room full of guests just across the hallway. Loath though she was, Janice removed her hand, but not before her tongue, with wild abandon, forced an entry into the inviting softness of Natasha's open mouth.

*   *   *

Drained of the last dregs of her emotions and with passion now spent, Janice, white-faced, sat beside Natasha, the enormity of what she had just done slowly crystallising and bringing with it a sense of shame and disgust.

'That was very bad of me, Natasha,' she said as the full portent of her action became ever clearer. 'I took advantage of you in a way that was unforgivable. What must you think of me? And more to the point, what must I think of myself?'

'But Janeece,' said Natasha, taking hold of her hand, 'I love you and eet was very nice ... perhaps later I come to you, *non*?'

'As a release of tension,' said Janice, looking at her, 'I can only say I've never known better, but nevertheless ...' this time avoiding Natasha's eyes, 'it could be construed as abuse. I just wanted you, with no thought for what you've been through. It was utterly selfish of me.'

'No, Janeece, it was not like that, you are my dear friend. As poor Olga used to say, sex itself is only another form of domination. That is the attraction it has for me, the feeling of power and being in control. Love-sex is so different. It is, after all, the only medium we have of physically expressing our love.'

Janice's eyes widened in wonderment. Here was a young girl whose background was so different from her own, expressing herself with a maturity, and yes, a dignity, far beyond her years.

Realising that some answer was required of her, Janice, gathering her thoughts together, decided frankness was her only option.

'Natasha,' she began, 'I find you enormously attractive ... I know as a mature married woman I should control such feelings – even banish them altogether.' A pause, as she groped for words. 'But we are what we are,' she finished lamely.

Silence followed, then as the reality of the situation returned to her, Natasha, her voice quivering, turned to Janice and said, 'What am I going to do, Janeece? Those men, sooner or later are going to catch me and send me back to Kolomyja. If they do, I think I shall die.'

Janice stood up and, smoothing her dress, looked down at her.

'Now, about these men, Natasha, I give you my word they are not going to take you away. I'll move heaven and earth first . . . I intend to speak to Daddy tomorrow – he knows people in high places, strings can be pulled. Believe me, nobody is going to send you away or hurt you.'

'Oh, Janeece, thank you, you're so good to me.'

Again, so childlike, thought Janice, as Natasha's face positively glowed with happiness.

'From tonight, you're staying here. You're to go to your bedroom, take a bath and go to bed. I'll send Henry up with a tray for you, you must be starving.'

'But I'm not hungry, really I'm not.'

'Rubbish, after a hot bath you'll feel differently. Now upstairs with you, and I simply must get back to my guests. God knows what they must be thinking.'

'What about Igor, Janice, can he stay here too?'

'Igor – but he's not with you?'

'I know, you see we had a row, he forbade me to come . . .'

'And you came anyway.'

'Yes.'

'What is it with you and this Igor?'

'I feel safe with him – the woman said he would always protect me and I could trust him with my life.'

'Is he your . . . lover?' Surely not, thought Janice, as soon as she had said it. Even in an evening as bizarre as this one, such a possibility was impossible to digest.

'No,' replied Natasha, without hesitation. 'But I'm very fond of him.'

'Where is he now?'

'At the cottage.'

'You mean where you ran to after those men . . .?'

'Yes.'

'Do you have the phone number of the cottage?'

'Yes.'

'Right, let me have it and I'll ring him in the morning. I've a few questions I should like to put to your Igor – if that's his real name. Now, bed for you, and I must join my guests.'

'You're so kind, Janice.'

* * *

As Janice entered the dining room the waspish voice of Hilda greeted her.

'At last, our hostess appears!'

'Not now, Hilda, I'm not in the mood for it,' replied Janice, as she took her seat at the head of the table.

'That's all very well for you, but I do think we should have been shown a little more consideration,' the waspish tone now replaced by one implying hardship bravely borne.

'Hilda,' Janice's tone was a red light flashing, 'I've had a girl shot in my drive, there are police crawling around everywhere, my husband is nowhere to be seen ...'

'Probably gone off with that Gollitzin woman, nothing would surprise me where she is concerned.'

'That's enough of that,' Big George's booming voice intervened, 'we've no grounds for thinking that, I say, and anyway I think it's all pretty exciting like an Agatha Christie novel – we don't know what's going to happen next.'

'Oh, do shut up, George, it's painful enough without your ridiculous comparisons,' said Hilda, with a look of ill-concealed venom.

'Natasha,' said Janice, looking directly at Hilda, her voice icy calm, 'is tucked up in bed.'

'Tucked up in bed! You mean to say that women is still in the house? Well, heaven help us all ... how could you, Janice! As I've said all along, bringing that Gollitzin woman into your home was inviting trouble, and I've been proved right.'

'Oh, I don't know,' said Emma, looking across at Hilda and clearly not wishing to be left out of such an exhilarating tirade. 'I think she is fascinating.'

'I found her extremely interesting,' came the quietly spoken voice of Audrey. 'You need someone like her to liven up your dinner table, I think Janice should be congratulated,' she said, looking anywhere but at Hilda.

'I must say I agree with Audrey,' said Ben, manfully ignoring the shaft of hostility now directed at himself as well as his wife. 'After all,' he continued, 'what happened tonight may well have a simple explanation, some lunatic on the loose for example.'

'No doubt, all will be revealed in God's good time,' contributed Peter, disregarding his wife's raised eyebrows at such a pious observation.

'I do hope Henry has looked after you all,' said Janice, in a brave attempt to bring normality back into the proceedings.

'Wonderful meal, Janice, as always,' said Big George.

'Well, you ought to know,' cut in Hilda, conscious that by getting at her husband she was on much safer ground. 'After all, you ate most of it!'

'Shall we all adjourn to the drawing room for coffee,' suggested Janice, struggling to regain her role as hostess. 'I for one am desperate for a cup.'

'But you've had nothing to eat at all, girl,' objected Hilda, now adopting a more conciliatory tone of voice, 'you must eat something.'

'Possibly later, but not now,' replied Janice, rising from the table.

'Excuse me Ma'am,' Henry's voice from the doorway stopped any further remonstrations from Hilda. 'Sir Humphrey Charters is in the hall and wishes to speak with you.'

'Oh God, not now,' murmured Janice, as the bulky frame of Sir Humphrey strode into the room.

'What the devil has been going on? I've just left my little girl in Hendon General recovering from an operation to remove a bullet from her shoulder...' towering above the diminutive Janice, he was the epitome of the outraged father. In spite of everything, Janice had to smile to herself; Penelope Charters described as a 'little girl ' had a certain irony about it.

'We're all terribly upset about it, Sir Humphrey, and are totally at a loss as to why it happened.'

'Indeed you should be, and I want an answer to a few questions,' he continued, glaring balefully at Janice. 'What's this I hear about you entertaining some Russian woman? If nothing else, it's damned unpatriotic.'

'If you are referring to Miss Gollitzin, she is a friend of the family.'

'Some friend I must say,' as, looking at the guests, his eyes fastened on Emma, who, just as Sir Humphrey entered the room was rising from the table. Her dress, as Janice had noted earlier, was not the most suitable for the occasion, being a size too small for her bulbous figure and served more to emphasise, than to discreetly conceal, her full, heavy breasts. This, when combined with make-up equally unsuitable, gave out a clarion call unmistakable in its message.

'So, you're the Russian bit I've been hearing about,' he said, addressing her, his fleshy face the mirror of indignation. 'You're the one he was really after, and looking at you, I can well understand why.'

Emma, stunned, turned to her husband, 'Peter,' she began, only for Janice to come to her rescue.

'That is Mrs Peter Canning who, with her husband, are guests of mine, and if you are going to continue to insult us I must ask you to leave.'

'Not until I've had my say.'

'I think you've said enough already.'

'Quite right,' squeaked Hilda, 'you tell him, Janice.'

'I want some answers,' Sir Humphrey's voice rasped on.

'Then I suggest you speak with Chief Inspector Reynolds at Hendon Police Station.' Then, turning in the direction of the dining room door, and in a clear resolute voice, Janice, although inwardly shaking like a leaf, called 'Henry, Sir Humphrey is leaving. Will you please show him out.'

'All right, I'm going, but don't think this is the last of it,' said Sir Humphrey as he pushed past Henry and out into the hall.

'I'm sure it isn't,' said Janice, sighing with relief at the sight of his fast-disappearing back.

11

Tumult

The cottage was no longer the desirable residence it had once been. But, situated in a small wood immediately adjacent to the A3, it was the ideal bolt-hole for Charlie and Natasha. Earlier that evening, at Natasha's insistence that she attended James Webster's birthday party, he had driven her there. Now, back in the cottage, he contemplated an evening of solitude with a measure of satisfaction. If nothing else, Charlie was a man utterly content with his own company.

As he rose from the battered armchair, the remains of its stuffing escaping from numerous holes, Charlie Tuttle, with the expertise of long practice, fed a magazine into his 9mm Luger. Then standing fully upright, with his sixteen-stone frame balanced evenly on the balls of his feet and with both hands clamped on the butt, he lined up the sights on a small damp patch, one of many smearing the stone walls of the cottage. With the index finger of his right hand now curled around the trigger he gave an audible sigh, as though he and the gun were a single entity, and gently squeezed.

The report, followed by a further two in quick succession, although stupefying in the close confines of the room, seemingly had no effect on him as, lowering the gun, he strode purposefully over to the patch and, with a contented smile, examined the two-inch round hole. Satisfied, he returned to the chair and pulling close an equally decrepit table, covered with a miscellany of cleaning materials, produced a much smaller gun from the rear of his waistband. Although in no way comparable in size with the Luger, being squat and easily covered by the palm of his hand, it was handled no less reverently as he placed it within easy reach at his side. Where Charlie Tuttle was concerned, his guns were as much part of him as his right arm and, he would argue, in certain circumstances far more useful.

With a mix of cordite fumes and cigarette smoke surrounding him, Charlie carefully began stripping down the Luger and from habit ensured each part was removed in a sequence which would facilitate its reassembly. On such occasions he was inclined to allow his thoughts to dwell on problems currently facing him.

Foremost in his mind were the difficulties surrounding Natasha. He remembered his promise to the Duchess, was it really but a few weeks ago? As he clasped her frail hand in his, he had assured her that Natasha's safety would be paramount. 'She is such an innocent in all this, Charlie. At times I feel so dreadfully guilty that she has become involved.' Yes, all would be well, he had reassured her with a confident smile – a confidence now he was far from feeling.

Whereas the expected had been allowed for, it was the unexpected in the transformation of Natasha herself that was proving the fly in the ointment. How do you control a young girl? A girl upon which nature had lavished such gifts, a girl who in the space of three months had seen her life become nothing less than a fairy tale – a fairy tale where all dreams come true. Already, as he had witnessed tonight, she was challenging his authority, and in spite of his dire warnings had insisted on going to the Webster's party. He could speak to Sergei, but he already had an uncomfortable feeling that he was equally at a loss as to how to handle her.

With the Luger reassembled, he returned it to the shoulder holster, which nestled under his left armpit, its weight as ever giving him a sense of bonding with something that, although inanimate, was totally reliable and dependable. As he lit another cigarette his thoughts went back to Elizabeth. He recalled their first meeting, arranged by the CIA, in that private clinic in Berne shortly after his world had been blown apart. Their proposition and hers was a lifeline, a rope thrown to a drowning man, and although outlandish, it had been accepted with gratitude.

Rising from the chair, he moved across the room to his cloak. A gift from a professional magician it had, at various times, served him well. Within its folds of dark heavy cloth were a myriad of pockets and other clever devices whereby even large objects could be concealed.

From an inner lining he removed a package and with it returned to his chair. Carefully removing its oilskin covering, secured by a length of bootlace, he spread the three manilla envelopes it contained on the floor in front of him. Selecting one, he opened it gently and removed an embossed sheet of paper. Settling back as comfortably as possible within the limitations of the chair, and lighting yet another cigarette, he began to read.

He had little doubt as to its authenticity. At the top the name of St Petersburg had been rather crudely erased, something a forger would have improved upon. In its place was the word Leningrad all but covered by an official stamp bearing the words *Bureau of Registration Sub-district Four*. The paper recorded the marriage of *Eugenia Alexandra Fyodorovna to Oberst Helmuth Handrick of Fliegerkorps 1*. The date of the marriage was given as 11/11/1941. He was aware that during the war the Germans failed to take Leningrad, but in their prevailing optimism at that time such an anomaly meant little. If anything, it lent even more credence to the document being genuine. Attached was a further certificate. This one bore the stamp of the German Eagle and the address of the Public Records Office, Berlin. It was a certificate of registration of the birth of *Natasha Alexandra Handrick*, the date of birth was given as *17/8/42*.

After returning the two documents to their envelope, Charlie Tuttle, eyes fixed on the ceiling above, began a low whistle, a sign to those who knew him well that he was deep in thought.

Without needing to open it, his mind turned to what was contained in the largest envelope. A copy of the last will and testament of the Duchess Elizabeth Fyodorovna, younger daughter of the Grand Duke of Hesse-Darmstadt, and sister of the last Empress of all the Russias. He recalled the degree of servility adopted by the solicitor's clerk as the will was witnessed by two nondescript employees of the firm. Since that day in Zurich he had done some historical research, his knowledge of such matters being severely limited. If the Duchess Elizabeth was to be believed, then by direct lineal descent from her grandmother, the Empress Tsarina, Natasha's great-great-grandmother was none other than Queen Victoria! The portent of such a fact, if it were true, was mind-blowing. Natasha Gollitzin, or, to be correct, Natasha Handrick could be the sole direct descendant of the house of Romanov and, as such, a relative of the House of Windsor – the British Royal Family...! Shades of Anastasia, but in this instance, far more was going for Natasha than the woman who turned up in Germany claiming to be the Tsar's youngest daughter.

As he lit another cigarette his gaze went to the last of the three envelopes. Again there was no need to open it, he was all too familiar with its contents; it was Natasha's mother's birth certificate and in copperplate writing gave her mother as *Her Royal Highness, Princess Eugenia*; under occupation (this tickled Charlie) were the words *Princess of the Royal House of Romanov*.

If it was a forgery, contemplated Charlie, it was a bloody good one. Yawning, he looked at his watch, time to get some shut-eye.

* * *

Sergei Poznansky, with his concern as to Natasha's whereabouts uppermost, ignored his inbred caution and agreed to meet Mikhael Derevenko in his room. It was the act of a man who, temporarily at least, had become overwhelmed by the turn of events. For such an act of gross stupidity there could be but one forfeit.

Barely had Derevenko entered when, in response to Sergei's agitated enquiry about the money, he, motivated in part by his years of hatred for all that Sergei stood for, brought his gloved hand just behind Sergei's ear with such power and fury as to all but crush the delicate bone structure connecting the cranium to the veterbrae. Sergei, without a sound, slid slowly to the floor at the feet of his assailant.

Working quickly and to an obviously prepared plan, Derevenko, using lengths of cord he had brought with him, soon had Sergei tied to the only chair in the room. Satisfied, he now turned his attention to an old vacuum cleaner standing in a corner. Ripping out the flex, he inserted the plug into a convenient wall point, enuring it was controlled by a switch, but not before he had bared the ends of the flex of all insulation. Then, watching Sergei through narrowed eyes, he lit a cigarette.

Low moans coming from his prisoner told him that Sergei was regaining consciousness. Tearing off a length of pillowcase, he leant over and with brutal force rammed it down Sergei's throat. Moving over to the small wash basin, he filled a jug of water and, with a coldness that mirrored the temperature of the contents, poured it over Sergei's head. For the first time since entering the room, Mikhael Derevenko spoke.

'Now, my friend,' he purred, 'as they say in England, the boot is on the other foot. You would do well to tell me where the plan of the gold is kept.' Sergei's eyes, his only medium of expression, stared blankly back at him.

From his years of experience gained in the arts of interrogation and from the responses of those undergoing unspeakable pain, a doubt crossed his mind. Had he hit him too hard? Peering closer into the emptiness now looking back at him, he cursed in a flurry of Russian. Probably the blow had damaged the brain stem – if so, Sergei Poznansky was as much use to him as the vegetable he appeared to have become.

With barely suppressed rage, he turned his attention to search the room. Cupboards, drawers, suitcases, not even Sergei's bed escaped his ruthless ransacking, all done swiftly and systematically, but no photograph. As he was leaving, and almost as an afterthought, he turned and looked back at the stricken Sergei.

107

Approaching him for the last time he produced his snub-nosed pistol, the same one Sergei had seen before on Waterloo Bridge, but this time there was a subtle difference: attached to the end was a bulbous addition of black metal. With the gun pointing at Sergei's forehead there followed a distinct plop, similar in sound to the opening of a magnum of champagne. It is doubtful if Sergei Poznansky heard the report, and if he had, he would have been the first to admit he had nothing to celebrate.

* * *

The shrill ringing of the telephone awoke Charlie. Knowing it could only be Natasha, he reached across his makeshift bed and spoke into the mouthpiece.

'You want Igor?'

'Don't play the halfwit with me, Igor, this is Janice Webster. I think you should know Natasha is staying with me until all this blows over.'

'Blows over?'

'Of course, you don't know. My brother's girlfriend was shot here last night. Not fatally, thank God, but needless to say, all hell's been let loose. It's obvious to me that whoever it was was after Natasha – Igor, are you still there?'

'I'm here, Mrs Webster.'

'Right, here's what I want you to do. Pack all Natasha's things and meet me ... where are you, Igor?'

'Er, near Godalming.'

'Igor, you don't have to be cagey with me. Anyway, from the telephone number Natasha gave me I knew you were in that area, so Hammersmith should suit you fine. Meet me in the car park opposite the bridge say in two hours, and Igor...'

Yes, Mrs Webster.'

'I want a few answers to a few questions, you get my meaning?'

'I do.'

'Good – and Igor, oh, to hell with it ... what is your name?'

'Charlie Tuttle, Mrs Webster, rhymes with scuttle.'
'All right Charlie, remember, I'm on your side, OK.'
'I'll try to remember, Mrs Webster.'
'You can dispense with the Webster, Janice is the name.'
' All right . . . Janice,' but the silence told him the line had gone dead.

* * *

In a café close to Hammersmith car park, Janice Webster eyed the man who, until the unburdening of Natasha's story the night before, she had known as Igor, with considerable interest. It was all but impossible to believe that this person, wearing a blue check suit and matching tie, was the mumbling character, Igor. Late forties, early fifties she guessed but, with men, it was never easy to estimate their age. Some women might well find him attractive; he certainly had that masculine look she associated with rugby players. Sipping his coffee and smoking a cigarette, he appeared the epitome of serenity; impassive and seemingly indifferent to her and the reason for their meeting.

'You've been in the services, haven't you?' she said as an opening gambit.

Placing his cup back on its saucer, he appeared, at last, to be aware of her presence.

'On occasions.'

'Now come on, Charlie, no evasiveness – cards on the table.'

'French Foreign Legion, the International Brigade.'

'Spain?'

'Madrid, during the siege.' Allowing her to digest this morsel of information, he again became silent.

'Charlie.'

'Yes, Mrs Webster.'

'Charlie, if you call me Mrs Webster again I shall scream!'

'Yes . . . Janice.'

'Charlie , who shot the girl?'

Silence again.

'Charlie, you know, don't you?'

'I could make an educated guess.'

'Tell me ... please.'

'It wouldn't mean anything to you if I did.'

'Try me.'

'A Red agent called Mikhael Derevenko.'

'You mean a Commie?'

Once more silence ensued as, stubbing out his cigarette in an ashtray, he immediately lit another.

'Worse, a hangover from the old Bolshevik days.'

'Was he after Natasha?'

'Undoubtedly.'

'Was it you who compelled her to dye her hair?'

'Perhaps I hinted that a change might be for the better.'

'It probably saved her life.'

'Well, I'm grateful for that.'

'Charlie, she's told me quite a lot about the Duchess and this business of being the heir to the throne of Russia – is it true?'

'Most of it.'

'If I'm to help, Charlie, you must tell me everything.'

'I may not know everything,' he said, producing yet another cigarette from a battered silver case.

'God, you're being difficult, aren't you?'

Through a cloud of cigarette smoke he replied, 'It might be better if you don't know everything.'

'Rubbish.'

'Look, one thing at a time, my concern is keeping Natasha out of harm's way. Derevenko will certainly try again.'

'Oh, God , do you really think so?'

'Knowing the type, certainly.'

'Wouldn't she be safer, all things considered, if she were in custody?' For the first time Janice saw the real man behind the façade of assumed indifference. His eyes, until now devoid of expression, flashed with such an intensity of feeling that any

110

doubts she may have had that he was just a man of straw were immediately dispelled.

'And have her back in Moscow within hours . . . ? NO.'

After such an emphatic pronouncement he again returned, much to Janice's annoyance, to his infuriating impassive self.

'I think you and I should pay a call,' he said after a pause.

'A call on whom?'

'Sergei Poznansky. To all intents and purposes, he is her legal guardian appointed by the Duchess. I know where he is.'

Janice rose from the table and followed him out of the café, wondering, as she did so, what further revelations were in store.

'You follow me up,' he said, as they reached her car.

'Anything you say, Charlie,' she said, welcoming his decisiveness. As she looked at him, a shadow of concern passed over his face.

'Tell me,' he said, leaning on the bonnet, 'last night, did the police interview Natasha?'

'No, they didn't, she couldn't be found. Hiding, as it turned out, in the library, of all places.'

'But they took her details, name, address, that sort of thing.'

'Well, yes, they did.'

Again the sleepy grey eyes flashed.

'Then she is in grave danger. What a fool I've been not to realise earlier, we must get to her at once and pray God we're in time.'

'Charlie,' Janice's voice reflected anxiety as he hurried her round to the driving side of the car, 'what is going on?'

'Simply this, by now they will have tied her in with the woman from St John's Wood – the name Gollitzin is a dead giveaway, there's an extradition order out for her. Now no more questions, just drive like Hell . . . I'll be right behind you.'

*   *   *

Janice remembered little about the journey. She knew at one time she touched fifty miles an hour, but always Charlie was right behind her. It was, therefore, with a tremendous sense of relief for her own safety that she finally approached her driveway. Spotting two police cars at the top, she did a frantic swerve and carried on down the road. Mercifully, Charlie anticipated her manoeuvre just in time and drew up behind her in the adjacent slip road.

'Did you see them?' she enquired breathlessly.

'I did, at least that tells us she must still be in the house. Now you go up the drive as normal – I'll take the path leading to your back door. If things are bad, leave it to me.' With that, he was gone, his long legs quickly taking him out of sight.

Janice swung the car round, ignoring the heavy bump as its rear end rode up the kerb and drove back up the road they had just left. Turning into her driveway, she parked immediately in front of the two police cars. Then, quickly straightening her hair in the hall and ignoring Florrie's explanations regarding the arrival of two strange men, entered the library.

'Ah, Mrs Webster, how nice to see you again.' It was Chief Inspector Reynolds speaking. 'May I introduce you to Mr Egerton of the Home Office?' The man who was obviously Mr Egerton extended his hand.

'Good morning, Mrs Webster.'

Janice inclined her head but ignored the proffered hand. At that moment her first concern was Natasha, standing forlornly at his side. No handcuffs, she noticed with relief.

'We were just explaining to Miss Gollitzin, Mrs Webster, the extradition order has been temporarily lifted. This has been done at the request of Hendon CID in connection with last night's affair, Miss Gollitzin being a material witness.' From his voice, thought Janice, Mr Egerton suffered badly from adenoids.

'Well,' acknowledged Janice, 'that is a relief.'

'However, Mrs Webster, there is another matter.' It was the Chief Inspector again. 'I have just charged Miss Gollitzin with being an accessory to an act of grievous bodily harm. She will be required to appear at Marylebone Magistrate's Court at eleven, tomorrow morning. Without doubt her case will be adjourned to the Crown Court; we shall not oppose bail, but a surety will be required.'

'Thank you for that, Chief Inspector. I shall of course go surety, and my father will ensure she is represented.'

It was then Charlie entered the room accompanied by an obviously anxious Florrie.

'This gentleman...'

'It's all right, Florrie, thank you.'

Then, turning to the two men, she said blandly, 'This is Allan Green, a partner in my father's practice.' And addressing the newcomer, 'Everything is fine, Allan, I have all the details.'

'Good,' commented Chief Inspector Reynolds, 'then we have no need to keep you any longer.'

'There is one thing, Chief Inspector, any news about last night?'

'The investigation is progressing, Mrs Webster – now good day to you.'

'Well, what do you think, Egerton?' said Chief Inspector Reynolds as they walked to their cars.

'The girl doesn't know if its Pancake Tuesday or Ash Wednesday, that's for sure, but I have to admit she's a nice piece of skirt, did you notice those eyes? Sent shivers down my spine, they did. As for Mrs Webster – now there's one sharp lady.'

'I agree, she knows a lot more than she is telling. You know she is the daughter of George Lawrence, don't you?'

'The QC?'

'None other, probably the best criminal advocate in the country.'

'I thought he had retired.'

'More or less, he owns the largest law firm in the county – but you can bet your bottom dollar that if his daughter is involved in something shady he'll soon be back. Have to tread carefully on this one, Egerton, what with Lawrence on one side and Sir

Humphrey Charters on the other ... I ask you, who would be a policeman?'

As they reached their cars, Chief Inspector Reynolds turned to his companion.

'What did you make of the latecomer, Allan Green? Bit out of breath, wasn't he? And did you notice his shoes? Covered in mud, they were – funny way to enter the house through the back garden...'

'I wondered if you had noticed that,' replied Egerton, 'could be he is the fly in the ointment.'

'The martial arts gentleman?'

'I would lay odds on the possibility.'

'You know, Egerton, I think you've missed your vocation.'

12

War Cry

'This memo,' said Colonel de Quincy, holding up an official-looking piece of paper, 'is from the Palace, Class A circulation. It's a request for more information about the Gollitzin woman and her claims. We know why, don't we, Teddy? The Royals are worried as a consequence of their total inertia to help the Tsar and his family back in 1918. The last thing they want is to be caught out again. If she is the granddaughter of the last Tsarina, then by natural descent she is a relative of theirs.'

'Precisely,' agreed Captain Farrar, 'Princess Alice, mother of the Tsarina, was the daughter of Queen Victoria.'

'You've been doing some research into this haven't you, Teddy?'

'A little.'

'Good, it may prove useful. I see tomorrow,' looking down at his diary, 'I have one Dmitri Sokolov coming to see me.'

'Yes, he's Grand Chairman of the Russian Nobility Association, to give him his full title, and sir, what he has to say may prove very helpful.'

'I'm aware of what he is and who he is, Teddy, and yes, I do agree the interview may prove very revealing.'

Ignoring his Chief's somewhat petulant demeanour, Captain Farrar carried on.

'What of the Home Office in all this ... sir?'

'They're floundering. I gather they have received the same

memo from the Palace and are playing it very cagey. You'll be glad to know they have temporarily lifted the extradition order on Gollitzin.'

'I'm pleased for that.'

'Yes, I thought you would be,' said the Colonel, smiling for the first time. 'But you won't be so pleased to learn she is still in deep trouble.'

'In what way, sir?'

'She's due at Marylebone Magistrates tomorrow morning – accessory to an act of grievous bodily harm, you remember the Home Office Official . . .'

'I don't see how they can make that stick. After all, all she did was run off.'

'There's another matter, Teddy, read this from Hendon CID, copied to us by the Home Office. You'll find it very interesting.'

Captain Farrar picked up the report and quickly read it.

'An attempted murder – the daughter of Sir Humphrey Charters – I don't believe it!'

'It's there in black and white, Teddy, and what the report fails to mention is that the Gollitzin woman was in the house at the time.'

Gazing upwards, as if meditating, the Colonel fell silent and then, reaching a conclusion, he rose from his desk.

'I'm inclined to put two and two together and make four out of this, Teddy. The girl,' glancing down, 'Natasha Gollitzin, was the real target.'

'Derevenko?'

'Most probably. At least we know now, if that is the case, why he is over here.'

'Should we pull him in, sir?'

'Won't be easy, we've no photographs of him on file. In fact we know precious little about him, that is where this fellow Sokolov may be able to help.'

'Do you think he'll try again?'

'Teddy, if that is why he is over here he will most certainly try again.'

'Could we not use the girl as bait?'

'Risky, but it might be worth a try. However, first of all we need to know a lot more than we do – I want dossiers on all who are involved in the Monarchist Association. Let's build up a picture, Teddy, right now it's mostly conjecture.'

'I'll have everything by tomorrow morning, sir.'

'Good for you, Teddy – and there is some consolation in all this. At least the Bear has been thwarted, there is nothing they can do to drag her back to Moscow whilst she's facing criminal charges here.'

'That was going through my mind, sir. Strange, isn't it, that back in Moscow they're pulling strings to get her back, whilst over here one of their agents is running round attempting to shoot her!'

'That is precisely why we need to know a great deal more, Teddy.'

'Amen to that.'

* * *

Bill Webster studied his wife from across the library. Outwardly, he was reading an updated edition of *The Law and the Countryside* to which he had contributed. His thoughts, however, were more concerned with the recent turn of events than the particular page in front of him dealing with 'Trespass'.

Natasha was becoming a nuisance – she could even be construed a threat to his marriage. She and Janice were inseparable. Conversations between them ceased whenever he appeared, and by their subtle attitude of indifference they made it obvious that he was excluded from their deliberations. His best defence, he told himself, was to act as if had noticed nothing untoward. But as their relationship became ever more exclusive, depression and a mounting fear began to assail him. The knowledge that Janice had put up five thousand pounds bail money for Natasha had only served to increase his fears.

117

'How long is Natasha staying with us?' he called across. Janice looked up, as if she were noticing him for the first time.

'As long as it takes,' came the perfunctory reply.

'That's no answer.'

'She's nowhere else to go and, in any case, I don't see how it is inconveniencing you. Daddy considers it's better she is with us, what with the surety and everything – and anyway, I enjoy having her around.' The barb in her last few words was not lost on Bill.

'Where is she now?'

'She's gone out with Igor to visit a friend, a Mr Popolsky, or something like that, they'll be back for tea.'

'I'm not so sure it's safe having her around,' he said, walking across to her, 'especially now the police are convinced the gunman was after her.'

'We're safe enough with Igor around.'

Janice bit her lip, she realised at once that was a foolish remark to have made. As expected, Bill pounced.

'Igor...? What's he got to do with it?'

'Oh, nothing I guess. Now I must go and have a word with Florrie, you know Peter and Emma are dining with us this evening.'

'No, I didn't know,' said her aggrieved husband.

*   *   *

The late evening paper said it all, the large black lettering leapt out at Janice as she picked it up from the hall mat. *Russian dissident shot to death* was the headline. *Sergei Poznansky, confidant of the late Tsar Nicholas and childhood friend of Tsarevich Alexi, was found dead in his one-bedroomed flat in North London late last night. Mr Poznansky, a supporter of the exiled Russian Monarchist Movement, died from a bullet in the head. It was believed he had been dead at least two days. Inspector Huggins, Marylebone CID, denied reports that the murder was connected with the recent shooting of Miss Penelope Charters, daughter of the well-known City financier, Sir Humphrey Charters, one-time confidant of the Tsar and his family.*

Suddenly feeling quite ill, Janice sat down on one of the hall chairs.

*   *   *

Captain Edward Farrar was still drinking his morning coffee when the telephone rang. It was a senior official at the Home Office. The plum-voiced caller extended the Home Secretary's compliments and would Sir Rupert attend a meeting that afternoon at the Home Office.

'Should I come along?' enquired Captain Farrar, hopefully.

'On this occasion, yes Teddy, bearing in mind that your knowledge of the last Tsar and Tsarina is much greater than mine. Dig out all you can on the Russian, Sergei Poznansky. Undoubtedly,' he said, tapping last night's evening paper, 'the cat is really among the pigeons this time. I'll meet you there at 1500 sharp, it might be as well to bring the file on Charlie Tuttle. You should find it under Personnel, classification B, look around the late forties.'

'As you wish, sir,' said Captain Farrar, 'and I had better cancel your meeting with that fellow Sokolov.'

'Yes,' replied his Chief, somewhat regretfully, 'but do arrange another appointment.'

'Will do,' called Captain Farrar halfway through the doorway.

*   *   *

The Home Secretary coughed politely and looked round at the gathering.

'Thank you, gentlemen, for attending at such short notice. However, looking at each one in turn, 'in view of last night's shooting, I considered it expedient that an early meeting should be called, particularly now the press are fishing around. Now one or two of you already know each other, so I will dispense with formalities other than to say we have two representatives of the Metropolitan Police present, Chief Inspector Reynolds from

Hendon CID and Inspector Huggins of Marylebone CID. To assist your deliberations you each have a "fact file", which by now I hope you've read. This contains all the information we have up to the present.

'Gentlemen,' the Home Secretary continued, 'it seems we have a gunman loose in London, and what is rather disconcerting, he appears to be one of our Russian friends. Finally, gentlemen, and this is not contained in your file, I was approached this morning by an unimpeachable source offering to exchange the gunman for Miss Gollitzin. Miss Gollitzin, I am given to understand, is a Soviet citizen who entered this country illegally. I also understand she is currently on bail awaiting trial on very serious charges. Gentlemen, I now invite your observations.'

'The source offering the exchange, Minister...'

'At present that is classified for my eyes only – I'm sorry, on this occasion, Sir Rupert, you'll have to use your imagination!'

Brief smiles of amusement spread round the gathering at this aside.

'I take it, Minister,' volunteered Chief Inspector Reynolds, 'that we all accept that the same gunman who shot Miss Charters also shot Poznansky?'

'Well, as you know, Chief Inspector, Forensic has confirmed that the bullets came from the same gun, although, to be absolutely certain, we need to have the weapon.'

'Thank you, Minister.'

'As I understand it, Minister,' it was Sir Rupert speaking, 'the shooting of Miss Charters was a mistake?'

'It would appear so.'

'So there has to be a motive possibly connected with Miss Gollitzin?'

'Almost certainly.'

'With regard to the motive, our enquiries are continuing,' stated Chief Inspector Reynolds, pompously.

Chief Superintendent Alfred Biggs, MBE, Head of Special Branch, looked up.

'It is my opinion, Minister, that there is a war going on between the KGB and some Russian dissidents in London. A look at the fact file and what I've heard earlier confirms this ... the prize they are fighting for is the Romanov gold. It does exist,' looking at each of the gathering as if daring contradiction, 'and is not, as many believe, a hoary old chestnut. Therefore, Minister, my recommendation must be that we do not accept the offer of an exchange until we have more facts to work with.'

'Reluctantly, Chief Superintendent, I am inclined to agree.'

'Her Majesty may have something to say if she were handed over ... sir,' it was Captain Farrar, his voice expressing his pent-up indignation.

'I beg your pardon,' said the Home Secretary, looking over the tope of his glasses. 'May I enquire who you are and which department you represent?'

'This is Captain Edward Farrar, Minister, my Number One at Section 10.'

'Do you agree with your Number One, Sir Rupert?'

'I think what Captain Farrar is trying to say is that the Gollitzin girl has claim to the Russian throne, Minister, and therefore if her claim is genuine she is related to Her Majesty.'

'Minister,' said the Chief Superintendent, 'I understand that such a claim is not even recognised by her own countrymen.'

'Thank you, that I feel clarifies the matter. Now my recommendation must be that bail on Miss Gollitzin be rescinded – you will please attend to that, Chief Inspector – and subject to certain conditions, Miss Gollitzin will be taken into custody pending the outcome of our further enquiries and investigations ... I take it we are agreed?'

'Agreed, Minister.'

'Thank you, gentlemen, the meeting is now closed.'

'Oh, Sir Rupert, can you spare me a moment?' asked the Home Secretary as the others filed out.

'Certainly, Minister.'

'I'm just a little concerned at the remarks of your man Farrar. Is there anything in this woman's supposed connection with Her Majesty?'

'Well, Home Secretary, if, and I say if, her claim is genuine, then she would be the great-great-granddaughter of Queen Victoria.'

Sir Rupert told Captain Farrar afterwards that at this point a subtle change came over the Minister's expression.

'Do you think we're being hasty, then, taking her into custody?

'Minister, I've thirty years' experience in Intelligence behind me, and if I advise caution it is purely because I have learnt there is usually more to these things than meets the eye.'

'What would you suggest?'

'Establish her bona fides – in that respect, Minister, I think I know a man who can settle the issue beyond doubt.'

The Home Secretary, deep in thought, said nothing for a few moments then, reaching a decision, he said, 'I'll put the matter on hold for a few days, Sir Rupert. This is between Reynolds and the two of us, you understand?'

'Certainly, Minister.'

'And, Sir Rupert...'

'Yes, Minister?'

You will keep me fully informed, won't you – about the man you mentioned?'

'As you wish, Minister.'

*   *   *

Janice Webster eyed Charlie as she poured out tea for them both.

'I'll take Natasha a cup in a moment, she is simply devastated about the news of this man Poznansky – what exactly happened, Charlie?'

'On our way to see him, I fortunately stopped to buy an evening paper, and there it was, so back we came.'

'Was the man close to her, Charlie?' asked Janice, having seen how upset Natasha was.

'I think she relied on him to a great extent,' replied Charlie, deep in thought, 'but that's not the point. I think it has finally come home to her how vulnerable she is. Another factor we should bear in mind is that your telephone is probably being tapped.'

'Bloody cheek!'

'Something you're going to have to get used to – there are no ground rules when it comes down to this sort of business.'

'But the girl's done nothing, Charlie!'

'That's as maybe, but in their eyes she is the fulcrum of what is going on at the moment – and she can be got at ... remember that. As I see it, Janice, it's not so much the gunman we need to worry about but our own officialdom.'

'I don't follow you?'

'Natasha is a Soviet citizen. The Russkies, if all else fails, will quite happily negotiate to get her back ... and not because she may have a claim to the throne; they're playing for much higher stakes ... the Romanov gold.'

'Oh, God no, not more complications. Charlie, what are we to do?'

'To stay one jump ahead, and to give us more time, why not lodge her with the caterers, Henry and Marlene?'

'Surely not?'

'It's the one place they won't think of looking – I will go along with her, and you could visit – providing you're careful.'

'They're always short and would do anything for money, but Marlene, she's got such a mouth.'

'She's also a romantic, she'll believe whatever I tell her – and don't forget I'll be there."

'All right then.'

'Where do they live?'

'Dagenham.'

'Couldn't be better, I know it well.'

'Then perhaps we should pay them a call and sound them out.'

Their conversation was brought to an abrupt end by the ringing of the telephone.

'Please,' said Janice, as she lifted the phone, 'not more trouble.'

'Jan, Daddy here. I want to see you and Miss Gollitzin in my office first thing. I'm going for a Judicial Review regarding the order – this will slow things down. I'm also looking into the question of asylum. If, by returning to the Soviet Union she is under sentence of death, assuming we can prove that, then we've a good chance.'

'Oh, Daddy, that would be wonderful.'

'Anyway, keep your chin up, it's not all over yet by a long way.'

'You heard that, Charlie?' said Janice, smiling. 'For the time being Natasha stays with me ... and so do you.'

'That is very good of you. You know you could drop all this if you had a mind to – after all, what is she to you?'

'I'm very fond of her, Charlie, and ... not for the reasons you're thinking.'

'You mean the bedroom ...?' For a few moments he looked at her then, turning away, he said, 'I think tomorrow I'll visit an old friend.'

Welcoming the change of subject, she faced him again.

'Who?'

'The Head of MI10, Sir Rupert de Quincy – I worked with him years ago.'

'Be careful, Charlie, you know they're looking for you.'

'To be precise, Mrs Webster, they're looking for an old man with grey, thinning hair, a big nose and dressed in a black cape.'

'You know, Charlie Tuttle,' she breathed, 'you should try smiling more often.' With that, and standing on tiptoe to reach up to him, she gently kissed him on the cheek.

Looking down at her, he said, 'I've been wanting to say something to you for the past ten minutes.'

'What did you want to say, Charlie?' she replied, again moving closer to him.

'Don't you think you should take that poor child her tea?'

'Damn you,' she replied ... but her eyes said something very different.

13

. . . of Mice and Men

'Isn't it time you got a new carpet in here?'

Sir Rupert de Quincy looked up.

'Well ... Charlie Tuttle of all people ... how the Hell's name did you get in here?'

'Used the key you gave me, Rupert.'

'I might have known. You of all people know how difficult it is to get funds even for having the locks changed.' Reaching under his desk he produced a bottle and, with something of a flourish, two glasses. He filled them to the brim with two large measures of Haig whilst kicking the one spare chair in Charlie's direction.

'Take the weight off, Charlie, we've a lot of catching up to do.'

Aroused by the bonhomie emanating from his Chief's office, Captain Farrar put his head round the door.

'Come in, Teddy,' invited Sir Rupert, 'there is someone here I would like you to meet,' and as Captain Farrar entered the room, 'Close the door behind you. We don't want the world to know who is here, do we, Charlie?'

'No.'

Then, as Sir Rupert rose to his feet, 'Teddy, may I introduce Charlie Tuttle. Charlie, meet my Number One, Captain Edward Farrar.'

Introductions completed, Sir Rupert once again rummaged in his desk and produced another glass. Pouring out a liberal measure, he handed the all but overflowing glass to his Number One.

'A toast, gentlemen,' he said, raising his glass. 'May fortune always favour the brave...' and then, as if reciting a poem, both Charlie and Captain Farrar added, 'And the devil take the cowards.'

'Remember that, Charlie,' said Sir Rupert, placing his glass on the desk.

'There are some things you never forget.'

'Now, Charlie, you haven't just breezed in here by accident, have you?'

'I need your help.'

'In what way?' replied Sir Rupert somewhat warily, as he glanced at the bulge under his friend's left armpit. 'You still carrying that 9mm Luger, Charlie?' he enquired, ignoring the earlier request.

'Yes.'

'And the Biretta?'

'Of course.'

Turning to his Number One, Sir Rupert, as if anticipating troubled waters, commented, 'I was with Charlie when he lifted that Luger from a dead German airman after the raid on Guernica, wasn't I, Charlie?'

'You were.'

'Doesn't Mr Tuttle know weapons are forbidden in here?'

'He probably does,' interceded Sir Rupert, 'but I wouldn't advise you to try and take it off him. Anyway, enough of this, what I want to know is what sort of help he wants.' Now looking directly at Charlie, 'What is the problem?'

'What have you got on a KGB agent by the name of Mikhael Derevenko?'

'So you are involved ... I knew it. What did I say, Teddy, only a day or so ago? That it had all the hallmarks of Charlie Tuttle.' Then, wagging his index finger, 'Mind you, Charlie, you did hit that Home Office laddie awfully hard.'

'Somewhat out of practice, Rupert.'

'Right, so you want all we've got on Derevenko, in exchange for what?'

'All the dope as to what is going on in London at present – one killing and one attempted – the whole works.'

'Now we're talking, Charlie.'

'There is one other thing, Rupert.'

'Such as?'

'No charges, civil or military, in other words complete immunity from prosecution for both myself and the girl, Natasha Gollitzin.'

'You name a high price.'

'The goods are worth it, Rupert, many times over.'

'If what you're saying is true, then you'll be aware that my department is only involved because we screened Derevenko initially. Primarily, it's Home Office business. My influence . . .' he broke off.

'Come off it, Rupert, we both know strings can be pulled. The information I have goes right to the top.'

'Tell me.'

'Royalty no less, plus a little matter of twenty million in gold.'

'Charlie, I gave up in believing in fairy stories a long time ago.'

Charlie shrugged his shoulders, 'Have it your way, then . . .'

'What you did to that man was GBH,' interrupted Captain Farrar. 'I don't see how the Chief can hope to circumnavigate that.'

'Just supposing, Charlie, there is something in what you're saying,' continued Sir Rupert, ignoring his Number One's outburst, 'I would need more than just your word.'

'Once I have your assurance on no charges, Rupert, I'll give you all the information I have about the gold, royalty, the lot.'

'How do we know you're not bluffing?' It was Captain Farrar, anxious to regain lost ground in the eyes of his Chief. 'As for myself, I don't believe a word of it.'

'Teddy, I appreciate your opinions when I've asked for them. Until them, please leave them out. And I think it might be better if you withdraw.'

'Yes, I think it might be better, Teddy, that you withdraw,' mimicked Charlie, revelling in the man's discomfiture.

Captain Farrar stood up and, preparatory to leaving, drained his glass, but not before he had looked directly at Charlie.

'The Chief has often told me how much he admired you. Having met you, I can only say I'm not impressed!'

Eyes that until now seemed incapable of emotion, flashed ominously.

'Take a tip from me, Farrar, don't play with the big boys until you've grown a bit.'

'I thought you were leaving, Teddy,' interposed Sir Rupert, his annoyance at the verbal exchanges obvious.

'As you wish, sir.' The tone was icy.

'Don't take it to heart, Charlie . . . he's very young you know,' said Sir Rupert, as Captain Farrar slammed the door behind him.

Charlie, ignoring the comment, walked towards the door. 'You've got just two days, Rupert, full immunity or no deal.'

*   *   *

Dmitri Sokolov's dining room reflected the sombre mood that had overcome him since learning of the death of Sergei Poznansky. The one lone bulb high in the ceiling lit the centrepiece, his dining table, in a harsh glare, which was made more pronounced by the equally dark shadows that engulfed the rest of the room.

Although doing his best to conceal his present state of mind from the others, it was nonetheless obvious to Paul, Vladimir and Magyar that the present Dmitri Sokolov was not the same optimistic planner of a few weeks before, when they had each been besotted with his dreams of riches simply waiting to be picked up. Again, as at their previous meeting, it was Paul who assumed the mantle of spokesman.

'I don't see why the murder of Poznansky should deter us, Dmitri, after all there could be many reasons why he was killed.' Vladimir and Magyar nodded their agreement.

129

'He was killed for what he knew,' said Dmitri, his fingertips tapping the table top. 'What is important,' he continued, looking at each in turn, 'is that we know he knew about the gold – the question is how much he told his killer or killers.'

'There is one thing that comes out of this,' said Paul, 'at least we know now that it's not a fairy story ... the gold does exist.'

'I hope you're not doubting my word, Paul,' said Dmitri testily.

'None of us doubt your word, Dmitri, and we are all well aware of the risks,' said Magyar, 'but I say we carry on.'

Silence followed until Paul, anxious to reinstate himself as the spokesman for the other two, rose from his chair and leant across the table.

'Look, Dmitri, on the way over here – no, we were not followed,' he said, anticipating Dmitri's question, 'we agreed, the three of us, to carry on whatever the risk. We would be fools not to.'

'So be it then,' replied Dmitri, as if relieved that the decision had been taken for him. Then, as if within the dark recesses of his mind uncertainty still plagued him, he vented his spleen on Magyar.

'Do you have to puff on that infernal thing? My room will smell for weeks, thanks to your wretched pipe.'

Magyar removed the offending object from somewhere beneath the matted hair of his beard and was preparing to launch himself at Dmitri when again Paul intervened.

'Leave it, Dmitri, let us get on with the plan ... and as for you, Magyar, blow the filthy stuff out the window or something.'

Magyar, with a show of great reluctance and lack of consideration for the carpet, hammered the contents of his pipe against the heel of his shoe before addressing Dmitri.

'The trouble with you, Sokolov, is that you've been in the West too long, you've gone soft. This enterprise is going to need all our determination and guts to see it through. Are you up to it, Dmitri?'

'Of course,' Sokolov replied, 'now let's get down to business ... I've had another look at the photographs ...'

'What photographs?' challenged Paul. 'This is the first we've heard of photographs.'

In quiet tones, Sokolov relayed the finding of the tattoo on Natasha's thigh and the subsequent photographs taken by Sergei Poznansky, who was convinced the tattoo was a plan of where the gold was hidden. Enthralled, the trio listened. It was Paul who broke the silence.

'I wouldn't place too much reliance on Poznansky's judgement.'

'He was killed for it,' reminded Sokolov.

'He could still have been wrong – after all, we are assuming he was killed because of the gold, we're not sure.'

'Come, come, Paul, what other reason could there possibly be?'

'Well, he was a monarchist after all...' Paul tailed off.

'No, gentlemen, I think we can take it he was killed because he knew where the gold was buried.'

'All right then,' said Paul, after further silence, 'now tell us more about the photograph.'

Sokolov cleared his throat. 'At first, as I told you at our earlier meeting, everything pointed to Appenzell. Now, I believe that was wrong. It was the deliberate intention of the Duchess to mislead – in case, gentlemen, Natasha Gollitzin, and with her the tattoo, fell into the wrong hands.'

'Bloody old cow,' exclaimed Magyar, relighting his pipe.

Sokolov ignored the interruption. 'No, I was not fooled by her. The gold, my friends, is not at Appenzell...' pausing to allow the maximum of impact, Sokolov then bent forward as if addressing each of the three in turn. 'It's buried where the Gollitzin girl came from originally...' His mouth, as if savouring something extraordinarily special, only allowed the word to escape in drawn-out pieces, 'Kol-omy-ja, gentlemen, in the cemetery at Kolomyja.'

* * *

Dinner had passed quietly, and Janice sensed that it was with a feeling of relief that her guests gathered for coffee and brandy in the drawing room. A subdued Natasha still held the centre stage. Although her bewitching smile was less frequent, her eyes continued to retain their hypnotic intensity. Charlie, reflecting on his visit to Sir Rupert the day before, was sitting with Janice on the chaise longue, having been introduced to Peter and Emma as an old friend of Bill's. Bill, to Janice's relief, pleading pressing business, had departed earlier that afternoon, still sulking at Natasha's continued presence.

Janice, as she had been at dinner, was aware of Charlie's unease. All attempts by Emma to engage him in conversation continued to prove fruitless, much to Janice's amusement. She guessed that Emma found him both attractive and mysterious. For a repressed suburban housewife like Emma, such a combination would act like an aphrodisiac of considerable proportions. All evening, as expected, the main topic of conversation had been the attack on Penelope Charters. Both Peter and Emma vied with each other to recount the lurid details to Charlie. A Charlie, however, who to their dismay adopted an attitude, by now well-known to Janice, of seeming indifference to even the most gory parts of the incident.

Finally, both gave up and turned to their hostess.

'Are the police any nearer an arrest?' asked Emma, sipping her brandy.

'I really don't know, Emma, all they tell me is that enquiries are continuing...' The appearance of Florrie's ample frame interrupted any further embellishment.

'Madam,' she said, her whole body, like her voice, quivering with excitement, 'madam,' she repeated, 'I think we have a prowler outside. I saw the kitchen door handle turn just now, and before that...' but she got no further. Charlie, gun appearing in his hand as if from nowhere, strode purposefully across the room to the light switch. His voice, no longer the indecisive monotone that had infuriated Emma all evening, had a cutting edge to it as sharp as a razor.

132

'Everyone on the floor and not a sound.' With that the room was plunged into darkness.

Janice, now crouching on the floor, felt a rush of cold damp air against her face and sensed rather than saw the billowing of the curtains which told her the French windows had been opened ...

*   *   *

Vladimir Semichastny placed the report in his out tray and, looking beyond Alexis Sternov, seated opposite him, fixed his gaze on the narrow window panes of his office. Through the badly stained glass he watched as the first snow of winter fell on Moscow's streets.

'Mikhael Derevenko has betrayed me,' his voice, though quiet, had a chilling edge to it as he continued to watch the ever-increasing flakes of snow, now gathering at the corners of the window frames.

'I am not surprised, comrade, it is a case of greed overcoming his duty to the State.'

Semichastny made no comment but continued with his own complaint. 'Not only has he betrayed me, but he has made our interest in the Romanov gold obvious to the West.' Again, his fascination with the gathering snowflakes seemed to distract him.

'What do you propose, Comrade Semichastny?' Reluctantly, two colourless eyes, devoid of expression, turned their gaze on Sternov.

'You will fly to London, Comrade Sternov. As my representative, you'll be given unlimited powers ... your first task will be to eliminate Derevenko and, with the help of our agent within the Duma, learn all you can about those who intend to recover the gold ... once we know that we will sit back and await their coming.'

'What of the girl, Gollitzin?'

'I'm getting conflicting opinions. Without doubt a fifth daughter was born to the Tsarina, that much is certain. Whether she had a

133

child and that child is the Gollitzin woman remains a grey area. I've come to believe that Vladimir Gollitzin was protecting her with his story of the gypsy girl. I know that he was involved in providing a safe house for the daughter of the Tsarina back in 1918, that much is certain – his confession proved that.'

Sternov had a mental image of Vladimir Gollitzin, broken under some unbearable torture, going to his death. Collecting himself, he changed the subject. 'I will fly to London tomorrow evening, Comrade Semichastny.'

'Good, and Sternov, do your duty.'

'Have no fear, comrade, the job will be done.'

'The rewards are high, as are the penalties for failure. Pay particular attention to your sealed orders, to be opened only when you reach London – orders more in keeping with your undoubted abilities.'

The hidden menace in Semichastny's parting words were not lost on Sternov as, without further comment, he left the room.

* * *

'Minister, I have here the dossier on Charlie Tuttle.' It was Sir Rupert de Quincy speaking in an office adjoining the Cabinet Room at 10 Downing Street. It was a day or so after the minor fracas in Sir Rupert's office between Charlie and Captain Farrar.

'Regrettably, Minister, it is incomplete, as for many years we believed Tuttle was killed in the Congo.'

'This man, Tuttle, you say he can establish the Gollitzin woman's credentials?' HM Home Secretary anxiously searched Sir Rupert's face for any signs of uncertainty.

'Without doubt, Minister.'

'Then read me his dossier.'

Sir Rupert cleared his throat, 'I'll read just the salient points if I may, Minister. Tuttle has had a very varied career, which at times included dark areas of which we know little . . .'

'All right, Sir Rupert, but do get on with it, I'm due in the House in half an hour.'

'Born 1912, Harrow 1926, graduated in foreign languages at Balliol and entered Military Intelligence 1932. It is here, Minister, we have a slight problem. Rumour has it that a titled lady was involved. In any event he absconded from our Embassy in Cairo, and nothing was heard until he turned up in the French Foreign Legion around 1933/34. In 1936 he was serving in the International Brigade. I know because I was with him during the siege of Madrid.'

'All very interesting,' said his listener dryly. 'Pray continue.'

'1939 enlisted in the Yorkshire Yeomanry as a private and saw service leading up to the debacle at Dunkirk. Gazetted, June 1940, with Military Medal. 1941 became one of Colonel Buckmaster's originals and with Maclean parachuted into Yugoslavia and was with Tito until the end of the war. Nothing known after that until he appeared in the Belgium Congo as a supporter of Lumumba. From there, Minister, it is mostly conjecture. We do know he was captured by the rebel troops and tortured horribly, ending up in a clinic in Berne. That would be around 1956/57.

'The rest we assume – at some time he entered the service of the Grand Duchess Elizabeth, sister of the late Tsarina, as bodyguard-cum-Man Friday. Nothing more until he arrived in my office two days ago.'

'Do you still consider he has all the answers, Sir Rupert?'

'If any man has, he has, Minister, at a price.'

'Price, what price?' said with a sniff he did nothing to conceal.

'Complete immunity from prosecution for himself and the girl Gollitzin.'

'That is really out of the question, Sir Rupert. How could I possibly square it with the Met, not to mention Immigration?'

'That's the bill, and knowing him as I do, he will accept nothing less.'

'Sir Rupert.'

'Minister.'

'In your opinion he has all the answers, particularly where the crown is concerned?'

'Most certainly.'

'Then,' said with a sigh, 'we must do what we must do. Thank you, Sir Rupert, I'll get back to you shortly.'

'As you wish, Minister.'

14

A Life for a Life

To Janice, it was as if time stood still. Crouched behind the chaise longue she was vaguely aware of a body nearby, and it was only by hearing intermittent sobs she identified it as Emma. Further to her right was the rotund shape of Florrie made distinctive by her white coat. Of Natasha there was no sign. The freezing air continued to buffet her face and arms with its breath of bitter cold, a reminder, though none was needed, that something, apart from the icy wind, was stalking unhurried and uninhibited through her drawing room.

It was at the precise moment, when the possibility of sudden death had occurred to Janice, that the bullet smashed into the back of the chaise longue. It was then her body froze with abject fear as the realisation came to her that someone impersonal and unknown was intent upon destroying her.

The report, like a crash of thunder, seemed of little consequence as her body tensed to an unimaginable extreme as it awaited the next and final bullet ... to be followed, she was sure, by a blanket of darkness stretching to eternity.

To her tremendous relief, the following explosion, but seconds after the first, was a world away from her. This time it was accompanied by a tearing sound as though giant hands were severing a piece of cloth. Then a shattering noise penetrated her senses as the curtain above the French windows crashed to the floor.

Other sounds, more mundane and recognisable in their substance, began reaching her.

'Oh God preserve us,' wailed the unmistakable voice of Florrie as Janice, surprised at her own sudden calmness, shouted across.

'Control yourself, Florrie, and ring for the police.'

From somewhere beyond the windows, a voice, immediately identifiable to Janice as that of Charlie, shouted, 'All right everybody, it's over.'

Janice, rising to her feet, rushed in the direction of the voice, only to fall headlong over a soft, recumbent form, which, as lights flooded the room, she saw was the body of a man. As she leaned over him a pair of sightless eyes returned her curious gaze, the trickle of blood now emerging from a small round hole between his eyes telling its own story.

* * *

'You say this gun,' said Chief Inspector Reynolds, holding the Luger with his pen through the trigger guard, 'is yours, Mrs Webster?'

'Yes, Chief Inspector.'

'You have a licence for it?'

'Well, no, but I always intended to get one,' said Janice, rather lamely.

'Where did you get the gun?'

'I bought it from a friend of a friend ... years ago.'

'And you say, as he looked across at the French windows and the broken curtain rail, 'you shot the intruder,' the Chief Inspector walked over to the chaise longue, 'from here.' Janice felt rather than saw the two questioning eyes looking at her.

'Yes, that's right, Chief Inspector, after he had shot at me.'

'The room was in darkness at this time?'

'Yes, it was.'

'Something of a lucky shot, straight between the eyes, wouldn't you?' say?'

'I suppose so,' replied Janice, aware that her hastily conceived plan was falling apart at the seams.

'Do you know what this is, Mrs Webster?' said the Chief Inspector, holding up a cylinder-shaped object the size of a thimble.

'I'm not sure.'

'I will tell you. It is the cartridge case expended by your gun. Curious, wouldn't you say, that it was found by one of my officers, not by the chaise longue, but in the garden beyond the French windows?' The silence that followed was to Janice timeless.

'I put it to you, Mrs Webster, that what you are saying is nothing but a product of your imagination.' He paused, then, as she watched with fascinated eyes, he placed the cartridge case in a thin cellophane envelope, sealed it, and put it in his pocket.

'What I want to know is who it was out there,' nodding in the direction of the garden, 'who really did the shooting. In other words,' as he turned towards her, 'the name of the person you're protecting.'

'But I'm not, Chief Inspector.'

'Oh come, come, do give me credit for some intelligence, surely you don't expect me to believe such a cock and bull story.'

They were both beyond the French windows now, and as the raw cold of the December night penetrated Janice's thin dress a feeling of intense loneliness came over her. Charlie was gone, disappearing into the night after their hurried discussion and in response to her entreaty for him to get to Hell out of it. Leave me your gun, she had pleaded, I'll say it was self-defence – they won't know the difference. But, with so little time to perfect such a plan, it was obvious the Chief Inspector did know the difference. What of the others? Perhaps they would support her story, but she knew, when pressure was applied, one or more would quickly crack.

'I'm waiting, Mrs Webster, for your explanation as to how the cartridge case from your gun, fired, or so you tell me, from over by the chaise longue, found itself out here?'

Ignoring him, Janice walked back into the room followed by the Chief Inspector. Her mind, glad of the respite such a movement gave her, was surprisingly lucid. Turning to the drinks trolley she poured herself a large brandy. As the warmth of the drink flooded through her, she rounded on him.

'Well, you're not getting one. In fact, Chief Inspector Reynolds, I have no intention of answering any more of your bloody questions until I have spoken to my father. I'm sure, Chief Inspector, with your experience you are aware of the penalties for wrongful arrest.' Janice found the brief frown that clouded his face very comforting.

'Then, I've no alternative but to ask you to accompany me. . .'

'Really, Inspector, to accompany you where?'

'Hendon Police Station, where there is every likelihood you will be charged with, at the very least, accessory to murder.'

'Murder? Chief Inspector,' replied Janice, now even more amazed at her calmness, 'a man bludgeons his way in here, fires at me and only misses by the proverbial inches, and you dare to suggest I shall be charged with murder because I shoot back.'

'If I thought that, Mrs Webster, we would all be tucked up in our beds by now. No, I want the name of the person who did such a professional job out there,' pointing in the direction of the garden, 'and before the night's out I intend to get it.'

* * *

When Florrie had burst in, Peter had again been lusting over Natasha, her charms made no less potent, as far as he was concerned, by the change of hair colour. On Charlie's shouted command and as the lights went out, he had grabbed Natasha's waist and pulled her to the floor. With his body half-across hers, the thought flashed through his mind that if he were going to die, what better way? Gently moving until he was fully on top of her, it wasn't until the first report, followed swiftly by the second, that she began to whimper.

The whimper, so close to his ears and combined with the heady scent of her perfume, acted on him like an aphrodisiac. Until that moment he had been content to remain prone but, as if taking on a life of their own, his hands began to explore the recumbent body beneath him. It was, therefore, with a feeling of deep frustration that he greeted the lights coming back on and the need for them both to struggle to their feet.

Seeing Janice rushing towards the French windows and his wife and Florrie still huddled together with eyes glued on the retreating Janice, gave him his opportunity.

'Quickly, Natasha, we must hide, there may be more of them.' Her response was encouraging.

'The library,' she breathed. Holding her by a limp arm he led her through the drawing room across the hall and into the library, quickly shutting the door behind them. With just one small lighted table lamp, the room was in semi-darkness. Moving ahead of him, Natasha crossed to the side furthest from the door, where there was a recess between two high bookshelves. Smiling back at him, she squeezed into the narrow aperture. Peter, with a quick look over his shoulder, followed. 'We'll be safe in here, Peter, I've hidden here before,' she chuckled.

Moving swiftly and with the thought that his earlier pent-up frustration would soon be appeased, he reached out for her and pushed her deeper into the opening until her back was against the wall. Then, as his head came down, his mouth avidly searched for hers.

'Peter, no,' she said, not very convincingly, as her mouth made no attempt to avoid his.

Such objections as they were only served to goad Peter further. As his mouth closed on hers the pressure he applied forced her lips apart. Soon his tongue, patient until then, seized its opportunity and entered the open portal. As she wriggled her hips in obvious anticipation, Peter, now all but beside himself with an all-consuming lust, revelled in the increasing wetness of her mouth as her own tongue welcomed the intruder ever more lasciviously. He was to have the bitch again, she, the sensual, the gorgeous, Natasha. It was not surprising that he barely heard Janice's voice.

'Natasha, is that you in there?'

First Peter and then Natasha emerged from between the book-shelves, to Janice's astonishment.

'Peter,' said Janice, contempt in her voice, 'your wife is worried as to your whereabouts, she is waiting in the dining room.' Peter, as he straightened his tie, hurried out of the room. 'And Peter,' she called after him, 'I should do something about that lipstick if I were you.' Turning, she looked at Natasha. 'Natasha, Natasha, what are we going to do with you?' she said with a wicked smile, moving closer.

'Janeece, it was not my fault, eet was Peter, he, how you say...'

'I know exactly how you say,' Janice replied, 'you know one day, Natasha, your sexual appetite is going to get you into...' It was then she noticed the Chief Inspector.

'You're waiting for me?' Her voice, though resonant, was calm.

'Not exactly, Mrs Webster. I thought I should mention that I see no point in you coming to the station tonight, or should I say this morning,' having looked down at his watch. 'Tomorrow is another day, and doubtless we shall all see things more clearly then. However, no doubt you and the other witnesses will hold them-selves in readiness for further questioning, and do give further thought to the position you find yourself in. We've identified the dead man as...' looking down at his notebook, 'a Russian national by the name of Mikhael Derevenko.'

Without so much as the blink of an eye, Janice replied, 'Good, then I will say goodnight. Chief Inspector.'

'Goodnight, Mrs Webster.' Then, as if noticing Natasha for the first time, 'Ah, Miss Gollitzin, our paths cross again.' Natasha did her curious little bob.

'I trust you are well?'

'*Très bien*,' she replied.

As the Chief Inspector crossed into the hall, both heard him mutter, 'Beware the child who carries the mark of Satan.'

'I didn't know you were a religious man, Chief Inspector,' said Janice, as she collected his coat from the hallstand.

'I'm not, Mrs Webster,' nodding in the direction of the retreating Natasha, 'but two murders and an attempted, all involving that young woman, does make one think – there's gypsy blood there, if I'm not mistaken.'

'Really, Inspector, Miss Gollitzin is a dear friend of mine.'

'I'm sorry if I offended, Mrs Webster, but take a tip from me, be wary of her. As a judge of character, after all it's my job, she's a bad 'un.'

'Thank you, Inspector, I wish you goodnight.'

For the the second time that night Janice discovered, for some indeterminate reason, she was shaking.

*   *   *

Sir Rupert lazily picked up the telephone, and even before he tucked it under his chin, leaving his hands free, he recognised the voice.

'It's me, Charlie, any news of our little arrangement?'

'I think, Charlie, circumstances have changed somewhat since our last discussion.'

'In what way?'

'The killing of Mikhael Derevenko for one.'

'Mikhael Derevenko wanted killing,' replied Charlie.

'He probably did, but you cannot turn North-West London into your own private shooting gallery,' accompanied by a quiet chuckle, 'it's not allowed.'

'Nothing that has happened since we saw each other has changed the situation regarding the girl or the gold.'

'I don't disagree with you, but complete immunity in what has become a murder charge, and a Soviet national at that, is something of a tall order – even allowing for what you're offering in exchange.'

'I'll say this once, Rupert, and you can pass it on to you know who. The KGB will soon replace Derevenko, I suspect they probably guessed he had turned and therefore was a liability. The girl remains the key and, where she is concerned, my responsibility.'

'Well said, Charlie, but we would have had Derevenko in the end. All you did was pre-empt the outcome.'

'Do you really expect me to believe that? Yes, you would have got him in the end, after a bloodbath, that is. There wouldn't, as you say, have been one corpse in North-West London, but half a dozen.'

'Charlie...' but even as Sir Rupert uttered his name the line went dead.

'No need to guess who that was,' said Teddy Farrar, a sheaf of papers clutched to his chest.

'Yes, it was our friend,' replied Sir Rupert with an audible sigh.

'We're tracing the call, should know in a minute or two.'

'Pointless, Teddy, he's probably adopted some outlandish disguise which will fool anyone – he's far too clever to be caught napping like that.'

'What happened to him in the Congo, sir? You never did tell me.'

'He was captured by the rebels, so the story goes, and handed over to their women. What they can do with a knife, Teddy, would make a surgeon blush with envy. Anyway, he was no good to any woman after that...'

'You mean they –'

'Exactly, Teddy, they cut off his balls – but they left him his penis as a reminder of what he was missing.'

'How ghastly.' Silence followed as Teddy Farrar digested the full impact of his Chief's words.

'Hasn't he any weaknesses, sir?' said Teddy, with emphasis on the 'any'.

'Who, Charlie? None that I know of except perhaps an overwhelming sense of loyalty.'

'Then all we have to do, sir is watch the girl and she'll lead us to him.'

'Thank you, Teddy, I had already worked that one out. As it

happens, we now have another problem which, I have to admit, compared with Charlie, has greater consequences for us all ... Starstreak. Here, read this report from Derby.'

'It's sheer bloody incompetence,' commented Teddy, as he returned the paper to his chief's desk, '... sheer incompetence.'

'I agree, but the question that concerns us is were they after details of the power unit, the RR100. That's what makes the Soviet Mig nothing more than a carthorse compared to the NATO Starstreak. It's Derby for us first thing tomorrow, all right, Teddy?'

'I guess it's a case of having to be,' replied a reluctant Teddy, who studiously ignored his chief's raised eyebrows. Then, as though relieved to change the subject, 'Dmitri Sokolov is waiting to see you in there,' nodding in the direction of the ante-room.

'Show him in, then,' replied Sir Rupert, sharply.

'Thank you for coming to see me, Sokolov, please sit down. You are aware, are you not, that Her Majesty's Government has respected your Association being domiciled in this country, always providing that your activities do not create embarrassment with the Soviet Union. Now, Sokolov, just such embarrassment has been caused between our two governments, and the matter remains to be resolved. Sokolov, it is very much in your interests to tell me all you know about the girl Gollitzin.'

'It is very simple, Sir Rupert. Natasha Gollitzin sought the endorsement of the Association and the Duma regarding her claim to be the true heir to the throne of the Romanovs.' Sokolov spread his hands as if in supplication, 'We refute her claim, there is no evidence to support it, and even if there were, the true heir, as you well know, is the son of the Grand Duke Michael, Prince Michael.'

'Yes, yes, Sokolov, I'm aware of all that, but answer me this, why is the KGB so keen on liquidating her?'

'You mean the recent murder of Poznansky, her guardian, and the two attempts on her life.'

'Precisely.'

I am as ignorant as you regarding their motives, Sir Rupert.'

'Could it be the Romanov gold, Sokolov? It does exist, you know, a further ingot turned up in Zurich only last week.' Sokolov swallowed deeply and for a few moments appeared lost for words.

'There could be a connection, Sir Rupert...'

'Don't fence with me, Sokolov, you damn well know there's a connection.'

Looking decidedly uncomfortable, Dmitri Sokolov mopped his forehead.

'If you say so, Sir Rupert.'

'I do say so, and therefore, Sokolov, if you value your residence in this country, I would advise you to be utterly frank with me. One word, just one word, Sokolov, could see you on your way back to the Motherland. Now, may I suggest you begin again?'

An ashen-faced Sokolov nodded in agreement.

*   *   *

'Was he very revealing?' asked Captain Farrar as be stood before his chief.

'As expected, Teddy, he was very cagey until I threatened him with deportation, then he was much more amenable. Undoubtedly he knows about the gold, and probably where it can be found. But there are still far too many unanswered questions. I cannot believe that the Grand Duchess's plan, years in its preparation, was based on the assumption that the Duma would fall over themselves in accepting the Gollitzin woman as heir presumptive, not without indisputable evidence.' He paused. 'But they might if there was a sweetener of twenty million in gold. We're back to Charlie Tuttle, Teddy – whether we like it or not, he is the only one with all the answers.'

146

15

Ashes to Ashes

Sergei Poznansky's funeral was held at the Russian Orthodox Church in London. It had been delayed because of the obduracy of the police in releasing the body for burial. In spite of Janice's concern about her safety, Natasha insisted on attending.

'Sergei was my dear friend,' she said simply, in reply to Janice's misgivings, 'and in any case the man Derevenko is dead, so what is there to fear now?'

'It means I shall have to again cancel that appointment with Daddy. Still, Charlie seems so sure he can handle everything, perhaps there's no need to see him.'

So Janice had agreed, even though the nagging thought persisted of how much she would miss Charlie's reassuring presence at her side. He had said he would be close by, but with Charlie that could mean anything.

In accordance with the religious custom of the Orthodox Church, the coffin was open. Sergei was lying on white velvet cushions, and although impervious to his surroundings, still retained the expression of surprise when Derevenko had administered the first blow. As the initial rites of the funeral service began, a red-eyed Natasha looked around at the chief mourners. She immediately recognised Dmitri Sokolov, one or two of the Duma and, but feet away, the Comte and Comtesse de Toulouse with their daughter, Mademoiselle Celestine. Across from her, doing his best to be inconspicuous, was Chief Inspector Reynolds accompanied by another man who Natasha guessed was a policeman.

A slight interruption in the service, together with the obvious agitation of those officiating, heralded the entrance of the Prince Michael and his entourage. Wearing the regalia of a Prince of the Royal House of Romanov, he strode purposefully forward until level with the casket and, leaning over, he kissed Sergei's forehead. Then, to the astonishment and delight of Natasha, he moved over and stood by her side.

It was Janice, standing on her other side, who inadvertently brought Natasha's smile of welcome for the Prince to an abrupt end by tugging at her arm and indicating, by the slight gesture of her head, the suitably attired figure of Charlie Tuttle, in an attitude of repose and surrounded by other members of the undertaker's staff.

'Isn't he the absolute limit,' she whispered to Natasha. But Natasha's whole being was far removed from poor Sergei, the service, and even Igor, as she still called him. Her mind was completely absorbed in the knowledge that within touching distance was the most devastatingly attractive man she had ever met.

*　*　*

As the group of mourners awaited their cars for the short journey to Highgate, the Comte de Toulouse strolled over to Dmitri Sokolov, who had acknowledged his presence at the funeral with the briefest of nods.

'You are well, Dmitri?'

'Fine, Henri, fine.'

'I'm somewhat upset, Dmitri, that I've heard no word from you about our little scheme.' In consideration of where he was, Henri chose his words with care.

'This is hardly the time or the place, Henri,' replied Dmitri, somewhat flustered.

'Then might I suggest we arrange a time and a place,' persisted

148

Henri. 'The Comtesse and I are in London until tomorrow afternoon; we are staying at the Royalty Hotel, room 151. Shall we agree noon tomorrow?'

'As you wish, Henri.'

'I do. You'll be interested to learn that I received twenty thousand sterling for the small gift Igor brought from Appenzell. You know what I'm talking about, don't you?'

'Of course, of course.'

'Then noon tomorrow?'

'Noon tomorrow.'

*　　*　　*

'What was that all about?' said Paul, as their car pulled away, 'particularly that bit about money.' Magyar, whose taxi it was, half-turned in the driving seat.

'Yes,' he added, 'twenty thousand sterling,' he paused. 'What's going on, Dmitri?'

'I explained all that some time ago, it's to do with the plan to drive into Appenzell and lift the gold. We all agreed how ridiculous the plan was.'

'You never mentioned the money, Dmitri, where has it come from?' The underlying suspicion in Paul's voice was obvious.

'If you must know,' answered Dmitri, his tone a mirror of his impatience, 'it was smuggled out of Switzerland with the girl and Sergei when they fled. Frankly, I had forgotten about it.'

'Forgotten about twenty grand,' said Magyar, pleased to be able to use an Americanism. 'I find that hard to believe.'

'You were not planning to do the dirt on us were you, Dmitri?' said Paul icily. 'I wouldn't advise it unless you want to join Sergei Poznansky in there,' as Magyar swung the car through the iron gates of Highgate Cemetery.

*　　*　　*

149

It was the morning after the funeral of Sergei Poznansky when the Home Secretary called a further meeting in his offices at St Anne's Court. A rather flushed Chief Inspector Reynolds was speaking.

'What you are asking, Home Secretary, could be construed as obstructing justice. The Crown Prosecution Service confirmed only yesterday that Charlie Tuttle, Janice Webster and Natasha Gollitzin all had a *prima facie* case to answer.'

'I am fully aware of that, Chief Inspector ... perhaps Chief Superintendent Biggs,' nodding in the direction of the Head of Special Branch, 'may care to explain the situation.'

'Thank you, Minister.' Alfred Biggs cleared his throat. 'Gentlemen, with the killing of Mikhael Derevenko the whole question of criminal proceedings has to be subverted in the interests of security. Derevenko was a top Red agent sent over here for a specific purpose. We now know that he has been replaced by an even more senior KGB operative by the name of Alexis Sternov. Sternov arrived at Heathrow late last night on Aeroflot flight 156, direct from Moscow. It is unprecedented, certainly in my eighteen years in Special Branch, for the KGB to operate so openly. Our intelligence gathering confirms that the woman, Gollitzin, is at the centre of their interest. Why...? We are still not sure, but the arrest and detention of those named by the Minister will serve no useful purpose at this time. Information is so sketchy that the woman herself could be working for the KGB and the matter of the Romanov gold be merely an extremely clever cover for something far more sinister ... for example, gentlemen, the break-in at Derby ... do I need to say more?'

'Your opinion, Sir Rupert?' invited the Home Secretary.

'I have, Minister, far too much respect for the Head of Special Branch to challenge his statement. However, I am inclined, based on what we know at Section 10, to believe that it is the Romanov gold. Having said that, I can fully understand the Chief Superintendent's concern. As a matter of interest, Minister, I've looked into the incident at Derby, and as far as is known at this time security was not compromised. It was nothing more than a minor burglary.'

'I find Sir Rupert's optimism difficult to digest,' muttered the Chief Superintendent.

'Have we received any formal protest over the death of Derevenko?' enquired Sir Rupert, deaf to the mutterings of the Head of Special Branch.

'Nothing, Sir Rupert.'

'With East-West relations the way they are, I find that strange indeed.'

Chief Superintendent Biggs stood up.

'Through you, Minister, may I ask Sir Rupert a vital question?'

'You may.'

'Is Charlie Tuttle still working for Section 10?'

'Through you, Minister, Charlie Tuttle, although a field agent some years ago, has no connection with my department now. I would add, though, in my estimation he is something of a loose cannon, and if anyone knows all the answers, he does.'

'Pull him in for questioning, then, ' said the Head of Special Branch.

'Were it that simple,' replied Sir Rupert, smiling.

'Yes, we know his terms, don't we, Sir Rupert?' added the Minister, making no attempt to restrain a sniff. 'Well, gentlemen, I think we have had some frank exchanges concerning the problems facing us at the moment. I have to say, that I do not make a habit of giving reasons for my decisions,' a wintry smile crossed his face, 'except in the House. But in this instance I did conceive it necessary to explain why the charges are to be set aside – at least for the time being. On another matter altogether, I have received a note from the Palace indicating that a senior member of the Royal Family wishes to meet with Miss Gollitzin.'

A profound silence met this announcement.

'Until our investigations are far more complete, Minister, I have to advise that such a meeting would he highly inappropriate,' volunteered the Head of Special Branch. 'On the grounds of security alone.'

'I assure you, Chief Superintendent, such advice will be forwarded from my office. May I now repeat, gentlemen, no criminal charges are to be processed in respect of the three named. They will, however, he retained on file.'

'One further question, Minister.'

'Certainly, Sir Rupert.'

'Department 10 is aware of the involvement of Miss Gollitzin and Charles Tuttle, but may I enquire as to the part,' referring to his notes, 'Mrs Janice Webster is playing?'

'I can probably assist Sir Rupert regarding that,' stated the Chief Inspector.

'Pray do so.'

'It would appear Mrs Webster met Miss Gollitzin through the party and social circuit of North-West London. Since then, they have formed a very close relationship, with Miss Gollitzin living with the Webster family. May I add here that certain actions of Mrs Webster have left her open to serious criminal charges – such charges are detailed in my report.'

'Through you, Minister, may I ask the Chief Inspector if Mrs Webster represents a threat to security?'

'No, my assessment of her is that we have here a bored upper-middle-class suburban housewife of above-average intellect who has been catapulted into a situation of high adventure. Further, from my observations of her I do not rule out the possibility of a sexual liaison with Miss Gollitzin. Finally, Minister, Mrs Webster is the only daughter of George Lawrence.'

'George Lawrence QC?'

'Correct, Minister.'

'I frequently meet him in the Carlton.' Sir Rupert fought hard to conceal a smile at this disclosure. 'And what is more,' continued the Home Secretary, 'he is a friend of the PM. Why wasn't I informed of this before?' The Home Secretary's raised eyebrows were evidence of his loss of composure.

'Until recently, Minister,' it was Chief Superintendent Biggs coming to the rescue of a decidedly uncomfortable Chief Inspector, 'she was viewed as an acquaintance of Miss Gollitzin's, nothing more.'

'Notwithstanding, Chief Inspector Reynolds should have at least drawn my attention to such a connection.'

'May I endorse your comments, Minister,' said Sir Rupert. 'My department had no knowledge of the Webster woman's involvement until now.'

The Home Secretary now assumed the caricature of a schoolmaster addressing his class as he wagged his index finger at the gathering.

'Gentlemen, gentlemen, we must have the most comprehensive exchange of information at all times. I appreciate there are several independent representatives present: Military Intelligence, the Metropolitan Police and Home Office Immigration Services,' looking across at Clive Egerton, who, as the junior present, had contributed nothing to the meeting, 'and of course, Special Branch. All of you are involved to a greater or lesser degree, therefore the closest liaison is essential. Gentlemen, we are faced with an agenda which has the widest political implications: at any moment it could blow up in all our faces, I trust you all appreciate that.'

The gathering nodded.

'In consideration of the possible ramifications of the KGB's activities now going on, I propose a code name which will be adhered to in all future communications on the subject. The code name will be "Romanov" ... most appropriate I feel, and for future counter-espionage activities connected with this unfortunate business, "Operation Romanov" will be applied.'

Again the gathering nodded.

'I now require from you all a day to day update on all matters related to the Gollitzin woman and her associates. From you, Chief Superintendent Biggs, and you, Sir Rupert, observations relevant to national security, not forgetting Derby and particularly their new man, Sternov.'

'As you wish, Minister,' they answered in chorus.

The Home Secretary then rose, joined quickly by the gathering, signifying the meeting was at an end.

'Sir Rupert, would you clarify a point for me?' It was Chief Inspector Reynolds speaking as they walked towards the lift to take them down to the vestibule.

'If I can.'

'Was it Tuttle who shot Derevenko?'

'He has said as much.'

'But that's a capital charge – I must say I think the Minister is taking a lot on himself.'

'National Security, Reynolds, National Security,' replied Sir Rupert, 'he really has no alternative given the facts.'

'Well, I don't like it . . .'

'Reynolds, have you signed the Official Secrets Act?' asked Sir Rupert as their lift descended.

'Of course.'

'Then I suggest you remember that.'

*　　*　　*

'Right, Teddy,' said Sir Rupert on his return to his office. 'The gloves are off with a vengeance.' He then gave his Number One a brief of the meeting with the Home Secretary. 'Remember, Teddy, the code name is "Romanov", to he repeated on all communications.'

'That's fine, sir, I've already logged it.'

'Good. Now I want one of our best men put on Sternov. Arrange for a dossier, photographs, the lot.'

'What about Barstairs, Chief, he did a good job on that chappie from Libya.'

'Yes he did, a trifle young but still very capable – yes, have him briefed, Teddy, and tell him I want daily reports.'

'As you say, sir.'

'And, Teddy.'

'Sir.'

'Get me that phone number Charlie left us, the one through which I can reach him, he needs to know about "Operation Romanov".'

'Is that wise ... sir?'

'Teddy, just do it.'

* * *

It was the room that but a few nights ago had witnessed the meeting of Sokolov and his coterie of selected members of the Duma. From its centre the single electric light bulb continued to bathe the occupants with an unshielded intensity and, as if in mute protest at Magyar's indiscretion, the carpet still retained its blackened smudge of ground-in ash.

However, Dmitri Sokolov's attitude was different. Gone was the façade of resolute determination, substituted by feeble subservience to his lone companion, Sir Humphrey Charters, KG, OBE, whose bulk smothered rather than occupied one of the three chairs which, with the attendant table, constituted the room's quota of furniture. Sir Humphrey's voice, seeming to emerge from a tortuous passage deep within an expansive chest, was nonetheless distinct.

'I've waited half a century, Sokolov, for this opportunity, and nothing is going to stop me. You know what I'm alluding to?'

'The Romanov millions?'

'Exactly, and you, if you'll pardon the expression, can join me feeding from the same trough. Incidentally, I'm aware of your own scheme to recover it...' Laboriously, as Sokolov watched, Sir Humphrey lit a cigar extracted from a silver case and, as if everything was subservient to such an exercise, puffed strenuously before continuing '... you're following a trail that can only lead you to the gates of Lubyanka...' more generous puffing, 'and they'll close behind you for a very long time – you get my meaning?'

155

Sokolov's eyes betrayed the abject fear the word 'Lubyanka' provoked. Gathering himself, he replied, 'Naturally, Sir Humphrey, the Nobility Association would only be too delighted...'

'You can cut the nobility stuff, this venture has nothing charitable about it – either you're in or out. I haven't all night, so make up your mind.'

'Sir Humphrey, I don't doubt your intentions or abilities,' said as two hands rubbed each other in an act of self-conscious humility, 'and I'm aware of how highly Tsar Nicholas thought of you in the old days, but couldn't you give me some idea of your plan?'

'Plan? Who said anything about a plan?'

'I don't understand...'

'Sokolov,' whispered Sir Humphrey, his head shrouded in cigar smoke and so quietly that his avid listener had to edge forward to hear him, 'I'm not searching for it, I'm recovering it... recovering what I buried.'

16

Charlie is my Darlin'

Janice was sitting in the drawing room, alone with her thoughts, when the telephone rang.

'Daddy here,' came the clear voice of her father. 'Good news, all charges have been dropped. Ben rang me a short while ago ... it appears to be all over.'

'All the charges – it's unbelievable. Daddy, are you absolutely sure?'

'No doubt at all. There is one thing, though, you still have to attend the coroner's inquest, won't be for a while, probably towards the end of the month. But don't worry, I'll come along with you.'

'You're a sweetie, I'm so relieved.'

'Jay?'

'Yes, Daddy.'

'A word of advice, drop your relationship with the girl, no good will come of it.'

'I'll give it some thought, I promise. I'm so very grateful ... and, Daddy, before you ring off, does this mean Charlie Tuttle is in the clear?'

'Well, my concern was only for you, but from what Ben said it was all charges, so it must include him. I don't see how they could proceed against him alone.'

'Thank God ... love and kisses.' As she returned the receiver to its rest, Bill walked in.

'I take it that was your father?'

'It was, and why aren't you at the office?'

' I've taken a half-day. Well, can you blame me? The last time I was away, you were shot at!'

Janice chose to ignore the sarcasm.

'Where's Natasha?'

'Gone to the hairdresser.'

'Alone?' Her tone betrayed anxiety.

'Of course she's alone. Really, Janice, it's all becoming too much, this cops and robbers scenario, when is it going to end? We've already had one tragedy with poor Pen, not to mention the man shot on our patio . . .'

'Hopefully, it has ended.'

'Good, when is Natasha leaving us then?'

'Bill, we've been through all this before, she's going nowhere, at least not this side of Christmas.' A pause. 'Charlie will tell me when it's safe for her to do so.'

'That's another thing, who the hell is Charlie? When he first came here he was Igor – I find it all so confusing.'

'Bill, you're becoming a bore.' Then, as if talking to a rather stupid child, Janice continued, 'Charlie is, or was, a secret agent working for British Intelligence – he had to adopt a disguise, that's all.'

'Now we are getting into the realms of fantasy. Whatever next?' he said peevishly.

'Believe what you like, make of it what you like, I really don't care,' replied Janice as, rising, she began walking towards the door.

'Well, I'll admit I'm no man of action, that role has obviously been filled, but it is my home,' spoken at the retreating figure of his wife.

'Don't count your chickens,' she said over her shoulder as she quietly closed the door behind her.

* * *

158

The day after, Janice and Charlie, in response to an urgent call from her father, were seated in the plush offices of Lawrence, Graham, Ellis and Hone in Baker Street. Shortly, the great man himself appeared and, as he hurried to his desk, his opening remarks were not encouraging.

'I can only spare you a few minutes, Jay, I'm terribly pushed today.' Charlie studied him with interest. So this was Janice's father, a man with the reputation of being one of the best criminal lawyers in the country. Looking at his steel-grey eyes, which, without apparent effort, seemed to penetrate through to one's soul, Charlie acknowledged that he would not care to face him in the witness box.

'So this is Charlie Tuttle,' he said affably, extending his hand. 'I've heard a great deal about you.'

'It's good to meet you, sir,' responded Charlie, accepting the proffered hand. Then, without further preamble, George Lawrence turned to his daughter.

'Jay, I'm hearing things, this business you've got yourself mixed up in is not so straightforward as I first thought. It's all very well, even commendable, to ... er,' he paused, 'to reach out and help a poor woman who is being hounded.' Again the pause. It seemed to Charlie, listening to the preamble, that the great man was no longer in his office but making a plea in some court of justice.

'I don't understand,' Janice's face mirrored her concern.

'Very simply this, it's not just the Home Office who are involved but British Intelligence as well – your friend could well be working for the KGB.'

'Oh, Daddy, really ... that's preposterous.'

'Nonetheless, it's what I've been hearing.'

'Sir,' interceded Charlie, 'you have my word nothing is further from the truth. Our concern,' looking at Janice, 'concerns the lifting of the charges. This places Miss Gollitzin in grave danger.'

'In what way?' Immediately Charlie sensed, from his tone, an element of antagonism.

159

'Because the Home Office will now accede to the Soviets' request for her to be extradited.'

The silence that followed was to both Charlie and Janice almost unbearable.

Charlie decided to continue. 'You see, sir, the fact she was facing criminal charges here was, in effect, her protection.'

'I see, I see,' he replied, with a shake of the head. 'She entered the country illegally?'

'She did.'

'That does present a problem – she's a Soviet citizen?'

'She is.'

'Daddy,' interceded Janice, 'why all the questions? You know all this.'

'Just a refresher. I am at present involved in a very complex murder trial.'

'I'm sorry, Daddy, I should have realised.'

Pointedly, George Lawrence looked down at his watch. 'Well, briefly,' he began again, 'the only recourse we have is to again formally request asylum ... you say she's under sentence of death if returned to the USSR?'

'As good as,' commented Charlie laconically.

Again silence. Then George Lawrence, leaning forward, looked directly at Charlie.

'The problem we face with illegal entry is that, in itself, it is not a crime. By that I mean there is no trial, and, consequently no defence, apart from appeal. Normally, in most cases, the miscreants are just sent back from whence they came.'

'Oh, Daddy, no,' it was Janice's plaintive voice, 'you must do something.'

'I always knew,' observed Charlie, 'that Natasha had more to fear from British officialdom than anything else.'

'You say, Mr Tuttle, that she's not working for the Soviets?'

'Definitely not.'

'Well, there may be others you'll have to convince apart from me. I have a contact at the Home Office and I'll see what can be

160

done, but,' looking at his daughter and rising from his desk, 'you may have to accept the inevitable.'

'No, never,' said Janice, close to tears.

'I'll ring as soon as I have something positive, now I really must go.'

As they emerged from the warmth and comfort of the office into the cold grey drabness of the December day, Charlie could not help noticing the tears streaming down Janice's face. As he slipped an arm round her waist she looked up at him.

'Cheer up,' he said understandingly, 'the game's not over yet, I still have a few cards to play.'

'Charlie,' as she snuggled closer to him, 'you must save her.'

'I never intended anything else,' he said, as he hailed a taxi.

* * *

They arrived at Janice's home just in time to meet Natasha coming towards them down the drive. But once again, much to the chagrin of Charlie, it was a different Natasha. In place of the blonde tresses her hair was again as dark as pitch.

'When did that happen?' said Charlie, his annoyance obvious.

'Yesterday, in the afternoon, she went to the hairdresser on her own – I had no idea,' replied Janice.

'Brilliant, that's all we need, and where do you think she is off to now?'

'I just don't know, Charlie, we cannot make a prisoner of her.'

'Believe me, before this business is over with we may well have to.'

'That would be nigh impossible.'

'Difficult, but not impossible,' chided Charlie.

'There is one solution,' said Janice timorously.

'What's that?'

'Find her a husband, that way she would become a British citizen. Are you married, Charlie?'

'No.'

'Well?'

'Janice, I would give my life for her, but marriage, that's too drastic.'

Janice smiled wryly. 'You mean you would die for her but not marry her – I'm sure she would be flattered if she knew that!' Charlie went silent. Janice, after further thought, returned to her suggestion.

'It would not have to be binding, Charlie, just the means by which we could foil the Home Office.'

'Janice,' said Charlie, looking straight at her, 'if Natasha marries she can kiss goodbye to any pretensions she has as heir to the Romanov throne.'

'As if that matters, Charlie.'

'It mattered a great deal to an old friend of mine. So much so it cost her her life.'

'I'm sorry . . . Charlie?'

'Yes.'

'What about those cards you still have to play?'

'I'm thinking about them – perhaps the time has come to play a few. Do you mind if I think aloud for a few moments?'

'Be my guest.'

'I'm beginning to wonder if I've been guilty of underestimating the Duchess Elizabeth.'

'In what way, Charlie?'

'Oh, it's just a niggle . . . but it won't go away.'

'Tell me, perhaps it will help.'

'Well, for one, why after our flight from Appenzell was Sergei so short of money he had to go cap-in-hand to the Comte de Toulouse? Surely, money was the least of Elizabeth's worries. Another thing, I know all about Natasha – marriage certificates, birth certificates, the lot, except one thing . . .'

'Such as?'

'Who the grandfather was.'

'You mean who fathered Princess Eugenia?'

'Exactly. It's not beyond the powers of reasoning to say he could still be alive. If he is, who is he and where is he?'

'But Natasha said that the Duchess told her Gregor Rasputin was her grandfather – after all, she has his looks.'

'I've never accepted that.'

'Charlie, we're just going round in circles, is it so important?'

'Only this, if we knew it might answer a lot of questions.'

'You are wonderful, Charlie, I believe I'm falling in love with you.'

'Time enough for that when this is all over.'

'Is that a promise?'

'I never promise what I cannot deliver, Janice.'

'We'll see about that, Charlie Tuttle,' said with a mischievous wink.

'Yes, indeed we'll see about that,' he replied, aping her wink. Then suddenly she sensed a change in him. Gone was the hilarity of moments before and in its place it seemed as if a darkness had descended, blotting her out. Looking into his eyes she saw they were focused, not on her, but somewhere far away, and even as she watched a shadow of great sadness passed over them.

Instinctively, she knew that whatever it was she could never play any part in it. Straining on tiptoe, she reached up to him and with great tenderness brushed each eye with her lips.

* * *

Alexis Sternov studied the paunchy figure with some disdain.

'I trust, Sternov,' said the Ambassador, 'that you will not embark on a series of stunts which were the earmark of your predecessor. Such mayhem does not make a difficult job any easier.'

Why was it, thought Sternov, that when so-called stalwarts of the regime spent any time in the West they became passive nonentities. Still, he was the accredited Ambassador to the Court of St James, miserable little runt that he was. So perhaps a little deference for his position wouldn't go amiss.

'You are referring to Mikhael Derevenko?'

'Indeed I am, he disclosed everything and achieved nothing.'

'Comrade Semichastny and myself are aware of that, Your Excellency.'

The mention of Semichastny's name brought about a subtle change in the attitude of the Ambassador; rubbing his hands together, he gave Sternov a thin smile. 'Of course, of course, your reputation, Comrade Sternov, is well-known. I have no doubt your mission will be achieved with panache as reflects an officer of the KGB.'

'Excellency,' began Sternov, 'what I have in mind will accomplish the tasks set me, without in any way causing you or the Embassy any disruption.'

'You have a plan?'

'Most certainly.'

'Do you require any assistance?'

'I have only one request.'

'That is?'

'Ask the British Government for the return of Derevenko's body. In death, Your Excellency, he will become a much greater patriot than he ever was in life.'

17

'. . . but by God They Frighten Me.'

Her Majesty's Minister for Home Affairs did not rise when Sir Rupert entered the room.

'Ah, Sir Rupert, do sit down. I assume you have the man Tuttle with you?'

'He's in the ante-room, Minister.'

'Good, then fetch him in, man ... I haven't all day,' he said somewhat petulantly. 'And understand this, Sir Rupert, I've gone as far as I'm prepared to with him – no more concessions.'

'I agree, Minister,' Sir Rupert replied, as he moved towards the door.

'So, you're Tuttle,' welcomed the Home Secretary, looking at Charlie's muscular frame with some admiration. 'I understand you can help us clear up some recent vexing incidents?'

Charlie said nothing, but began to loosen a bootlace securing a small parcel he had been carrying. Producing three envelopes from the package, he placed them on the floor at his feet.

'To understand the significance of what I'm about to tell you,' he began, 'I need to go back to the 1918 Revolution in Russia, and in particular its effect on those Romanovs who survived the aftermath.'

'You have an hour, Tuttle, and I am familiar with the events in Russia at that time, so please be brief.'

In a low monotone, Charlie, as if reciting a well-known story, began. As the dialogue progressed, Sir Rupert marvelled at the expertise with which Charlie marshalled the sequence of events. When Natasha Gollitzin's meeting with the Duchess Elizabeth entered his discourse, Sir Rupert easily visualised the occasion. A look at the Home Secretary confirmed how totally absorbed he was in what Charlie was saying. Soon, all three envelopes had been opened and their contents (with the exception of the last will and testament of the Duchess Elizabeth, a case of respecting her privacy Charlie had said, by way of explanation) examined. Loud exclamations, such as 'Incredible', 'Unbelievable!', came from both the Minister and Sir Rupert as each new piece of the outlandish story was revealed, like fragments of some puzzle. Twice the Home Secretary lifted the phone and cancelled previously arranged appointments. Looking at his watch, Sir Rupert noted that Charlie's explanation had lasted over two hours. Finally, Charlie, drinking from a glass of water offered by the Minister, lapsed into silence.

'Brilliant, Mr Tuttle, I compliment you. Your presentation, and in my profession I know something about presentations, was both remarkable and lucid. My congratulations.'

'Well done, Charlie,' muttered Sir Rupert.

'Thank you,' said Charlie, as he busied himself retrieving his papers.

'What do you make of that, Sir Rupert?'

'I can only think of one word, Minister, unbelievable – but I have no doubt every word was true.'

'Now, Mr Tuttle,' said the Minister, with a quiet sniff, 'I should like your opinion on one salient fact.'

Charlie, having recovered his documents and placed them back in their wrapping, gazed unblinkingly at the Minister.

'Assuming, as you told us, the late Tsarina had a fifth daughter and she in turn gave birth to a daughter of her own, what proof have we that Miss Natasha Gollitzin is that daughter? I do not doubt for an instant, from the evidence you have produced, that a child did exist. But are that child and Miss Gollitzin one and the same?'

'I have no doubt, Minister. Remember, I served the Duchess Elizabeth for eight years, during that time she talked of nothing else but her plans for Natasha Gollitzin.'

'Yes but, Mr Tuttle, that hardly constitutes proof. Now, regarding the Romanov gold, you've been rather reticent on that subject, the cause of all the recent hiatus. You say you know its location but you're not prepared to disclose it. You have told us that over half a million sterling has been deposited in the Suisse National Bank, but you won't tell us in whose name. You tell us that you put it there over a lengthy period of time, and I believe you. But I have to say this, you are still keeping a lot back. In one respect I am grateful to you, we now know the reasons for the interest of the KGB in all this, and I have to admit to a feeling of some relief that other matters of greater concern are not involved. Perhaps now, you will kindly leave us and, Mr Tuttle . . . thank you.'

'Well, Sir Rupert,' as the door closed behind Charlie, 'what now?'

'I have to admit, Minister, I'm as disappointed as you are. In my opinion, Tuttle is playing for time in the hope that someone overplays their hand.'

'In what way? And please, Sir Rupert, don't talk in riddles.'

'What we have here is a very complex plot. The main planks appear to be the girl, Natasha Gollitzin, and the Romanov fortune. We know, from what has happened, that the girl poses a threat to some whilst others are intent upon keeping her alive – possibly because of what she knows, or, more to the point, what they think she knows.'

'You're not making it any easier, Sir Rupert.'

'Simply, Minister, because it's mostly conjecture.'

'One thing does worry me,' said the Minister, as he picked up a ruler from his desk and absent-mindedly began to bend it. 'Why is the KGB so interested in the gold? After all, they're putting a lot of effort into something which even now may be no more than a myth.'

'Here, I have to disagree with you,' replied Sir Rupert, 'there is too much evidence to the contrary. The gold does exist, Minister.'

'What should we do about Tuttle, Sir Rupert?' he said as he replaced the ruler on his desk.

'At the present time, Minister, I would recommend no action. After all, he is no Communist, and might well be the one person capable of bringing matters to a head.'

'If you say so, Sir Rupert, if you say so.'

* * *

'Charlie,' Janice said, the following evening. 'Tomorrow we're having lunch with my godmother Hilda and her husband, George. Peter and Emma have been invited,' and then as something of an irrelevant afterthought, 'and of course Bill.'

'It's not really my scene, Janice...' but Janice cut in quickly, 'I'm taking Natasha, and I always feel more comfortable when you're around. So please come.'

'Well, if you put it like that, all right. I have to admit that my protection of her has not been all it should have been – I guess I'm getting too old for this sort of thing.'

'Too old, you, nonsense, after what you did to that pig Derevenko?'

'I was just lucky, Janice, I saw him before he saw me.'

'Well, whoever saw who first it was a tremendous shot, especially so in the semi-darkness.'

'Thank you for that.'

'You're welcome – and you will come, won't you?' Moving closer to him, 'not necessarily for Natasha's sake but for mine.' She pressed her body against his.

'How could I possibly refuse?' he said, as she reached upwards, her slim arms already encircling his neck.

'Kiss me,' she breathed, 'kiss me like you've never kissed any woman before.' He smiled down at her then, gripping her at the waist, lifted her bodily off her feet. For what to Janice seemed an eternity of time his eyes held hers before, with a force which utterly consumed her, his mouth crushed against hers.

'Wow, Mister Tuttle,' she said, her breasts heaving as he lowered her to the ground, 'what have I been missing these past weeks ....? And what a tongue!' Her arms moved upwards again as she mouthed, 'More please.'

'Janice,' he said, stepping back, 'Bill's in the next room.'

'Bill, who's Bill?' she replied dreamily, her arms already around his neck.

* * *

Janice could be forgiven her desire to bask in the unprecedented limelight her involvement with Natasha and Charlie had brought about.

Standing in Hilda's drawing room in a most commanding position, with the gathering attentive and sated after several sherries, she was in her element. Sharing the three-seater sofa were Bill, Emma and Peter, across from them, Charlie and Natasha. George and Hilda occupied two of the four armchairs. For George, the position was ideal, giving him an uninterrupted view of where Natasha's long legs reached her hips. It was for Janice a unique opportunity to disclose to her captive audience how, with the help of Charlie, she had taken on the might of the Soviet Union. How they had thwarted that monolithic giant by their cunning and expertise and, by way of a little spice, her realisation that the 'war' still remained to be won and therefore help was needed.

As her audience sipped their sherries Janice's description of the death of Mikhael Derevenko, given for the benefit of George and Hilda, and the fact that Natasha, although incognito, was a Russian Princess, created an atmosphere of amazed incredulity as illustrated by the frequent 'Oos' and 'Ahs' greeting each extra-ordinary revelation.

In particular, the party were astounded by the exposure of

Natasha's manservant, Igor who, far from being the bumbling moron so familiar to them, had, by some metamorphosis, become Charlie, secret agent extraordinaire.

Hilda, by frequent nods of her head, let it be known that she alone had anticipated such revelations. A bookworm, with a prodigious appetite for spy stories, the disclosures coming from her goddaughter were manna from heaven. Squinting through her bifocals, first at Natasha and then at Charlie, it was obvious that any preconceived opinions she once held, particularly about 'that woman', had been discarded utterly and irrevocably.

'You poor child,' she cooed, as she joined Natasha on the sofa, 'How perfectly dreadful for you.' Then, in a sickly sweet tone normally reserved for small children and animals, she said, 'but as a royal princess, you must expect attentions from those who are motivated by jealousy and greed.' But it was to Charlie, who with the resigned look of one accepting his fate, she directed her most outrageous comments and eloquence.

'Brilliant, my man, brilliant. Such bravery deserves the highest recognition. It is men like you who made this country great, it is men like you who carved out of the jungle and swamps the great British Empire, it is . . .'

Phyllis, Hilda's maid, announced lunch, and put an end to what had become the most embarrassing moment in Charlie's life.

Janice, seated at one end of the table, gauged the reaction of the now intrigued party. Hilda, as Janice expected, was already, metaphorically, armed to the teeth and ready for battle. Emma, eyes wide in admiration for Charlie (she would have to watch that one, thought Janice), had become, quite openly, his slave. Big George, although out of his depth, was still hopelessly enamoured with what was now even more desirable – a live and kicking royal princess. Peter continued to be Peter. It was interesting, recalled Janice later, he was the only one who had questions about the Romanov gold during her discourse – not that he had learnt anything. But, without doubt, he was weighing up what was in it for him. Then there was Bill, her 'imitation man' as she now called him – a nonentity.

Janice smiled to herself now for the announcement. 'Dear friends,' she said, rising to her feet. 'I give you a toast … Charlie and Natasha.'

'Charlie and Natasha,' they chorused.

'I now invite you all,' continued Janice, 'to pledge yourselves to their protection against any who would do them harm, so that, in the fullness of time, Natasha, dear Natasha may attain her birthright and become a true royal princess of the House of Romanov.'

'We so pledge,' declared Emma and George; the others mumbled incoherently.

Janice lowered her glass with a feeling of intense satisfaction – now for some substance to that pledge.

'Hilda?'

'Yes, Janice.

'In the event that a safe house is required for Natasha, can she come here?' Janice's use of the terminology 'safe house' would, she calculated, appeal to Hilda's fevered imagination.

'Most certainly, our cellar, properly prepared, would be ideal.'

'No question,' boomed Big George, anxious to get in on the act, 'and I've got a shotgun you know – heaven help the bastards … my apologies, ladies … if they come within range of that.'

'Quite,' replied Janice, with difficulty avoiding Charlie's eyes.

'We could have her,' chimed in Emma, as she smiled across at a somewhat subdued Natasha. 'We've no cellar, but I am sure she would be safe with us.' Only Bill remained silent, his jaundiced expression, however, speaking volumes.

*　*　*

'That was unnecessary,' said Charlie, as they drove home. 'You've broken the first rule of espionage, secrecy, by your behaviour today.'

'Charlie, don't be cross with me, we may need their support before this business is finished.'

Choosing to ignore her excuse, he continued to remonstrate with her. 'You totally ignored my warning signals, and, another thing, if you need allies you vet them first. You don't jump in with both feet. It may be of interest to you to know that I do not trust,' holding up five fingers and ticking them off, ' Bill and Peter, and to a lesser degree, Emma. That, leaving us out of it, is three out of the five you blabbed to this morning.'

'But Charlie, three already knew about Derevenko, and they were present when Pen got hers.' The use of such an idiom as 'got hers' made Janice all but gasp. She really was into intelligence jargon now, a fully committed agent … she smiled to herself at such a thought.

'Nevertheless,' he replied, 'I do think it would have been better to have kept quiet. We could always have approached one of them if need be.'

Charlie stretched his feet and closed his eyes, the warmth of the car after Hilda's excellent lunch inviting sleep. Janice, however, was not to be denied.

'What did you think of Hilda?'

'She's all right, she's a fighter.'

'Takes one to know one, eh, Charlie?'

'Something like that,' again closing his eyes.

'And Big George?'

'Harmless – he's so anxious to bed Natasha he would do nothing to hurt her.'

'You don't miss much, do you, Charlie?'

'It doesn't pay to in this game.' Glancing in her mirror, Janice satisfied herself that Natasha was curled up asleep, then, giving Charlie a sideways glance, 'and what about me, how do I measure up?'

'Not bad.'

'Thank you, I'm very flattered,' she paused, then, 'May I ask you a personal question?'

'Keep it short.'

'Do you want to bed me? You can if you want to.'

'That's one complication I can do without.'

'How very flattering you are today ... Charlie?'

'What now, Janice, can't a man get some sleep?'

'Just one more question, then I'll shut up.'

'Fire away.'

'Have you slept with Natasha?'

'I've been sleeping with Natasha for months.'

'Charlie, do you know something?'

'Oh God, what now?'

'You're a pig.'

As they swung into Janice's driveway, they both noticed Bill's car had arrived before them.

'He's wasted no time,' said Janice, as she drew up behind it.

18

The Judas Apostles

By dint of explaining his preference for the simple things of life, Alexis Sternov had refused the Ambassador's offer of a guest room in the Embassy, He had, instead, opted for a sparse single room within the staff quarters. This, as an earlier reconnoitre had quickly established, although offering the barest essentials, did have one distinct advantage, a short passage from its door led to the rear entrance. This offered him the facility of entering and leaving the Embassy in some privacy. True, there was an armed guard, an aged incumbent responsible for security, but him apart, Alexis's comings and goings could enjoy complete anonymity – sufficient compensation for the loss of the lush furnishings of a guest room.

Stretched out on the narrow bed, his huge bulk all but flattening the thin mattress, Sternov, jacket removed and his red braces hanging loose, contemplated a large bluebottle making slow progress across the ceiling. Leaning over, he picked up his Mauser automatic pistol from an adjoining bedside table, lined up its sights on the now stationary fly and gently squeezed the trigger. The resultant click was so unobtrusive that the object of his attention, having completed its observation of the immediate surroundings, continued its meandering.

A discreet knock an the door interrupted any further distractions, and with lightening speed, born of long practice, Sternov reunited the pistol with its magazine. Then, with the gun trained on the door he called, 'Enter.' In response to his bidding, a small man wearing a heavy winter coat and clutching a cloth cap entered the room.

' Ah, Mordici Bogrov, you got my message, then?'

'Yes, Comrade Sternov, I came immediately.' Sternov, sixteen stone and over six feet, continued his large man's contempt for small men. As his visitor eyed the Mauser still pointed at him, his hands holding the cloth cap began a ritual reminiscent of someone ringing out wet washing, as they nervously screwed it into an ever smaller ball.

'I have a job for you,' said Sternov without further preamble, as he replaced the Mauser on the side table.

'I am at your service, Comrade Sternov.'

Ignoring such assurance, Sternov continued, 'The job requires great care and patience . . . do you drive, Bogrov?'

'Yes, comrade.'

'You have a vehicle?'

'No, but I know where I can get one.'

'Good . . . from your reports you are familiar with a woman calling herself Natasha Gollitzin?'

'Bourgeois trash.'

'Exactly. I want round-the-clock surveillance on the woman, and Bogrov, this is the tricky bit. I need to know her movements – in advance, note that. And, most importantly, who will be with her.'

'I understand.'

Sternov now moved to his jacket hanging on the bedpost. Fishing in a pocket, he produced his pipe and a wad of tobacco; slowly he began to fill the pipe, his eyes however, never leaving the, by now, more relaxed Bogrov.

'You will need money, look into the top drawer,' pointing as he spoke in the direction of a battered chest of drawers. Bogrov, relieved at being given the opportunity to escape those pitiless eyes, moved to the chest and quickly opened the drawer. He soon produced a thick roll of notes which he held aloft for Sternov to see.

'Five hundred pounds in used notes. Should you need more let me know,' said Sternov, with total indifference.

'That should be ample, comrade,' he said ingratiatingly.

Having lit his pipe, Sternov stretched his full length on the bed and watched as the smoke curled upwards towards the now motionless fly.

'How is your family, Bogrov?' he asked, after once again studying the insect. 'Are they still living in Minsk?'

'Yes,comrade.'

'They are well?'

'Yes, comrade.'

'Then you will want to keep them that way?'

'Of course, Comrade Sternov.'

'You would do well to bear that in mind, Bogrov.'

'I understand, comrade.'

'And, Bogrov.'

' Yes, comrade?'

'You might, just might, get that exit visa you're so anxious to obtain for them . . . you get my meaning?'

'That would be wonderful. It is something . . .' but Sternov interrupted him.

'Close the door quietly when you leave, Bogrov.'

'Certainly, comrade.'

'And, Bogrov . . .'

'Yes, comrade?'

'Do give my best wishes to the Duma, won't you . . .' the harshness of his voice betrayed his true feelings.

* * *

'Well, Dmitri,' said Paul, 'you've taken your time getting back to us. Now what happened between you and the Comte de Toulouse and, more to the point, what happened about the money?'

'Yes,' chimed in Magyar, 'don't tell us you've again forgotten about the money – Jesus, twenty grand, and he told us he'd forgotten about it.'

'Do you have to repeat yourself, Magyar?' said an obviously stung Dmitri, 'you know it's the first sign of...' pointing to his head.

Vladimir , silent until now, looked from one to the other, then, in a voice of righteous indignation, said, 'Will someone tell me what this is all about?'

Dmitri Sokolov raised his glass to his lips and wearily looked at his three hand-picked conspirators. What a sad, dispirited trio they were, he thought. Particularly Magyar, with his matted beard and bloodshot eyes. Even Paul, by far the most intelligent and therefore the one to watch, seemed to have lost his enthusiasm for the venture and was mere concerned about a piddling twenty thousand than the millions just waiting to be picked up.

'Well,' repeated Paul, 'or are we going to have to wait all night in this flea-bitten hole Magyar has the gall to call home?'

'The twenty grand,' replied Dmitri, 'as Magyar chooses to call it, is going into the coffers of the Nobility Association. Without doubt that is what the Duchess Elizabeth would have wished.'

'Why, have you asked her?' said Paul , his voice thick with sarcasm.

'That would be difficult,' joined in Magyar ironically, 'seeing she's been dead these months.'

'And who is Chairman of the Association?' said Vladimir, mirroring Paul's sarcasm and beginning to make some sense of the conversation.

'It is my wish,' said Magyar, in a high falsetto voice, mimicking what he thought was the voice of the Duchess, 'that the money should go to further the aims of the great Nobility Association ... Nobility Association, my arse.'

'I would remind you all that the money is held by the Comte. Therefore, if it's his decision to give it to the Association, the money will go directly to the Treasurer – I won't even see it.'

'If you believe that you'll believe anything,' said Magyar, draining his glass.

'All right then,' said Paul, anxious to resume the role of

spokesman for the other two. 'All right, we'll accept that, now let's get on with the plan.'

'I guess what you've never had you never miss,'' said a morose Magyar, 'but a word in your ear, Dmitri: cross me and I'll slit your throat – and enjoy doing it.'

'What a happy, trusting band we are, gentlemen,' commented Dmitri dryly, making light of the threat. 'Just the sort of trusting relationship we need if we're ever going to pull this off.'

'Oh, shut up, Dmitri,' they chorused.

With a sigh of seeming resignation, Dmitri Sokolov reached into the inside pocket of his voluminous overcoat and produced a letter. 'I've had this from your brother in Zurich, Vladimir,' he said, laying the envelope down on the table.

'Don't tell me they've finally let him out?' responded Vladimir. 'I thought he had another year at least to serve.'

'He's out, and he's been to Kolomyja, gentlemen,' said Dmitri, unable to hide a note of triumph in his voice. Silence greeted this announcement. It seemed, from their expressions, that the very mention of the word 'Kolomyja' had re-cemented their fragile comradeship. And what up to now had been a scene of childish bickering became one of concentration and anticipation.

'What did he say?' asked Paul, his voice hushed and the glow of returning enthusiasm already lighting his eyes.

'It's in code.' The three nodded in unison.

'It's not even addressed to you,' exclaimed Magyar, holding up the envelope.

'Don't be a bloody fool, Magyar, of course it's not addressed to me, don't you know all our mail is intercepted...' Dmitri was pleased for the opportunity to get back at Magyar.

'Get on with it, Dmitri, the suspense is killing me,' said Vladimir.

'He confirms the map is rubbish. There are three possibilities within the cemetery at Kolomyja, infant burials around the relevant time confirm this ... gentlemen, the gold awaits us.'

Such was the significance of Dmitri's statement that it was met with awe by his compatriots. All, until that moment, had nurtured a lingering doubt that the gold did exist, and each, in his own way, had prepared for that. But now, the knowledge that the riches were there and that they alone knew where, was overwhelming in its portent.

'Is it buried . . . deep?' asked a breathless Magyar, as he scurried round replenishing their glasses.

'How deep is a grave?' replied Dmitri, all but emptying his recently filled glass, and delighting in the consternation his declaration had caused.

'You mean we're going grave-robbing?' exclaimed Paul, brow deeply furrowed.

'What the Hell – if there's one thing for sure, the dead can't hurt us,' contributed Magyar, with a mirthless smile.

'There is one thing worrying me,' volunteered Paul, his brow still deeply furrowed. 'If it was that easy for Vladimir's brother, why haven't the KGB been on to it years ago?'

'Because they didn't know what I knew,' replied Dmitri softly.

'You mean,' said Magyar, having resumed his seat, 'that even the Bolshies knew nothing about it?'

'Nothing.' From the look of intense concentration now mirrored in Magyar's face it was evident, to Dmitri, a doubt was emerging.

'Try pulling the other one, you don't expect us to believe that, surely?' Still relishing the rising consternation his words had initiated in all three, Dmitri rose from the table and helped himself to another drink.

'You've never met the Duchess, have you?' he said, swilling his drink round and round in the bottom of his glass, 'Well, I have. It's just the sort of hiding place that would appeal to her, in particular, her sense of humour. Not to mention her delight in putting one over the hated, the detestable Bolsheviks.'

'Come on, Dmitri, put us out of our misery, tell us how she did it,' said Paul, quickly joined by the other two.

'All in good time. But the one thing I will tell you is that recovering it will be a doddle, the problem will be getting it out of the country.'

'Dmitri,' it was Paul speaking, 'I am getting the feeling that we're going after the lot, no more talk of the odd ingot or two ...'

'Surely, Paul, why should any of us settle for thousands when we can have millions?'

Slowly, ever-widening smiles spread across the faces of all four as if each, in his mind's eye, was already seeing the riches to come ...

* * *

As Dmitri drove home a smile creased his face – yes, he considered, he had carried that off very well and exactly as Sir Humphrey had instructed.

'Tell them just enough to light their enthusiasm, but no more.' Well, he had done just that. The letter from Vladimir's brother, he chuckled to himself, was clever – fortunately not one of them had demanded to see it, fools that they were. Paul, as always, would need careful handling, but he was confident now he was over the worst. A tricky situation had turned out very well, and he was sure Sir Humphrey would be pleased.

19

The Fifth Column

'Thanks for coming in, Peter,' said Bill, 'I've been wanting to have a quiet word with you since Sunday.'

'You mean the luncheon?'

'Indeed, and my wife's rallying call to arms in support of Natasha and the pseudo-secret agent she's got in tow.'

Peter noted that no attempt was made to hide his evident animosity. It was his first visit to the offices of Lawrence, Graham, Ellis and Hone, and it would have been less than natural for him not to compare the surroundings with his own shared office above a laundrette in Edmonton.

'I think it went a little over the top,' he chose his words carefully as he was, as yet, uncertain of Bill's motive in asking him there.

'A little over the top,' mimicked Bill, 'I consider it was a downright impertinence taking advantage of friends in that way – who the devil does Janice think she is? Here we have a Russian woman whose antecedents are, to say the least, questionable, literally taking over my home, my wife and my friends.'

As Bill paused for breath, a discreet knock on the door heralded his secretary's entrance with coffee. Peter, inevitably, compared the silver tray, with its bone china cups and saucers, with the cheap homespun mugs used in his own office. As for Bill's secretary, even her plain black dress and sparse make-up did little to hide a face and figure more in tune with the front page of a fashion magazine than the leather and mahogany of a solicitor's office. Bill certainly knew how to pick them, he thought, as deftly she leant across him to pour just the right amount of coffee and milk. Her perfume, reflected Peter, was both elusive and captivating, an effect achieved only by the most expensive brands.

'I know the feeling,' he volunteered, as he studied the rotating hips of the withdrawing secretary.

'Then don't you think we should do something about it?'

'I don't see what we can do. Emma is completely enamoured with both of them – talks of nothing else.'

'Peter, I'm going to tell you something now in the strictest confidence. You won't let me down, will you?'

'You have my word, Bill,' said as he placed his cup and saucer on the edge of the highly polished desk.

Leaning across, and in a voice little above a whisper, Bill said, 'Janice has become a lesbian, she regularly sleeps with Natasha, and, for all I know, the man Charlie Tuttle as well!'

Peter, swallowing deeply, temporarily lost the power of speech, as Bill, evidently delighted in having someone to confide in, continued.

'I'm certain, Peter, that the three of them want me out. God knows Janice has dropped enough hints.'

'Surely not?' replied the somewhat recovered Peter. Although still trying to absorb such heady stuff, he was aware of a sense of glee at the thought of Bill Webster being pushed out into the cold harsh world, a world with which he himself was so well acquainted.

'Now, Peter, I think the same thing could happen to you. Don't be upset if I tell you I've noticed the strained state your marriage is going through and, without doubt, it's down to those three again.'

'What do you suggest, then?'

'Obvious, we join forces against them ... for our own survival. And we are not alone.'

'I don't understand.'

'Sir Humphrey Charters, Penelope Charters's father, is furious that nothing was done when Pen was shot. He's mouthing "cover-up" and could prove a very useful ally – he has friends, Peter, high-powered friends. What I suggest is we feed him information that will send Natasha packing and, hopefully, Charlie Tuttle to jail. Are you with us?'

'Well, I don't want to do anything that might harm Emma.'

'How could it possibly harm her?'

'No, I suppose not,' then, 'eh, Bill, do you think there is anything in this talk of gold bullion?'

'Peter, you've put your finger on it. All this talk about Natasha being a princess is eyewash. It's just a brilliant cover, what they are after is the gold.'

'Do you really think so?'

'I'm positive.'

'What if it were found, would there be a reward, the usual ten per cent?'

'I would think so; I'm sure the Russians would show their gratitude.'

'You mean they would give us something substantial – money?'

'I'm sure of it.'

'Peter?'

'Yes, Bill?'

'I noticed you looking at Rachel, my secretary.'

'Very nice, if I may say so.'

'You fancy her...? I can fix it for you, she's pretty hot stuff..'

'I think I should like that.'

'Consider it done. I'll be in touch.'

$*$ $*$ $*$

As soon as the door had closed behind Peter, Bill pressed the switch on his intercom.

'Rachel, get me Sir Humphrey Charters, and when I've finished come in.'

After a brief delay, the harsh gritty voice of Sir Humphrey came on the line.

'Bill Webster here, Sir Humphrey. Just a few words, I've had a chat with Peter Canning ... he's with us.'

'Good man. Now Bill, I'm pursuing that line of enquiry you suggested. It may well be there was collusion between the three of them. You, perhaps, could assist me further on that one.' A short break in the conversation as Sir Humphrey broke into a coughing fit then, as he cleared his throat, 'Sorry about that, caught it somewhere last week. As I was saying, I'm convinced that it was more than coincidence that on the day Pen was shot the Gollitzin woman had had her hair dyed.'

'You may well be right, Sir Humphrey.'

'I'm damn sure I'm right – you know what, Bill, I think Pen was set up.'

'It will probably take some proving, but I'm inclined to agree with you.'

'Anyway, Bill, I'm seeing Andrews the detective fellow again tomorrow. Up to now he's been very evasive, but I'll keep after him.'

'Right, Sir Humphrey, I'll be in touch ... and good luck.' As he replaced his receiver, Rachel walked in. But it was a somewhat different Rachel from the one Peter had met ... no longer was there the obsequiousness so evident earlier; instead, an air of self-confidence prevailed, its existence born of the knowledge that she had Bill Webster in the proverbial palm of her hand. As she reached his side she leant across him and helped herself to a cigarette from a silver cigarette box. Lighting it, she inhaled deeply, then, pulling up the hem of her dress, sat down on the edge of his desk. She looked at him quizzically.

Bill Webster, ignoring the ample display of creamy thigh, attempted to instill a note of authority into his voice.

'Peter Canning,' he began, as she, with the tip of her shoe, began to rub gently just below his navel.

'What about him?' she replied, through the billowing cigarette smoke.

'I should like you to take care of him.'

'Oh, Bill, not another fool, can't you find me someone with a bit of . . .' with that she gestured obscenely.

'He's all right, is Peter. In any case, you'll do well out of it, as you always do.'

'When?'

'One night next week – just the once, I promise.'

'If you insist,' she said resignedly, 'but I want a good dinner first and, if I say so, a decent hotel.'

'It will be done,' he said as she walked towards the office door. 'And Rachel, it's important – you'll give him a good time, won't you?'

'Don't I always?' she replied as she closed the door behind her.

* * *

'Do you realize, Charlie, that two weeks tomorrow is Christmas day? I've done absolutely nothing in the way of preparation.' Charlie, in the process of buttering a slice of toast, said nothing. Bill, his head appearing from behind his morning paper, could not resist an aside.

'I had noticed,' he said, with a flamboyant rustle of the newspaper. 'Usually by now, the tree is up, cards have been sent, shopping done,' then with heavy emphasis, 'but this year . . .'

'Oh, you poor dear,' retaliated Janice, helping herself to more bacon from the silver serving tray, 'don't worry, you won't miss out on anything.'

Natasha, turning to her hostess, the devastating smile once more evident, said, 'I love Christmas, Janeece, even back in Kolomyja it was the one time when everyone was happy.'

'How very nice,' said Bill scathingly, then, looking at his watch, 'I'm off, do let me know if anything is needed, Janice, won't you – you know, Christmas puddings, perhaps a turkey or two . . .'

'Sod off,' said an irritated Janice under her breath, then, as the door closed behind him, 'He really gets to me these days, Charlie, he really does, he's like an old woman with his moans and groans.'

'Well, his life has been somewhat turned upside down,' commented Charlie, with a pointed look in the direction of Natasha. Taking Charlie's hint, Janice turned to Natasha.

'As a Christmas treat from me, Natasha, how would you like to go to Covent Garden and see *Swan Lake*? It's running for a short season, now, until just after Christmas.'

Natasha clapped her hands with delight. Her face reminded Janice of when a child saw Christmas tree lights for the first time.

'*Magnifique*,' she said.

'Good, that's settled then, I'll book the seats this morning.'

* * *

'You're cross with me, aren't you?' said Janice, having run Charlie to earth in the library later that morning. He looked up as she, not to be ignored, prised the book he was reading out of his hands. 'My,' she said as she returned it to him, 'you're not going all intellectual on me, are you, Charlie? Tolstoy's *War and Peace*, that's going it a bit, surely?'

'Is that wise?' he said, ignoring her banter. 'Taking Natasha to Covent Garden?'

'You certainly come straight to the point, don't you, no "Where have you been, Janice?" or "Have you been busy, Janice?"'

'You know they've replaced Derevenko?'

'Charlie, no,' she said as she crumpled rather than sat down on the nearest chair. 'When?'

'A few days ago, one of their top men.'

'Who told you?'

'Does it matter?'

'God, when is it going to end?'

'When they get what they want,' replied Charlie, as he returned Tolstoy to the bookshelf.

'I've got two lovely seats. We'll be able to see every movement, and in any case I cannot let her down now.'

'You may have to.'

186

'No, Charlie, just this once I'm putting my foot down, we're going.'

'Not if I say no.' Seeing the steeliness creeping back into his eyes, she knew she was all but beaten.

'Charlie, this is no life for a young girl, shut up here all day, never allowed to go anywhere...'

He cut in brusquely, 'Do you want her dead? Or worse, shipped back to Moscow?'

'All right, all right, you know best... Charlie?'

'Now what?'

'I don't think I can take much more of this.' Silence followed then, rising to his feet, he took her by the shoulders.

'Janice, that's not you talking. All I'm asking is we don't take risks, certainly not unnecessary risks. However, if it's so important to you then OK, but on one condition, I take you and bring you back and...' producing the Beretta from his waistband, 'you carry this with you at all times.'

'But, Charlie, I've never carried a gun in my life. Come to think of it I know nothing about guns at all.'

'Then it's time you learnt, come on upstairs to my bedroom.'

'Charlie, I thought you would never ask me...'

* * *

'Florrie, this carpet is going to have to be cleaned, I keep telling Bill, but as usual, nothing happens.'

It was later the same morning, the gun tuition having proved a fiasco.

'I don't know, mum, would you like me to have a go at it? You can buy stuff nowadays, powder like, no water, no mess,' replied Florrie, as she examined part of it with a critical eye. 'As I was saying, mum, 'e was a real gent, bought me three stout 'e did. Now, as you well know, mum, I'm not a drinker but I do like my bottle of stout, perhaps two if I'm feeling a bit frivolous – but never three, mum.'

187

'Florrie, were you serious about that powder? Do you really think it would do the job...? I suppose we could try a small piece – that, over by the door, is by far the worst.'

'I 'ad to laugh on the bus going 'ome. If my Alf got know, 'e'd be furious – mind you, mum, 'e never buys me a stout, not 'im, mean old skinflint that 'e is. Not that 'e need 'ave worried, mum, the feller reminded me of a ferret, yer know all sharp features, and another thing I've never been attracted to small men. Now Alf...'

'There you are, Charlie. Any luck – did you manage to mend it?'

'No, the firing pin is broken, but I know a gunsmith in Dagenham who may be able to fix it.'

'Does it matter?'

'It does to me.'

'Yer know, mum, I think 'e fancied me. Some men like the fuller figure, as Alf always says, more to get hold of.' With that, Florrie's whole body, beginning with her podgy face, began to shake with laughter.

'Florrie,' said Janice, responding finally to the event so succinctly described by Florrie, 'I'm surprised at you.'

'Well you know, mum, you're never too old,' laughter again not far away. Charlie, having recovered his Tolstoy from the book-shelf, sat down on the nearest seat.

'I hope you're not intending to sit there for the rest of the morning. Florrie and I are cleaning in here.'

'I wonder if 'e'll turn up tonight, 'e said he would.'

'What's this all about?' enquired Charlie, looking up whilst wiping his nose with a large handkerchief.

'It's nothing, Florrie's made a conquest, that's all ... have you got a cold, Charlie?'

'Oh, mum, you are a card ... but if 'e keeps the stout coming, who knows?'

Charlie put the book down. 'Who's buying you stout then, Florrie?' before sneezing heavily into the, by now, limp handker-chief.

'It's someone she met in her local ... Charlie, I suggest you take a Beechams before that gets a hold of you.'

'Well?' said Charlie, looking at Janice as Florrie left the room.

'Charlie, it's nothing, just some man she met in the pub who bought her a couple of stouts – seems it made her night ... now about that Beechams?'

'Did she describe him?'

'Said he was small and reminded her of a ferret.'

'It wasn't Sternov, then,' said Charlie, more or less to himself.

'Sternov, who's Sternov?'

'Their new KGB man.'

'You know, Charlie, I think you're beginning to get paranoid about this business. he was obviously some silly old fool who took a fancy to her, there's nothing in it.'

'Janice, have you looked at Florrie lately? She must be all of fourteen stone ... now, if it were Marlene, I could understand it.'

'Charlie, you're chasing shadows.'

'Pray you're right, Janice.'

*　　*　　*

'You will adore *Swan Lake*, Natasha,' said Janice, the day after her words with Charlie. 'In so many ways it is a reflection of your own life. Have you heard of Tchaikovsky? He is one of your country's greatest composers, you're in a for a treat. Just wait until you see the ballroom scene, it's breathtaking.'

'I hope it isn't sad, the ending I mean.'

Both she and Janice, ably assisted by Florrie, were busily picking what few flowers were still in bloom in Janice's extensive garden.

'Is it sad, Florrie?' said Natasha, as she transferred her collection to Florrie's flower basket.

'No good asking me, love, it's way over my 'ead, I much prefer a good thriller, you know with blood everywhere. When are you going?'

189

'Friday night ... I'm so excited! I've never been to anything like that before in my whole life.'

'Well, I hope you enjoy it, but as I said, I'm afraid it would be a bit too highbrow for me.'

'I think it's about to rain,' said Janice, as she strolled over to them. 'And in any case,' looking at the basket, 'I think we've enough.' Then, as she moved with the other two into the kitchen, 'Collect the vases up, Florrie, we'll have just about enough for the downstairs rooms.' Florrie, with Natasha in tow, went to do her bidding. As they left the kitchen, Charlie entered.

'I must say, Charlie, you haven't been your scintillating self these last couple of days. Much more, and a girl could go off you.'

'It's this cold – and I'm not happy about the trip to Covent Garden.'

'Surely you're not still on about that? You're like a dog with a bone, Charlie, really you are. In any case, there's no way I can let her down, she's still talking of nothing else – in the garden just now she was asking questions ...'

He cut in, 'Talking about it in the garden – why don't you shout it from the house tops, let the bloody world know.'

'Och, you have got one on.'

'Janice, you've known all along I've been against it. Why, for heaven's sake, take unnecessary risks?'

'Charlie, for once–'

He interrupted her again. 'I know, I know, you're putting your foot down. Did I ever tell you about the siege of Madrid?'

'No, but you're about to,' she said dryly.

'Franco was at the gates, do you know what he said?'

'Well, as I wasn't there ...'

'He said, "I've four columns outside the city and a fifth column inside."'

'So?'

'As then, Janice, it's the fifth column that worries me ...'

20

The Snatch

The steady drip drip of the rain water as it overflowed from the downpipe onto the patio's stone floor did little to soothe Charlie's nerves and seemed to him to be the perfect illustration of his own heavy cold. Blowing heavily into a tissue, he peered through a chink in the curtains at Janice's rain-sodden garden and made a mental note to allow an extra half an hour when he went to collect them from Covent Garden. It was a night, he thought, when God himself would have pondered twice before venturing forth in search of lost souls.

Again he looked at his watch and, with the need for the additional time, worked out how long his journey would take. It was at that moment the telephone rang, its strident note magnified by the prevailing stillness of the room.

'Charlie Tuttle?' It was a voice he recognised but could not put a name to.

'Speaking.'

'Just a quiet word in your ear, Charlie. Something is on tonight but we don't know what.'

Charlie, utterly taken aback, was about to ask who was speaking when the click told him whoever it was had hung up. It was then, as if on cue, a roll of thunder shook the house and the drip, drip, drip, so infuriating earlier, transformed itself into a deluge. Through the mist of concern his mind had become, the name of the caller came to him like a douche of the ice cold water now rampaging outside. It was Teddy Farrar ... no time to weigh up the whys and wherefores. It was a tip-off, almost certainly genuine, and for Natasha's sake, not his.

* * *

For Janice, the music of *Swan Lake*, particularly the waltz and the violin solo in the *andante*, were as enjoyable as the ballet. But her greatest pleasure was in watching Natasha's reactions which, as the scenes and music changed, went through the full range of expressions: from deep solemnity to sheer delight bordering on ecstasy. She was right to have brought her; never, she thought, had Tchaikovsky been so appreciated – and by one of his own. She savoured the triumph she would experience when she got home and told Charlie how right she had been.

Emerging from the brightness and warmth of the theatre, they were confronted by scenes of chaos. The rain, whipped up by a violent and relentless wind, had reduced what, but a few minutes before, had been a regulated and cosseted collection of people into a mass of struggling individual groups, each striving to obtain protection from the elements. Like sheep on a hillside they huddled together, as if, by doing so, their nearness to each other would somehow provide shelter from the raging storm.

The inevitable queue of cars developed, their brilliant lights revealing the all-engulfing curtain of rain. Janice, holding Natasha's arm, squinted into the harsh glare of headlights, desperately seeking their car and, with it, the reassurance and security of Charlie. It was then, above the shattering noise of the storm, she heard the screaming and with it, clearly and distinctly, her name being called. Tentatively she looked across in the direction of the sound, and saw a small group of people standing over a body writhing on the pavement. Again she heard the cry, 'Janice...' Releasing Natasha's arm, she walked hesitantly towards the scene of the commotion, but when she had taken but half a dozen steps, some sixth sense caused her to stop and turn back to Natasha, now

192

standing alone on the edge of the kerb. A black car, its bonnet a glittering wetness in the headlights of other cars, had stopped immediately beside her, its rear door open. Janice watched stupefied as two arms emerged and enveloped Natasha. Their embrace was of such force as to all but lift her off her feet and, as a consequence, devoid of balance, she assisted rather than hindered as the arms, now secure in their purchase, dragged her into the car.

With Janice's high-pitched screams of 'No' whisked away on the wind, the car, as if propelled by some hidden force, accelerated away from her and, cutting out from the line of slowly moving cars, moved to the centre of the road, narrowly missing a taxi in the process. Continuing to scream, Janice ran along the edge of the pavement and, for one brief moment, caught a glimpse of Natasha's face through the rear window. A face of beseeching intensity, before a gloved hand holding something white covered the face and it disappeared from view. Then it was only the tail lights of the car, soon impossible to follow, as they mingled with countless others before they too disappeared from view into the maze of London's traffic.

Motionless, Janice stood by the side of the road; the rain, having penetrated her thin coat, now soaked her skin with its icy touch. Faceless people, some grouped together under umbrellas, stopped and stared at her before moving on. Looking back, still unbelieving, Janice saw a tiny evening shoe lying where the car had stopped, its earlier shiny newness and bright gold braid now reduced to a pitiful sodden remnant of its past elegance.

Her car drew up, a door opened and an ashen-faced Charlie leant across.

'Get in,' he said, in a voice she barely recognised. Sinking back into the cushions, it was as if a dam had burst as she broke into uncontrollable sobbing.

'You can cut that out,' he said brutally. By a masterful effort of self-control, she clawed her way back to something approaching normality.

'Charlie, why are we turning?' she asked. 'The car's in front of us.'

'Was, you mean . . . in any case, I know where it's going.'

'Where, Charlie?'

'The Soviet Embassy, Hyde Park Gate.'

'Oh dear God, no.'

*   *   *

'Right,' said Charlie, as soon as they arrived home, 'upstairs with you and into a hot bath, then we'll talk – in the meantime I'll see to the fire.'

Without a word, Janice slowly climbed the stairs. No delightful innuendo this time, he mused; she would need all of his cheerful optimism to get over this, and, he had to admit, that was one commodity in rather short supply at the moment. He had, he knew, been very hard on her in the car and, being frank with himself, he wondered whether the outcome would have been so different had he been with them.

What had happened had been the classic snatch, perfected decades ago in the days of the Chicago mobsters, prohibition and the likes of Al Capone. If they hadn't taken her tonight, he guessed, persistence eventually would have had its reward – after all, he couldn't possibly have watched over her day and night. In every respect they had had the advantage. For them it was merely a case of picking the right time and place, and again, he had to admit, they had certainly done that.

Sitting in a comfortable armchair and gazing into the roaring fire with his mind full of the disaster, he hardly noticed Janice join him.

'Where to now, Charlie?' she said, her voice little above a whisper. 'In any case, she's probably dead already.'

'If I'm certain of anything, Janice, it's that she is still alive and probably will be for some time to come.'

Huddled in her dressing gown and with her legs tucked under her, Charlie thought how small she looked and how vulnerable.

When, however, he had offered his opinion that Natasha was still alive, a change had come over her. Once gain that determined look he had got so used to, shone through in her eyes.

'Charlie, do you really think so? You're not just saying that.'

'Sternov is an ex-colonel in the Red Army. He will do everything by the book, it's what is known as discipline. If his orders are to bring her back to Moscow, that's exactly what he will try to do. I suspect they will have drugged her, but killed her? No.

'Now, Janice, I want you to clear your mind of everything else except what happened tonight. I want you to go over it bit by bit, every movement you made and, in particular, everything you saw. So, away you go.'

'The oldest trick in the world,' he said, when she reached the point of hearing her name being called. 'It's called a diversion, to take your attention. You have to hand it to them; their timing was inch-perfect.' And he added, as an afterthought, 'The weather was on their side, too.'

'You mean they planned it that thoroughly,' she exclaimed unbelievingly.

'Yes, based on information they had secured from Florrie's friends, the ferret.'

'Oh, God, Charlie, she must never know, poor old thing, she meant no harm.'

'Ninety per cent of the time they never do – but remember what I said about the Fifth Column?'

'What are we going to do?'

'Get her back, of course.'

'Charlie, how?'

'Well, to begin with you're going to bed.'

'And you?'

'I've got a delivery of milk to do and, like all good milkmen, I've got an early start, so away with you.'

'No way, whatever you're intending to do I am going along with you, and this time, Charlie Tuttle, I am really putting my foot down.'

195

'From here,' he said, laughing for the first time that night, 'you've certainly got a pretty foot, and certainly well worth putting down.'

* * *

'Janice, when we get close to Hyde Park Gate, watch out for a milk float.'

'You're not going to shoot someone, are you, Charlie?' said Janice, an undercurrent of nervousness in her voice.

'Hopefully, that won't be necessary,' then, looking across the road, 'the very thing, Uniform Dairies, pull up alongside him.'

'Good morning,' said Charlie, as they drew up level with the float, 'may I have a word?'

'What's up, guv – are you lost?' came the reply from a figure who, with black oilskins done up to the neck complete with hood, resembled more some medieval monk than a milk roundsman.

'Are you interested in earning a hundred pounds?' said Charlie, having stepped from the car.

'A hundred nicker, you must be joking! What's the catch?'

'No catch, I just want to borrow your float for a few minutes and make a delivery – it's for a bet – you do deliver to the Soviet Embassy, don't you?'

'I do.'

'Well then?'

'No funny business?'

'Good Lord, no, in fact my wife,' nodding in the direction of Janice, still sitting in the car, 'will stay with you. Here's fifty pounds and another fifty when I come back.

'On one condition,' said the roundsman, warily. 'I sit in the float with you.'

'All right, but only I make the delivery.'

'Done.'

Just inside the doorway was the expected security guard – his open mouth and crumpled uniform testimony, as he lolled back in his chair, to the rigours of watch-keeping. Charlie smiled, he was in luck, but such luck was tempered in the knowledge that within the sentry's reach was an AK47 assault rifle. Placing four bottles of milk gently on the floor, he moved quickly along a passageway with attendant doors either side. Breathing heavily he stopped at a junction; which way, he pondered. It was at that moment the wrath of the guard could be heard. Charlie, impervious to the shouting, kept going.

Disappointingly, every door he tried was locked. Reaching the end of a passageway he was about to try another, leading off at right angles, when a voice in thick Russian spoke from behind him.

'Move another inch and I'll blow your head off.'

Charlie turned and faced a huge man clad in a black stormcoat which reached almost to his ankles. The gun, inches from his head, he quickly identified as a Mauser automatic pistol. Studying the man again, it occurred to Charlie that here was the epitome of a Hollywood secret agent, only this was no film, and the gun held unwaveringly at his head was real.

'Alexis Sternov, I believe?' said Charlie in a friendly tone.

The man neither agreed nor disagreed but replied, 'You are?'

'Charlie Tuttle . . . rhymes with scuttle.'

The man seemed unimpressed and, lowering the gun, said as a statement of fact, 'You shot Derevenko.'

'He needed shooting,' replied Charlie.

'Then we have something in common, because if you hadn't I would have.'

Warmed by this apparent understanding, Charlie grew more confident.

'Can we talk . . . somewhere private?' he ventured.

'In here.' The man opened the door at right angles to the passage, the door, Charlie surmised, that Sternov had emerged from but a few moments before.

'You *are* Alexis Sternov?' repeated Charlie, once inside the room.

'I am.'

'Good, I want to talk to you about the girl.'

'What girl?' A pause then, 'I'll have that gun inside your breast pocket . . . now.'

Charlie handed over his Luger butt first. Placing Charlie's gun on a side table, Sternov added the Mauser alongside it.

'That's better, said Charlie, 'one doesn't converse well with a gun at one's head.' At that moment the sentry rushed in.

'Is everything all right, Comrade Colonel?'

'Fine, you can leave us, but report back to me in thirty minutes.'

The watchman, with a questioning look at Charlie, quickly left the room.

Sternov, in the meantime, walked over to a wall cupboard.

'You like vodka?'

'Never drink anything else when in Russia,' replied Charlie, attempting to inject some humour into the situation. His reward was a deep-throated chuckle.

'You English,' he said, as he filled two glasses, 'are so predictable – not like your weather.' Turning and facing Charlie, 'I quite expected something like this.'

'Then you admit she's here . . . listen, Sternov, she knows nothing about the Romanov gold. Now I do, and I am prepared to tell you all I know in exchange for her.'

'In exchange for a common gypsy girl? Because that's all she is, someone lower than a kulak.' This was accompanied with a smile, the smile of a poker player who knows he holds all the aces.

'I'm prepared to trade, Sternov, even on your terms,' repeated Charlie, already aware of how sparse his trade goods were.

'But she does know where the gold is, otherwise you wouldn't be here.'

Charlie looked at his adversary helplessly. 'You admit she's here,' he said, doggedly trying again.

'Russia is a big place, my friend.' Again the smile. 'And may I remind you, Tuttle, that here you're as much in Russia as if you were standing on the steps of the Kremlin itself.' The implicit threat was not lost Charlie. Sternov continued, 'I like you, comrade, and because it took courage to come in here I will give you a tip: go back to your milk round.' With that he picked up the Luger and expertly removed the magazine, then, using his thumb as a lever, he flipped its shells from their housing on to the floor before handing the gun back to Charlie.

'Go and deliver your milk,' he said, with a noticeable twinkle in his eyes, as he opened the room door.

'What about the girl?' said Charlie desperately.

'She is well.'

'You're not just saying that?'

'You have my word.'

'Thank you for that, Sternov,' said Charlie, surprised to find warmth entering his voice.

'Until we meet again, comrade,' said Sternov, holding out his hand.

'Until we meet again,' replied Charlie, accepting the offer. It was only when he got outside that Charlie realised he hadn't drunk his vodka.

* * *

Slowly he walked across the road to his waiting car, the milk float and an anxious looking milkman.

'Did you get the money?' said the roundsman, 'they always pay on a Saturday.'

'No I bloody didn't,' said Charlie as he drew level with him.

'Fine milkman you turned out to be, mate ... yer see, it's not such a straightforward job as people think.'

'I'm sure you may well be right,' said Charlie, handing him his fifty pounds.

'I'm 'ere every Saturday, guv, if you want to try again,' he said, as he struggled to find his pocket hidden within layers of clothing.

'I somehow don't think that will be necessary,' said Charlie, as he opened the car door.

Then as the float began to trundle down the road, the cheerful recipient of the hundred pounds waved a farewell, his parting words, carried on the wind to a despairing Charlie, accompanied by loud laughter. 'A hundred quid – and it's not Christmas until next week!'

Fascinated, Charlie watched as the float made an erratic course across the road in the direction of the Embassy, its veering from side to side testimony to the delirious mood of its driver. He was tempted to watch the reception the gleeful milkman was sure to receive at the Embassy entrance, but having looked across at Janice's irate face, decided enough was enough.

'I've just realised something,' he said, ignoring her question, 'when he emptied the magazine, there was still a round in the chamber...' mumbling to himself, he pulled the gun from his inside pocket and examined it, then pointing it out of the window he gently cocked it – sure enough, a round appeared, bright and shiny.

'I must be getting old, Janice, what a fool I've been, I might have got her out after all.'

'I don't know what you're on about,' she said as she turned the car, 'it's all double Dutch to me. One thing I do know is that she's still in there, and it looks like that's where she is staying – why don't you admit it's hopeless?' She paused. 'I don't think I've ever been so tired in my life or so utterly depressed.'

'No point in talking like that. Yes, I'll agree, they've been very clever, but snatching her was the easy part – they've still got to get her out of the country – that, Janice, will be a great deal harder.'

'In what way?' her voice reflected a slight change of mood.

'Firstly, there are only two direct flights to Moscow each week, they wouldn't risk anything but a non-stop flight. Secondly, she won't go willingly, so they will have to conceal her in some way. Thirdly, unlike when they snatched her, they can't pick their time, they will be governed by the flight times. As a consequence of that, not all the cards are in their hands.'

'How do you know there are only two flights a week?'

'Because I've taken the trouble to find out.'

'You make it sound like a game, Charlie, instead a matter of life or death for poor Natasha.' The irritation in her voice was obvious to him.

'In some ways it is a game. All right, they've won the first hand, but there's a long way to go yet.'

The rest of their journey was spent in silence, Charlie still retaining his measure of optimism, whilst Janice sank ever deeper into an abyss of despair.

'Why not ring the police?' she ventured, as they entered the hallway.

'Won't do the slightest good. By the time British justice grinds into action, she'll be back in Moscow.'

'Then I'm going to ring Daddy and see what he can do.'

'All you'll get will be a load of platitudes; it won't do any good, believe me.'

'It's better than doing nothing.'

'Curiously, I found myself liking him.'

'Liking who?' she said as she dialled.

'Sternov.'

'God preserve us, you're not going soft on me are you, Charlie?' But Charlie was already halfway up the stairs.

21

A Call to Arms

It was the morning after Charlie's abortive attempt to free
Natasha. Alone in the kitchen, he contemplated the future over a
large mug of coffee, glad of the opportunity to be alone with his
thoughts – thoughts which seemed only to act as mirrors of his
utter despair.

'So you couldn't sleep either?' was her opening remark as
Janice, swathed in a dressing gown, joined him.

'There's coffee in the pot,' he replied, ignoring her question.
Helping herself to a generous mug-ful, she joined him at the
table.

'Charlie...?'

'Not now, Janice, just leave it.'

With both her hands wrapped round the mug, Janice surveyed
him. 'How are the mighty fallen – so, you're giving up on
Natasha, then? Leaving her to whatever fate has in store for
her.'

'I didn't say that.'

'Well, what else am I to think?'

'I'm working on it.'

'You're going to have to come up with something – and soon, if
you want my opinion.'

'What help did your father offer?' he said as his eyes met hers
for the first time.

'As you forecast, just a load of platitudes – I loathe it when he

202

talks down to me.' Silence followed, then, 'Charlie, will you be absolutely honest with me?'

'Haven't I always been?'

'Well, yes, but you do tend to lean on the optimistic sometimes ... Charlie?'

'Now what?'

'Do you really know where the gold is hidden?'

'In one word, no. But someone does, and it's that fact which is worrying me.'

'I don't follow.'

'Simple ... why bury something in the first place?'

'Go on.'

'So that, when the coast is clear, you can go back for it. Someone, probably close to the Duchess, has been biding their time with the view of doing just that.'

'How does all this help Natasha?'

'Because, Janice, I am more and more certain there is a silent player in all of this and has been for some time.' Janice, eyes uplifted to the ceiling, seemed to be in an act of meditation as Charlie continued. 'It has to be someone who was close to the Romanovs – very close.'

'And alive,' added Janice, recovering from her reverie.

'Exactly.'

'But, Charlie, that's all very well, but what about Natasha?'

'I haven't told you before, but I received a tip-off last night, I think it was Farrar, Rupert's Number One. I intend getting back to him and see what more he can tell me.'

'Oh, Charlie, do, and quickly.'

'It's too early, first thing after breakfast – what do they say about the early bird ...?'

* * *

'Thank you for that, Farrar.'

'For what, Tuttle?'

'Last night, the tip-off.'

203

'It wasn't for you, it was for the girl.'

'Whatever, they got her just the same.' Silence followed, then, 'Anyway, Farrar, may I speak to Sir Rupert?'

'He's away in Scotland, won't be back before the New Year.'

'Then you're her only hope.' Again silence.

'What do you want to do? Invite the Foreign Office to send a note of protest? Please, one of your agents has kidnapped a Soviet citizen, may we have her back?' Captain Farrar's voice was the embodiment of sarcasm.

'Surely there is something you can do?'

'Listen, Tuttle, you went into this with your eyes wide open, now things have gone wrong, you want me to bale you out. Yes, possibly a note of protest could be sent through channels. That itself would take at least a week – with the Christmas recess coming up, even longer. By then it will all be over and she'll be back in Moscow.'

'Farrar, something has to be done.'

'I gather they're holding her in their Embassy?'

'If I'm sure of anything, I'm sure of that,' replied Charlie.

'Well, short of sending in the SAS, I don't know what,' came the reply. Then, 'Listen, Tuttle, much against my better judgement...'

'Yes, I know, for the sake of the girl,' Charlie commented dryly.

'Quite. As I was about to say, you can have a few words with Richard Barstairs. He's been tailing Sternov for the past few days. I'll put him on.'

Janice, with a questioning look in her eyes, was standing alongside Charlie in her hallway. Leaning across, he whispered, 'I think we may be getting some help,' then, as she was about to say something, Charlie put his finger to his lips.

'Richard Barstairs speaking.'

'Barstairs, you know the form, is there anything you can tell me that might help?'

Barstairs came straight to the point.

'Sternov made two visits to an undertakers in Kensington. I

have their name – Peace and Serenity, they're in Old Church Road, upper-crust firm, you know the sort of thing, very select.'

'Anything else?'

'Sorry, Tuttle, nothing of any significance, all mundane stuff. I'll put Captain Farrar back on.'

'Now, Tuttle, I really have to get on with some work . . .'

'One final question, Farrar, why an undertakers?'

'Of course, you wouldn't know, Derevenko's body is being flown home. The Home Office has given permission. Now, hold on a minute, I'll give you what detail we have. Yes, here it is – next Wednesday, Aeroflot Flight 162, direct to Moscow from Heathrow, ETD 2100.'

'Thank you for that, Farrar.'

'And Tuttle . . .'

'Yes?'

'Good luck.'

'Well?' said Janice, as he replaced the receiver to its rest. For a few moments he ignored her, a faraway look in his eyes.

'I'm not sure,' he said quietly. 'It may mean nothing, but it could mean everything. Anyway, it appears we're going to have to call on a firm of undertakers. In the meantime, give George and Hilda a ring. I've a gut feeling they may come in useful shortly.'

'Yes, sir,' said Janice, rising to her feet, 'anything is better than just sitting here. Oh, by the way, two letters arrived this morning for Natasha. I've taken the liberty of opening them – would you believe she's come into some money? Twenty thousand to be exact, left in the will of poor old Polski . . .' He interrupted her.

'You mean Poznansky.'

'Well, I cannot get used to these Russian names. Anyway, they say, subject to probate, that's what he's left her, plus some accrued interest.'

'So, he didn't forget her after all, dear old Sergei. Mind you, it was not his money. It came from the Duchess . . . and the other letter?'

Taking it out of its envelope, she read it aloud to him.

'An invitation from none other than Prince Michael, heir pre-sumptive to the throne of the Romanovs, to join him at a weekend house party on the fifteenth of January, nineteen hundred and sixty four. Wow, they're even going to send a car to collect her! Charlie, we've got to get her back, she would be over the moon if she knew about this.'

'Janice, in the words of someone I cannot for the life of me remember, I have only just begun to fight! And another thing, I believe I know how they are planning to get her out of the country – ingenious, but then not so ingenious because I've guessed it.'

*   *   *

'Chief, Teddy here.'

'Yes, Teddy, I trust it's important, remember I said no calls unless it was imperative.'

'I thought you ought to know. Sternov's got the girl.'

'When did this happen?'

'Last night.'

'Charlie must be slipping . . .'

Captain Farrar broke in on him. 'He wasn't with her at the time. Barstairs says it was planned to a T, all over in seconds.'

'Well, I always knew Sternov was no slouch.'

'That's not all, Tuttle was on the line a few minutes ago, beg-ging for help.'

'No way, Teddy, at least not yet, it may well turn out to our advantage. I'll be back in London Tuesday, in the meantime don't forget a report to the Home Secretary coded "Romanov".'

'There's something else, sir. I wouldn't have bothered you with it, but . . .'

'Spit it out, man.'

'Sir Humphrey Charters is raising Cain, demanding answers to questions. Chief Inspector Reynolds doesn't think he can hold him off much longer.'

'That old goat.'

'Old goat he might be, sir, but he's a powerful old goat.'

'Granted. Include it in your report to the HS. Anything else?'

'Nothing that won't wait.'

'Right then, I'll see you Tuesday ... oh, Teddy, any problems with our friend, pull him in – the elastic has finally run out.'

'Will do, sir.'

The keenness in Teddy's voice, thought Sir Rupert, as he put the phone down, boded ill for Charlie Tuttle.

*   *   *

Charlie Tuttle, wearing the grey livery of a chauffeur, sat idly turning the pages of a sombre-coloured brochure, its design and content intended to convince readers that Peace and Serenity conducted funerals with grace, compassion and humility – allied, as frequently mentioned, with the expertise of over one hundred years' experience. On the glass-topped table in front of him, miniature coffins, called caskets in the brochure, of varying size and grandeur, had names such as Tranquillity, Peace and Remembrance etched in copperplate writing on their sides. Surrounding him was the muted sound of a lone flute and pervading everything a sweet perfume reminiscent, Charlie recalled, of the hothouse at Kew Gardens.

Sitting opposite him, attired in black with a veil that reached to her waist, was Hilda Fawcett. The requirement to adopt a suitable grieving expression had presented no difficulty for Hilda. It was, after all, but a reflection of her permanent disposition. Charlie, noticing the opening of a door at the far end of the room, gave Hilda a surreptitious wink, as a man, dressed in a black morning suit, approached them, making no sound as he walked across the thickly carpeted room.

'Mr Henry de Witt will see you now,' he whispered, this accompanied with a low bow in Hilda's direction.

Mr de Witt rose from behind his desk as Charlie and Hilda were ushered into the room by Black Morning Dress.

'Do sit down,' purred Mr De Witt, as their guide positioned two chairs, a quite unnecessary procedure, as Charlie remained standing.

'May I present,' commented Charlie, 'the Grand Duchess Rodzinski,' indicating the, by now, seated Hilda. 'The Grand Duchess speaks only a little English,' he continued, 'so I have been instructed to represent her wishes.'

'Of course, of course,' Mr de Witt continued to purr, 'I see the Duchess is in mourning.'

'Yes,' replied Charlie, 'for her brother, the late Mr Mikhael Derevenko.'

Charlie cleared his throat whilst Hilda, acting on the cue of 'brother', produced a white lace handkerchief and, as it fluttered like a caged bird from behind her veil, began extravagantly dabbing her eyes. Pausing for a few moments to allow this single expression of grief to be digested by Mr de Witt, Charlie continued.

'His Excellency the Soviet Ambassador has informed the Grand Duchess that the funeral arrangements for Mr Mikhael Derevenko are being conducted by Peace and Serenity.'

'That is so,' replied Mr de Witt, his face now assuming an expression of deep humility and sadness.

'The Grand Duchess Rodzinski is horrified,' (at this point Hilda made even more extravagant gestures from behind her veil), 'that no blessing has been arranged prior to the body being returned to Moscow for burial, and the Grand Duchess would appreciate a few moments of contemplation alone with her brother.'

'But surely, hasn't Mr Sternov explained matters to the Duchess, the body is not here, it is at the Soviet Embassy.'

'Regrettably,' replied Charlie, his tone of voice implying that the mere mention of the name Sternov was beyond the pale, 'the Duchess is aware of that but is not in agreement with it. You see, the Grand Duchess Rodzinski does not recognise his side of the family.'

'I quite understand,' came the soulful reply.

208

'Therefore,' continued Charlie, warming to his task, 'the Grand Duchess is prepared to meet any additional costs involved whereby the cortège, on its journey to Heathrow, stops at the Russian Orthodox Church, 67 Ennismore Gardens, SW7 to permit a short blessing and to allow the Duchess the opportunity of bidding farewell.'

Mr de Witt selected a grey folder from several others scattered on his desk. Then, with something of a flourish, he rearranged the glasses perched on the bridge of his nose. Speaking softly, he began, 'Ah, I have the itinerary here. The late Mr Derevenko...' this brought about a suitable wail of anguish from Hilda, which gave Charlie a few moments of trepidation. There was such a thing, he thought, as overplaying one's part. Mr de Witt, with what passed as a sympathetic smile in the direction of Hilda, continued. 'As I was saying, the late Mr Derevenko will join Aeroflot, Flight 162, departing Heathrow at nine p.m. this coming Wednesday. Our instructions are to collect the deceased from the Embassy at six p.m. And,' here Mr de Witt closed the folder with a gesture of finality, 'we have special dispensation, granted by the Home Office, for the casket to be sealed within the Embassy by a customs official. This will permit the minimum of delay at Heathrow. Therefore, for any short service at the Russian Orthodox Church the casket will have to remain closed, perhaps you would explain this to the Duchess.'

Charlie in faultless Russian explained it all to Hilda, who, by way of reply, spoke rapidly in what little Russian Charlie had managed to teach her. This, were it translated, would have bemused Mr de Witt as it merely said, '*Good morning, I think we are going to have some snow.*' Fortunately for both Charlie and Hilda, Mr de Witt did not speak Russian.

'The Grand Duchess has noted that your charges are in guineas. She has, therefore, instructed me to initially offer one hundred guineas for this service, which she will pay now, and a further one hundred guineas on completion. That is, Mr de Witt, conditional on Mr Sternov not being informed of this arrangement.'

'Do assure the Grand Duchess Rodzinski that Peace and Serenity are frequently requested to observe discretion in these matters, and her wishes will be respected. For my part, I must insist that any delay in Clapham is kept to a minimum – say twenty minutes?'

'That should be ample,' replied Charlie.

With the formalities concluded, Charlie and Hilda, suitably ushered out by Morning Dress, stepped into the cold drizzle of a bleak December day.

'Well done, Hilda,' said Charlie as George's vintage Rolls drew up alongside them.

'Yes,' replied Hilda, 'but do you think it offers any hope?'

'Put it this way, our chances of getting her back have increased tenfold in the past hour.'

'Pray God you're right,' said Hilda as she slid into the car beside Big George.

*   *   *

As Charlie surveyed the group seated in Hilda's drawing room, each avidly listening to his plan, he knew he was putting Natasha's future in the hands of amateurs. Dedicated amateurs, to be sure, in their desire to rescue her, but amateurs nonetheless. They were, he knew, up against the best in Sternov, and that apart, he was constantly beset by doubt – supposing his hunch was wrong? If that were the case, it would be all up with Natasha. He looked again at the group, their willingness and dedication all too obvious as, with their rapt attention, he went over the plan yet again.

'Remember, George, the pantechnicon must be in the right position at the corner of Swallow Drive. I cannot emphasise enough how vital it is that their back-up car is taken out. Any questions, George?'

'No questions – if need be I'll fling myself in front of it...'

'Stop being so dramatic, George,' said Hilda, interrupting him. 'This operation reminds me of a recent spy story I read, *The Four Chessmen* it was called...'

Charlie adroitly intervened, 'Quite, Hilda, but I do assure you there is no need for George to fling himself in front of anything.' Hilda made no attempt to hide her disappointment.

'Janice, you know how vital it is that you draw off at least two of the bearers once we're inside the church?'

'Don't worry, Charlie, in the get-up I'm planning to wear I could probably inveigle the priest himself outside.'

'I have to admit,' smiled Charlie, 'that the broken-down car and the stranded maiden in distress, as ploys go, is as old as the hills, but it rarely fails.'

'Now, Hilda, as I go to work on the coffin I want plenty of wails from you, anything to cause a distraction.'

'No worries there, Charlie, being married to George all these years has given me plenty of practice.'

'Charlie,' said Janice, 'opening the coffin will mean breaking the customs seals, won't it?'

'I'm afraid so, but we've no choice.'

'That in itself is a criminal offence, surely?'

'No question,' boomed George, 'once those seals are in place it's what they call bonded. I only hope you're right, Charlie, and she is in there . . .'

*   *   *

In his backroom at the Embassy, Sternov stretched his ample frame and lumbered across the room to answer the phone.

'Sternov here.'

'Mr de Witt, Mr Sternov, Peace and Serenity. As you suggested, we have done some checking.'

'Well?'

'You were right in your assumption. The Grand Duchess is a fraud.'

'As I suspected,' said Sternov, allowing himself a thin smile.

'Do you wish us to ignore her request?' Sternov hesitated, his attention drawn to his room companion, the bluebottle, who by now thoroughly familiar with most of its surroundings, had decided to explore the furthest high corner of the room. Within seconds it was enmeshed within the coils of a silken web, its loud incessant buzzing witness to its distress.

'Are you there, Mr Sternov?' the resonant tone of Mr de Witt was totally at variance with his normal quiet voice.

Sternov was about to reply when a movement, just beyond the struggling fly caught his eye, as the owner of the web descended his shiny stairway and quickly enveloped the luckless bluebottle in ever more strands of sticky restraints.

'No, Mr de Witt,' said Sternov, 'leave things as they are.' Then, as he slowly returned the phone to its rest the desperate buzzing of the captured fly reached a crescendo, only to suddenly cease. Looking up, all Sternov saw of the once energetic and exploratory bluebottle was a shrouded black blob hanging from endless tentacles of gossamer threads. As he returned to his bed, Sternov stretched himself to his fullest extent and then, for no apparent reason, began to sing. It was a song the few who had survived Stalingrad would have immediately recognised, for it was the Song of Victory.

22

Nemesis

As the moment of truth approached, Charlie was beset with feelings of dread. What if he was wrong...? Walking towards the coffin, now reposing on a low altar in front of him, he knew that failure would ensure his present and future becoming one meaningless entity, and all his assurances to those who had put their trust in him would have been but empty vessels.

Why was it, he wondered, that places of worship held him in awe and seemed intent on draining him of his self-belief...? Was it the same with other men, he wondered – were their innermost thoughts like his at this time, overcome in the knowledge that something empyreal was present and that they, too, were but mere mortals subject to the dictates of an all-powerful but invisible being?

Recovering his composure and dismissing those dark doubts to the back of his mind, he approached the coffin. So far, he mused, the plan had worked like a charm – the back-up car following the hearse had, as intended, become ensnared in a melee of vehicles, their drivers venting their frustration in a cacophony of sound, leaving only Mr de Witt and his bearers to be dealt with.

Behind him walked Hilda, outwardly immune to his diverse theological thoughts and clutching, as if her life depended on it, the toolbox. On reaching the coffin, he turned and gave her a smile that was intended to boost her confidence, knowing, as he did so, that it was his own confidence that had, with each step, been draining away.

Scrutiny of the coffin's lid established there were ten screws, three each side and two at each end. The screws at the head and rear were each tagged with a customs seal. Its black lettering, beneath the insignia of the crown, left him in no doubt of the seriousness of what he was about to do.

He leant across the coffin to collect a screwdriver from Hilda, but, keen though he was to begin the task, a sound to his right caused him to look up. Standing motionless a foot away was a priest, his heavy habit and high hat as black as pitch, relieved only by a gold neck chain from which hung a massive metal cross. To his left were Mr de Witt's four bearers.

In an offhand voice, which to him seemed the quintessence of nervousness, Charlie said, 'Just opening the coffin for you to give a blessing, Father.'

If the priest replied at all, Charlie didn't hear him, as a commotion away to his right immediately took his attention. The clear voice of Colonel Sir Rupert de Quincy echoed hollowly within the confines of the church.

'All right, Charlie, that's enough. This time you've gone a bridge too far.'

Emerging from a small doorway were Sir Rupert, Captain Farrar and a police constable. Charlie froze; already two screws had been removed, and the process was proving a lot easier than he had expected. Turning away from his task, he confronted the trio now but yards away. As he drew his Luger, the feel of it in the palm of his hand seemed to instantly banish all his earlier fears.

'Don't make me use this, Rupert, I will if I have to . . .'

'You are only making matters worse, Charlie. Give me the gun and put an end to this nonsense.'

With that, Sir Rupert took a step forward. It was then that Janice, entering the church for the first time, took a hand in matters. Precariously balanced on her ridiculously high heels she ran up to Charlie, and said breathlessly, 'Give me the gun, Charlie – you deal with the coffin.'

Without a word, Charlie passed her the Luger.

'Mrs Webster, I believe,' said Sir Rupert, his words measured. 'I hope you know the gravity of what you're doing?'

Teddy Farrar, quiet until now, couldn't resist adding, 'This time, Tuttle, they'll lock you up and forget where they've put the key.'

Charlie, calm at last, started on the last screw. As he did so, a pigeon, obviously alarmed by all the disturbance, fluttered up in front of him and in swirl of flapping wings disappeared into the void high above.

Totally unperturbed by this and all else around him, Charlie passed the last screw to Hilda and with it the screwdriver. Hunching his shoulders, he prepared to raise the lid when one of the bearers detached himself from his companions and came over to him.

' 'ere,' he said, 'I'll give you a lift with that,' at the same time moving to the head of the coffin. Charlie nodded his appreciation.

Once free, the lid was comparatively light and Charlie and his helper had no difficulty in swinging it round and resting it against a convenient pillar. He knew, even before the light-blue-coloured muslin was drawn back from the body, that his hopes were dashed.

There, his face like that of a painted gargoyle, was Mikhael Derevenko. All the cosmetic prowess of Peace and Serenity had been unable to obscure the neat round hole in the centre of his forehead, now resembling a puncture mark made by some obscene insect.

Charlie, completely stunned, managed, by an effort of will, to avoid meeting Janice's eyes, which now expressed the full gamut of the agony of failure and a growing despair for the future. Hilda, unable to look at what represented their shattered hopes, simply bowed her head.

* * *

Sir Rupert, having joined him by the coffin, spoke quietly but firmly.

215

'I trust you're satisfied, Charlie. You have done enough damage to Anglo-Soviet relations for one day – now you would oblige me by placing yourself in the hands of the constable here.'

At that moment Mr de Witt, a passive onlooker until then, stepped forward.

'I really must protest in the most strongest terms at this desecration, Sir Rupert. In twenty years I have never witnessed anything so utterly disgraceful and I will expect, on behalf of Peace and Serenity and my client, the most abject apologies ...' and then, after a moment's thought, 'and suitable compensation.'

The spell, if such it was, was broken by the sound of a loud voice from the entrance, as Alexis Sternov strode into the church, dressed in the ceremonial uniform of a colonel in the Red Army.

'Ah, the milkman again ... have you found what you're looking for?' Without waiting for Charlie's reply, he turned to Sir Rupert.

'Colonel de Quincy, I believe? Head of Section Ten, British Military Intelligence?' Although somewhat taken aback, Sir Rupert soon recovered.

'Alexis Sternov, Colonel, Soviet Military Attache,' he replied, extending his hand. Sternov inclined his head back in the direction of Charlie before clasping it.

'Have you seen this, milkman?' he said, as he unfolded a newspaper from under his arm.

Charlie, desperate to avoid his accusers' eyes, focused on what seemed to be the dancing newsprint in front of him and, thankful for any reprieve, however short, read the headlines.

'Man throws himself in front of tube train'

With a questioning look, Charlie turned and faced Sternov.

'Try page two, milkman.'

Charlie obediently turned the page.

'Girl claiming to be a Romanov princess found wandering on Thames Embankment'

216

'You don't mean...'

Sternov shrugged his massive shoulders. 'I've always said she wasn't worth the price of her seat back to Moscow.'

Sir Rupert interrupted. 'This mess, Sternov, will have to be sorted out – what will be the attitude of the Soviet Embassy?'

Making no attempt to hide the glimmer of a twinkle forming in his eyes, Sternov faced Charlie, now standing behind him, before once more facing Sir Rupert.

'From the Soviet point of view,' he said, making an expansive gesture of finality with his hands, 'the least said the better.'

'I'm inclined to agree,' replied Sir Rupert, 'particularly now the girl has turned up – wouldn't you agree, Charlie?'

Charlie nodded, then, 'Where is she now, Alexis?'

'Hammersmith Hospital, and before you ask me, she's quite well.'

Charlie looked at the beaming faces of his co-conspirators, each eagerly reading the paper before, almost in unison, they cried out.

'We'll fetch her, Charlie, leave it to us.'

Ignoring the scramble for the entrance, Sir Rupert moved across to Charlie. 'It looks as if you've got away with it again, Charlie.'

Giving a half-smile, Charlie said nothing.

'Constable Perkins and Mr de Witt, will you join me?' invited Sir Rupert, as he moved in the direction of the door from which they had so recently entered.

'Perhaps we should take the hint, milkman,' said Sternov.

'Obviously,' replied Charlie, 'we're no longer wanted, and in any case Sir Rupert will sort it out ... we English are good at cover-ups.'

Sternov's laughter, swelling from deep within his chest, was infectious, and Charlie joined in.

'Alexis?'

'Yes, my friend.'

'Will you answer a couple of questions?'

'It depends on the questions, comrade.'

217

'Is your interest in the girl finished?'

'We are rarely interested in common gypsy girls for long.'

'Then why bother with her?'

Sternov sighed, 'Orders.'

'You know where the gold is, don't you, Alexis...? You've copied the map, haven't you?'

'If you say so.'

'Alexis, who tipped you off about Covent Garden?'

'You said two questions, comrade, but I will say this much, the KGB has a very long arm. I think that's enough for now, milkman.'

It was at that moment that Sir Rupert rejoined them. 'Mr de Witt is anxious to leave for Heathrow. But before you go, Sternov, I wish to confirm that as far as my government is concerned, this incident never happened.'

Surreptitiously, Charlie and Sternov exchanged a wink. Sternov, face impassive, stared at the high ceiling where the pigeon, again divorced from such mortal matters below, continued to circle in long lazy sweeps.

'Curiously, Colonel de Quincy, I can remember nothing after we left the Embassy. However, may I make a suggestion?'

'Please do.'

'To avoid similar unfortunate incidents, please inform your government that the question of the Romanov gold, if it exists, is an internal matter of the Soviet Union. Any further interference will be viewed with grave concern by my government. Oh yes, and my friend here, who I'm told is not an agent of British Intelligence...'

'That is so.'

'In that case, I trust the agreement we've reached will extend to him regarding all matters connected with this, er, unfortunate affair.'

'You have my word, Colonel Sternov, no action will be taken.'

With that, Colonel Alexis Sternov, hero of the Soviet Union, marched from the church as if he were taking part in a May Day

Parade in Red Square. When he reached the porchway he momentarily stopped and turned, then, standing stiffly to attention, raised his arm in a military salute. Sir Rupert waved a limp arm, but Charlie, having watched his departure, sprang to attention and with equal military precision returned the salute. Strangely, the pigeon chose that moment to abandon its aimless circling of the high ceilings and, as if saddened by his departure, followed Alexis Sternov out of the church and into the gathering darkness of the late winter day.

* * *

'Where is she?'

'Upstairs in bed – it's nothing short of a miracle she hasn't gone down with pneumonia, considering she was only wearing that thin dress – as it is she has a touch of hypothermia, but the hospital said providing she's kept warm, she'll be all right in a day or two.'

'Thank God for that. Can I see her?'

'She's asleep, sleeping off whatever they pumped into her. Best to leave her for a while.'

'Drugs?'

'Undoubtedly.'

'Well,' said Charlie, divesting himself of his coat, 'there's one good thing that's come out of all this, the KGB are no longer interested in her.'

'Is that what your Commie friend told you?'

'That's a bit unfair, Janice, he's not my friend in any sense of the word, but we do respect each other. Being a woman, you wouldn't understand.'

'Well it looked to me like an old pals reunion – hello milkman – are you well, milkman . . . I don't know what Sir Rupert made of it all.'

'Better that sort of relationship than the other.'

'Yes, I suppose you're right. I'm just very tired, Charlie, you'll have to understand, emotionally I'm just utterly exhausted with it all.'

'Of course I understand, but like Natasha, you'll be fine in a day or so.'

'Charlie?'

'I'm listening.'

'Why did they let her go?'

'Simple, she knows nothing of what they were after. Sternov said as much to me.'

'Do you believe they intended to ship her home in that coffin?'

'Yes, I'm convinced that was the plan, but when they realised she was of no help to them they let her go.'

'But what of the tattoo?'

'A fake.'

'But Sergei thought it showed where the gold was hidden and was killed for his pains . . .'

'Sergei believed what he wanted to believe – sometimes that can be a very dangerous game.'

'What now, Charlie?'

'A stiff brandy, then sleep. Things will be clearer in the morning.'

'I admire your optimism,' she said as she stifled a yawn, 'and Charlie, two pints and one cream in the morning . . .' her laughter followed her up the stairs, only dying as she closed the bedroom door behind her.

23

The Impossible Dream

Gathered yet again around his dining room table, the intrepid trio of Paul, Vladimir and Magyar waited impatiently for their leader's pronouncement in the quest for the Romanov gold.

'Tonight, gentlemen,' began Dmitri Sokolov, surveying the large map spread out in front of him, 'we make the final preparations. You each have a map, so follow carefully the details I'll be giving you – it would help, Magyar, if you turned yours the right way round.'

'All right, professor, keep your hair on,' responded Magyar sourly.

Ignoring him, Sokolov continued, 'You will be pleased to learn that, in spite of your aspertions cast on me at our last meeting, my Association is prepared to invest ten thousand pounds in our little enterprise.'

'How much . . .?' said Magyar.

'I've just told you, ten thousand pounds.'

'No. How much do they want?'

'Oh, I see. Well, in the circumstances I suggested a one-quarter share.'

'What, a full quarter?' exclaimed Magyar, looking at Paul and Vladimir for support. Such intervention was scotched at once by Sokolov.

'Bearing in mind we're not putting anything into the pot, I don't consider a quarter share excessive.'

'No,' replied Magyar, 'oh no! We're putting nothing in the pot except our skins.'

Paul, silent until now, came to the rescue. 'I think that's fair. But what about Vladimir's brother and his helpers.'

'For heaven's sake, man, we're going after twenty million, there'll be plenty for everybody'

'Yes,' replied Magyar, after some thought, 'and the more who know about it the greater the danger.'

Ignoring him, Sokolov continued. 'Now, gentlemen, if you study the map you will see a red line, representing a main road running south from Kolomyja. Follow this down and you come to a town called Kielce. Have you all got that ... you, Magyar?'

'Yes, I've got it.'

'Good, then there is hope for us all.'

'Less of the sarcasm, Sokolov, not all of us lectured at the Leningrad University, you know.'

Again, Sokolov ignored him. 'Nothing much of interest in Kielce, gentlemen,' he said, looking at each in turn, 'except that it has a brickworks. That in itself may not strike you as of any great interest; however, the bricks produced there are exceptional. They are what is known as non-porous, or in the trade as blue bricks, and they are exported all over the world. This country imports all it can get its hands on ...'

Looking at the trio seated round him, it was becoming obvious that the penny had dropped. Paul was about to say something when, with an imposing gesture, Sokolov waved him down. 'Let me finish, Paul.' Then, delving into his inside pocket, he produced an official-looking document. 'This, gentlemen, is an Export Licence granted by the Ministry of Trade in Warsaw, it allows us to purchase three thousand of those blue bricks, or if you like, four and a half tons. And this, holding up another document, is an Import Licence granted by our own Board of Trade.'

With glints of admiration beginning to appear in their eyes, Paul, Magyar and Vladimir leant forward in their chairs. For the first time since it was envisaged, all three began to see that the scheme, which up to now had been little more than an impossible dream, was gradually becoming more and more viable.

'That's very clever,'said Magyar, slowly repeating, 'that's very clever indeed.' Then, after a few moment's thought, 'But you still haven't told us where the gold is hidden, Dmitri.' The growing respect in his tone of voice was not lost on Sokolov.

'All in good time, Magyar, all in good time.'

'All right,' commented Paul, 'but just assuming everything goes well, we've still to get it out of the country and that won't be easy.'

'Nothing will be easy in this venture, Paul, but there is a very good chance we'll get away with it. You see the Ministry of Trade in Warsaw were most helpful. They even recommended a Polish shipping line used by the factory in Kielce – they have weekly sailings from the port of Gdansk.'

'What about Customs?' interrupted Magyar.

'Do you really believe, Magyar, that Customs will be interested in a consignment of bricks?' Silence followed, as each of the three contemplated the likelihood of such a prospect.

'I have to admit,' said Paul, the first to emerge from his reverie, 'it does sound feasible.'

'At what stage do we load the gold?' enquired Vladimir, silent until now.

'After Kielce,' replied Sokolov, 'and should we be intercepted on our way to Kolomyja, we can always plead we've lost our way – after all Gdansk is roughly the same direction. I cannot emphasise enough, gentlemen, the least possible time we have the gold on board the better. I trust, Magyar, you see the logic of that?'

'Yes, I'm with you,' replied Magyar, rubbing his hands with glee, 'all we've got to do is clear out the grave, load up and run for home ... I like it, I like it.'

'I wish it were that simple,' commented Sokolov, dryly, 'but I have to admit you've got the general idea.'

'What about a drink in celebration?' suggested Magyar, still in the throes of delirium at the thought of how easy the whole enterprise was becoming.

'Celebration of what?' said Sokolov coldly, his patience clearly all but exhausted.

'That we've cracked it.'

'Paul, do take him in hand ... for the sake of my sanity. Yes, we will have a drink,' directing Vladimir to the drinks cabinet, 'but not in celebration, there is still a lot to be thought out,' said as Vladimir quickly dispensed their drinks.

'Firstly, we have to hire two three-ton trucks. You, Magyar, will drive one and Vladimir the other. Paul and I will travel by car.'

Magyar, banging his now empty glass on the table, wiped his beard with the back of his hand, and to Sokolov's chagrin was again his awkward self.

'Why won't you drive one?'

'Because,' Sokolov began, an edge to his voice, 'I do not hold a heavy goods vehicle licence, and in any event I shall have all the paperwork to take care of – satisfied?'

'Yes,' replied Magyar, after a moment's thought, 'but it's we who will be shot at if anything goes wrong.'

'Magyar, if anything goes wrong we will all be shot at.' Paul, quiet until now, intervened. 'You're getting on my tits, Magyar, we're all wanted men inside the Eastern Bloc, which, if you've forgotten, includes Poland. We all know the risks we're running, but for twenty million I, for one, consider it's worth it.'

'He's getting a quarter of it,' corrected Magyar, pointing at Sokolov.

'So, Magyar,' continued Paul, 'are we to assume you're having second thoughts? If you are, say so now, there are plenty willing to take your place.'

The others nodded their agreement.

A suitably chastened Magyar remained silent then, rising from the table, helped himself to another drink.

'Well?' said Sokolov, as Magyar drained his glass.

'You know me,' said Magyar, again wiping his beard, 'I've been for it from the beginning, and I've no intention of pulling out, as you put it.'

224

'Magyar ... we know too much for each others good – I trust you get my meaning,' said Sokolov brutally.

'You do get Dmitri's point, don't you, Magyar?' said Paul quietly.

'Dmitri, there's no reason to threaten. I'll admit I'm a little slow on the uptake but I'm loyal, believe me I am,' responded Magyar.

'Right,' said Paul, 'now no more nonsense. Let's hear the rest of the plan ... I assume we're going overland? The outward journey, I mean.'

Once again, Dmitri Sokolov reached into his inside pocket and produced yet another buff envelope.

'Here, my friends,' his conciliatory tone of voice, so different from his earlier pronouncement, was not lost on the trio now avidly eyeing the envelope held aloft. 'Here are your visas for entering and leaving Poland. Your names are, for obvious reasons, fictitious.' With that, Dmitri Sokolov, as if he were a conjurer reaching his finale, spread them out in front of him.

'You're a genius, exclaimed Paul, holding his documents up to the light. 'If they're forgeries, they're brilliant forgeries. How on earth did you manage it?'

'No more for now – and remember, all of you, not a word, not a whisper, you understand?'

Three heads nodded in unison.

24

Skeletons Hop Out of the Cupboard

Charlie, lighting another cigarette, patiently awaited what he confidently expected would be a salvo of recrimination from Sir Rupert. All the signs were there; the tardy acknowledgement when shown into his office – in response to the perfunctory summons he received whilst still at breakfast – and now the silent treatment, reminding him when, as a schoolboy, he had suffered the headmaster's displeasure.

Sir Rupert finally raised his eyes from the contents of a brown file he had so diligently been studying.

'From Washington, Charlie, only received it this morning.' Charlie said nothing but continued to stare fixedly at a portrait of the Queen adorning the wall behind Sir Rupert's desk.

'Time to come clean, Charlie.'

'If you're referring to the church business yesterday, I thought it was agreed with Sternov to forget it.'

'No, I'm not referring to that, disgraceful though it was,' he paused, 'no, what I want to ask you is far more serious, top-level stuff in fact.'

Now what? thought Charlie.

'Charlie Tuttle,' said Sir Rupert in slow, measured tones, 'are you still working for the CIA? Before you deny it, may I tell you I have your dossier here,' tapping the brown file with his forefinger. ' I have to say it is most revealing and answers many questions.'

'I thought you were going back up to Scotland, Rupert . . .'

226

'Charlie, just answer my question.'

'Was, not still, Rupert.'

'At last we're getting somewhere, and do stop me if I'm wrong. You were recruited by them after the Congo affair, right? And, Charlie, the Duchess Elizabeth just didn't pluck you out of that clinic in Berne, did she? You were seconded to her for a specific purpose, right?'

'It's all water under the bridge, Rupert.'

'I don't think so, and I'll tell you why – everything you've done in this country since your, eh, reappearance, ties in nicely with the disclosures detailed here.' Again tapping the file, 'Disclosures I can only describe as staggering in their audacity and typical of the CIA.'

Charlie, lighting another cigarette, said nothing.

'Did you really think they could get away with it?'

Exhaling smoke in the direction of the Queen, Charlie disdained a reply.

'It's no good remaining dumb, Charlie, I want some answers.'

'All right, Rupert, I'll give you some. You say it was staggering ... so was the Kennedy assassination, but it happened.'

'You cannot compare the planned killing of Nikita Khrushchev with that.'

'Why not? They had a go at Castro – poisoned cigars, I'm told!'

'Well ...'

'Exactly, you see, Rupert, the planned murder of Khrushchev had far more going for it. An heir to the throne of the Romanovs in waiting, a populous weary of Communism ...'

'Charlie, everything points to the Soviet Union being more united than ever.'

'Then perhaps you should have told the CIA?'

All right, we'll leave that alone. Now, more to the point, what part was the Duchess Elizabeth supposed to play?'

'Surely, that's obvious.'

'It hadn't a hope, Charlie, you must have known that?'

'What, Rupert? With a sweetener of twenty million!'

227

'You mean the Romanov fortune?'

'I do. With that sort of money, anything is possible.'

'I have to admit,' replied Sir Rupert, rubbing his chin, 'that does change matters considerably ... but what of you, Charlie? What course of action are you still deemed to play in all of this? I see from the file you have the simulated rank of,' turning a page, 'a Major in the US Army.'

Charlie shrugged his shoulders, then, 'The pay is good, Rupert.'

'You utterly exasperate me, Charlie. So, in other words, you're still in the pay of the CIA?'

'Yes, but to calm your nerves, Rupert, the initial part of the operation is null and void – it died with Kennedy.'

'The second part?'

Charlie again shrugged his shoulders.

Silence descended on the room as the two men looked at each other across, what seemed to them, the void of an expanse of desk.

'Charlie,' again the measured tones, 'what is in this file,' again the tapping with the forefinger, 'is explosive. Earlier today I spoke with the PM. I share his view that the plot and its intended execution were appalling in the extreme. Therefore, and note this well, Charlie, any attempt by you to process any part of it, I shall, without any hesitation, recommend your deportation.'

'Is that it?' said Charlie, rising.

'That is it, Charlie, as you so succinctly put it.'

*   *   *

With Tolstoy's *War and Peace* open on his knees, Charlie watched as the light from the grey winter's day slowly changed to the ever-increasing gloom of early evening. Beyond the picture window of Janice's library, the garden was becoming a panorama of deepening shadows, each one dark and forbidding. Fascinated, he watched, as what minutes before had been the vague outline of a leafless tree was now transformed into a stark effigy of whatever his imagination might wish it to be. The arrival of Janice interrupted his self-imposed reverie.

'You should see the dress Natasha's bought for the fifteenth, it's out of this world,' then, looking hard at him, 'and how did things go with Rupert Bear this morning?'

'So so.'

'You mean you're not going to tell me?'

'Janice, I've a lot on my mind at the moment.'

'All right, but at least answer me this – is Natasha safe now?'

'Without taking anything for granted, I would say yes.'

'Well, I guess we should be thankful for small mercies. Incidentally, and to change the subject, who did tip off Sternov about Covent Garden?'

'Undoubtedly the ferret, or, to be more precise, one Mordici Bogrov.'

'What a ghastly name. Anyway, I intend to have it out with Florrie, she's to watch her tongue in future . . .'

'Don't blame Florrie entirely. Sure, the initial information about Covent Garden almost certainly came from her, but you're missing something.'

'Such as?'

'My cold – which meant I was out of the picture at the crucial stage. That information came from someone much nearer home.'

'So, if Bogrov didn't pull the plug entirely, who did? Charlie, no ifs or buts, you know, don't you?'

'I could make a reasonable guess.'

'Start guessing.'

'Well apart from you, me, Florrie and . . .' his voice tailed off.

'Of course, Bill. I should have realised – what a low-down thing to do, how could he?'

'I said it was only a guess, I could be wrong.'

'I've never known you to be, Charlie Tuttle. You can leave this one to me . . . the scab.'

'Janice, it's better left unsaid.'

'You're the oracle, I'll say nothing for now ... but it won't be easy.'

'More to the point, Janice, is who he fed the information to? I'm pretty sure it wasn't Sternov.'

'Who then?'

'That, my dear, is what the Americans call the sixty-four thousand dollar question.'

* * *

'Sir Humphrey, how nice,' but Bill's voice lacked conviction.

Sir Humphrey's reply was barely a discernible grunt as he lowered himself into the first available chair. Dispensing with formalities, he leant forward.

'Damned uncomfortable chair, you should tell Lawrence so. Now, the Gollitzin affair, what a fiasco. What have you got to say for yourself? You said it couldn't fail.' Like bright tiny buttons his eyes flashed ominously above puffy cheeks.

'Sheer bad luck, Sir Humphrey, sheer bad luck, and the incompetence of the KGB. I played my part.'

'Their man Tuttle, smart man from all accounts,' continued Sir Humphrey, as though he hadn't heard Bill's excuse. 'But I've a few tricks of my own up my sleeve. I'll fox him, believe me, I will. Do you know poor Pen can't lift her arm above her waist...? Loved her tennis, did Pen ... out of the question now.' He paused, if only to draw breath, giving Bill an opportunity to speak.

'What about the police?' he ventured timidly.

'Police,' snapped Sir Humphrey, 'fat lot of good they are.' His face took on a reddish hue. ' No, it's down to me now – you've had your chance, Bill, and you and the KGB muffed it.'

'Did you know,' said Bill, anxious to change the subject, 'she's been invited to stay with Prince Michael, the Russian Pretender?'

'What, that penniless idler ... all I can say is they deserve each other.'

'Can I get you a coffee, Sir Humphrey?' invited Bill ingratiatingly.

'A double malt would suit me better.'

'No problem,' replied Bill, welcoming the opportunity to escape from those searching piggy eyes for a few moments.

'Right,' said Sir Humphrey, as his drink was passed to him. 'This is what I want from you, Bill, a full dossier on the girl – in particular what credentials she has that support her claim to the Romanov throne.'

'It won't be easy,' replied Bill.

'Damn it, man, do you want to be rid of her or don't you?'

'Of course, I –'

But Sir Humphrey cut in, 'Then get on with it, and this time I want results.' With that he drained his glass and strode towards the office door. 'You've got a week, Bill, you know where to find me.'

The door had barely closed behind him when Rachel rushed in.

'So, that was Sir Humphrey Charters,' she said, as she occupied her favourite position on the edge of Bill's desk, with the usual display of creamy white thighs, 'is that his Rolls out there?'

'Well, it certainly isn't mine,' responded Bill cynically.

'Why can't you fix me up with someone like him?' she pouted.

'Because he's way out of your league.'

'Rubbish . . . I've never met a man yet who was.'

'You know, you and Natasha Gollitzin would make a fine pair.'

'Natasha Gollitzin, who's she when she's at home?'

'That's exactly what I've got to find out . . .'

*   *   *

One airport, she guessed, was much like any other, but this was different, it was Heathrow, England. Silently she followed the crush of people towards the sign which read 'Arrivals'. Then, as if it were a single entity, the forward motion of the crowd ceased, the reason soon becoming obvious.

231

Now she patiently waited her turn, for queues were as much a part of life as the air she breathed. Shuffling forward, she assessed the two uniformed men standing behind a low desk at the head of the queue. She knew any form of officialdom was to be feared, although, she had to admit, they appeared pleasant enough as they smiled at each fresh individual. In one hand she clasped her passport and entry visa, and with the other her one piece of luggage, a suitcase of some vintage tied up with yards of string.

As her turn approached she was increasingly aware of the heat being generated by the slow-moving crowd of people – a heat additional to the building's many hot-air vents. For some unknown reason the queue stopped dead, and again she lowered her suitcase to the ground. With her hand temporarily free of its encumbrance, she eased her fingers around the edges of her high, tunic-like overcoat, the collar of which was already damp from perspiration and was chafing her neck. Once more movement commenced, and she realised only two or three individuals were ahead of her. Again she looked at the two uniformed men, but this time she noticed a grey-suited man standing apart. Her instincts warned her that he was the one to fear, it was always those in plain clothes with a cultivated disinterested look who were the real danger. Secret police, she surmised, but she had experienced no problems leaving Warsaw or, for that matter, Frankfurt when she had changed planes.

'Passport please,' said a voice, and then, 'complete the form.' She stared at the pink piece of paper thrust in front of her before a stubby finger assisted her by indicating the relevant part.

A bored voice said, 'Port of origin.'

She stared blankly back, she knew it was far better to assume a pretence of ignorance – after all, it went with her appearance.

Again the bored voice, impatient now, 'Where . . . did . . . you . . . fly . . . from?'

'Warsaw,' she replied, trying her hardest to appear calm as the grey-suited man moved over to them and was handed her passport and visa. Without expression, he studied them.

'Address in the United Kingdom?' once again the stubby finger pointed, but to no avail.

The voice was pained, 'Where ... will ... you ... be ... staying?'

She filled in the name – Russian Institute.

Satisfied, the stubby finger moved down the form. 'Full name and address in Poland ... here.'

Laboriously she wrote it down. It was at that point grey suit took over.

'You realise your stay in the United Kingdom is restricted to one month?'

She nodded. With that he handed back her passport and visa ... then with a smile that never reached his eyes, he said, 'Welcome to the United Kingdom, Miss Valma Gollitzin.'

* * *

It was Janice speaking, her legs tucked up snugly beneath her and her head resting comfortably against the high-backed sofa. 'I wonder what this New Year is going to bring?'

'More of the same,' replied Charlie mischievously.

'Oh, Charlie, no ... I couldn't go through all that again.'

He looked up from his contemplation of the flames from the log fire leaping high into the chimney.

'Sorry, that was a nonsensical thing to say, I'm sure the worst is over now – certainly where Natasha is concerned.'

'She's changed, Charlie, she's not the girl of a few months ago, surely you must have noticed?'

'You could hardly expect anything else, considering what she's been through. Think for a moment. A young impressionable girl plucked from a background of squalor and confronted with the stuff dreams are made of ... Is it any wonder she's changed? Her indoctrination at the hands of the Duchess would have turned most heads – one minute nothing more than a peasant girl, the next heir to the throne of the Romanovs. And it didn't stop there, once in the West she is fawned upon, admired, chased by every man . . .' he paused, giving Janice a sideways look, 'and woman . . .'

'You know about that, don't you?' she said, rising from the sofa and crossing to the drinks trolley. 'It's something I deeply regret, believe me. If I could put the clock back . . .' spoken, as she poured herself a brandy, then, 'will you have one?'

'Well, if it's confession time, perhaps I'd better.'

'Charlie,' she said, handing him his drink, 'you know I'm in love with you, don't you?'

'Janice, keep to the subject – we were talking about Natasha.'

'There are times, Charlie Tuttle, when I could willingly strangle you.'

'Where is she now . . .?'

'There you go again, Natasha, Natasha, Natasha – if you must know, she's in her bedroom.'

'She spends far too long alone up there, it's not good for her.'

'That's what I meant when I said she had changed. She's no longer the outrageous bouncy girl I first knew.'

'Well, considering the ordeal she's been through . . .'

'It goes deeper than that. I wonder if it has anything to do with the drugs they used. After all, she says she remembers nothing or hardly anything.'

'You have to realise that such events were bound to leave scars. When I think back to the Duchess and all those grandiose pictures she painted of her future – power, status, luxury beyond the girl's wildest dreams, but with little mention of the greed and hatred inevitably in train, is there any wonder?'

'Charlie, I don't think I have ever heard you so open with your thoughts before, you've always been the strong silent type. I must say I welcome the change.'

'Perhaps it might have been better if she had stayed back in Kolomyja,' said almost to himself as he drained his glass.

'What, condemned to a life of prostitution, surely not?'

'Yes, you're probably right . . . then there is the other matter that is worrying me.'

234

'Such as?'

'Her inheritance, twenty thousand, she's going to have to be told.'

'Not another crisis.'

'To tell a young girl with her background, she's got that sort of money will take some getting used to.'

'Perhaps we should cross that bridge when we come to it, Charlie. That latest letter points out the difficulties with the probate – Sergei was a Russian citizen, you know, and there was that small matter of illegal entry.'

'She'll get it sooner or later.'

'I hope you're right. Charlie, may I ask a personal question? She keeps you out of her bedroom now, doesn't she?'

'You mean since I'm no longer Igor?'

She nodded.

'Yes, I suppose she does, bedtimes are private affairs nowadays...'

Moving to the drinks trolley, Janice picked up the decanter and returned with it.

'Another,' pouring a large measure into his glass, and then, her voice husky, 'let's get pissed and go to bed.'

'Were it that easy...'

'Why not ... what's wrong with me? I've a good body, everyone says what lovely legs I've got – look,' with that she hoisted her dress to her waist. 'There, Charlie, have a good look and see what you're missing.' Without a word he got up and moved to the window – silently she watched him. Had she gone too far this time, she wondered?

'One day you'll learn why,' he said, his back towards her.

'Yes, I know, you've got a little wifey tucked away somewhere,' she said, her voice petulant.

'Nothing is further from the truth,' he replied, rejoining her on the sofa.

'Charlie, I'm a young woman, or haven't you noticed? I cannot exist without some physical show of love from the man I care about and who I know cares about me ... you must understand, I want to feel you deep within me, your arms around me ... please, Charlie, what is wrong?'

'Nothing, Janice, certainly not with you. One day I will tell you, but not now ... I will say this though, everything you've said is true, you are the most gorgeous, lovable creature I've ever met, and far too good for me.'

'Don't come that rubbish, if what you are saying were true you would have been fucking me long ago ...'

'Janice, I'm surprised at you.'

'Well, at certain times such words are the only ones that spell it out.'

'What are you going to do about Bill?' said Charlie, ignoring the outburst.

'That's typical of you, anything to change the subject.'

'No, Janice, I'm serious. In some ways I feel sorry for him, he's had a lot to put up with.'

'I shall deal with my beloved husband in my own way. He's not getting away with it ... satisfied?'

'There you both are,' Natasha's voice had their heads turning in the direction of the drawing room door. 'The house is so quiet, I wondered if you were out.'

'No, sweetie, come and join us and tell us your plans for the fifteenth.' Natasha, needing no second bidding, quickly sat down between them, but her usual devastating smile was missing.

'I'll leave you two alone for now,' said Charlie, rising to his feet. 'I've a letter that needs writing.'

Janice had the distinct feeling that he was only too glad of the opportunity to escape from her.

'Have I interrupted something, Janeece?' said Natasha, as she eyed Charlie's fast-disappearing back. 'No, Natasha, you haven't interrupted anything – more's the pity. Now, tell me all your plans for your visit to the Prince.'

'Oh, Janeece, I'm so excited, he's so handsome and so, how you say?'

'Sophisticated?' suggested Janice.

'*Très bon*, exactly that.'

'Well, don't rush your fences, Natasha, take it gently.'

'Supposing he doesn't like me . . .'

'I've yet to meet a man who doesn't consider you ravishing.'

'Ravishing – what does it mean?'

'It means, desirable . . . wanted, gorgeous . . .'

'But, Janeece, you don't seem to want me anymore . . . you never come to my room and love me like you used to.'

Janice looked hard at the incredible loveliness of Natasha, now sitting beside her, and again that itch began to stir high up between her legs, a sensation that would not be stilled.

She learnt forward, her mouth searching for that provocative, enticing crimson opening . . . Natasha, somewhat taken aback at the suddenness of it, could only murmur a few words of encouragement before Janice's lips found hers.

* * *

'Surprise, surprise.'

'What now, Teddy?' replied Sir Rupert somewhat impatiently.

'This "Pink" from Immigration, last night's arrivals at Heathrow.'

'What of it . . . anyone we know?'

'A certain name rings a bell,' said Teddy in an offhand manner.

'I know it's the season for party games, but I'm not in the mood for one right now – spell it out, man.'

'Valma Gollitzin arrived on Pan Am Flight 406 from Frankfurt at 2200 last night . . . port of origin, Warsaw.'

'I don't believe it . . . give me that.'

'There it is, chief, in black and white, or should I say black on pink.'

'Now, what are they up to this time, I wonder?' said Sir Rupert, reading the pink notification form.

'Restricted, chief – one month UK only.'

'So I see, and staying at the Russian Institute.'

'Not at the Russian Embassy,' volunteered Teddy.

'I suppose it could be a coincidence...' said Sir Rupert doubt-fully.

'No, they're up to something, sure as eggs,' contributed Teddy. 'Do you think we should tip the wink to you know who?'

'Teddy, stop talking in riddles,' said Sir Rupert, obviously annoyed. 'If you mean Tuttle, say so.'

'It was only a thought,' said an aggrieved Teddy.

'No, I haven't got over that gun being levelled at my head yet ... let him stew in his own juice.'

'My sentiments entirely, chief.'

'There is one thing, I should be interested in knowing what reason she gave for the visit. Get on to Immigration, Teddy, and ask them for a sight of her visa application.'

'Now?'

'Now, Teddy. I've a feeling things are beginning to build.'

25

A Meeting of Minds

She didn't need the proverbial snow on her boots, or to be carrying the hammer and sickle, for Bill to realise at once that the woman standing at the front door was Russian. Usually, answering the door bell was left to Florrie, but as he was leaving the house anyway, the accepted ritual was, on this occasion, ignored. Even before the door was fully open the woman spoke.

'My name is Valma ... I come from Warsaw last night ... I wish to speak with my sister, Natasha.'

Perhaps after all he had been through, Bill thought afterwards, he could be forgiven for being completely taken aback. It was several seconds before the full import of what the woman had said crystallised in his mind. Then, in the knowledge that providence had given him an unprecedented opportunity, he gathered himself together.

Quickly assuring the approaching Florrie that she was not needed, he ushered the visitor into the library.

'Natasha is out at the moment with my wife,' he found himself saying as he looked at the woman. In that instant he was reminded of wartime newsreels depicting women digging tank traps on the approaches to Moscow – the same massive shoulders were in evidence together with a face, he smiled to himself, that, rather than launch a thousand ships, would more likely sink them.

The woman's response was incisive. 'Then I will wait.'

'You said your name was ... Valma?' his ingratiating smile

239

achieved little in the way of response. 'Is there anything I can get you, a cup of tea perhaps . . . or coffee, while you wait?'

'You have coffee?'

'Yes indeed,' he replied, as he moved to the bell push before turning back to her, 'Perhaps you would prefer a vodka?'

'You have good Russian vodka?' her eyes, he noticed, becoming alive for the first time.

'The very best,' he said, thankful that his offer of vodka had clearly been more attractive to her than either tea or coffee. He must, he reminded himself, keep this manifestation, that had emerged out of the blue as it were, to himself – it might well prove the answer to all his problems. It would have been the height of folly to have allowed Florrie to get even an inkling of what had dropped into his lap. Where Janice and Natasha were concerned, it would be at least another hour before they returned from the hairdresser, and, as Christmas Eve was tomorrow, there was every likelihood that a spot of last-minute shopping would extend that time considerably. One thing he must do, he realised, is to get the woman – Valma, was it? – away from here before then. He turned to her.

'Where are you staying – er – Valma?' he enquired, as he poured a further generous measure of vodka into her glass, the first having speedily disappeared.

'Hobbom,' she answered, lowering the empty glass, 'the Russian Institute,' as a pink tongue emerged from between thick lips in search of any remnants of the vodka.

Bill replenished the glass. 'Holborn,' he said, ' I know it well. Are they looking after you?'

'I have my own bed.'

Silence followed as Bill once more studied the woman claiming to be Natasha's sister. Her appearance would not go unnoticed in Carnaby Street, but then that was a minor consideration. It was what she might know that was all important.

'Listen, Valma,' he began, 'I wish to have a long talk with you about Natasha . . . but not here, you understand?' Valma nodded.

'Supposing I take you to good hotel, good food, plenty of,' nodding in the direction of the vodka bottle, 'and money for shopping?'

'Money,' she exclaimed, 'you give Valma money?'

God, he thought, had he put his foot in it – her next words quelled his fears.

'How much money?'

Again doubt assailed him, frantically he considered what would appeal without disclosing how desperate he was. 'A hundred pounds,' he said, anxiously searching her face.

'When will I see Natasha?' she said cunningly, as her eyes looked anywhere but at him.

'Tomorrow,' he said, still anxious to appease her, 'tomorrow will be so much better.' Silence again as she digested this.

'We go to hotel now?'

'Yes, yes, why not?' replied a relieved Bill.

'Tell me, you wish to sleep with Valma when we get to hotel?'

By an incredible effort he concealed his astonishment, and aware of the vital need not to offend her, replied, 'Yes, but later.'

From her reaction it was obviously the expected reply, as, with what was meant to be a smile but was more a smirk, she answered, 'Good, I think I shall like Englishmen.'

Having recovered somewhat from the shock of her offer, Bill said, 'Right, I'll go and phone for a taxi, you wait here.' Then, as he handed her the vodka bottle, 'We'll go to the Institute first and pick up your luggage – all right?'

But he got no reply as Valma, having dispensed with the glass, was now holding the bottle up to her mouth. One thing he was sure of, conjectured Bill as he lifted the receiver, she couldn't possibly be Natasha's sister . . . but that was not to say she didn't know a lot about her . . . perhaps even enough to cook Natasha's goose for good. Excitedly, he ordered the taxi.

* * *

241

'Who was that at the door, Florrie?' asked Charlie, as he watched the taxi pull away, the figure of Valma in the back being partially concealed by Bill.

'I only caught the odd word, sir, but I believe she was a foreign lady – she was asking for Miss Natasha.'

'Was she now – you're certain you haven't seen her before?'

'Certain . . . but I'll tell you one thing, Mr Webster couldn't get her away fast enough.'

'Thank you, Florrie, and, Florrie, not a word of this to your mistress or Miss Natasha for that matter – you understand?'

'I've seen nothing, Mr Tuttle.'

'Good girl.'

At that moment the phone rang.

'It's for you,' said Florrie, handing him the receiver, 'someone called "Suckerlove" – I can't get used to these weird-sounding names,' she said as, wiping her hands on her apron, she ambled away in the direction of the kitchen.

'Charlie Tuttle speaking,' he said.

'I prefer to call you Igor,' replied a voice.

'Have it your way,' replied Charlie, still unsure as to who the caller was.

'It's what Igor knows that interests me,' continued the voice.

'I've got it now . . . it's Dmitri Sokolov, isn't it?'

'It is, and I've an interesting proposition to put to you.'

'To me or Igor?' Charlie replied.

'Igor, preferably.'

'I should have guessed as much. Purely a shot in the dark, Sokolov, but would it have anything to do with the Romanov gold?'

'My, you're quick, but then I've been told you are.'

'Get on with it, Sokolov.'

'Not on the phone – but could you meet me – say tonight, Room 232 at the Cumberland Hotel, around seven?'

'I don't know what I'll be doing tonight.'

'Oh, come, come, Charlie . . .'

242

'So it's Charlie now...'

'Charlie or Igor, one or the other – or both for that matter.'

'Yes, Sokolov, as I'm curious to know what you're cooking up I'll be there, but don't count your chickens.'

'You haven't heard the proposition yet.'

'Well, I'll say this much...' but Sokolov was no longer there.

* * *

'Sir Humphrey?' Bill's voice was exultant, 'You'll never believe this.'

'Believe what?' replied Sir Humphrey testily.

'Natasha Gollitzin's sister has turned up, literally out of the blue. Knocked on my door this afternoon asking for Natasha ... her name is Valma. Flew in from Warsaw last night and, Sir Humphrey, she's undoubtedly on the make, no money, and what's more, there's no love lost between them...'

'All right, Bill, calm down, we've had false dawns before, but I must say this is interesting – what have you done with her?'

'I got her away from the house sharpish, no one saw her, and I've put her in a hotel in Victoria.'

'Good man, this could well be the break we've been looking for. You say she has no love for her sister?'

'No, the impression I got was that she was both envious and jealous.'

'Excellent, couldn't be better. Now, I shall have to cancel a couple of appointments tomorrow afternoon – not to worry, though ... I'll book a room at the Carlton, say fourish. Bring her there, Bill.'

'A word of warning, Sir Humphrey, she's got an appetite for sex, particularly Englishmen.' He grinned into the mouthpiece. 'I had to go to bed with her to keep her sweet.'

'So you've shafted her already – what is it with these Russian women, is it their diet?'

'Could be – I'll say one thing, what they lack in finesse they make up for in energy.'

243

'Some sacrifice then, Bill.'

'You haven't seen her, Sir Humphrey.'

'Well, I've that pleasure to come ... see you tomorrow.'

Of all people to have as an ally, Sir Humphrey Charters would be the last on his list, thought Bill, as he replaced the phone. The man was known throughout the square mile of the City for his callousness and greed. On the board of countless companies, he was reputed to be a millionaire several times over. Ruefully, mused Bill, he had no known vices except one, if that could be called a vice, his adoration for his daughter, Penelope. But Bill had to admit, if anyone could bring Natasha Gollitzin crashing down it was Sir Humphrey. Yes, ruminated Bill, Natasha may have survived the worst the KGB could do, but Sir Humphrey Charters was a different proposition altogether.

*   *   *

Why the Cumberland Hotel? mused Charlie, surely Sokolov's own office in Holborn would have been more convenient – and less expensive. After walking down several corridors, all carrying that impersonal identical look he always associated with large hotels, he eventually found room 232.

'Thank you for coming, Igor ... or should I say Charlie?' was the greeting.

Charlie ignored the barely concealed sarcasm and contented himself with giving Sokolov a brief nod. He had been in two minds whether to keep the appointment at all, but curiosity had got the better of him. His innate instinct for scenting trouble and the certainty that Sokolov was cooking up something had been the deciding factors.

'So, Sokolov, what's the score?'

'First a drink,' said Sokolov, producing a hip flask and taking a long draught before passing it to Charlie. The contents hit the back of his throat like a hot poultice before filtering down to his stomach, where they immediately began to inflame his very vitals.

244

'What on earth was that, Sokolov?'

'Good isn't it – best Russian vodka ... straight from the Urals. I'll tell you one day how they distil it.'

'Don't bother,' replied Charlie, 'leave it to my imagination,' as he returned the flask. 'Now, what is this all about?' he began again.

'Simply this, Charlie. You remember the ingot you produced when we were with the Comte de Toulouse back in August?'

'I could hardly forget.'

'Well, at the time you feigned ignorance as to where it came from ... I think you knew. For months now I've been preparing a plan to recover the cache, with your help, Charlie, it can't fail. You see, I know that the tattoo Sergei Poznansky got so hot under the collar about, and which cost him his life, was nothing more than what you English call a red herring – planted by the Duchess Elizabeth. Poznansky believed it because he wanted to believe it, but I wasn't fooled.'

Charlie stifled a yawn, much to the annoyance of Sokolov.

'You may pretend disinterest if you like, Charlie Tuttle, but I know differently. I'm offering you a decent slice of the cake, all I want from you is protection.'

'Protection? What exactly do you mean?'

'If the going got rough, Charlie, you would look after me and, eh, my interests.'

'But I need to know the plan.'

'Of course, of course,' replied Sokolov, rubbing his hands together before again producing the hip flask and handing it to Charlie. He, with a shake of the head, declined – his body juices having finally extinguished the first conflagration, he had no wish for a repeat. Sokolov, in no way deterred, took a further large measure, much to Charlie's admiration. And then, declining any second bidding, outlined the plan he had hatched with Paul, Vladimir and Magyar.

'You're saying, Sokolov, that the gold is buried in the cemetery at Kolomyja?'

'That's where it is, Charlie, buried with a child who died back in 1918.'

'How can you be sure?'

'Because, Charlie, and mark this, the man who buried it is my sponsor.'

'And who might that be, Sokolov?'

'None other than Sir Humphrey Charters, one-time financial adviser to Tsar Nicholas himself.' By a supreme effort of will, Charlie managed to curb his amazement at this disclosure. Even so, an element of his astonishment could not be completely hidden – much to the delight of Dmitri Sokolov.'

'Surprise, surprise, Charlie?' Then briskly, 'Now you can see why I need you. I do not altogether trust Humphrey Charters; his reputation speaks for itself.'

'You'll be taking one Hell of a risk, you know that don't you, you'll be well behind the Iron Curtain. One slip and it will be . . .'

'More reasons why I need you – you speak the language like a native and know the country, particularly around Kolomyja.'

'That's as maybe, Sokolov, but the risks are enormous.'

'So is the size of the pot waiting to be picked up, Charlie.'

'I need to sleep on it, Sokolov, I'll get back to you.'

'Not Sokolov, Charlie, Dmitri. After all, if we're going to be partners . . . and another thing, Charlie,' said as he tapped his nose with his forefinger, 'you will respect my confidence, won't you? It's fair to say my life may depend on it.'

'You have my word . . . Dmitri.'

26

The Leopards Show Their Claws

'Valma, may I introduce Sir Humphrey Charters. He has been anxious to meet you since your arrival.'

Sir Humphrey, in a voice Bill barely recognised, murmured a few words of greeting. Valma, with an exaggerated show of reluctance, got off the bed and gave him a brief nod before lowering herself into a chair.

'Bill, surely you could have found something better than this,' said Sir Humphrey, looking with obvious distaste at a room badly in need of redecoration and boasting only a bed and two chairs. 'I know I decided against the Carlton for our meet, but this...'

'I thought it would be safer here.'

'Perhaps you're right ... anyway, let's get down to business. What have you said to her so far?'

'That we want to know all about Natasha.' The sound of her sister's name galvanised Valma out of her trance-like state, as quickly she rose from the chair and moved to a battered suitcase. Heaving it on to the bed, she soon produced from its hidden depths a handbag, which she clutched to her chest before returning to the chair.

'What have you there?' said Bill, as if addressing a child. Far from soothing her, as he intended, his approach only infuriated her, as with a glare which completely unnerved him, she spat out a reply.

'Valma clever, Valma speak good English, Valma not a kulak.'

'Go steady, Bill, I think you should let me handle this,' said Sir Humphrey, giving her what he judged was a smile of understanding before pulling up the unoccupied chair and sitting opposite her. Then, probably intended as no more than a gesture, he placed his hand on her upper thigh. Immediately placated, Valma, in response, gave Sir Humphrey an outrageous wink whilst moving his hand inside her skirt. By a supreme effort of will Sir Humphrey continued to smile, though to someone more discerning than Valma, it would have seemed more glacial than warming.

'You have something to show us, Valma?' he managed, continuing to smile.

'Yes,' she grinned, whilst with a dexterity obviously gained from long experience, she spread her legs and moved his hand further up the inside of her skirt. 'Valma has Natasha's death certificate.'

It was Sir Humphrey who kept his cool, in spite of the shock of such a statement – Bill, with an expression of utter bewilderment, sank down on the edge of the bed.

'I – don't – quite – understand,' said Sir Humphrey, his breathing becoming distinctly irregular, as, with the ease of practice, she now directed his hand against her inner thigh and commenced movements with her hips which could have but one interpretation.

'Valma talk later,' she whispered hoarsely, as she eased herself forward, positioning her bottom on the edge of the chair seat.

Although everything about her was coarse and ugly, Sir Humphrey found himself becoming more and more aroused. His hand, no longer requiring persuasion, began movements of its own – fiercely kneading and rubbing against the rough material cloaking her innermost thighs. Her actions now became even more blatant as with her free hand, the other gripping the side of the chair, she delved inside his overcoat and commenced an exploration of her own.

To the watching Bill, Sir Humphrey's eyes became increasingly glazed and his face a blotchy red, clear indications of the progress of Valma's hand. Pushing her away, he stood up and began to

248

undress. Stimulated by such obvious intent, Valma, slipping off her skirt and what to Bill appeared to be some sort of medieval shift, clambered back on to the bed. Then to the amazement of both men, spread her legs wide and gave an implicit invitation to Bill that, as far as she was concerned, although it was a double bed, she would not consider it amiss were it occupied by the three of them. He, conscious of the fact he had lied earlier to Sir Humphrey regarding having relations with her, pretended tiredness and sank down in the chair just vacated by Valma.

With a gruff, 'Not a word to anyone, Bill,' Sir Humphrey ponderously climbed on to the bed and straddled her. Bill, by an effort of will, kept his thoughts to himself. Such thoughts, he had to admit, placed a doubt in his mind as to just how genuine was Sir Humphrey in his desire to avenge his daughter's injury ... and what was more crucial, was this the way to glean the information from the woman? One thing was sure, the obscene expletives forthcoming from the bed only added to his doubts.

*　*　*

'Charlie,' said Janice, pulling a face at the empty coffee pot. 'A penny for your thoughts?'

'Yes, I will have another cup.'

'Silly, that isn't what I asked you ... Charlie, is there something I should know?'

'I intended to keep it from you, but yesterday, whilst you and Natasha were shopping, we had a visitor.'

'So?'

'It was a she asking to see Natasha.'

'What of it? Could be anyone.'

'I've a feeling it was someone a lot nearer home ... by that I mean Kolomyja. Natasha has a sister, you know.'

'God, not another Natasha, I couldn't stand it.'

'I think a call to Rupert might not come amiss – let's find out just what we're up against.' With that he went across to the kitchen extension and began to dial. Janice, without a word, joined him.

'Charlie here, Rupert, is there anything I should know? Particularly concerning recent arrivals in the UK?'

'In spite of making a career of embarrassing your friends, you have the nerve to come knocking for favours yet again. I really do despair of you, Charlie,' replied Rupert, his voice plaintive. 'And, in spite of all your promises, you've really told me very little, and now this latest revelation that you're working for the CIA, the CIA of all people . . .' Charlie removed the phone from his ear and made a grimace in the direction of Janice.

'You know, Rupert, this phone isn't secure . . .'

'That's your worry, not mine.'

'Anyway, I'm really sorry about the CIA, Rupert, truly I am, but in the circumstances I had little choice.'

'That's as maybe, but I shudder to think what the outcome might have been if Sternov had not been so conciliatory. And Charlie, in spite of promises, you've really told me very little about the Romanov affair – or, to be more precise, the gold. In many ways you've been too clever for your own good, and now, to top it all, you're scratching around for information yet again . . . this time the answer is no.'

'Believe me, I've reasons for thinking matters are coming to a head, and all I want is one more tiny scrap of information – really to confirm what I already suspect. And, Rupert, surely you don't want another Derevenko on your hands?' Silence ensued, giving Charlie the opportunity of exchanging a sly wink with Janice.

'One small piece of information you said, Charlie?'

'The tiniest.'

'All right, for the last time,' came the tired voice of Sir Rupert, 'but I warn you, step out of line once more and I will recommend deportation – after you've served your prison sentence, that is.'

Charlie, realising it was in his interest to ignore the implicit threat, went straight to the point. 'Anything in the "Pinks" over the last few days, Rupert?'

'How did you know about the pink forms – we only introduced them a year or so ago?'

'Because on arrival at Heathrow I went through the same procedure,' he replied, struggling to contain the note of triumph in his voice. Again the silence, and again Charlie took the opportunity to smile down at Janice as she slipped an arm round his waist and returned his smile with her usual look of adoration.

'There was one, Charlie, and I suggest you take a deep breath.' A rustle of papers followed before Sir Rupert spoke again, this tine in measured tones as if reading. 'Pan Am Flight 412, 22nd December,' a pause as he cleared his throat, 'ETA 22.00, confirmed, from Frankfurt, one female, port of origin ... Warsaw. Doubtless, Charlie, you would appreciate the individual's name?'

'And address in the UK, please, Rupert.'

'Valma Gollitzin – UK address, the Russian Institute.' Sir Rupert had the satisfaction of hearing Charlie's sharp intake of breath before he continued. 'Another arrival due tonight may interest you ... Alexis Sternov is returning as Assistant Military Attache.' This time Charlie's sudden silence invoked a question from Sir Rupert.

'Are you still there, Charlie?'

'I'm here, Rupert ... and thank you.'

'What is it, Charlie?' asked Janice, removing her arm from his waist. 'You've gone as white as a sheet.'

Charlie, saying nothing, sat down in the convenience chair by the phone.

'Another Gollitzin has surfaced,' he said, 'Valma, she's staying at the Russian Institute.'

'So what?'

'That's not all, Sternov is flying in tonight...' his face had assumed a look she knew well, denoting he was deep in thought. Finally he said, looking at her as if for an answer, 'He told me himself he had no further interest in the girl.'

'Perhaps he's changed his mind,' she said with a shrug of the shoulders, 'there could be many reasons for his return. And Charlie, what's all this about the CIA?'

'Not now, Janice, not now, explanations later.' Then, after a pause, 'I think we'll need to watch over Natasha very carefully these next few days.'

'Oh, Charlie, I'm so sick of it, when are we to get some peace?'

'Another thing,' he said, as if he hadn't heard her, 'I believe it's time we had a face to face with Bill.'

'There, what have I been saying for days?' said Janice, thankful for something to get her teeth into. 'I shall ring Daddy tonight and settle his hash for good.'

*   *   *

As Christmas celebrations go, it was a non-event in the Webster's household. The saying 'You could cut the air with a knife' flashed through Charlie's mind as he surveyed the group now sitting in Janice's drawing room, sipping their after-dinner liqueurs. The meal had also been an unending strain and taken in almost complete silence but for Bill. He felt, in spite of his contempt for the man, some sympathy for his beleaguered state and the manner in which he had pretended nothing was wrong. Throughout dinner he had talked of some case he was working on, seemingly unaware of the waves of hatred being generated by Janice opposite him. Soon, Charlie knew, from Janice's earlier decision, the storm would break. A storm of hurricane proportions.

Natasha, sitting beside Janice, had seemingly recovered her *joie de vivre* and appeared to be immune to the tensions surrounding her. With the return of her dazzling smile, Charlie had to admit she once again exuded a fascinating mixture of bewitching beauty and youthful innocence. Not for the first time, he wondered why it was that one human being should be so richly endowed.

Charlie's gaze switched to Bill, now leaning over several pages of foolscap spread out on the floor, his briefcase open on the sofa beside him. Janice's voice, although only reproachful, came across to him like a streak of forked lightning before the crescendo of thunder.

252

'You've got something to tell us, haven't you, Bill?'

'Something to tell you . . . I don't understand,' came the reply.

'I think you do . . . I believe the name she gave you was Valma Gollitzin.'

Charlie, experienced more than most in the arts of concealment, again found himself admiring Bill, who had retained his composure.

'Valma Gollitzin, I don't understand.'

Janice, aware that her thunderbolt had not had quite the desired effect, shrugged her shoulders, Natasha, with a quizzical expression, looked up.

'Janeece, I don't understand . . .'

'Hush, sweetie,' Janice replied, 'explanations later.' Then like a cat, bored with the mouse as a plaything, she moved in for the kill . . .

'All right, Bill, have it your way. I want you out of my house by Monday morning and, as Daddy wants you to clear your desk first thing, you're going to be a busy little man.'

In such cases ruminated Charlie, it was usual to use a blindfold. Janice, in full cry, had no time for such a ritual. Again, Charlie had a measure of admiration for the man as, looking up, he said, 'I cannot say this is unexpected . . .' The mouse was all but dead, or if you preferred it, thought Charlie, the cat had done its job . . . now it was just a case of finishing him off. Janice did this without pity or compunction.

'And you can hand me the keys of the Jag – get yourself a taxi.'

Sweeping his papers into his briefcase, Bill allowed himself one venomous look at Natasha before, briefcase under his arm, he strode from the room. It is doubtful if Bill heard his wife's parting salvo, as, helping herself to another Cointreau, she muttered, 'And good riddance to bad rubbish,' before turning to Charlie with a broad smile of triumph.

'I must say,' remarked Charlie, as he closed the drawing room door behind the retreating figure of her husband, 'I've witnessed quite a few executions in my time but that was as cold-blooded as they come.'

'He had it coming,' was the spirited reply, 'you said so your-self.' Natasha, wide-eyed, looked from one to the other.

'What is happening, Janeece...?'

'Nothing to worry your lovely head about,' comforted Janice, and then to Charlie, 'Tell her, Charlie...'

'Time will tell – hopefully there is no need for concern,' replied a rather reluctant Charlie.

'Is that the best you can do?'

Charlie, stung by her tone stood up. 'You're right, what's the point of pussyfooting around. She's not over here for health reasons – I suspect blackmail at the very least.'

'Thank you, Charlie, now you've upset Natasha.'

Natasha, tears beginning to run down her cheeks, looked at Charlie, then, accepting the proffered handkerchief from the consoling Janice, fired a broadside of her own.

'If you're talking about Valma she is a wicked, wicked woman, she has always hated me...' her diatribe finished abruptly as Bill re-entered the room.

'Your keys,' he said as he threw a bunch of keys at Janice's feet. Then, in a reproachful tone, 'I have no wish to stay where I'm not wanted.' Janice, however, was not to be outdone.

'That's good coming from you, you've only been tolerated in this house as long as you have because we've had more pressing matters to attend to.'

Bill, by this time having reached the doorway, turned back and, ignoring her remarks, launched a vicious onslaught of his own. Pointing at Charlie, he said, 'Oh, yes, my dear Janice, you think he's got balls, but, if you ever do get him into bed, you'll find that's one part of his anatomy he's missing, wouldn't you agree, Natasha?'

As the door closed with a bang behind him, Janice, her eyes like saucers, looked at Charlie in bewilderment. To her dismay he said nothing but moved across to Natasha and, bending down, placed his arms round her shoulders.

'We've come through worse than this, Natasha, Just trust me.'

254

It was then, as Janice looked on at the dog-like devotion now clearly showing in Natasha's eyes, that understanding came to her. She did not, she realised, have a monopoly where Natasha's affections were concerned – or for that matter, Charlie's. Yes, she thought, it had been a most revealing and momentous evening.

*　*　*

'Well, what now?' said Bill, as he looked at Sir Humphrey Charters quietly sipping his drink whilst reclining in a large leather chair, his feet resting on a footstool. It was the day following Bill's clearance of his desk. 'I've lost my home, my partnership, and my wife – a full house, as they say in poker.'

'Stop whingeing, Bill, I'm sure you're well rid of her.'

'Yes, it's all right for you to say that, but how am I to live? She's even taken the car...'

'You should have been more subtle, Bill, and as you've mentioned poker, kept your cards a little closer to your chest. By the way, I went back to her hotel last night, took a large bottle of vodka with me ... she sure loves cock and booze.'

'Did you find out anything more?' asked Bill, his voice rising.

'For heaven's sake, man, keep your voice down, this is the Carlton after all – the Home Secretary himself is sitting over there.' Sir Humphrey's tone had a distinct edge to it.

'Perhaps it would help if I were offered a drink.'

'Of course,' said Sir Humphrey, beckoning to a white-coated waiter, 'I'm sorry about that.'

Bill, somewhat mollified, whispered, 'Did she say anything more?'

Ignoring him, Sir Humphrey spoke to the waiter now hovering in attendance.

'Two large malts ... soda or water, Bill?'

'Eh, water, please.'

As soon as the waiter had withdrawn, Sir Humphrey leaned

forward in his chair. 'You know, Bill, it is a fact of life that your usefulness to me no longer exists.

'What are you getting at?'

'Simply this, if you're no longer a member of the household, as it were, how can you possibly feed me information?'

'In other words, Sir Humphrey, you're giving me the bum's rush.'

'I wouldn't put it quite like that, but you must admit circumstances have changed somewhat...'

'Perhaps, Sir Humphrey, it might be better for you to appreciate how much I already know.'

'Don't be subtle with me, boy, if that was intended as a threat, say so.'

'Surely it doesn't have to end like this. I can still be useful to you in many ways.'

'Name one?'

'Well, I'm not thinking straight at the moment – this has come as something of a shock.'

'Of course, of course, and incidentally, in case you're short of the readies, here's a cheque for five hundred. Now I've got a date with a lady...'

'Valma?'

'You've got it in one, my boy – she may be nothing to look at, but what she has got she knows how to use.'

'Good luck, then,' said a somewhat chastened Bill as he placed the cheque in his wallet.

'I don't need luck, Bill, just a bottle of good vodka and plenty of energy,' he said as he hoisted his bulk from the chair.

It just shows you, thought Bill, as he watched Sir Humphrey take his leave ... nodding to a person here ... stopping and saying a few words there, how little they really knew him. A man of no publicly known vices, conjectured Bill, but he certainly had one hidden vice – the knowledge of which he would quietly tuck away as an insurance policy ... it might well be useful one day.

27

Whodunit?

It was the time of day, sometimes called the quiet hour, when the light slowly dims and nature pauses in anticipation of the approaching night, that Charlie awoke from an uneasy sleep. Looking across at the recumbent figures of Janice and Natasha asleep on the sofas, he envied them both the ability to switch off whatever their anxieties ... anxieties that continued to plague him even in sleep. The emergence of Sir Humphrey Charters into the arena added rather than diminished the complexities of an already intricate situation – a situation that had already prescribed a need for his unremitting resolve to see it through.

As if his thoughts had communicated themselves to her, Janice, yawning, looked across at him.

'Switch the light on, Charlie, there's a dear,' and then, 'Good heavens, is that the time? I'll fetch the tea.'

With the light on, Charlie busied himself drawing the curtains. Natasha, by now also awake, was just in time to see Janice depart in the direction of the kitchen.

'Charlie, I'm so frightened, why has Valma come to England?' Her eyes, rounded and appealing, added substance to that fear.

'That is what I intend to find out, believe me, Natasha...' but, with hands clasped to her ears, as if in dread of what she might hear, Natasha rushed from the room, all but colliding with Janice and the previously prepared tea trolley as she did so.

257

'What's bugging her?' said Janice, as she trundled the trolley into the room.

'I don't know, it's one thing after another, as soon as one threat is out of the way another appears.' Pouring the tea, she looked across at him.

'Well?'

Changing the subject, he said, 'Dmitri Sokolov has invited me to join him and Humphrey Charters and go for the gold.'

'Sir Humphrey Charters ... Penelope's father?'

'The same.'

'I don't believe it.'

'Neither did I, at first, but now it's beginning to hang together. You see, back in the old days he was financial adviser to the Tsar, so if anyone knows where the gold is hidden, he does.'

'Surely you're not going to help them?'

'Of course not, but nevertheless it niggles. It's as if all the pieces of the puzzle are in front of me now and all that is needed is to get them sorted in the right order.'

'Have you ever played Whodunit, Charlie?' she said as she joined him on the sofa with her tea. 'I used to play it with Daddy years ago, and it's quite something. We shall need a pen and writing paper...' With that she got up and moved to her writing desk.

'I don't feel much like games, Janice...'

'Shut up and do as I tell you,' she replied, as she rejoined him armed with a pen and pad. 'To begin, we'll do an analysis of each piece of the puzzle – fire away.'

'You're a clever girl, Janice.'

'Never mind that, question one.'

Charlie, sitting back, fixed his gaze on the ceiling.

'Firstly, why did the Duchess appear to have no interest in Natasha for so long? It was only in the latter two years that she even began to pay for her French and English lessons.'

'Think about it, Charlie.'

'There could only be one reason: she knew the true heir to the throne was dead.'

'Logical, so almost certainly correct,' said Janice, busily writing.

'Second question, what brought Natasha into the picture? It could only have been Elizabeth's decision to resurrect her original plan. After all, why not play the cards Fate had dealt her?'

'I think you've got it in one, boy, everything points to that.'

'But, Janice, we're no nearer to completing the puzzle.'

'Oh, yes, we are. Think for a minute, put yourself in the shoes of the Duchess. An aged, feeble old woman constantly in fear of her life, with the bitterness and hatred of the Bolsheviks eating away at her over the years, her one hope of ousting them gone with the death of her niece's child. Then word reaches her about Natasha – not an ugly duckling, as she might have expected, but a swan. So she concocts a new plan much the same as the first, but substituting Natasha in the role of heir to the throne.'

'Then what Sternov told me, you accept as true, and Natasha really is only a gypsy girl . . .'

'Bought . . . for . . . a . . . handful . . . of . . . roubles,' they said in unison.

'Accept that,' said Janice, 'and the rest is easy.'

'It does have one flaw, though,' remarked Charlie.

'Such as?'

'Why continue to pay Daddy Gollitzin for all those intervening years?'

'I admit that is a point, but for the Duchess the payments were little more than pennies, and at the back of her mind would always be the thought that she might rescue a few chestnuts from the fire.'

'You could be right.'

'I'm sure of it – her new plan was nothing more than an outlandish confidence trick. To an enfeebled woman . . .'

'She never struck me as being enfeebled,' said Charlie, interrupting her.

'I'm not implying she had lost her marbles, far from it, but her wish for revenge had festered and become ever more compulsive over the years. To her, in her desperate state, one infant was much like any other...'

Silence followed as Charlie considered Janice's point.

'Charlie...'

'I'm listening.'

'Tell me, you were there – when the Duchess first met Natasha, what was her attitude towards her?'

'For the first few minutes it was as if Elizabeth was sizing her up.'

'You mean like an interview for a job or something?'

In that moment the commanding words of the Duchess came back to him, 'Turn around girl, and walk over to the bureau...'

'Yes, exactly like that.'

'There you are then, from that moment a new heir to the throne was born.'

'But ... what ... about ... Sir ... Humphrey ... Charters?'

'I'll admit he is something of a fly in the ointment...'

'All the time I was with Elizabeth I never heard his name mentioned, yet there must have been collusion between the two of them.'

'Think like Elizabeth,' said Janice, sucking the end of her pen and pausing to allow Charlie a few moments thought before continuing. 'Then, inevitably, however much she tried to justify herself, there would be an element of guilt. Therefore, to salve her conscience, what would she try to do with what was left of the Romanov fortune?'

'Give it back?'

'Exactly that.'

'But how?'

'You're making it easy for me, Charlie. You're asking just the right questions ... she had but one choice, bury it with the infant, the true Romanov – and who helped her do that?'

'Sir Humphrey Charters. That answers the question why poor old Sergei Poznansky, supposedly her guardian, was so short of money ... Elizabeth was not so well-off as everyone thought.'

'No doubt at all. But she tried to make amends at the last minute by giving you the three ingots.'

'So,' said Charlie, somewhat distantly, 'the residue of the Romanov gold IS buried back in the cemetery at Kolomyja.'

'If it exists at all, Charlie, that's where it is, and if I may say so, game, set, and match to me ... there is something else, I'll tell you in a moment after I've persuaded Miss Misery Guts to join us.'

In Janice's absence, Charlie mentally went over her assessment of the puzzle. Certainly, he had to admit, her conclusions might well be close to the truth, they certainly matched what Sokolov had told him – but if the ingots were buried in the cemetery at Kolomyja, then recovering them might be well-nigh impossible ... unless ... but that was too preposterous to contemplate, or was it? At that moment, Janice returned with a fresh pot of tea.

'She won't come down,' she said as she poured.

'I'm not surprised, she's badly frightened with the appearance of her sister. Getting back to the puzzle, Janice, it does have one flaw.'

'Such as?'

'Why did Elizabeth keep Sir Humphrey under wraps ... even from me?'

'Difficult one, that. I don't think for a minute it was lack of trust in you, her later actions proved that.' She thought for a moment. 'Perhaps it was something to do with misplaced loyalty to him. I don't know what else.'

'You could be right.'

'By the by, I had a telephone call today from Wills Willoughby, trying to reach our errant gentleman.'

'And who or what are Wills Willoughby?'

'Only one of the biggest brokers in the City. They've appointed Bill to their legal section, would you believe?'

'What of it?'

'Well, I thought you should know that on the Board of Wills Willoughby is an old friend of ours, Sir Humphrey Charters ... I can see from your expression that like me two and two have made four – or rather, two and one have made three.'

'You mean Charters, Bill and Valma?'

'Yes, and each has a motive for bringing down Natasha. Perhaps individually they present no great threat, but collectively they could be dynamite.'

'All right, Janice, what would you suggest?'

'You're asking me...'

'Well, you seem to be the one with the ideas.'

'I would go for the weakest link. It's close, but I think the girl Valma just edges Bill.'

'She'll take some finding. They will have stowed her somewhere out of harm's way.'

'Would Sir Rupert be able to help?'

'I doubt it. They will have the Russian Institute as her address, but the bird will have flown long since.'

Janice, obviously deep in thought, again occupied her favourite position in front of the fire.

'According to Florrie,' she began again, 'when Valma came to the door she asked for Natasha... right?'

'Point taken.'

'Therefore, we could use Natasha as bait.'

'We've still got to find her.'

'Come on, Charlie, start using some of your expertise.'

'Well, in my opinion, it's a job for a private dick.'

'A what?'

'A private investigator.'

'Right then, let's get off our backsides and find one. And now, we must get ready for Hilda and George ... after all, it is New Year's Eve, and so far I've done nothing by way of preparation.'

'But they're only coming for drinks.'

'Charlie, it is New Year's Eve. I have to offer them something, and I've no Florrie to help me.'

'Well, to begin with, Natasha can come down here and lend a hand.'

'Agreed, and as you're the one with the charm, you go up and fetch her.'

*   *   *

Hilda, followed by George, his hands clasped behind his back like some Prince Consort, entered the room, Janice following. 'As a special treat,' she gushed, ' I've prepared a champagne punch...' If she heard at all Hilda gave no indication as, in obvious haste, she moved across to Charlie. No doubt at all, mused Janice, somewhat annoyed at the lack of response. Charlie, in Hilda's eyes, had become a true knight errant as if he were patently a throwback to the days of King Arthur. Gazing up at him admiringly she held out a limp hand, which Charlie, to Janice's utter amazement, lifted to his mouth and soundly kissed. Hilda, obviously delighted, sat down on the sofa nearest the fireplace, smoothing down her dress as she did so.

'Janice,' she said in her authoritative voice, 'tell me all the news since I last saw you. I'm sure a great deal must have happened.' Then, looking around, 'And where is Natasha?'

As if on cue, Natasha entered.

'You won't believe this,' she said, barely into the room, and full of overwhelming excitement and exuberance, 'Michael just rang, he's brought forward our dinner engagement to tomorrow week, and I've accepted.'

'I didn't hear the phone,' said Janice vaguely, attempting to come to terms with the outburst, then, 'you might have had a word with me first, and in any case...' but she got no further as Hilda's shrill voice interrupted.

'Michael, what Michael?' She patted the seat beside her. 'Come over here, Natasha, and tell me all about him.'

With her words ignored, as well as the champagne punch, Janice, much happier when she was imparting news, took over. 'He's the Grand Prince Michael, heir to the Romanov throne.'

'You mean *the* Prince Michael?'

'None other.'

Hilda's eyes, magnified by her bifocals, blinked excitedly. 'How wonderful. I trust we shall have an opportunity of meeting him in the not too distant future, Janice. I'll never forgive you if we don't.'

Helplessly, Janice looked across at Charlie, but it was Big George, quiet until now, who burst forth, 'Now there's a thing, I say, there's a thing. Royalty no less, you'll have to watch your Ps and Qs now, Natasha.'

'There's no need for your peculiar brand of wit, George, thank you,' admonished Hilda as she patted Natasha's knee. 'In any event, Natasha is a princess in her own right, aren't you, my dear?' Giving Natasha's knee an extra squeeze, 'Tell me, child,' she continued, 'is he as handsome as they say he is? And where did you meet him?'

'Not in Sainsbury's, I'll warrant,' cut in George laughingly as he joined Natasha and Hilda on the sofa, ensuring, as he sat down, he had as much knee contact with Natasha as possible.

Janice, obviously disgruntled at the frequent interruptions, moved to her favourite position for announcement, in front of the fireplace.

'Apart from the likely possibility I am now going to have to entertain a prince,' exasperation was in her voice as she looked at Natasha, 'other problems have arisen. Natasha's sister has arrived in England, and she's out to make mischief.'

'She's not my sister,' exclaimed Natasha, her enthusiasm and enchantment whilst describing Michael to Hilda changing to barely controlled anger.

Hilda's questioning eyes again focused on Natasha.

'You've never mentioned a sister before.'

'I have never been asked,' replied Natasha petulantly.

'Surely,' said George, relishing the opportunity for further banter, 'not another Natasha . . . it's impossible.'

'Hilda, George, do you really want to hear all the news or don't you? Because if I'm interrupted once more I shall scream.'

'Of course we do, Janice dear, that's why we're here.' Charlie, alone on the periphery of the gathering, avoided meeting Janice's eyes by gazing intently at the ceiling.

'Hush everybody,' said Hilda, anxious to placate her hostess, 'you carry on, Janice.'

At that precise moment, George, anxious to be helpful, lumbered to his feet and picked up the tray of champagne flutes with the intention of handing them round. Janice, her feet astride and her jaw set determinedly, screamed at him, 'I have an announcement to make . . .'

George, halfway across the room, stopped dead. With his hands trembling, the tray of glasses, until then finely balanced, became alive with a melody of their own not unlike a prelude to 'Jingle Bells'.

'I am divorcing Bill, and as soon as that's over Charlie and I are to be married,' said Janice, somewhat wild-eyed.

For the first time that evening silence descended, except for the continuing close harmony of the champagne flutes, which, to their open-mouthed audience, became ever more precariously balanced on the silver serving tray. Perhaps it was a mistake for George to attempt to return them back to the trolley, because in doing so a collision with a grim-faced Natasha, bent on leaving the room, was inevitable. The resounding crash of splintering glass, allied to a bouncing silver tray, could only be compared to the clash of cymbals and thundering cannon that concludes the *1812 Overture*.

* * *

'Well, Mrs Tuttle?' said Charlie, gazing at the dying embers of the fire, 'You've certainly made a hit with Natasha tonight.'

'So what? It's time she realised she hasn't got a God-given right to every man in creation.'

'I wouldn't argue with that, but it is customary for the lady to wait until she is asked before announcing a marriage.'

'How flattering you are tonight, Charlie. Much more, and a girl could go off you.'

'Actually,' looking at his watch, 'it's two in the morning and I'm off to bed.'

'Charlie, before you go, you know she's in love with you ... a woman can tell.'

'Natasha, with me! You must be joking – what about her prince?'

'Flash in the pan, it's you she really cares about ... Charlie, answer me truthfully, do you care about her?'

'God, Janice, what's got into you? Of course I care about her, I should have thought that was pretty obvious.'

'Yes, but I don't mean in that way...'

'Janice, I'm tired, and I'm going to bed. If necessary we'll finish this conversation some other time – that's if it's worth finishing.' With that, Charlie got up and walked towards the door, stopped and looked back. How small she looked and how vulnerable curled up in that massive armchair. He had, he realised, been very unkind, quite unnecessarily so.

'Janice,' he whispered.

'I thought you had gone to bed.'

'Well, actually, I was waiting for you...'

'You know, Charlie Tuttle, you're a pig, but you're a very lovable pig, you're also a very tired little pig ... I can wait ... and oh yes, Charlie, Happy New Year!'

28

Head to Head

Her greeting was very different to the welcome he had become accustomed to. Even the brandishing of the, by now, *de rigueur* bottle of vodka, made little impact on her attitude of cold aloofness.

'You've brought Valma package?'

'Package...? I don't understand...'

'Comrade Sternov – you understand now?'

'You mean...'

'Valma to be given package, Valma take to Moscow.'

Nonplussed, Sir Humphrey sat down on the nearest chair.

Delighted at his consternation, Valma elaborated.

'Comrade Sternov clever, diplomatic bag not safe – Valma safe. Now, you go fetch package.'

'On your word alone? Really, Valma, do you expect me...'

'Sir 'umphrey, I have little time, you fetch now and give Valma, Valma has only to ring,' she said as she moved towards the phone.

'Yes, I'm beginning to see it all now, your supposed visit to your sister...'

She all but spat at him. 'Natasha is not my sister. Valma has no sister.'

'Exactly, all that was a cover for the real reason for your visit, very astute I must say. All right, I'll have the package, as you call it, here later tonight, but you can tell Alexis I'm not best pleased.

'Good, now you give me vodka and we fuck.'

For the first time in his life, Sir Humphrey Charters was at a loss for words.

* * *

Within two days, the private investigator presented a detailed report of Sir Humphrey's movements.

'For someone supposedly with a great deal to hide, he has been most indiscreet, commented Charlie, reading the report, ' and a flat in that corner of the woods must have cost a pretty penny.'

'What's that to him?' Janice had replied, 'He's got oodles of money.'

They decided it was imperative to visit the flat as Valma might well be there, but persuading Natasha to accompany had been difficult.

'Please, Janeece, I don't want to see her . . . I never want to see her . . .'

'It's for your own good, honey, we have to find out what she's up to,' was Janice's reply.

'Charlie,' Natasha had pleaded, ' I hate the woman and she hates me, Charlie, please . . .'

'I don't like it any more than you do, Natasha, but Janice is right. We must know what she is up to.'

The address pinpointed by the investigator was close to Belgravia, in a ten-floor block of luxury apartments.

'We've no guarantee that she's here, Janice, so keep your fingers crossed,' he said as they had stepped into the lift.

'Rubbish, Charlie, three visits in two days and always un-accompanied, it can only mean he's got her here . . . charming little love nest, I must say. He probably can't believe his luck,' she elucidated with a knowing smile.

'We shall soon find out,' Charlie replied, pressing the bell.

* * *

'What's going on, Vladimir?? We've heard nothing for weeks.'

'Do you always live like a pig, Magyar?' replied Vladimir, surveying a sink of dirty dishes whilst running his finger along a cracked and peeling mantelpiece before wiping it on a towel hanging forlornly on the back of a chair. ' I don't know any more than you,' he said, finally replying to Magyar. 'The last thing I heard he was having trouble getting the vehicles.'

'If you ask me,' said Magyar, plaintively, 'the whole business has blown up in his face and he hasn't the guts to tell us.'

'Could be, but don't underestimate our friend Dmitri Sokolov. If something has turned up that is more promising, it's goodbye Vladimir and Magyar.'

'What about Paul?'

'Paul will stick to him like glue – they're two of a kind ... probably consider themselves a cut above us.'

'If he has betrayed us, then God help him.'

'Who, Paul?'

'No, both of them.'

'Come down to earth, Magyar, what could you do? Come to that, what could either of us do?' Looking at him, Vladimir wondered how anyone ever got into his ramshackle taxi, what with his tobacco-stained beard and creased shirtfront liberally spotted with food stains ... 'Why don't you do something about your appearance, Magyar?' he found himself compelled to say.

'Put a sock in it, Vladimir. You didn't come here to look for dust on my mantelpiece or to find fault with my appearance, or if you did, you're madder than I am.'

'All right, Magyar, point taken. Get the bottle out and we'll talk.'

'Now that's more like it ... you should remember, Vladimir, that where I was brought up we had an earth floor and the rain peed in through the roof. At least this place is an improvement on that.'

Ignoring him, Vladimir, after careful inspection of the chair offered him, sat down.

'No glasses, Magyar?'

'There are a couple in the sink.'

'No, thank you, I'll drink from the bottle.'

'I was going to anyway,' replied Magyar, lifting the bottle to a web of a beard-covered mouth. Vladimir watched incredulously as the bottle, almost perpendicular, seemed glued to Magyar. Only the pressing need for air finally outweighed the attraction of its contents. Lowering the bottle, Magyar wiped the driblets from his beard with the back of his hand belching loudly.

'Have you been hearing things?' he said, gathering his breath and passing the bottle to Vladimir.

'I have,' replied Vladimir, ignoring the obvious with difficulty.

'Tell me.'

'You remember the Gollitzin woman?'

'Hardly likely to forget her ... I still go to bed at night wondering what it would be like to ...'

Impatiently, Vladimir interrupted him, 'I know, I know ... well, her sister has come visiting.'

'What, from the Union?'

'No, Poland.'

'Same thing.'

'Anyway, she's over here, and what is more, some bigwig from the City had a meeting with Dmitri.'

'Who told you that?'

'I've got a friend in the Nobility Association – and that's not all. Dmitri also had a meeting with someone from British Military Intelligence. An hour or so afterwards our dear Dmitri was very excited. All right, I'm not saying we should think the worst,' looking at Magyar's mournful expression, 'it may mean nothing.'

'You know differently, otherwise you wouldn't have told me.'

'Possibly.'

'No possibly about it, Vladimir, he's up to something, and that something doesn't include us.'

'What do you suggest?'

Later, Vladimir often had cause to wonder why he had so easily surrendered the initiative. But then, whatever his faults, he knew that between the two of them Magyar was by far the stronger and therefore likely to be the most unforgiving . . .

* * *

As the door inched open, Valma's podgy face appeared. She was about to say something when her eyes fastened on Natasha – her mouth formed an 'O' followed by, 'Nat . . . ash . . . a.'

Surprisingly, it was Natasha who took the initiative. 'Yes, it's me, Valma, let us in.'

'No one allowed in,' came the cryptic reply.

'Rubbish,' contributed Janice, not to be outdone

But it was Charlie, deciding further words were pointless, who put his shoulder against the door and pushed. Accepting the inevitable, Valma backed away.

In faultless Russian, Charlie took charge. 'You wanted to see your sister . . . we've brought her to you.'

Gathering herself together, Valma let forth in a torrent of Russian. Janice, glancing at Natasha's face, needed no interpreter to get the gist of what was obviously a venomous tirade.

With Valma fully occupied addressing her sister Janice pushed past her and strode across the hallway into what was apparently the sitting room. As Charlie followed with Natasha and Valma bringing up the rear, the flood of abuse continued. Finding themselves chairs, the trio sat down. After carefully emptying an ash tray into the open hearth, Charlie, with characteristic calm, busied himself lighting a cigarette, and neither he nor Janice expected Natasha's sudden lunge at her tormentor.

Obviously goaded beyond endurance, she stood up and launched herself at Valma, slapping her hard on the cheek. As if a cork had been replaced in a bottle, the flow of insults emanating from Valma ceased and a look of incredulity came over her face. Then, to the astonishment of all, she sat down and began a low wail. Compared with her previous stream of invective it was, thought Charlie, something of an anticlimax.

Drawing on his cigarette, Charlie exchanged a wink with Janice before, in consoling tones, he addressed Valma and with a gesture of sympathy took her hands in his. Janice, aware that her support was needed, stood up, moved across to the erstwhile miscreant and, with the aid of her handkerchief, attempted to stem the flow of tears. Natasha, meanwhile, remained haughtily to one side, her vague mutterings accompanied by glares of glacial proportions whenever she caught her sister's eye.

With a semblance of order restored, Charlie continued his dialogue, which produced a few whispered words in response from the, by now, chastened Valma. Their low-key conversation continued for some time before Charlie turned to Janice and Natasha.

'She's prepared to accept our offer of two thousand pounds to fly home tomorrow night – Charters has been full of promises, but so far nothing has been forthcoming, so she is, to say the least, a little disenchanted with him.

'A bit sudden, isn't it? This decision to fly home just like that...'

'Not really, Janice, it's as I suspected, she came over to get money from Natasha.'

'I hope you're right, but I've got my doubts – it's all too pat for my liking. And anyway, is there a flight tomorrow night?'

'Yes, it's the weekly from Manchester. I checked – direct to Warsaw.'

'What guarantee do we have that she won't be back?'

'We don't.'

'Seems a bit one-sided to me.'

'Janice, two thousand pounds will give her half a million roubles at current exchange rates – more than she could earn in a lifetime... I don't think we will have any more trouble from her.'.

'If you say so.'

'I do say so... now I suggest you and Natasha leave. I will stay with Valma whilst she packs, and we'll go to Manchester tonight.

Tomorrow you bring up the banker's draft – she won't be able to take sterling out – you follow?'

'Well, I only hope I've that much in my account . . .'

'I'll make it right with you in a day or so.'

Rising, Janice, still looking doubtful, walked across to Natasha. 'Come on, sweetie, it's time we went,' then, looking across at Valma, she couldn't help noticing the gleam that had replaced the earlier tears. With a glance at Charlie, who was again engaged in conversation with Valma, she permitted herself one final barb, 'I hope you know what you're doing, Charlie, and take a tip from me, watch her.'

Charlie, if he heard, said nothing, but Valma, whose knowledge of English was patently greater than she was prepared to admit, was already responding to Charlie in a manner, much to Janice's chagrin, that could have one interpretation . . .

*   *   *

'Shall I serve tea now, ma'am?' enquired Florrie as they made their way into the drawing room. 'And will it be just for the two of you?'

'No tea, Florrie, I need something a little stronger,' then glancing across at the white-faced Natasha, 'and so does she, by the look of her.'

'Oh, and, Florrie, Mr Tuttle won't be back tonight – and I've got an early start tomorrow. Just a breakfast tray will do.'

'As you wish . . . Mr Tuttle, is he all right?'

'He's fine, thank you, Florrie,' replied Janice, as she poured herself and Natasha a large brandy each.

'Drink this, it will put the colour back in your cheeks,' she said, passing the glass to Natasha.

'Oh, Janeece, it was awful, that dreadful woman . . .'

'Well, I have to admit she wouldn't rate very highly in the popularity stakes, and I only hope Charlie knows what he's doing.'

'You worry, Janeece?'

'To be frank, I do, it was all too easy – call it feminine intuition if you like, but she collapsed just a little too conveniently for my liking. You know, Charlie has one great weakness,' she continued, 'he doesn't understand women and their wiles . . . I cannot get away from the feeling that Valma pulled one big act.' Silence followed as they both sipped their brandies and contemplated the significance of Janice's last few words. It was Natasha who finally spoke.

'You confuse, me, Janeece.'

'Well for one thing, why would two thousand pounds tempt her, when Sir Humphrey Charters could match that ten times over and not feel the pinch?'

'It ees a lot of money, Janeece.'

'By your standards, yes, but nevertheless something is bugging me; what, I cannot put a finger on . . . yet. I just wish Charlie were here to talk to,' her voice trailed off.

'Valma has always been a mystery,' said Natasha, accepting the offer of another brandy.

'In what way? Tell me about her, Natasha, it might prove useful.'

'She was always going away. Then, when she came back she would boast of places she had been to . . . Paris, Rome, Berlin, even Helsinki – she was lying, of course.' Natasha paused to drink from the replenished glass.

'This is interesting. Anything else, Natasha? Think, girl.'

'When she came back she always had plenty of money. Occasionally she would give me some, but not often. Once she gave me a handful of French francs, she did it out of spite, what could I do with them?'

Janice, placing her drink on a nearby table, stood up and walked across to Natasha then, looking down at her, she said, 'Natasha, you're sure about this, the French francs, I mean, and the boasting?'

'Of course, Janeece, I would not lie.'

'Oh, God, I cannot reach Charlie until the morning.' For a few moments she paced the room before turning back to Natasha.

'If necessary, would you repeat what you've just told me?'
Natasha nodded her head.
'Wait here, I'm going to make a phone call. I think Charlie, the idiot, could be in grave danger from that woman.'

*   *   *

Sir Rupert de Quincy's sigh was clearly audible. 'Mrs Webster, if this is to do with the Romanov gold...'
'Sir Rupert, please listen. I have reason to believe Charlie's life may be in danger.'
A throaty laugh came back at her and then, after a pause, 'Mrs Webster, I trust you haven't rung to tell me something I've known for years.'
'Sir Rupert...' Janice swallowed deeply, controlling with difficulty her rising anger. 'Sir Rupert,' she began again, 'I've no wish to waste your time, or for that matter mine, but I think you should know that Valma Gollitzin is not quite what she appears to be.'
'Really, Mrs Webster, I cannot say that interests me a great deal.'
'Supposing I were to tell you that Valma Gollitzin is a much-travelled young lady, who, in the course of the last two years has been to Rome, Paris and Berlin – last year even Helsinki, hardly a tourist spot wouldn't you agree? I find such globe-trotting difficult to associate with a poor peasant girl or kulak, as I believe they are called.'
'You mentioned Helsinki ... last year?'
'Quite definitely.'
'Who told you this?'
'Natasha ... you remember, Natasha, don't you, Sir Rupert?'
There followed an indecipherable conversation, interspersed with lengthy silences, that Janice guessed was with Captain Farrar. Then Sir Rupert was back on the line. But now a different Sir Rupert: this time there was a distinct air of suppressed excitement in his voice.

'Mrs Webster, where is Charlie?'

'He's with her.'

'Mrs Webster, that is not what I asked ... where is he?'

'Some hotel in Manchester – I won't know until the morning.'

Again there followed, what seemed to Janice, an interminable silence.

'Mrs Webster, are you there?'

'Yes, Sir Rupert.'

'You're calling from home.'

'Yes.'

'Right, I should like to bring you and ... Natasha, into the office. A car will fetch you within the hour.'

'But it's past seven, Sir Rupert, we haven't eaten yet.'

'You said you thought Charlie might be in danger?'

'Well, yes I did.'

'Supposing I agreed with you...?'

'You know something, don't you, Sir Rupert?'

'Mrs Webster, I'm aware you haven't signed the Official Secrets Act, so I must choose my words carefully – let me say this, from what you've told me, there is every chance Valma Gollitzin is an agent of the KGB.'

'Oh God ... no,' murmured Janice almost incoherently, as Sir Rupert rang off.

* * *

Valma Gollitzin sat cross-legged on the bed, nursing a half-bottle of vodka she had inveigled Charlie into buying. Their journey from London had been uneventful, with very little conversation, although Charlie had become increasingly aware of her mounting interest in him. The hotel had the advantage of being close to the airport. As such, it provided rather spartan comfort – welcoming the weary traveller but not encouraging him to remain longer than was strictly necessary. It was, reflected Charlie, about as impersonal as a dentist's waiting room.

The thought of keeping his companion sweet for the best part of twenty-four hours worried him, as did the riddle of the full ashtray back in Belgravia. Valma didn't smoke. Sir Humphrey, if he did, would probably smoke some exclusive variety or, more likely, a cigar. What he had seen in the ashtray was neither. It was the remains of half-smoked pipe tobacco and, from its smell, a particularly pungent brand.

From his years of experience in Intelligence, Charlie knew that to ignore the seemingly innocuous was to do so at one's peril. Why pipe tobacco? In spite of attempts to shrug it off, the feeling of unease persisted.

'You're Charlie Tuttle, aren't you?' she said, putting the bottle to one side.

Charlie noticed that her demeanour had undergone a change in the past few minutes. Curious too, he thought, that until now names had not entered their conversation.

'If you say so,' he replied, and then, 'Who told you, was it Sir Humphrey?'

Charlie remembered that when he was registering she had asked to make a phone call to Sir Humphrey and he hadn't objected. She said nothing but lifted the bottle once more to her mouth. He, somewhat relieved the discussion had ended, continued to leaf through the house magazine, adorned with colour photographs extolling other hotels in the chain. Placing the bottle again at her side, she slid off the bed and walked towards him, then, as if changing her mind, moved across to her suitcase resting on the luggage rack by the door. Out of the corner of his eye Charlie watched as she began to untie the string fastening. Opening it, she began to rummage inside. As she had her back to him, he could see nothing of what was obviously interesting her until she turned and faced him. Clasped firmly in her right hand was an automatic pistol, its black barrel glinting in the electric light and made more sinister by a bulbous addition. Familiar with handguns, he knew at once he was looking at a Breda Magnum fitted with a silencer. Spreading her legs, her left hand quickly

277

joined her right before both gripped the butt. As she laughed, Charlie nonchalantly lowered the magazine to the floor.

'Charlie Tuttle,' she sniggered, 'how does it feel to be outwitted by a simple kulak?'

Aware that his jaw had stiffened and his mouth had suddenly become as dry as a desert, Charlie smiled. It was, he knew, more a grimace than a smile – the grimace of a man who could clearly see a stubby finger curled around a trigger, the slightest pressure from which would send him to eternity.

Whilst appearing calm, he returned her unblinking gaze ... his thoughts those of a drowning man. After all he had been through, was his life really going to end in this sterile hotel room and at the hands of this insufferable creature? Her pitiless eyes told him that she was one of that obscene group that enjoyed killing for its own sake. He smiled, at the same time whetting the inside of his mouth with his tongue.

'Would you allow me one last cigarette – and then perhaps we can talk?'

'Hand me your gun, butt first,' was her reply, his request ignored.

Dutifully, Charlie handed her his Luger, which she promptly threw onto the spare bed.

'I really do hand it to you, Valma, you've been very clever. Tell me, you didn't come over to England just to upset Natasha, did you?'

She smirked, obviously delighted with the compliment. Then, 'You may have your cigarette.'

It was not through pity she agreed, but rather the opportunity this gave her to prolong what for her was entertainment of the most perverse kind. One hand removed itself from the gun and began a ritual of its own by disappearing beneath her dress and commenced movements which he could only identify as masturbation. Charlie, meanwhile, with shaking hands made abortive attempts to light his cigarette, much to her continued amusement, as evinced by even more furious gyrations from underneath her dress. Charlie, aware that his only salvation was to get her talking, began again.

'You're not really Natasha's sister, are you, Valma?'

'Natasha is a slut ... why should she be the next Empress? She is just a bastard gypsy girl, a throw-out, sold for less than a hundred roubles.'

Thankfully, Charlie noticed that after that tirade the gyrations beneath her skirt had subsided somewhat. But, almost at once their tempo began again. This time, he sensed there could be but one ending.

In a gesture of supplication, Charlie slid from his chair and on to his knees. With both bands raised, one still clutching his unlit cigarette, and with a face he hoped was the epitome of abject fear, croaked in a voice he barely recognised, 'Please, Valma, please don't kill me ...'

He realised that with his pseudo-attitude of sheer terror he had got a couple of feet nearer to her. Her flushed face confirmed what he suspected that on reaching her climax she would pull the trigger ... he had, at best, but a few more seconds.

'Sir Humphrey,' he said, looking beyond her at the door.

It was the oldest trick in the book – but it worked. For one split second of time she glanced in the direction of the door ... it was all he needed as he launched himself at her. The plop of the discharge and the searing pain in his upper left arm, if anything, spurred him on.

Fortunately, his lunge had knocked her off-balance, and the weight of his body did the rest. Sprawled on top of her, his right hand forced her gun hand back. Two further plops, near to his ear, told him how close it had been. She fought like a tiger, but his initial impetus proved conclusive. In spite of the searing pain which climbed his arm like red-hot coals, he got a vicious punch, with all his weight behind it, into her midriff. She gasped, reminding him of a punctured tyre, and her body seemed to drain of strength. Using his knee like a blacksmith's anvil, he brought her gun arm down with terrific power – his reward was her scream as her arm was broken. From then on it was easy. Now on his feet, his good arm circled her throat. Turning her body so that he was behind her, he drove his knee with tremendous force at the base of her spine whilst twisting her neck. The sickening sound of her breaking bones assured him it was all over.

Throwing her body from him, he staggered in the direction of the bathroom, but not before picking up the Breda and his Luger. Then, pausing once more, he finally lit his cigarette...

*   *   *

Examination of the wound in his upper arm was proof, if it were needed, of how lucky he had been. Even the slightest divergence of the bullet's trajectory, and a main tendon would have been severed, leaving his arm useless. The thought of overpowering Valma with only one arm didn't bear thinking about. Reaching for the phone, he ordered a half-bottle of Scotch and some cigarettes then, using the remains of the vodka, he liberally doused the injury before making a rough bandage. It was then he noticed the deep bite marks on his left thumb, further evidence of the struggle she had put up. Luckily, the bleeding from the worst of his wounds was not heavy, but the arm was already stiffening up, as evidenced by the difficulty he had in lifting her body on to one of the two single beds.

Ensuring she was well covered, he eased himself on to the other bed and looked at his watch. If his calculations were right, he had about half an hour before the arrival of her visitor – just sufficient time to examine that suitcase...

Scattered beneath a conglomeration of odd bits of female attire were two small brown paper packages. Selecting one, Charlie quickly removed its covering then, squinting, held it up to the light. It did not require his professional eye for him to realize that he was holding a roll of film. Tiny lettering indicated there were twenty-two exposures, with the other identical roll, a total of forty-four exposures in all. Smiling to himself, Charlie conjectured that although Valma could be considered a tourist, it was highly unlikely, when the films were developed, he would be looking at the Tower of London or the Houses of Parliament.

Whistling between his teeth, Charlie continued his investigation of the suitcase, which soon revealed a brown manilla envelope, the contents of which had him taking a long draught from the whisky bottle and reaching for another cigarette.

The stamp of the German Eagle and the words Public Records Office, Berlin, swam before his eyes, but not before the lettering recorded the death of one *Natasha Alexandra Handrick on November tenth Nineteen Forty Two* ... one more piece of the puzzle, he thought, as looking at his watch he realised he hadn't much time. Gritting his teeth against the pain, he clambered on to a chair immediately below the room's centre light and, working quickly, soon completed his task. Still no sign of the expected visitor as, completely exhausted, he stretched out on the unoccupied bed; even this slightest of movements was excruciating. Then the knock came'...

'It's unlocked,' he called, his good hand gripping the butt of the Luger. Agonisingly slowly the door opened, and as it did so Charlie lined up the sights. He was perfectly positioned, having arranged the dressing table and mirror so as to see his caller long before the caller saw him. As a consequence, it was Charlie who spoke first.

'I was expecting you, Alexis.'

'Obviously, milkman, you have the gun,' replied Alexis Sternov, as he eased his bulk past the dressing table and into the room. The uniform of a Colonel in the Red Army had the effect of enlarging his already massive frame.

'May I?' he said, as he lowered himself into a chair and removed his cap. Charlie, ignoring the request, spoke quietly but firmly.

'Keep your hands where I can see them, Alexis.'

As if he hadn't heard, Sternov delved into his bulky overcoat pocket and pulled out a tobacco pouch and pipe, then, as if having an automatic pistol levelled at him was an everyday occurrence, he began slowly filling the pipe. Looking across at the shapeless form occupying one of the two beds, he said,

'Hannah...?'

'I don't know who the hell Hannah is, that's Valma Gollitzin ... or was.'

Sternov began to laugh. It started with a rumble from deep within him before erupting into a gale of sound which reverberated from floor to ceiling. Charlie, as Sternov's head went back, had a dentist's view of a row of gold teeth. The laughter finished abruptly as it had begun.

'Of course, comrade, I keep forgetting, you're no longer with Military Intelligence.'

'Haven't been for years, Alexis.'

'Then we might be able to strike a deal, eh, milkman?'

By now, Sternov had the pipe alight and Charlie was reminded of the pungent smell he had noticed in Belgravia.

'A deal ... what sort of deal?'

'I'm a man of few words ... shall we say twenty thousand sterling for the film, milkman. I assume you have it? And, incidentally, looking at you she obviously gave you quite a fight – good girl was Hannah, she'll be missed.'

'Like a rattlesnake, Alexis.'

Again the laughter swelled up.

'Yes, I have the film, but no deal, Alexis.'

'Because I like you, Englishman, I'll make it another ten thousand in cash.'

'Very tempting, but no dice.'

'You're a fool, milkman, a nice fool but a fool nonetheless. What loyalty have you to the British Secret Service? They did nothing to help over the girl. We know your history, the Spanish Civil War, your time in the French Foreign Legion, the Congo – the Duchess. Throughout your life your loyalty has been to the underdog ... time for a change surely, my friend, neither of us is getting any younger...'

'Would you betray the Soviet Union, Alexis?'

'For me it is different. I'm a military man, I swore an oath.'

'Sorry, Alexis, but the films remain with me.'

'Milkman, you leave me little choice, only one of us is going to leave this room with them.'

'No, Alexis, it is you who's the fool. You're in no position to dictate terms, but I am ... now listen to me. Accept you've lost and get away from here while you can. I have no wish to be the cause of your downfall, after all you cannot be blamed for her failure. He nodded at the recumbent form on the adjoining bed.

'She deserved success,' muttered Sternov, giving Charlie the impression the man was talking to himself. 'It had everything,' he continued, 'an ingenious cover for poor Hannah – jealous of her sister and the wish to get even through blackmail. And Sir Humphrey Charters, pig of a capitalist, fell for it ... but then, he has eyes only for the Romanov gold.'

'What part did he play?' enquired Charlie.

'You don't know, milkman?'

'I wouldn't have asked if I did ... though I can guess.'

'Then it's better you don't know.'

'He got the film, didn't he, Alexis? Detailed drawings, filmed of course, of the advanced Rolls Royce R100, the power plant for the new NATO fighter, the Starstreak.'

'And you pretend, milkman, you're not working for any intelligence agency...'

'I'm not – at least not now.'

'Not even the CIA?'

'How did you know about that, Alexis?'

'Everything has a beginning ... you must remember, Charlie Tuttle, we've been on to the Duchess Elizabeth for more years than I care to remember, and, coming back to the R100, who did tip you the wink on that one?'

'A report on Rupert's desk – as simple as that.'

'You mean the Chief of MI10, British Intelligence? How careless of him.'

'Not really, I am quite well versed in reading writing upside down!'

Again the eruption from deep within Sternov.

'Alexis.'

'Yes, my friend?'

'Do you know where the gold is hidden? And, when you had the girl, what did you make of that tattoo?'

'Everything points to the cemetery at Kolomyja but, during the war, it was fought over twice – I don't have to tell you what artillery fire can do to a burial ground. Everything was destroyed, burial records, the lot. As for the tattoo, well, it was put there for a purpose, but what purpose?'

Charlie's arm was bleeding again. He could feel the warmth as the blood trickled down, saturating his shirt sleeve, and the nauseating pain kept returning in waves, each one worse than the last. Also, more worrying, he was finding it difficult to keep Sternov in focus.

'You need a doctor,' said Sternov, leaning forward, 'and you won't shoot me, my friend, not in cold blood, I know you too well for that.'

'Don't tempt me, Alexis, those films stay with me.'

For the first time since Sternov entered the room, both men were silent. In spite of the ideological gulf between them, each had respect for the other, but it was Sternov who was the more desperate.

For such a large man, he moved with incredible swiftness. Ostensibly leaning forward to empty his pipe against the sole of his shoe, he sprang. It was, thought Charlie in retrospect, the manner of the attack that deceived him. Instead of launching himself in a direct assault – had he done so, there could have been but one result – he threw himself to the floor below Charlie's immediate vision and, with his arms outstretched, reached the edge of the bed. With one massive heave, the strength coming from the enormous power of his shoulders, he tipped it upwards and away from him, sending Charlie sprawling in a flurry of bedclothes.

Standing, Sternov hoisted the bed off Charlie, and picking up the Luger, removed its magazine before hurling both across the room. Satisfied, he leant over Charlie.

With the sane pungent smell, this time close to his face, Charlie opened his eyes.

You all right, my friend?' said Sternov anxiously. Charlie struggled to a sitting position.

'You know, Alexis, you really should do something about your breath.'

Again the booming laugh rang out as Sternov rearranged Charlie's pillows.

'What a shame, milkman, you're not on our side ... now where are the films?'

'They were under the pillow.'

Sternov reached down and recovered the two small packages, then moving across to the phone, he spoke over his shoulder, 'I'm going to ring for a doctor, that bleeding has got to be stopped.'

'Thank you,' replied Charlie, sensing darkness closing in.

'On second thoughts, my friend, I don't think that would be very wise – here, let me see what I can do.'

But Charlie never heard him – he was swimming in what seemed to him a sea of clinging mud, and no matter how hard he struggled it gradually sucked him down into ever-increasing blackness.

*   *   *

Through a haze alternating between light and dark, Charlie slowly realised the room was full of people. Sounds, at first vague and then more distinct, seemed to hover over him. Shadows, some intangible, some with substance, appeared and disappeared and then, as if a sudden materialisation had occurred, he saw Janice's face and heard her voice.

'How bad is he?'

'Well, one thing I can tell you, Mrs Webster, whoever put that bandage on him knew what they were doing – without it he would have died hours ago. As it is, he's lost a lot of blood. ... don't worry, the ambulance will be here any minute.'

By an immense effort of will, Charlie squirmed to a half-sitting position.

This time he recognised Sir Rupert's voice.

'Hold on, Charlie, the medics are coming...'

'Damn the medics, Rupert, will someone give me a cigarette?' It was then that Janice, still at his side and between sobs, said, 'Did that bitch do that to you, Charlie ... may she rot in Hell.'

'I'm afraid so, but then she's not looking too good either.' Then, turning to Sir Rupert, 'He's got the films...'

'We know, Charlie, he won't get far,' but his voice betrayed his anxiety.

'You silly, gorgeous, lovely man,' began Janice again, 'I told you to watch her...' but she got no further as a commanding voice spoke.

'That's enough, Mrs Webster, we'll take over now, please.'

But Charlie would have none of it. As they manoeuvred him gently on to a stretcher, he clutched Janice's arm.

'Janice,' he said, with obvious effort, 'take this,' giving her the manilla envelope.

'What is it, Charlie?'

'Natasha's...' but once more, as the rushing sound returned and blackness closed in, he again surrendered himself to the void.

*　　*　　*

With Charlie on his way to hospital, Sir Rupert and Janice spoke quietly together.

'How bad is it really? she asked, her tearstained face begging for reassurance.

'His arm's a bit of a mess,' answered Sir Rupert matter-of-factly, 'and he's lost a lot of blood, but he should be all right.'

He was about to say more but stopped as Teddy Farrar joined them.

'Section One are on their way up to take care of the body, Chief, and I've spoken to the CC about the press.'

'What did the Chief Constable have to say?'

'He's quite happy to leave it all to us.'

'By the by, Teddy, get that gun to our people as soon as you can. Unless I'm mistaken, it's the one that killed our man Regan in Helsinki last year. Charlie was very lucky,' he said almost to himself, then turning to Janice, 'Mrs Webster, I have to get back to London shortly. May I say how very grateful my department is for all your help, and is there anything at all I can do?'

'I've no intentions of leaving Manchester without Charlie, Sir Rupert, but, as you know, Natasha is downstairs in the car...'

'Don't say another word, Mrs Webster, we'll drive her back to your home and I'll detail a man to look after her.'

'That would be such a relief – thank you so very much.'

'It's the least I can do in the circumstances. Regarding Charlie, I'm sure in a day or two, providing the hospital has no objections, I can arrange for an ambulance to bring him down to London. At our expense, of course – the sooner I talk with him the better.'

'Thank you for that, Sir Rupert.'

29

Conclusions

Pale-faced, with his arm in a sling, Charlie was again seated in Colonel Sir Rupert de Quincy's office with, as before, Captain Farrar in attendance. It was exactly a week since *The Incident*, as referred to by Sir Rupert.

'How are you, Charlie?' began Sir Rupert solicitously.

'Bit rough.'

'I won't keep you long – not with Mrs Webster fretting downstairs, but I do have one or two questions and some tidying up to do . . . also I've some news for you.'

'Good or bad?' replied Charlie laconically.

'Depends, how you view it,' was the dry reply, as he looked down at a bulky file emblazoned with the word 'Secret' in red ink.

'We've confirmed that Valma Gollitzin was a KGB courier with the code name "Hannah", and that her controller on this particular occasion was . . .'

'Alexis Sternov?' cut in Charlie.

'Alexis Sternov, precisely – as a matter of interest, what put you on to him, Charlie?'

'Pipe tobacco, he smokes an unusual brand.'

'Fascinating,' commented Sir Rupert, 'we should all learn a lesson from that, eh, Teddy?' Teddy Farrar nodded, somewhat reluctantly.

'So it was Sternov you expected at the hotel?' continued Sir Rupert.

'Or Sir Humphrey Charters,' added Charlie.

'By then you knew about the cover they had concocted?'

'You mean Valma and Sir Humphrey?'

'Who else?' said Sir Rupert, impatiently.

'Not until Alexis told me.'

'It threw us completely.'

'So I gathered.'

'Mind you, Charlie, we would have got them in the end.'

'Doubtless.'

'Of course you knew nothing about the films?'

'Not until I examined them. Even then, a lot of it was guess-work ... I assume he got back to Moscow with them?' Charlie couldn't resist that.

'For what good they are, the R100 blew up in its test bed yesterday ... kaput.'

'You know, Rupert, you really do have the luck of Old Nick.'

'That's rich coming from you, Charlie – did you know she got off three rounds? We found them in the adjoining room; fortunately it was unoccupied at the time.'

'Tell me something I don't know, Rupert.'

'Such as?'

'How did you know which hotel?'

'We didn't, we tried them all, that is, those close to the airport – as luck would have it, you registered in your own name ... for once.'

It became obvious that Sir Rupert was tiring of the question-and-answer syndrome as, in an act of finality, he picked up the folder and placed it in his desk drawer.

'You'll be interested to know, Dmitri Sokolov is being deported, it came through from Home Office this morning ... I did warn him ...' said as if an afterthought.

'Anyone else for the chop?' said Charlie, brightening and brazenly staring at Captain Farrar, indicating who he hoped it might be.

Sir Rupert ignored the implication. 'We're combing the

Nobility Association and the Duma – who knows what we'll turn up...'

'I must say my old department is getting ruthless,' said Charlie, a smile spreading across his face.

Such a remark and the earlier innuendo had not pleased Captain Farrar, who, until now, had been silent.

'You appear to have a good relationship with Sternov, Charlie. I hope you're not going soft on the Commies?' he said artfully.

'No I'm not ... but I do admire men with his courage and resourcefulness – a role model for you, Captain Farrar.'

'Anything else, Charlie?' said Sir Rupert, eyeing the colour rising in his subordinate's cheeks.

'Yes, Rupert,' said Charlie, rising from his chair, 'what is to be done about our friend, Sir Humphrey Charters?'

'Difficult one that.'

'I bet it is,' said Charlie, sitting down again.

'Slippery customer, knows all the right people, including the PM. We've known for some time he is not adverse to engaging in industrial espionage, but this is the first time he's really stepped out of line.'

'Well, throw the book at him.'

'Impossible without the girl ... Hannah I mean. He has been charged, but I doubt we can make it stick...'

'The more things change the more they remain the same, eh, Rupert?'

'Something like that,' said with a shrug of the shoulders.

*   *   *

'Well,' enquired Janice, as soon as they had found a café and ordered coffee, 'what gives?'

'Usual cat-and-mouse game so beloved by Rupert, but it was interesting to learn of Sokolov's deportation.'

'Was he mixed up in it?'

'At a guess, only on the periphery, but enough to incur Rupert's wrath.'

'It's all very confusing, Charlie.'

'Not really if you separate the two – Valma's hatred and jealousy for one, and the theft of the films for another. And remember, Sternov was pulling both sets of strings.'

'How?' Janice placed her coffee cup down as Charlie lit a cigarette.

'It was no coincidence that he and Valma arrived in the country within twenty-four hours of each other. She had been working for the KGB as a courier for at least two years, and for this particular job she had all the right credentials . . . hatred for her sister Natasha and supposedly, out for all she could get. An absolute gift for Sternov, and a perfect cover for lifting the film, which involved no less a person than Sir Humphrey Charters.'

'Yes, I can see that, but are you saying that part of it was a blind? The hatred for Natasha, I mean.'

'No, no, that's why it was so clever, as far as Valma was concerned she was killing two birds with one stone . . . she probably couldn't believe her luck when we offered two thousand pounds to see her off.'

'Did she intend catching the plane, then?'

'Most certainly, and with the film, we had presented her with a perfect cover – young girl returning home after a visit.'

'Then why kill you?'

'She had asked Sternov who I was . . . she had rung him from the hotel – not Sir Humphrey, as she led me to believe. He was not entirely sure I wasn't still working for military intelligence, and said so. That put the cat amongst the pigeons: for all she knew, I was waiting for an opportunity to kill her . . . so.'

'She got in first, or tried to.'

'Exactly, she jumped the gun and made a mess of it.'

'But, Charlie, how could you have rung me in the morning if you were dead?'

'Simple, she would have rung – and shot you the minute you stepped into the hotel room.'

'Thank you for that . . .'

'Don't mention it.'

'Yes, but surely Sternov could have finished you off.'

'Why bother? He had the films, and I was a dead duck, with her body in the next bed ... remember, I had every reason to want her dead and there was no possible connection with him.'

'I can see that, but why did he come rushing up – and not even bothering to change?'

'Come on, Janice, that's an easy one, he obviously couldn't be sure Valma could handle it ... and don't forget she had the films.'

'I have to say, I'm surprised you let him have them ...'

'Life insurance, I knew if he had them he wouldn't kill me – and you would be amazed what you can do with undeveloped film under a bright light.'

'Charlie, you didn't,' she said laughing. 'You exposed them. You really are fantastic.'

'Not fantastic, just clever,' he said, as she leant across the table and kissed him.

'Janice,' he said, lighting another cigarette, 'have you looked in that envelope yet – I assume you got hold of it?'

'Of course I did. Apart from some nonentities, there was an official-looking document in German. All double Dutch to me.'

'Back in Belgravia Valma told me she had Natasha's death certificate. It was up for auction ... that's what it is.'

'Natasha's death certificate, you must be joking?'

'Not *our* Natasha, but another pseudo-granddaughter of the Tsarina.

'Oh, no, Charlie, not another one ... and you know what that means.'

'I'm afraid so – but at least one part of the jigsaw fits ... at last.'

'But what of the gold?'

'Buried in the cemetery back in Kolomyja, and I mean buried. The cemetery was fought over twice during the war.'

'Do you know, I'm disappointed.'

'That's the romantic in you, buried treasure and all that.'

'What about the tattoo, Charlie, it must relate to something, surely?'

'I asked Sternov about that – he's as puzzled as we are.'

'Then there could still be hope?'

'Maybe. In any event, I intend to take another look at it.'

'We still have the crusade, Charlie … Natasha and the Duchess's hopes … we mustn't fail them.'

'After what we've been through, no way.'

'Charlie, you've no regrets, have you? You know, me and everything?'

This time it was Charlie who leant across the table.

*   *   *

It was the day after the debriefing in Rupert's office. Janice, still in her dressing gown, was bubbling over with her desire to tell Charlie of Natasha's visit to the Prince.

'I was like a gooseberry sitting there with the two of them,' she said, elbows resting on the kitchen table, sipping her coffee. 'I might just as well have not been there for all the notice they took of me.'

'Love at first sight, was it?' said Charlie, smiling.

'Well, maybe it's premature to say that, but they certainly created an impression on each other … would you believe over dinner he was feeding her wild strawberries?'

'Where Natasha is concerned, I would believe anything.'

'Anyway, where was I?'

'The wild strawberries …'

'Yes, then they moved to another room, without a word to me – by the way the house is vast – well, I heard music, so I followed and there they were, dancing, clinging to each other like two … oh, I don't know, I leave it to your imagination.'

'Now I'm really interested, tell me more.'

'Yes, I thought you might be, you dirty bugger. Anyway, I said to myself, what point is there in my staying, so home I came. I must say the meal was excellent but a little rich for my taste – champagne cocktails, caviar, roast pheasant...'

'And wild strawberries.'

'And wild strawberries,' said Janice laughingly. 'I must say,' she said as an afterthought, 'his manners were impeccable – except of course when he wanted to be alone with Natasha.'

'No passes at you?'

'What, when he had Natasha there, literally eating out of his hand? Not likely. All I hope is she doesn't succumb to him on the first night – I warned her, but you know Natasha.'

'Yes, if we know anything at all we know about Natasha's weaknesses,' said Charlie, pouring himself another coffee. It was an opportunity for them both to lapse into silence.

'Charlie,' said Janice, after a moment or two, 'a penny for them.'

'I doubt they're worth a penny.'

'Come on, tell me.'

'Well, I've been thinking...'

'Obviously.'

'Just how much is Sir Humphrey Charters involved in everything? Strange, is it not, how we keep coming up against him. Time and time again he pops up. ... is he the puppeteer? And are we all on the end of pieces of string? And what of Lady Charters, what must she make of it all?'

'He goes back a long way, Charlie, I mean to the Tsars.'

'That's just the point, even as far back as the Revolution. You know something of the family, Janice, what was he doing during the war?'

'I do know he was in Germany when the war ended, something to do with the Control Commission. Pen told me herself he made a bomb out of it.'

'In Berlin?'

'I believe so. As for Lady Charters, she died years ago.'

'Holding high rank and being a Peer of the Realm, he would have freedom of movement,' said Charlie, as if thinking aloud, 'and, with all the chaos in that part of the world at that time...'

'I think I know what you're getting at, Charlie. We're back to the gold, aren't we?'

'Until now we've always accepted that Natasha held the key, and rightly so . . . now I'm not so sure. He was in the right place at the right time, who's to say he didn't take advantage of the opportunity?'

'But he's a millionaire, Charlie, why would he bother himself with something that, even in those days, would have been very risky?' she said as she refilled their coffee cups.

'Purported to be a millionaire – have you seen his bank statements?'

'Now you're being silly.'

'Not at all. I think a much closer look at the Right Honourable Gentleman is long overdue . . . perhaps another call on Sir Rupert wouldn't come amiss.'

'Charlie,' said Janice, watching him light yet another cigarette, 'in your opinion how much gold is there?'

'Possibly a few million, but nothing like the twenty million being bandied about. You must remember the Duchess lived off it for years – and she lived well. As a matter of interest, I've got two ingots tucked away.'

'Two ingots, how marvellous. What are you going to do with them?'

'They're insurance for Natasha – in case things don't pan out.'

'You know, Charlie, I wonder if she really appreciates all you've done for her.'

'Who, Natasha or the Duchess?'

'Both,' replied Janice, smiling, 'but I read somewhere about the Romanov gold and the Tsars, they were supposed to be fabulously wealthy.'

'True, they were, but you must remember the Bolsheviks got hold of a lot of it, and also money was invested abroad. At the time of the Revolution this was frozen – still is for that matter.'

'How then did Elizabeth acquire her fortune?' said Janice, eyes wide with interest.

'She was fortunate, being German. Lenin was their favourite son at that time because he stopped the war, the Great War that is, between Russia and Germany. Therefore, the last thing Lenin wanted was to bite the hand that fed him, consequently, Elizabeth was more or less left alone.'

'And got her hands on some of it – the gold I mean.'

'Yes, something like that.'

She was silent for a moment, then, 'But where does Prince Michael come into this? As the accepted heir, why didn't the Duchess support him instead of Natasha – surely it would have saved a lot of hassle and been far simpler?'

'Because the Prince cannot claim direct lineage descent. He was only on the fringe of the Romanovs and, by bad luck, the Duchess loathed that part of the family ... and to his disadvantage, he has very little money.'

Janice was about to rise from the kitchen table when the full impart of Charlie's words hit her. 'So,' she said, 'put the Prince's expectation ... with Natasha's money ...'

'Exactly,' said Charlie, rising, 'you have a match.'

*   *   *

Later that same day, Peter Canning knocked discreetly on a door marked Legal Department with the lettering, W. Webster, just beneath it.

'Well, you seemed to have landed on your feet,' he commented, with an expansive gesture of his hands. 'Your own office and working for a firm with the reputation of Wills Willoughby.'

'Who's fooling who?' replied Bill. 'All this is just a front, it has no real substance ... look at my desk, as bare as a baby's bottom. No, Peter, when Charters gets round to it I'll be shown the door.'

'You mean ...'

'Just that. He has no time for people unless they're useful to him, and I'm afraid I've outlived my usefulness.'

'No bullion?'

296

Bill, by way of reply, gave a laugh expressing a mix of bitterness tinged with despair. He knew his bridges were burnt. Foolishly, he reflected, he had put all his eggs into one basket . . . Sir Humphrey Charters, and . . .

Peter spoke again, interrupting his thoughts. 'Surely he won't just abandon you?'

'I sometimes wonder, Peter, what planet you live on. Men like Charters have no conscience, only selfish arrogance. They see pity and compassion as human frailties to be avoided. Whilst the plan was alive I was necessary . . .' he raised his hands in an expression of hopelessness.

'That man, Tuttle, is responsible for all this, Bill. If it weren't for him, we might both be on our way to a fortune.'

'Maybe.

'Not only Tuttle,' continued Peter, warming to his theme, ' but Janice as well. You know Emma and I are *persona non grata* nowadays, Emma can't make it out . . .'

'Janice and I are washed up, Peter, she's suing for divorce.'

'No, Bill . . . I can't believe it . . . I'm terribly sorry.'

'No need to be, it's down to my stupidity. I should have had more sense than to take her and that bitch, Natasha, on.'

'I was right, you know,' said Peter, a faraway look in his eyes, 'to christen her the Black Orchid . . . but even now I can' t get her out of my mind.'

'That's because she peddles a particular brand of poison, Peter, you're not the only one to succumb.' For once Bill felt envious of his friend. His marriage, although rocky at times, had survived. So had his job, mundane it might be . . . whilst he . . .

'What is happening to Sir Humphrey? I hear he's out on bail,' questioned Peter, who, in spite of himself, was relishing news of the debacle.

'You hear right, he's supposed to be in big trouble, but knowing him, he'll wriggle out of it.'

Silently, the two men looked at each other, each, in his own way, trying to mask his disappointment, and in Bill's case, his devastation. Then, Peter, half-rising, said, 'So it's all over, Bill, all our hopes.'

Bill, taking his cue from Peter, stood up. 'Unless there's a miracle, I'm afraid it is.'

'How's your secretary, Rachel?' asked Peter, his face brightening.

'Shut up, Peter, for God's sake.'

30

Revelations – the Truth Will Out

'Stop fidgeting, Charlie. That's the tenth time you've looked at your watch in the last hour, and don't forget your appointment with the physiotherapist in the morning – I know you hate going, that's why I'm reminding you.'

'Thank you for that, Janice.'

'No need to be crotchety, the last thing we want is you with your arm in a sling longer than necessary ... was that the doorbell?' Even now, after a week or two of something like normality, Janice's nerves still jumped at the slightest provocation.

Florrie's head appeared round the door, her face displaying the usual worried frown she had now permanently adopted.

'That man Suckerlove is at the door asking for you, Mr Tuttle.'

'Who on earth is Suckerlove, Charlie?' questioned Janice, her eyes wide with curiosity.

'Dmitri Sokolov,' he replied with a smile, 'you remember, be offered me a sort of partnership...' his voice lowered, 'you know, the gold.'

'Show him into the library, Florrie, Mr Tuttle will be with him in a moment.'

Charlie had barely entered the library, followed closely by Janice, when the bleatings of a frightened man greeted them.

'They're deporting me, Charlie, you've got to help me ... my appeal has been turned down, and I've less than a week ... you know what they'll do to me when they get me back ... please do something, I beg you.'

'Calm down, Dmitri, calm down, getting into a state won't help.'

'Aren't you making rather a lot of it?' Janice's cool voice interrupted, 'Surely you've done nothing wrong.'

Sokolov gave what was meant to be a laugh but sounded more like a croak. 'Tell the lady,' looking desperately at Charlie, 'tell...'

'Janice Webster,' Janice volunteered calmly.

'Janice, may I call you Janice?' His flushed face now turned to her.

'Why not? It's my name after all.'

Charlie, for the moment on the periphery of the exchanges, detected a note of contempt in her voice.

'I only just escaped the last time ... tell her, Charlie ... you know.'

'I guess you were rather lucky,' said Charlie, looking across at Janice, a slight shake of his head remonstrating with her for her last remark.

Sokolov began again. 'You've got influence with the Intelligence people, Sir Rupert for one, a word or two from you may save me even now.'

'You know how they operate, Dmitri. It's simple, what have you got to trade?'

'Trade?'

'For example, Sir Humphrey Charters – Rupert would give a lot to know more about him ... and so would I, for that matter.'

Janice, earlier seeming to lose interest, now brightened up. 'That would be something,' she said, almost to herself.

For the first time since Charlie and Janice had entered the room, Sokolov was silent.

'Think, man,' encouraged Charlie, and then adding a hint, 'around the time of the Revolution, what was his connection with the Romanovs?'

'I wasn't all that close . . . I really don't know,' he replied hesitantly.

'You know, don't you, Dmitri, what was his speciality at the Court of the Romanovs?'

'I believe he handled investments for the Tsar and Tsarina . . .'

'And also the Grand Duchess Elizabeth, eh, Dmitri? What was the deal concerning the infant – you know, the Tsarina's fifth daughter?' If ever stark fear showed in a man's eyes, thought Charlie, never would he see a better example as Sokolov looked wildly around for some means of escape from his inquisitor. There was none.

'If I were to tell you, will you help me. . .?' he said at last.

'Put it this way, one good turn deserves another.'

'Oh, Charlie, may the Holy Mother of God bless you.'

Charlie looked away, the man was all but sobbing with relief.

In a voice little above a whisper, Dmitri Sokolov recounted the meeting he had with Sir Humphrey. Of the 'arrangement' they had agreed, whereby the gold, hidden there by Sir Humphrey all those years before, could be recovered.

'Only it's not all gold,' said Sokolov, delighting in the look of astonishment etched on his tormentor's face, 'apart from ingots, there are stocks and shares – all negotiable of course. Probably worth in excess of ten million at current stock market prices.'

It was Charlie's turn to be silent as he weighed up the startling disclosure. Looking at Sokolov's tense face, a mixture of pleading and triumph at the effect such revelations had achieved, he knew what he had heard was true.

'How do you know all this, Dmitri?'

'From the horse's mouth, as they say.'

'Charters?'

'I would rather not say,' replied Sokolov, recovering some measure of control, 'if a certain party got to know, I'd have as much to fear here as in Moscow.'

'And what about the child, Dmitri? What can you tell me about that?'

Ashen-faced, Sokolov looked across at Janice, her deadpan expression telling him little support was forthcoming there.

'The infant, Dmitri, I'm waiting...'

Moistening his lips, Sokolov began again. 'You mean the daughter born to Princess Eugenia?'

'Who else?'

'Vladimir Gollitzin agreed to look after her, she was ailing from birth and died within a few months.'

'So.'

'Vladimir, anxious to keep his retainer, replaced her.'

'Did the Duchess know?'

'She found out.'

Charlie stood and began to pace around the room whilst Janice watched him intently. If it were left to her, he guessed, she would order Sokolov out of the house. But that was not his way; he knew from experience that, given encouragement, the tongues of frightened men wagged incessantly, and such an opportunity had without doubt presented itself...

'Just one or two points need to be cleared up, Dmitri. For instance, if it were paper money, why didn't Charters bring it with him to England?'

'What, and be caught with it on him? No way, you must realise at that time anyone connected with the Romanovs was being hunted like dogs; the Bolsheviks would have skewered him if they'd got hold of him.'

'Finally, Dmitri, why lodge the baby with Gollitzin, of all people?'

'That part of it I'm not so sure about. In any event the kid died, so providing an ideal burial place for the cache.' Sokolov's smile reminded him of Valma's ... when she was holding a gun at his head.

'Did the Duchess know about the buried bullion?'

'Must have.'

'So there was collusion between her and Charters?'

'One must assume that,' replied Sokolov, somewhat calmer.

'Then why, Dmitri, did Charters remain silent when the Duchess pushed for our Natasha to be recognised as the true heir?'

'I think he always planned to go back and recover the gold and was just biding his time ... the last thing he would want would be publicity – for obvious reasons. You understand,' said Sokolov, his eyes as wide as saucers and making an expansive gesture with his hands, 'some of this is only conjecture.'

'What are the grounds for your deportation?' asked Charlie, changing the subject and sitting down.

'National Security ... but I've done nothing wrong.'

'That's a tough one to break, Dmitri. It takes precedence over anything and everything. I'm not surprised your appeal was denied and frankly, there are many who would say you're only getting what you deserve.'

'You mean you won't help me?' Sokolov's expression reminded him of an incident he had witnessed during the Spanish Civil War, when one of Franco's Fifth Column was executed. Then he had seen the same look in the eyes of the victim as the firing squad came to the 'Present'. Charlie swallowed deeply; executions, by their very nature, were not things he liked to be reminded of.

'It's finished ... all finished,' said Dmitri, whose tortured eyes again recalled for Charlie a rain-swept courtyard and the mental image of a forlorn figure tied to a tree. There followed a few moments of silence, broken only by Janice tapping her toe against the table leg expressing, Charlie had little doubt, her mounting impatience.

'All I can do,' said Charlie at last, 'is to speak to Sir Rupert, but I have to say, Dmitri, you're rather light in trade goods.'

Dmitri Sokolov buried his face in his hands.

* * *

'Well, Janice?'

'Well, Charlie? I have to admit our little game of Whodunit

wasn't far off cue. What often happens – and where we went wrong – is falling into the trap of bending the pieces of the jigsaw to fit the puzzle. But,' she smiled, 'we were right about the Duchess and her motives.'

'I have to admit, what Sokolov told us completely threw me. I would never had guessed in a million years the extent of Charters's involvement. I would love to have been a fly on the wall when Charters met Sokolov. Think of it, the two of them, sparring with each other and neither knowing how much the other knew,' he laughed, 'and so typical of Charters to try and entice Sokolov to do the dirty work for him.'

'So, what next?'

'I think I will take a trip to Kolomyja.'

'You're not serious?'

'Janice, stocks and shares are easily transportable, I could carry them under my arm.'

'Now I know you're mad ... and how, may I ask, are you going to get a visa?'

'I think Sternov might help me there.'

'You mean you're going to invite the KGB to help you?'

'Not help, collaborate perhaps is a better word.'

'You and the KGB ... well, in that case I'd better start knitting you some bedsocks 'cause you're going to need them where you're going.'

'What ... for Poland?'

'No, the Gulag ...'

*   *   *

(*The day after*)

Florrie strode purposefully into the drawing room, her apprehension evident by the agitated wiping of hands on her apron. Looking at Charlie reproachfully, she announced, 'Two foreign gentlemen are at the door asking for you and Miss Natasha.'

Charlie, jumping up, gave Janice a reassuring look. 'It's all right, Florrie, I'm expecting them … show them into the library, would you?'

'Two foreigners … now what, Charlie?'

'From the Suisse National Bank in Zurich. Come and join us – I've a feeling we're going to hear some good news for a change.'

'As if I wasn't,' replied Janice, as she followed him into the library.

Charlie inwardly smiled as he entered the room. It was strange how certain professions were reflected in the appearance of their practitioners. None more so than bankers.

The elder looking of the two spoke first. 'Monsieur Tuttle?'

Charlie nodded.

'My card.'

Charlie scanned it before passing it to Janice. The words, in gold lettering, read, *Suisse Nationale Banque, Zurich*. In smaller black type, *Pierre Fontaine*.

Recovering the card, the man spoke again. 'Permit me to introduce my associate, Monsieur Ferrer.' The other man inclined his head by way of acknowledgement.

Charlie shook the outstretched hand.

'You are Mademoiselle Handrick?' enquired the owner of the card.

'Good heavens, no,' replied Janice, somewhat confused but receiving a reassuring nod from Charlie. 'She's in her room, I'll fetch her.'

'That will not be necessary, for now, Madame…?'

'Webster, Janice Webster,' again the outstretched hand was shaken. A few brief moments of silence followed before Janice realised her duties as a hostess, giving Charlie an opportunity to assess one of his callers. He would give, he mused, a lot to know just how much Fontaine enjoyed the Duchess's confidence. He remembered, as Igor, her long telephone conversations, usually muted, with the Suisse Nationale. The man exuded an air of dependability, the sort most rich elderly women would he delighted to confide in … Janice interrupted his line of thought.

'Would you gentlemen care for a café?'

'Merci, Madame,' they said in unison as Janice moved to the bell-pull.

'You've suffered an accident, Monsieur?' asked Pierre Fontaine, obviously the spokesman of the two.

Charlie, touching the sling, smiled. 'It is nothing.'

'You could have fooled me,' muttered Janice, only to receive a glare of admonishment for her trouble.

'Now to business, Monsieur Tuttle. A business, may I say, that in some respects is a little delicate. You are probably wondering why Monsieur Ferrer is present, are you not?'

Monsieur Ferrer, until now on the periphery of the discussions, gave a weak smile. Charlie had already decided that he was of little consequence and probably never had contact with the Duchess. Dark, and with a receding hairline, he could be considered something of a lady's man – typical French, thought Charlie, who had already intercepted more than one admiring look at Janice.

Monsieur Fontaine, clearing his throat, continued, 'Under the terms of the will of the late Grand Duchess Elizabeth Fyodorovna, certain verifications are necessary. You are, of course, familiar with the person I'm referring to,' looking in turn at Charlie and Janice.

Both nodded.

'Pardon, Monsieur, Madame, but my instructions are explicit and the verifications required are,' he coughed unnecessarily, 'somewhat intimate for both yourself,' looking at Charlie, 'and Mademoiselle Handrick. I am sure, with so much money involved, you will appreciate the reasons for this. In your case, Monsieur Tuttle . . . forgive me, I trust I can speak freely?'

It was Janice who answered, 'We have no secrets, Monsieur Fontaine, thank you.'

'In that case, inspection of mutilation scars in the lower abdomen would be required and, where Mademoiselle is concerned, a tattoo on the inner thigh. Monsieur Ferrer is qualified to undertake such inspections.'

'Bully for him, and no big deal, eh, Charlie?' said Janice,

moving closer to him, aware of the sudden tensing of his body as exemplified by the stiffening of his facial muscles. A discreet knock on the door was followed by the ample frame of Florrie, balancing the usual silver serving tray.

For once, Janice was glad of the interruption as, turning to her visitors, she said brightly, 'Ah, your café has arrived, Messieurs.'

Placing the tray on a convenient table, Florrie nervously looked at Janice.

'That will do, Florrie, we can manage for ourselves, thank you.' With what appeared undue haste, Florrie withdrew.

'There is one further matter,' said the banker, delving into his briefcase and producing a large envelope; he then selected, from its numerous companions, a single sheet of paper.

'Before I disclose any further details, the Grand Duchess Elizabeth . . .' he paused, 'has directed that the following statement be read.' Clearing his throat, he began to read.

'*Until the yoke of Communist oppression is lifted from my beloved country and Russia recovers its soul then, when that time is reached, and I pray God it will be soon, one half of all monies forming my last will and testament will remain with my executors. To be presented, with my blessings, to whichever Romanov ascends the throne.*'

Charlie shuffled his feet. Often he had heard the Duchess speak in that vein – it was as if she were talking to them now, even from beyond the grave. He gave Janice a weak smile in response to her quizzical look . . . well knowing the possible ramifications of such a condition.

'Finally, Monsieur Tuttle, I shall require you to sign an affidavit to the effect that, and again I quote the Duchess Elizabeth, "*That the girl known as Natasha Gollitzin is in fact Natasha Handrick . . . daughter of Eugenia Alexandra Fyodorovna and granddaughter of the Empress of all the Russias, the Tsarina Alexandra. And further, that the girl present is the same girl we both welcomed to my home on the twelfth day of June nineteen hundred and sixty three.*" '

Janice's sharp intake of breath could clearly be heard by all in the room.

'You are prepared to sign such a declaration, Monsieur Tuttle?'

Charlie, already unscrewing the top of his pen, stepped forward. 'I am.'

'Good, now all that remains is for Monsieur Ferrer to examine Mademoiselle Handrick; you mentioned earlier, Madame, that she was in her room?'

'Indeed, Monsieur, shall I fetch her?'

'I would rather you stayed here. Janice, ask Florrie if she would kindly conduct Monsieur Ferrer to Natasha's room,' said Charlie rather pointedly, as Janice, without further word, left in search of Florrie, followed by the rather hesitant Monsieur Ferrer.

'How long was the Duchess Fyodorovna a client of yours, Monsieur?' asked Charlie brazenly. 'As her companion for the latter part of her life, I know Elizabeth trusted you implicitly ... and,' as Janice returned, 'surely Monsieur Fontaine, now business is over, would appreciate a cognac.'

'The Suisse Nationale has been serving the Romanovs since the turn of the century,' replied the banker smugly, as he accepted the offered glass from the dutiful Janice. 'Of course, in the early days we dealt with an intermediary, I still hear from him occasionally, Sir Humphrey Charters. Doubtless you've heard the Duchess mention him?'

'Frequently,' replied Charlie, endeavouring and succeeding in holding his astonishment and relieved to see Janice looking anywhere but at the banker.

The return of a somewhat flushed Monsieur Ferrer brought their conversation to an abrupt end.

'Satisfactory, Claude?' enquired Monsieur Fontaine, addressing his erstwhile companion.

'Perfectly, the tattoo clearly shows the five points advised by the Duchess Elizabeth.'

'Good, then,' looking at his watch, 'we will detain you good people no longer.'

'God, Charlie, I couldn't believe my ears, one half to be retained until . . . you know what this means, Charlie,'

'Yes, and unless I'm sadly mistaken, it opens up another can of worms. Now the question is, is the true heir alive? And if so, does our dear friend Charters know who she is and, more to the point, where she is?'

'Do you think that's possible?'

'I would say it's more probable than possible.'

'Charlie, that affidavit you signed, you realise the position it puts you in if Charters were to challenge it? I hope you realise what you've done?' Janice said as they watched their visitors make their way down the driveway to the waiting taxi.

'I gave my word to Elizabeth, Janice. I'm not about to start breaking it now.'

'Well, your word could land you in prison for the rest of your natural,' she said, as they made their way back into the library.

Stung by her words, Charlie replied. It was, she realised later, the first time she had ever heard him raise his voice. 'Only you and I know the truth, Janice. Valma's dead, Gollitzin's dead and poor Elizabeth, besotted with her scheme, is dead. Who's left to prove Natasha is not who we say she is?'

'Very likely Sir Humphrey Charters . . . you can count me out of it . . . Charlie, it smells to high heaven.'

'You're disenchanted with me, aren't you, Janice?'

'No, you silly man,' her tone more conciliatory now, 'I understand your loyalty to the Duchess . . . but there is a limit.'

Charlie moved over to Janice's writing desk. There he picked up two cheques and, brandishing them in front of her, read aloud, 'Pay Natasha Handrick the sum of five hundred and and twenty-one thousand pounds, three shillings and two pence.' Replacing it on the desk, he read from the other, 'Pay Charles Allen Tuttle the sum of one hundred and four thousand pounds, nine shillings and eight pence.'

At that moment, Natasha rushed into the room.

'Charlie, may I see my cheque ... isn't it marvellous ... I've rung Michael and told him ... oh, Charlie, it's all down to you, I do love you.' With that she flung her arms around him, causing him to wince with the sudden pain to his injured arm.

'All right, Natasha, enjoy this moment, but remember your obligations to the Duchess, it's really down to her you know,' he said, gently rubbing his arm.

'Has Monsieur Ferrer gone? He was veree nice, Janeece,' said with that look so well known to them both.

'Yes he has,' replied Janice, somewhat sharply, 'and if you're not careful, the ink will fade on that cheque if you stare at it much longer.'

Ignoring her, Natasha turned to Charlie. 'How many roubles is it, Charlie?'

'Oh, about five hundred million, give or take a million or two,' he said smiling.

With her usual childlike simplicity, Natasha kissed the cheque, then said, 'I must dash, I'm meeting Michael at the tennis courts.'

'See what I mean, Janice,' said Charlie as Natasha hurried away, 'I'm not about to destroy her dream, not to mention Elizabeth's, after what we've been through.'

'Charlie, that sort of money can only bring trouble, big trouble, you know that as well as I do – whatever was the Duchess thinking of?'

'It may be of interest to you that the Duchess gave me a copy of her will before I left Appenzell – there was no mention of such bequests. So, it can only mean they were added later, sometime after we left for Paris. All right, I'll abide by her wishes – as I have all along.'

'And been handsomely rewarded for it ...'

'That was unfair, Janice.'

'Don't you see, you've joined with Elizabeth in a conspiracy ... heaven knows where it will end, and if I appear ... well, upset about it, it's only because I'm worried about you.'

'Enough said, let's leave it at that. I know what I'm doing.'

'Pray God you do.'

'Listen, Janice, I do think you're looking for trouble. Think for a few minutes – the death certificate for the infant buried in Kolomyja has been destroyed. I have Natasha's birth certificate and her mother's marriage certificate ... who could possibly gainsay that she is not who she says she is?'

'I don't know, quite probably you're right. But I know this much, if you're wrong, Heaven help Natasha, because a fall from the heights she has scaled could prove fatal.'

'I would be there for her.'

'Charlie, you cannot spend the rest of your life protecting her. Soon it will be up to a husband to play that role – and rightly so. And in any case, what about me? I'm entitled to have you to myself, not permanently sharing you with Natasha ... there's another thing, I think you've already forgotten about Sir Humphrey Charters, for sure he knows a great deal more than we're giving him credit for...'

'You mean about the child at Kolomyja and his involvement with the Suisse National?'

'Almost certainly.'

'I had overlooked him.'

'Now do you see what I'm getting at"

'But it would only be his word...'

'That of a Peer of the Realm, Charlie?'

'A somewhat discredited Peer, if I may say so.'

'That's as maybe, but a Peer with many influential friends.'

* * *

The Grand Prince Michael put down the phone – what a relief that Lavinia was in Cannes. But, from what she had said, the reprieve was likely to be of short duration. He could still hear her rasping voice, reminding him of how often he had heard it over the years.

'Michael,' she had said, 'I shall be flying home at the weekend

... Really, talking of betrothal to a girl you've known but a few weeks ... this is my reward for leaving you alone in London ... I should have known better.'

He knew, from experience, that her last remarks were but the opening salvo ... for certain more was to come. Dismissing such thoughts, he selected a tie and gazed at his reflection in the. full-length mirror. It showed a tall, well-proportioned body ... his fair hair and blue eyes more than hinting at Aryan blood, a contradiction of his Russian ancestry. From his family history, he well knew there was more than a fair share of the Teutonic in his make-up. His mother, murdered in the bloodbath of 1918, was the daughter of a Prussian Prince, and his uncle had served in the Kaiser's Army.

He looked at his watch, and again dismissed Lavinia and her tantrums from his thoughts. With the knowledge that soon he would he reunited with his beloved Natasha, it wasn't that difficult. And what of her news ... her inheritance, over half a million pounds, it was incredible. It was all very well, he thought, for the Countess Lavinia, his self-appointed surrogate mother, to bleat away on the phone, but here was an opportunity to avail himself of a gorgeous bride with a dowry large enough to make any man's head swim. Only last week he had received a letter from the manager of Coutt's, telling him he was overdrawn ... again ... well, such irritations would soon be relics of the past.

One worry still remained, however. He was sure Lavinia would make much of Natasha's past. The story, implying she was a lowly gypsy girl, would provide her with all the ammunition she could wish for. As far as he was concerned the story, told him by Dmitri Sokolov, was an invention to besmirch the girl. Surely, if the Grand Duchess Elizabeth saw fit to leave her a fortune, that, for him anyway, was proof enough of her antecedents. There was, of course, the question of the accession. Here, he again smiled to himself. Even if she were the granddaughter of the last Tsarina, only a male was acceptable to the Duma.

Once more his thoughts returned to the money. In one stroke he would no longer be dependent upon Lavinia's somewhat restricted generosity. Five hundred pounds a month barely kept him in good wine – and then there was Natasha. Their lovemaking had reached heights he had never experienced before. She was that rarity amongst women (he had often heard spoken of when he and his friends were in their cups), a lady at breakfast and a whore at night. Yes, he had indeed been lucky, and the Countess Lavinia could do her worst, he was not to be done out of his good fortune … not if he had anything to do with it.

Changing his tie for the fourth time and again looking at his watch, doubts assailed him. What if there were others in the running? And what of this man Charlie she was forever mentioning…? Delay could be fatal, he must not be so naive as to think he was the only one, there were bound to be others.

The sound of a car drawing up outside heralded the arrival of his beloved. Throwing a jacket loosely over his shoulders and with a last look in the mirror, he rushed downstairs.

From a secluded window-seat, Michael watched her. If ever there existed the complete woman, then Natasha was it. Her arms cradled a mass of freshly cut flowers, some, he ruefully recognised as being Lavinia's prize blooms, husbanded, after months of care, in her greenhouse. (Such sacrilege had not gone unnoticed by the gardener working on the far side of the lawn.)

Gaily waving, she continued with her plundering intermixed with her usual devastating smile. Putting thoughts of Lavinia's outrage at such desecration to the back of his mind, he continued with his contemplation of Natasha.

Her every movement created mental images of such eroticism which, like some powerful aphrodisiac, initiated in him an all but uncontrollable desire and lust of a nature previously foreign to him. No, he would not delay, he would propose that evening and suggest a short engagement. The decision made, he strode through the open French windows and greeted her with an overpowering embrace.

* * *

'Well, Charlie, what is it this time . . . and how's the arm?'

Charlie realised the welcome was somewhat perfunctory but chose to ignore it. 'You could say I'm on a mission of mercy this time, Rupert. Dmitri Sokolov has been to see me . . .'

'When?'

The abruptness of the question startled Charlie, but he soon recovered. 'A day or so ago, if that has any significance.'

'Not really, but on this occasion you're a little late.'

'You haven't shipped him out already?'

'Not in the way you mean.'

At that moment, Charlie was aware that Captain Farrar had entered the room. Moving to his chief's side, he commented testily, 'Obviously, Tuttle, you don't read the newspapers.'

'Not one for papers,' replied Charlie.

'Then I wouldn't expect you to know,' intervened Sir Rupert, 'Dmitri Sokolov was fished out of the river late last night.'

Charlie's shock at the announcement was only too apparent. Gathering himself together, he stated rather than asked, 'Suicide?'

'Not unless he cut his own throat . . .' answered Sir Rupert dryly.

'Dead before he hit the water,' added Teddy Farrar.

'Here we go again . . .' commented Charlie, 'another investigation.'

'Not really,' replied Farrar, choosing to ignore warning looks from his chief. 'Pity, really, at times he was useful to us.'

Charlie, quickly realising his old antagonist was in an expansive mood, adopted a look of innocent curiosity. 'You mean you fed him information?'

'Something like that . . . but since the matter of the Romanov gold, he had become rather . . .'

'Expendable?'

'I think that will do, if you don't mind, Teddy. I'm sure Charlie is not really interested.'

'Oh, but I am, Rupert . . . do you know who did it?'

314

'It's a matter for the Met, Charlie, not really our concern.'

Charlie, adept at knowing when the shutters had come down, decided now was the time to unload the big one. 'Rupert, on another matter altogether ... the R100 film.'

Sir Rupert picked up his letter-opener and ran a finger along the blade, giving Charlie the distinct impression he knew what he was about to say.

'They ... were exposed, by me.'

'Do tell us something we don't know, Tuttle.' It was Farrar again, and this time his face radiated smugness. 'We intended Sternov should have them, but you buggered it up.'

'That's enough, Teddy,' remonstrated Sir Rupert, but it was all too late. Farrar, goaded on by his hatred of Charlie, had no intention of relinquishing such an opportunity...

'You knew then ... Sir Humphrey Charters...?' said an astonished Charlie.

'Exactly,' replied a triumphant Farrar. 'One of our best double...'

'Captain Farrar, that is quite enough...' said Sir Rupert, obviously infuriated, 'you're in breach of security, please leave my office at once.'

Farrar, suddenly aware of the possible ramifications of what he had just said, began to move away from his chief. It was Charlie, rising from his chair, who barred his way. For a few moments, he stared at both Sir Rupert and Captain Farrar. Then, in a tone that surprised even him, he said, 'As God is my witness, how do you two live with yourselves...? You didn't rush up to Manchester to save my bacon. Your only concern was your precious scheme, built on hypocrisy, deceit and faithlessness, and that I, in my innocence, might throw a spanner in the works.'

'Charlie, you've been expendable since the first day you stepped into my office ... good God, man, you of all people know the score.'

'And Sir Humphrey Charters?' queried Charlie, ignoring Sir Rupert's outburst.

The ensuing silence told him all that he needed to know. Reaching the door, Charlie turned and looked at them both.

'So, Charters at best is a double ... you know something, Rupert, I suddenly feel sick to my gut.'

As Charlie emerged from the offices of Section Ten, British Military Intelligence, and into the bright sunlight of a late January day, he took several deep breaths, the cold, clean air gently refreshing him but doing little to cleanse a sickening taste at the back of his throat. Then, as if some unseen phantom had embraced him with dark wings of age, he suddenly felt very, very old.

*   *   *

By prior arrangement, Janice was waiting for him in the café they used whenever Charlie called upon Sir Rupert.

As he approached her table, she half rose. 'Charlie, you look as if you've seen a ghost,' then, more seriously, 'More revelations?'

Placing his coffee on the table he sat down, lit a cigarette and, continuing to ignore her, inhaled deeply. Then, as if the smoke had some fascination known only to him, he watched it drift lazily towards the ceiling.

Finally, he spoke. 'You know, Janice, what I've learnt today is something I've long suspected ... I'm too soft for Intelligence work.'

'Well, you'll never convince me of that. In my opinion you knock Sir Rupert and that stupid man Farrar into a cocked hat. Now, what have they been saying?'

'Only that Sternov and Valma were set up, and that I, in all innocence, fucked it up.'

With widening eyes, Janice returned her cup to its saucer.

'You can't mean...?'

'That the films were a plant? Well, that's what they're saying ... they wanted Sternov to have them. Naturally, they would have been suitably doctored to give an entirely false impression of the power unit, the R100.'

Janice, her expression reflecting her attempt to digest the indigestible, reached across and gripped his hand.

'Tell me the worst. Was Charters involved?'

'My guess would be he was in on it from the beginning – probably works for Military Intelligence and in particular, Sir Rupert.'

'But he's out on bail.'

'So we were told ... also he was supposed to be a slippery customer ... all for our consumption, Janice.'

'Come to think of it, we saw nothing in the papers. For someone as well-known as Sir Humphrey...'

'Quite, and you never will, it was all part of the cover.'

'God, how devious can you get?'

For a few moments they were both quiet. It was Janice who broke their self-imposed silence. 'Does this mean he's still a threat to Natasha?'

'Could be, we would do well to be watchful ... he certainly knows about Kolomyja.'

'You know what, Charlie? The sooner she marries, the better.'

'Who, the prince?'

'Who else?'

'I'm not sure I follow you ...'

'No, you wouldn't – I hope you haven't ideas in that direction yourself?'

Charlie, ignoring the implication, changed the subject. 'They pulled Sokolov out of the Thames last night ... his throat had been cut.'

'How ghastly, the poor man! Do they know who did it?'

'"I got the impression they were not terribly interested ... but I would put my money on Magyar – one of the Duma, I'm damned if I know his surname.'

'Couldn't we have done more to help him?'

'No, Janice, no. He was a lost cause, believe me.'

'What a rotten business Military Intelligence is.'

'At the risk of repeating myself ... my sentiments exactly.'

'Let's go home, Charlie, and plan a wedding.'
'Which one?'

*   *   *

'Well, Charlie, what did you make of her?' said Janice, as her erstwhile guest's car swung out of the driveway. 'Personally,' she continued, 'I found her an insufferable prig ... that bit,' (here Janice did an excellent mimicry of the Countess Lavinia), ' "I've only just heard of this, er, affair since my return from Cannes ... Michael, in some ways, is such a secretive boy." '

It was a week since Charlie's shock meeting with Sir Rupert, and the Countess had wasted no time in confronting Natasha's closest friends following Michael's announcement of their betrothal.

'All I can say, after that little lot, is that I need a drink. The cheek of the woman ... "Of course Natasha's dowry will be useful ..." Who the Hell does she think she is? Elizabeth left that money to Natasha, not her precious Michael ...'

'Calm down, Janice, the boy's of age, there is really little she can do.'

'Frankly, I wouldn't mind telling her and her beloved to take a running jump.' Janice paused to gulp her brandy. 'And then that final piece about his good looks and what an impressionable young man he was. Bloody cheek ... not a word about Natasha ... I assume she has met her, though you could have fooled me.'

'They met the other evening,' replied Charlie. 'Natasha hardly mentioned it.'

'I'm not surprised, I shouldn't think the girl got a word in edgeways. One thing's for sure, half of Natasha's money must be invested out of their reach ... you and I can be Trustees.'

'I agree. I know she's promised Michael a hundred thousand the day they marry.'

'See what I mean, Charlie ... I'll ring Daddy in the morning, he'll know how we should go about it.' With that, and to emphasise

318

the point, her fist smacked hard into an open palm. 'That will put a stop to that.'

'I know little about a Russian wedding, what's the format?'

'To say the least, a Russian Orthodox wedding is somewhat different – nothing we can't cope with, but different. They've narrowed it down to two dates, but Natasha is keen for the twenty-ninth of February – it is a leap year you know, she says it's the romantic in her. Knowing her, she'll have her way.'

'That's less than five weeks.'

'I know, exciting isn't it? But that's when it will be, you can bet your boots on it. And after that's over and we're free at last...'

'Janice, you're plotting again.'

'Stop playing hard to get. After all, we're sharing a bed now and I'm sure Florrie is a trifle disgusted..."

'Yes, sharing a bed, but that's about all it is.'

'Oh, I don't know,' Janice giggled, 'we don't do too badly, and in any case there is that clinic in Harley Street ... I'm told they can do wonders these days.'

'Amen to that.'

31

Into the Bear Pit ...

Paul Vyrubova, Vladimir Kokovtsov and Magyar Stolypin gazed intently at Sir Humphrey Charters whilst digesting his every word.

'What has happened to our friend Dmitri, no one regrets more than I. But Dmitri is dead, gentlemen. However, the arrangement we had, of which each of you has a part, if you want it, is still very much alive.'

Paul had the distinct feeling, as the words came across, that Sir Humphrey could easily be addressing a board meeting. His tone was one of confidence tinged with an ego that made no allowance for contradiction.

'Whatever Dmitri told you regarding your individual share of the enterprise no longer applies ... each of you will receive two and one half per cent of whatever is recovered – I shall, of course, be paying all expenses. You have,' looking at his watch, 'two minutes, at the end of which you will tell me whether you're in or out.'

It was Magyar who, tentatively, raised his hand, again giving Paul the impression they were at nothing more than an annual board meeting with Sir Humphrey Charters as chairman.

'Well?'

'Could you ... do you think you could tell us how much ...' the request, to the other two, was agonisingly slow.

'How much is two and a half per cent?'

'Yes,' replied Magyar, lowering his arm.

'About one hundred thousand . . . each.'

'Sterling?'

'Well, certainly not roubles,' replied Sir Humphrey, with an expansive grin, which soon communicated itself to both Paul and Vladimir. As quickly as the grin appeared, it vanished as, with a glance at his watch, he spoke again. 'Are you in or out?' It was Paul, hastily assuming his usual mantle of spokesman, who replied.

'Naturally, we are upset over Dmitri, Sir Humphrey, but I'm sure I speak for all of us . . .' the violent nodding of two heads assured him of that, 'when I say all three of us are in.'

'Good,' replied Sir Humphrey, as if some important motion had just been carried to his satisfaction. 'You all have your twenty-eight-day visas, so I don't have to tell you time is short. We sail, with two vehicles, from the Port of London on the first– the SS *Eureka*. We should arrive in Gdansk on the eighth. From there we follow the plan given you by Dmitri. Although it's unlikely we shall need them, weapons, which I will supply, will be carried once we're aboard. Finally, gentlemen, I have given Paul,' nodding in his direction, 'a private number where he can reach me if necessary. No further contact is to be made, and I cannot emphasise enough the need for the utmost secrecy. Right, gentlemen, I now close the meeting.'

Paul admitted to himself afterwards that he was surprised Sir Humphrey had omitted the word 'board' before the word meeting . . .

* * *

'I have to say,' it was Magyar speaking, 'I get the feeling we're no longer amateurs, as we were with Dmitri, but professionals. He certainly gives confidence,' he said as he examined the contents of a buff envelope each had been given by Sir Humphrey. 'Look, there's even a hundred pounds in here.'

'What about the police? Paul, they're interviewing everyone, not to mention British Intelligence.' It was Vladimir, concern deeply etched in his face. 'I'm surprised he never mentioned that.'

'Keep your hair on, Vladimir, it will soon die down. After all, as if the murder of Dmitri Sokolov, a known Russian dissident, is going to cause any sort of stir – it will all be over by next week, won't it, Magyar?'

'I know what you're both thinking. I'll admit I said I would cut his throat if he shit on us – but he didn't and I didn't.'

'That's good enough for me, what say you, Vladimir?'

'Certainly. He's gone, and as far as I'm concerned that's the end of it.'

*   *   *

The departure of Natasha and 'My Prince' as she called him, marked the end of the small dinner party, hosted by Janice, in celebration of their engagement.

With the residue of guests gathered in the drawing room sipping their brandies, Janice turned to Hilda. 'Did you have to curtsy every time he approached you? I'm sure you embarrassed him dreadfully ... and why on earth did you continually address him as Your Royal Highness?'

'He is a Royal Prince, Janice, nothing can change that. And, anyway, because I prefer to observe etiquette gives you no reason to criticise.' Janice disdained a reply, but her arched eyebrows, directed at Charlie, spoke volumes. Ignoring the exchange, Charlie stood up and coughed politely.

'Perhaps now is the time to tell you,' looking anywhere but at Janice, 'that on the ninth I'm flying to Warsaw. From there I shall journey on to Kolomyja ... hopefully, at the end of it all, those things that have plagued us these past months will be resolved ... at least in time for the wedding.' He paused. 'I should be back by the thirteenth at the latest.'

'Surely, you don't think I'm going to let you go to Kolomyja alone, Charlie?' It was Janice, rising from her chair as if to add emphasis to her words.

'Kolomyja? You're going to Kolomyja, Charlie, what on earth for?' said Hilda, cracking her knuckles in agitation.

'If it's where I think it is,' said Big George, darkly, 'we might as well kiss him goodbye now.'

'Yes, Charlie, where exactly is it?' asked Hilda, leaning forward and adjusting her bifocals.

'It's on the borders of Poland and ... er ... the Soviet Union. I've been invited to go by Alexis Sternov, and I'm guaranteed immunity from arrest and the protection of his office. Now, does that answer all the questions?'

'You're not serious, Charlie,' said Hilda, moving to his side in a gesture of protection. 'Your life won't be worth a fig, surely you know that?'

'You may be right, Hilda, but that is where the answers are, and I know I won't rest until I have them.'

'Hilda,' it was Janice, her face flushed from emotion, 'you're wasting your time. If that's what he wants he'll go, whatever we say. I've done all I can to persuade him otherwise...'

* * *

The huge Zil limousine swung alongside the turbo jet as soon as it stopped moving. Charlie, stepping on to the tarmac, found himself surrounded by grey-clad figures who silently hustled him across to the waiting leviathan. A door opened and a voice he instantly recognised greeted him.

'Good to see you, comrade.'

Charlie smiled, 'And you,' he replied, before easing himself into the vastness of the car already permeated with the smell of strong pipe tobacco.

'You've eaten?' enquired Alexis Sternov, emptying his pipe against the sole of his shoe as the car accelerated forward.

'I had a meal of sorts on the plane, but frankly, I've little appetite.'

'That, comrade, I can well understand. Losing that little nymph of a gypsy girl to that bourgeois Prince Michael must be a terrible blow.' With that, a chuckle rumbled from within his broad expanse of chest, only to be extinguished as he settled back into the plush cocoon of soft leather, his huge bulk seemingly dwarfed amidst the massive extent of the car's interior.

As if on cue, the internal lights slowly dimmed. Charlie had the feeling he was living a dream and the only reality was the low whine of the engine and occasional soft buffeting of the wind. Leaning back, he closed his eyes. Sleep, like a silent predator, overcame him and, as the car hurtled through the night, permitted him a few hours' respite from the agony of knowing that this time there was no pulling back . . . he really was in the bear pit and up to his neck . . .

* * *

It was the lurching of the car that awoke him. Sternov, leaning forward, was barking orders to the driver, the glass panel separating them now fully open.

'Welcome to Kolomyja, Englishman,' he said, pipe gripped firmly between his teeth.

The car door opened and without further comment, he clambered out and met five men dressed in drab grey uniforms. Continuing to ignore Charlie, he walked with them towards a mound of earth lit by two large arc lights.

So, this was Kolomyja, thought Charlie, the cradle from where it had begun all those years ago. Involuntarily he shivered. Glancing away from the glare, he was aware of a line of trees stark against a glowing backdrop of reflected light from what was probably the town itself.

Looking again at the area lit by the arc lights, Charlie compared it with a stage. One specially prepared to enact a dramatic finale – with Sternov as director and he, Charlie, the audience.

As he moved towards the pool of light, he stumbled across a

small oblong box encrusted with white permafrost, with black earth clinging to it like barnacles on a ship's hull. It was a moment or two before he realised he was looking at a child's coffin. Ahead of him, Sternov was engaged in conversation with a further group of grey-clad men, but here there was a difference. Each was armed with what Charlie immediately recognised as an AK 47, their bayonets glinting, in the harsh glare of the lights, like the blades of some obscene guillotine.

As he approached, what had been moments before but three shadowy forms, now emerged as three men standing motionless, their heads bowed. Further beyond them were parked two trucks of World War Two vintage.

To complete the scene, a man appeared from behind a line of trees and stepped forward into the circle of light. Charlie, carefully stepping round another open pit, instantly recognised Sir Humphrey Charters carrying what appeared to be a duffle bag. Alexis Sternov, pipe still griped between his teeth, walked slowly towards him.

Charlie, with the reassuring pressure of the Luger against his armpit, waded round another morass of newly dug earth and joined them.

Sternov, ignoring Charlie's presence, was speaking. 'Well, Charters, your opinion?'

Holding up the duffle bag as if it were on display, Sir Humphrey Charters replied, 'They're as pristine as the day I buried them.'

'Their value?'

'Difficult to say, Alexis, but still freely negotiable – if I had to name a figure I would say...' he paused, 'ten million, give or take a million.'

'And the ingots?'

'As I suspected, Elizabeth's helped herself from time to time, but still over twenty, you'll need a pickaxe though, they're really bedded into the side of the coffin -- what with the permafrost...' he got no further as his eyes, as if hypnotised, stared at the Mauser pistol now levelled at him.

'You know, Charters, I really don't think I've any further need of you . . .'

'No, Alexis,' shouted Charlie, quickly moving in front of Charters, 'let me speak to him.'

'What now, milkman? Not more nonsense about the succession?'

'Charters,' said Charlie, ignoring the comment, 'answer me one question and I'll do all I can to save you.'

As if praying, Sir Humphrey Charters sank to his knees. His bulk seemed to shrink whilst his eyes, enlarged and grotesque, became mirrors of stark fear.

'What do you want to know . . . it's Tuttle, isn't it?'

'It is – Charters. Who is the true granddaughter of the Empress, and where is she?'

'Anything but that, Tuttle, anything but that.'

'Answer him, Charters, time is running out.'

'Promise me, both of you, no harm will come to her.'

'Answer him, Charters . . .'

'My daughter, Penelope, is the granddaughter of the . . .' Charters never finished. Two reports ended what conversation there had been as, before Charlie's unbelieving eyes, Sir Humphrey Charters pitched forward. Only the pungent smell of cordite and faint wisps of dirty grey smoke lingered, as if mute evidence of his passing.

As Sternov turned to Charlie, he returned the Mauser to the voluminous pocket of his military overcoat. 'You know, Charlie,' he said with a smile, 'you can be a traitor to one side and probably get away with it . . . but to both sides, no.'

Afterwards, Charlie reflected, it was one of the few times Sternov had used his forename when addressing him. Curious, he thought, that such an insignificant fact outweighed the incredible revelation and event he had just witnessed.

'What now, Alexis?' enquired Charlie, as two men lifted what a few minutes before had been Sir Humphrey Charters, Knight of the Realm, and pitched him into an open grave.

Ignoring the question, Sternov watched the 'burial', then with a throaty chuckle, turned to Charlie. 'There lies the real architect of the Romanov riddle.' Both men looked down at the crumpled remains of Sir Humphrey Charters, his eyes and features still reproachfully returning their curious gaze as if resenting this intrusion on his path to eternity.

So here, at last, was the confirmation both he and Janice had been looking for all these past months – the answer to the riddle; and answered where it had all begun, in this drab cemetery that served a nondescript town called Kolomyja. How simple the mystery, he thought, so easy now he knew all the answers. Two infant burials, not one, and both around the same time. One fostered on the Gollitzins by the Duchess, the other some poor waif picked up by Charters at a time when Europe was awash with the hopeless and nameless. Then the grand deceit, a forged death certificate purporting to show the death of the infant grand-daughter of the Empress . . . what better cover for his own precious daughter? In reality his granddaughter!

There remained, Charlie acknowledged, still some loose ends to tidy up, but the riddle of who fathered the fifth daughter of the Empress and was grandfather of the true heir apparent was now beyond doubt. Who could have possibly imagined that Penelope Charters . . . it was staggering. If only Janice were here – he could almost hear her saying, 'Well, Charlie boy, we came pretty close . . .' Indeed they had. Valma, for all her subterfuge, had been wrong, so had poor Sergei Poznansky and many others who had believed that Natasha was the true heir apparent. It was also certain that the Duchess herself had been fooled, certainly initially.

As for the lovely Natasha, she had, unknowingly, played the role of the gorgeous innocent, manipulated and used to achieve the dreams of an aged, bitter and vengeful woman. For certain, the red stain of the Romanovs had all but spread itself to her . . . now, what of the future? Perhaps the forthcoming nuptials would be the final consummation. Charlie drew a deep breath: was that the whispering of the wind now stealthily moving round the cemetery, or could it be the quiet chuckle of the gods themselves? For the second time that night, Charlie wished Janice was with him.

Charlie followed as Sternov, picking up the duffle bag, sauntered in the direction of the three men still standing quietly in front of the two trucks.

'Your decision, Englishman, do with them as you wish,' said Sternov handing him his Mauser.

'I don't shoot men in cold blood, Alexis, and I've seen enough executions in my time. No, the guilty have already been punished – let them go, Alexis.'

'As you wish,' replied Sternov, with a shrug of his shoulders, 'we've no reason to hold them, their papers are in order and...' here, that deep-chested chuckle began again, 'after all,' the chuckle merging into a burst of laughter, 'they've got the bricks they came for.' Charlie watched as Sternov, picking up the duffle bag, spoke to one of his men before walking towards the car.

'What now, Alexis?' It was at that moment rifle shots, three in quick succession, shattered the stillness and even the wind seemed to hold its breath at such a disturbance. Charlie, his eyes narrowed, looked across at Sternov settling himself down in the back of the Zil.

'They saw and heard too much, Charlie. I'm sorry, but that's how it has to be. You've asked a couple of times, what now? I will tell you.'

As the car swung round preparatory to leaving, Charlie, through the rear window, had a fleeting glimpse of three bodies, Magyar, Paul and Vladimir, disappearing into freshly dug graves.

'Four murders in as many minutes, Alexis, surely...' but Sternov quickly interrupted.

'Murders! I killed ten times that number in less at Stalingrad and still ate a good supper. No, my friend, in this business you strike hard and you strike first. Now, you're booked into a flight leaving Warsaw for Zurich in...' he looked down at his watch, 'four hours from now. I've arranged an appointment for you with

328

the Suisse National Bank with Pierre Fontaine. You will deposit the contents of this,' pointing at the duffle bag, 'Understood?'

Charlie nodded, then, 'In whose name, Alexis?'

'Your own,' he paused, then grasping Charlie's hand in a powerful grip, 'and, comrade, when in your opinion the time has come, the proceeds are to be presented to His Holiness the Patriarch of the Russian Orthodox Church in Moscow, with instructions that the money is to be distributed by the Holy Church to the poor and needy, from whom it was taken in the first place . . . I have your word?'

'You have my word.'

'Good, then there is nothing more to be said.'

'One question, Alexis: how are you going to square this with your boss, Vladimir Semichastny?'

'Simple, we recovered thirty ingots from the grave, more than enough to satisfy him . . . your share, an ingot, is in the bag.'

'Alexis, there was no need . . .'

'Rubbish, milkman, I've got one,' he said with a grin then, serious again, 'Most of what is in there are bonds and shares in the name of Tsar Nicholas. It will be up to the Holy Church how they negotiate them.'

Charlie smiled, 'One final question. How did you know where to dig? I realise Charters would have known, but he was hardly likely to have told you.'

'Ah, that was where your gypsy girl and her tattoo helped.'

'In what way?'

'We photographed and enlarged it then, using it in relation to the ground – you're a military man, you know what I mean – orientate is the word, I believe. But even then, because of the artillery fire during the war, it had destroyed almost everything, we used a compass.'

'A compass?'

'Yes, you're familiar with the Romanov insignia?'

'Not really.'

'In the centre is a sword. Orientate the map and place a compass

329

so that the pointer matches the sword, and you have a bearing . . . simple. Even then I opened twelve graves of infants buried between nineteen forty-two and three.'

'Yes, but how did you know you had the right one?'

'Again, the Romanov insignia . . . I knew they would never bury one of their own without it, and I was right, it was on the coffin lid.'

'Yes, but Alexis, the infant wasn't the granddaughter of the Empress.'

'All part of the grand deception, and very clever it was, you have to hand it to Charters and of course the Duchess Elizabeth.'

Silence followed, then a smile began to crease the face of Alexis Sternov, a smile quickly overtaken by a deep-throated chuckle. Then, as if ignited by the chuckle, there began an eruption of laughter of such infection as to have Charlie also red-faced with merriment. Their undiluted mirth all but rocked the car. When it finally subsided, Sternov's hand disappeared within the confines of his overcoat to emerge, much to Charlie's relief, holding a silver flask. Unscrewing the tope, he placed it to his mouth and drank, then, before passing it to Charlie, belched loudly.

'Not the special from the Urals I hope, Alexis?'

'No, milkman, this is even stronger. It's distilled from the blood of the heroes of Stalingrad.'

'Then I would be honoured to join you,' said Charlie, raising the flask to his lips. As he did so, his eyes met Sternov's as they both looked down at the duffle bag.

'You think this represents the Romanov fortune, don't you, Charlie?' said Sternov, as he touched the bag with the toe of his shoe. 'Well, it doesn't. What we have here is the Duchess's ill-gotten gains – the true Romanov bullion has still to be found, my friend.'

'I don't believe it.'

'Charlie, the Romanovs were the richest imperial family in Europe. What is here is small change compared to their wealth. You and I, Charlie, represent the best of both worlds – why then don't we pool our resources and go for it ourselves?'

330

'Alexis, assuming you're right, then Charters's granddaughter, Penelope Charters, who, for reasons of subterfuge he passed off as his daughter, being directly descended from the Empress, must be entitled to everything?'

'I wondered how long it would take you to work that one out.'

'Then she must be a millionairess...'

'A hundred times over – then some.'

'God, it's staggering, so Charters probably intended to reveal all...'

'He knew about the Duchess's cache but not the whereabouts of the main fortune ... if I thought he did, I wouldn't have shot him.'

'Alexis, before I think further of your proposition, you know I exposed the film of the R100?'

'You did me a favour. We were set up, Hannah and I. A great deal of damage would have been done if you hadn't.'

'No hard feelings then?' But already Sternov, eyes tightly closed, was surrendering to the warmth and gentle movements of the Zil as it sped through the gathering dawn light of the country-side.

32

Triumph and Tragedy

'Well?' said Janice, seated in the airport lounge and tapping the table leg with her foot. 'It seems the Romanov Riddle is about over – as I said about the gold some time ago, I've a feeling of disappointment that it is finished.'

'Not entirely ... I wasn't going to tell you this, but ...'

'Tell me what, Charlie?'

'Sternov's suggested we should join forces and go after the real Romanov fortune ourselves – what we found really was only what Elizabeth had salted away.'

'You and Sternov together?' said Janice, partly out of her seat, but sitting down again, her face the image of incredulity. 'Now I have heard everything. In all but name we're at war with the Soviet Union, and you're considering teaming up with one of their top agents – what is it with you two? Can anyone join your mutual admiration society?'

'All right, all right, it was just a thought.'

'Just a thought, he says ... you know, Charlie Tuttle, you never cease to amaze me. Aren't you satisfied? Natasha has her prince and a huge fortune, what concerns me is us. Charlie, what have we to celebrate?'

As if he hadn't heard her, and ignoring her questioning look, Charlie lit a cigarette then, watching a smoke ring curl gently towards the ceiling, spoke as if to himself.

'I don't understand why Charters decided to call her his

daughter and not his granddaughter. Seems a little odd.'

'Easy, that one,' replied Janice, by now well used to his reticence. 'To protect her of course,' her voice an indication of her growing impatience with him.

'And you know, Janice, Derevenko was on to her. It was not a case of mistaken identity, as we all thought, no way, he was far cleverer than even Sternov gave him credit for...'

'Charlie, I'm not interested now. Charters is dead, so you and Natasha are off the hook. You've got your ill-gotten gains, but I still find it difficult to accept Penelope Charters as the true heir.'

'That was unfair, Janice. If the Duchess were here now she would not change a thing, she would be over the moon with the way things have turned out.'

'Goody goody gum drops, then everyone is happy,' said Janice, smiling and rising from the table, but the smile noticeably never reached her eyes. 'Now let's go home, I'm positively starving.'

* * *

As if by arrangement, February the twenty-ninth dawned bright and clear with the early promise of possible sunshine to come. However, the Webster household barely noticed – there is, after all, very little sun at eight in the morning in late February.

Gathered in the kitchen, each clasping a mug of steaming coffee, were Charlie, Janice, Hilda, Big George and Ben and Audrey. Emma was also present, Janice having called a truce for this special occasion, but Peter had not been invited.

Janice, as usual, was holding court, but this time without her back to a fireplace. Florrie, bursting with excitement and energy, moved amongst them, replenishing empty mugs and dispensing egg and bacon sandwiches.

'Really, Janice, was it absolutely necessary to get us out of our beds at this ungodly hour? After all, the service isn't until twelve.' Hilda's objections were quickly smoothed over by Janice, her eyes darting from one to the other as if daring any further criticism.

'I wanted to be really sure you all knew the special jobs you have to do. A Russian Orthodox wedding is very different from ours...' Hilda again interrupted, 'You told us all that last night, we're not children you know.'

Apart from a venomous look, Janice ignored her and continued, 'Charlie and I have been to Hell and back these past months, and today, as much as it's Natasha's, it's also ours, and as God is my witness, nothing is to be allowed to go wrong.'

'Bravo,' contributed Big George, through a mouthful of sandwich. 'I, for one, would appreciate a reminder...'

Hilda rounded on him at once, 'My apologies, Janice, I was forgetting we have a simpleton amongst us.'

'Now,' said Janice, getting into her stride, and again ignoring the interruptions, 'First the crown-bearers, that's Charlie, George and Ben ... you three take up positions behind Natasha as the service begins. Charlie...'

'Yes, Janice.'

'You will have to move swiftly because you're escorting the bride to the west end of the church. There she'll meet Michael and the priest, and at that point your job is done. The exchange of rings and prayers will take place there, and then the priest will lead them both to the centre of the church where we will be assembled ... any questions so far? Good. Now the bridesmaids, that's myself, Hilda, Emma and Florrie – we've little to do but stand to the side of the crown-bearers.'

It was here a further interruption occurred as Florrie, by now overcome, took centre stage.

'Oh, ma'am, wot can I say ... such an 'onour 'as been done me ... to think I'm to be bridesmaid at Miss Natasha's weddin', when I told my Bert 'e couldn't believe it, 'e couldn't...'

'That's all right, Florrie, it was Natasha's special wish. Now you get upstairs and see if she is ready for the hairdresser ... she's coming soon, and tell her I'll be up shortly.'

With tears of joy streaming down her face, Florrie scurried away only, much to Janice's chagrin, to return almost immediately.

334

'There's a man at the door carrying a bunch of flowers and a package for Mr Tuttle ... 'e says 'e's from the Soviet Embassy.' Chest heaving, Florrie stood in the doorway, the portent of her announcement creating from what moments before had been Janice's discourse, complete silence.

It was Charlie who recovered first. 'Ask him to leave them, Florrie, and thank him.'

'Now where was I?' began Janice, but it was obvious her audience were no longer interested in her diatribe, as with necks craning they looked beyond her and through the half-open kitchen door. As if in response to their avid curiosity, Florrie reappeared, clutching a huge bunch of red roses to her ample bosom. Janice, her face the epitome of frustration, surrendered to the inevitable and sat down on the nearest kitchen chair.

As Florrie passed a small package to Charlie, they all gathered round her. 'Aren't they gorgeous,' said Emma, leaning over Florrie's still palpitating chest, 'and their scent, it's quite out of this world.'

'What's in the package, Charlie? Be careful, it might be a bomb,' said Hilda suspiciously, 'you know you're a marked man,' this time uttered in a tone designed to convey covert anxiety.

'It would have to be a very small bomb, Hilda,' said Charlie jokingly, as he placed it on the table, where it was immediately picked up by Janice.

'Thank you very much, Florrie, it's addressed to both of us.' Her frustration, mounting to irritation, was obvious as she tore open the package. 'It's from Alexis Sternov, Charlie, same sort of poem, here you read it ...'

Much to their frustration, Charlie read it to himself then, with a faraway look in his eyes, aloud. ' "*If you reach for the moon, you may just get as far as the top of the nearest high tree. But if you reach for the top of the tree, you may never even get off the ground.*" I believe it's an old Chinese saying,' he said distantly.

'How very odd,' commented Janice, peevishly, 'no sooner do we get rid of one riddle we have another.'

'I thought it very sweet, Janice,' said Hilda before adding a postscript, 'especially coming from a Russian – and a member of the KGB at that.'

'It's his way of congratulating us and, of course, Natasha,' added Charlie, carefully folding the note and placing it in the pocket of his dressing-gown.

'Now, I really must ask you to concentrate on the wedding,' Janice began again, 'as I said earlier...'

This time it was Big George, having devoured yet another sandwich, who interrupted. 'What's the name of the church, Janice? Just in case I get lost.'

Janice's expression would have demolished lesser men than Big George who, sublimely unaware of her agitation, began, in the absence of Florrie, to pour himself more coffee.

'It's the Russian Orthodox Diocese of Sourozh, Ennismore Gardens. You may remember, it's where we went to rescue Natasha.' Her sarcasm fell on empty ears.

'Ma'am,' said the plaintive voice of Florrie from the doorway, her arms still embracing the roses, 'I think the hairdresser has arrived...'

'Show her into the bloody library,' responded Janice, her face purple at this further intrusion, 'and tell Natasha she's here. Now, where was I? Oh yes, I come now to the crown-bearers. They stand behind the bride, and when you get the nod from the priest each of you hold the crown above Natasha's head in turn ... have you got that?' The three nodded in unison.

'What about the groom, isn't he crowned?' said Hilda, amidst barely concealed amusement from the gathering.

Tight-lipped, Janice turned to her, 'As I said last night, three members of the Russian Duma are carrying out those duties for their Prince ... no problem there. Now, the final act of the crown-bearers, after the bride and groom have drunk the wine, and with the priest leading, you walk round the table three times following the bride. Also remember, during all of the service the couple are holding lighted candles, so be careful.'

'Sounds terribly grand – much more so than our service,' said Emma.

'I wouldn't altogether say that,' replied Janice, as if casting pearls before swine. 'A lot of it is purely symbolic, but the last act, I'm told, where the bride and groom kiss the icon screen, is very moving. Now, finally, we are all due at the hotel at one-thirty – so, gentlemen, no stopping off for a quick one.'

'Pity none of the crowned heads of Europe have accepted their invitations, Janice, I mean, after all, Michael is royalty.'

'Just as well, Hilda, the mere thought . . .' here, Charlie spoke up. 'You cannot altogether blame them, in the present political climate.'

'Well, I think it's a shame,' finished Hilda somewhat lamely.

'One last thing, don't forget we all stand throughout the service,' continued Janice, beginning to show signs of strain in her attempts not to overlook anything, 'and remember, there's no choir or music, but you are all expected to sing.'

'You mean we can't sit down?' exclaimed Hilda, her eyes staring from behind her bifocals. 'That's a bit much, I'm not sure I can stand that long.'

'Would it be all right just to hum?' enquired Big George, still battling with yet another sandwich.

With a gesture of helplessness, Janice looked across at Charlie.

*　*　*

The Bentley slid effortlessly down the driveway, its noise utterly disproportionate to its size and, even to the keenest ear, all but inaudible. Engulfed in the luxury of the expansively luxurious soft leather seats, Charlie and Natasha sat side by side. The chauffeur, punctilious in his duties and resplendent in a grey uniform with silver buttons had, with a touch, released a drinks cabinet, which opened with consummate ease displaying a glittering array of decanters and their attendant glasses. From the car's bonnet fluttered a small pennant depicting, on a royal blue background, the double eagle of the House of Romanov.

337

'Natasha,' said Charlie, 'I've never seen you look lovelier...'
even those hypnotic eyes, he mused, seemed to have softened. Her
floral patterned lace wedding dress was meticulously hand-
embroidered with pearl and crystal beads, which, as the rays of the
sun caught them, flashed like tiny diamonds. It conveyed, he
thought, just the right image for a fairy princess. She gave no sign
of having heard his compliment, but her eyes, if anything, were
even softer as they looked at him.

'Charlie, when I'm married, will you come and live with me
and be Igor again?'

'Natasha, Natasha,' he said, taking her hand in his, 'Igor is the
past, so is Kolomyja and the Duchess, all in the past ... it's your
future now. Who knows what it may hold for you and Michael?
Everything Elizabeth wished for is coming true.'

'I know, but I don't want a life without you ... you must try and
understand, until now you've always been there...' her voice
faded and Charlie sensed tears not far away.

'I will never be far from you ... perhaps no longer in the same
bedroom,' he added with a chuckle ... but her face told him his
pathetic joke had done nothing to placate her. Her next question
was even more disturbing.

'Are you really going to marry Janeece?' Implacably her eyes
held his, their intensity of feeling causing a shiver of emotion,
which, like some fever, impregnated his whole being. He said
nothing but, like a drowning man grasping for some driftwood,
reached for the cabinet. Unperturbed, Natasha, lifting her veil,
inclined her head so her mouth was only inches from his ... he
barely heard her whispered, 'Kiss me, Charlie,' before her lips
pressed hard against his. As if possessing a life of their own, his
arms, but moments before reaching away from her, encircled her
waist and with uncharacteristic roughness pulled her to him.
Momentarily, all reason was lost as he bathed in sensations he had
believed he was forever denied. Then, through the turmoil engulf-
ing him, her voice reached out to him.

'Charlie, I don't want to marry Michael if it means losing

you ...' Like a man emerging from a dream, Charlie struggled for reality. There was no matter-of-fact Janice to help him, he was alone ... this incredibly lovely childlike creature, but inches from him, had made a declaration of her feelings, which, he knew, in many ways mirrored his own. Releasing her, he again, with hands shaking, reached for the cabinet. Pouring himself a brandy, he gulped it down, conscious that she was watching his every move.

Easing himself back in his seat, he closed his eyes, desperate not to look at her, his thoughts chaotic. At last finding a suitable reply he said, 'What you mean, Natasha, is you'll miss ...' he started again, realising he had to bring Janice into it by name, 'the security and love Janice and I have for you.'

She pondered this for a few moments, then, in a tone of voice of pure innocence said, 'I love, Janeece, Charlie ... and I love you.'

As if she had plunged a knife into him, the bitter realisation that soon she would be gone took hold ... no longer would he be her mentor, her protector. Never again would she turn to him with her simplistic questions or seeking guidance ... a new man, a stranger to him, would fulfil that role. For the first time he realised his world and that of Janice's would be that much emptier without her.

A voice penetrated through the dark curtain of his thoughts ... a voice rich in its cockney accent, 'We're 'ere, guv ...'

* * *

Never did a bride, thought Charlie, go to her wedding more willing in some ways and so unwilling in others. As they alighted from the car, Natasha gripped his arm with a strength that defied her femininity.

'Charlie, promise me now we'll never be parted ... not ever.'

As he gazed at her, ostensibly to check all was in order before their final walk to the church door, emotions again swelled within him. Was it possible he was in love with her? Could it be, that in spite of Janice and all she meant to him, such feelings for Natasha had merely been lying dormant these last months and that, like so

339

many before him, she had worked her spell on him? He, who until now had always considered himself immune to her magnetism.

As if a physical manifestation had emerged from the dark recesses of his mind a figure, entirely clad in black, walked towards them from the portico of the church. At once the being became, in his mind, an unknown someone who was about to snatch her from him, possibly for ever. Charlie stopped and faced her and from somewhere found the courage to look deeply into eyes still eloquent of her love for him. With a voice he barely recognised, he said, 'Natasha, darling, if thing's don't work out, you're to come back to me ... understand?' With eyes heavy with tears, she nodded and then, as if in that instant of time she had shed her youthfulness, her voice assumed a maturity of such intensity as to astonish him. 'Charlie, I love you, I shall always love you.'

The priest, who had patiently waited, now stepped forward and in an act of possession, offered her his arm and guided her over to the waiting Prince Michael. Charlie, swallowing deeply, looked away.

* * *

As the camera bulbs flashed, Natasha and her Prince emerged from the church. Janice, smiling, moved across to Charlie. 'Aren't they a magnificent couple?' she said, her eyes bright with success, 'and the service went off so well ... I'm delighted.' Then, frowning, 'Why are you looking so miserable?'

'Janice, I think you should know, I've fallen in love with Natasha and she with me ...' Speechless, Janice stared at him as if in some way he had become utterly unknown to her. Finally, her expression of sheer delight of moments before evaporated, to be replaced with one of incredulity.

'Nothing is going to spoil today,' she replied, 'we'll talk about it later.' With lips pursed, she moved away then, turning, said, 'God in Heaven, how are the mighty fallen, eh, Charlie? So even you have finally succumbed to her charms. But,' looking at her watch, 'may I say you've left it a little late ... one hour too late, to be precise.' Turning on her heel and without a second glance, she got into her car.

Charlie looked down at his well-polished shoes as he searched for his cigarette case – that empty feeling at the pit of his stomach told him all he needed to know – he had lost them both. Nothing was so final as those last few words of Janice's, nothing he could say or do would change anything in the slightest, it was over...

Was it for ever he had to relive those last few words they had exchanged? And was his mind stamped for eternity with the sight of her car in front of him turning into the main road, blindly, as if her sole motivation was to lengthen the distance between them ... whatever the cost? The hideous swerving, spinning, as she braked hopelessly late, followed by the splintering crash, the silence broken only by the cranking of the car wheels, as if reluctant to cease their turning.

His rush from his car ... an inner voice telling him, as he scrambled on all fours to release her, no one could have lived through that. Outwardly unmarked, her face looked up at him. She was not quite gone, and her words, though faint, were perfectly clear. 'Look after Natasha...' then, even as he tore at the wreck of what a few minutes before had been a car, her eyes took on a look he knew too well, glazed and vacant.

*   *   *

(*Two weeks later*)

Grief had cemented their various relationships, but it was to Hilda they had all turned. Diminutive Hilda, who had demonstrated that size was of no significance when strength of character and iron will were required. It was she who stepped in, when all had surrendered to the agony of their loss. Janice, throughout, they had all accepted, was the dynamo, the inspiration in the struggle to fulfil the dreams of an unknown Grand Duchess, who, privately, they considered may well have succumbed to senile dementia or

341

worse. But, collectively, they had allowed themselves to be swept along – Janice's fierce determination ensuring that. Then, when all seemed to have been achieved and their triumph was there to behold, she was gone.

It was Hilda who had arranged the funeral, stepping between April, Janice's divorced mother, and her father, George Lawrence, whose court rhetoric, as Hilda had delighted in telling, might well have brought him a fortune but whose resilience in the face of tragedy was found sadly wanting.

Charlie's grief was the more worrying. 'He's completely devastated,' she had told the gathering on the morning of the funeral. 'He won't be attending ... no flowers, nothing.'

'I say,' said Big George, 'suicidal? What's the point of that?'

'You oaf,' she had replied, 'can't you understand he won't accept he's lost her.' Then, almost to herself, 'Both of them.'

Silently they had filed into the church, she and Big George, Emma, Florrie, Ben and Audrey. Leading them were the Prince and Princess Michael. She, so recently radiant in white, was dressed entirely in black ... again the simile, reflected Emma, white and black, good and evil, it was as if they were her own personal shroud ...

*   *   *

'Mr Tuttle, your car is here,' said Florrie from the doorway, her face flushed, tears spreading over onto fat cheeks. 'Oh, Mr Tuttle, what are you going to do?'

Charlie stood up. 'Life has to go on, Florrie, that above all else she would have wanted.'

It was too much for her as, with head bowed, she buried her face in her apron.

'Now, Florrie, don't go on so, believe me I wouldn't change anything these past few months have given me. It was a privilege to have known and loved her...'

'Oh, God, Mr Tuttle ... don't.'

'Triumph and tragedy, Florrie, they often go hand in hand,' he said as he gave her a comforting hug.

'You will come and see me from time to time, won't you, Mr Tuttle?'

But he was back in Appenzell leaning over the Duchess's shoulder, as, in her lazy scrawl, she scribbled the words *'Bring the girl to me'*. Five innocuous words ... simple in their request, but what agony and ecstasy they had brought about. Now he had to pick up the pieces. This time the fragments were larger, the loss many times greater.

As he moved into the hallway, Florrie's gentle weeping following, he again heard Janice's voice, strident at times, full of love at others. Yes, he conjectured, they had prevailed ... but the price was all but unbearable. He paused, looking down the driveway at the waiting car, quiet sobbing continuing behind him as if the tears she were shedding were as much his as hers. Then, half-turning, he pulled out a crumpled piece of paper – through blurred eyes he read it again, digesting every word.

'Comrade,' it read, *'on the orders of the First Secretary, that area of the cemetery at Kolomyja, the subject of recent excavations, has been totally destroyed and all evidence alluding to it burnt. This has been done in the best interests of the State ... and, milkman, distribution of the cream found to continue in accordance with our agreement. Salutations, Sternov.'*

If only she were here to read it with him ... all the turmoil, the threats ended at last. Natasha was safe, but Janice was gone and he was alone, bereft. Then, as if all the pain and agony of his loss had suddenly swelled up, he stopped. With head raised and feet apart, he shouted, all his pent-up fury and heartbreak giving emphasis to every word, 'God damn you, Elizabeth, are you satisfied now? You have your Princess, you've won ... but it was never worth the price ... surely you knew, those few scribbled words were but an invitation from the Devil.'

343

EPILOGUE

St Petersburg, 1998

As the volume of music in the great St Peter and Paul Cathedral roe to a crescendo, she again squeezed his hand. 'Charlie,' she whispered, her head bent forward, 'isn't the Crown Prince magnificent in his regalia?'

'Yes,' he replied, a smile lurking at the corners of his mouth, 'as his mother, Natasha, he does you great credit.'

'Princess Natasha, if you please . . .'

'Do forgive me, Your Highness,' the smile now reaching his eyes, 'like many old men, I tend now to live in the past.'

'Charlie?' Her dazzling smile extinguishing any fears about the rebuke of a moment before. 'Who is the love of your life?'

He looked up at her. How could it be that ageing, like maturity, had passed her by? It was as if the gods themselves, having fashioned her, were so proud of their achievement they had disdained such mortal afflictions.

'You, of course. How could it possibly be anyone else?' he replied.

Bending down, she kissed him on the cheek, her face radiant. 'I've always known it,' she said. Then, as if such revelation had really little significance, her eyes again focused on her son standing but feet away from the eight tiny coffins.

As the sad, plaintive music penetrated ever deeper into the labyrinth of the great Cathedral, Charlie's thoughts went back over thirty years. Wouldn't she have loved to have been here – his

344

own dear Janice. For the hundredth time that day, he relived that terrible car accident. Again he heard her last and only words, '*Look after Natasha . . .*' he had watched by the roadside as her life ebbed away – how impotent he had been to help her on this most crucial of occasions. His impotency had been the joke of their time together; it had always been there, the only reason he had doubted the wisdom of marriage; and he was sure, if she had been spared, she would have come to accept it and his declared love of Natasha. Then, in her final moments, he was again impotent in that he could do nothing to save her.

And now, what of the present? What changes there had been. It was even feasible that a Romanov might once again reign supreme over mighty Russia, even an old woman's dream could yet be fulfilled. Back where it all began in 1963, who would have believed in the emergence of Mikhail Gorbachev – 'Here was a man,' Margaret Thatcher had said, 'I can do business with. . .'

As the music reached its final crescendo, Natasha placed an arm round him and with her free hand gently tucked the blanket more closely against his knees.

'Charlie,' she began again, 'I wish Michael could have lived to see this . . .' and then, as if the memory of his debauchery came flooding back, she began again. 'Charlie,' her face but inches from his, 'I'm glad I'm the love of your life.' He smiled, but the ache in his heart, unlike the dying sad notes of the music, persisted.